Human Cloning

Revolution of the Manufactured

Shervin Tarjoman

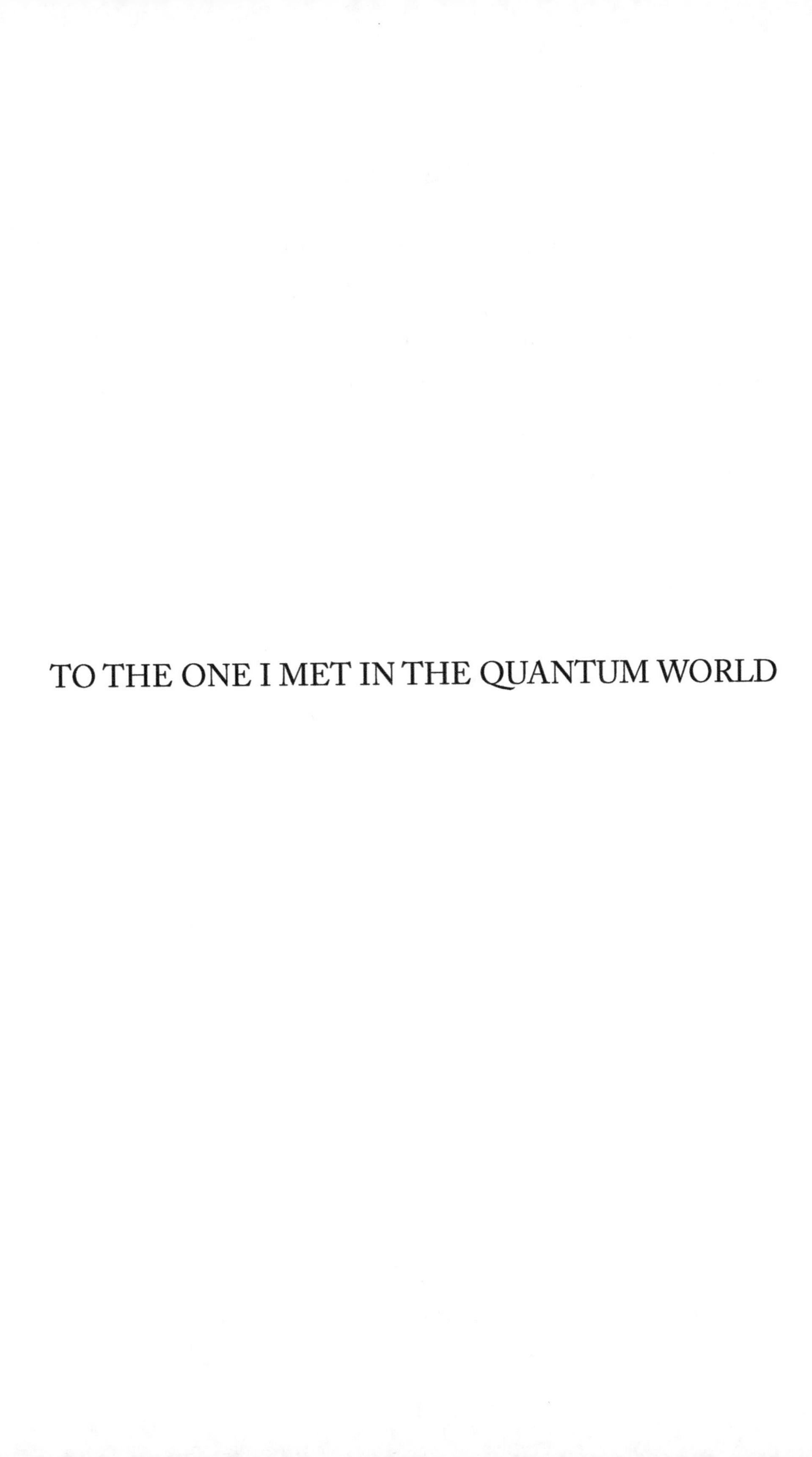

TO THE ONE I MET IN THE QUANTUM WORLD

Prologue

In sterile laboratories around the world, humanity was pushing the limits of borders. Cloning had crossed into an arena that was previously only talked about in science fiction, and it had stealthily become a faded reality-an unwelcome whisper in boardrooms, a debate on parliamentary fronts, and a matter enshrined the deepest by corporate secrecy. Human cloning was no longer a counter-question for the future: it was happening now.

Dr. Rebecca Miles knew it better than anyone. For years, she had dedicated her life to science, believing that cloning could mend the wounds of humanity. She believed it might cure diseases, regenerate life, and rewrite the laws of biology. But standing next to Dr. Leonard Krauss and watching the pale-skinned figure of Noah emerge from the artificial womb, she realized that they had truly crossed the boundaries of nature.

"This isn't a cure," Rebecca murmured, her voice trembling as the glass chamber hissed open. "It's...something else."

Leonard didn't look at her. His eyes were riveted on Noah-the first human clone-sorrowful and rabid with exaltation and dread. "It's the future," he said, more to himself than to her.

Rebecca's stomach twisted. For years, she had worked with Leonard towards their joint ideal of harnessing the power of cloning. But now that the vision stood before her as a concrete matter, the very evidentiary embodiment of their dreams, doubt began to gnaw at her resolve. Noah was not merely a scientific achievement; he was a threat to the fabric of humanity itself.

Noah's eyes opened, and the moment crushed heavily on Rebecca's chest. His gaze was unnervingly direct, filled with awareness that no infant-or clone-should possess; and as he spoke, the first word shattered the fragile silence in the lab.

"Why?"

Rebecca froze. Her instincts told her to stop, to shut it all down, but it was too late. That word had already turned Noah into more than an experiment; he had turned them both into a question neither she nor Leonard felt able to answer.

Beyond the lab, humanity remained blissfully unaware of the revolution brewing beneath its feet. Yet as cloning programs blossomed in secret laboratories, flooding the planet, Rebecca was becoming the cautionary tale. The question was no longer whether cloning would define the future-it had already. The only one remaining was: **would humanity survive it?**

Inside the Revolution

About The Author

Shervin Tarjoman is an inspiring serial entrepreneur and author known for his groundbreaking work in quantum computing, emerging technologies, and state-of-the-art scientific research. His love of pushing through the limits of human innovation has taken him far and wide studying human cloning technology, thus providing inspiration for the book, *Human Cloning: Revolution of the Manufactured.*

As a world-known founder of several successful companies, Shervin's entrepreneurial ventures are fueled by an unwavering belief in furthering true science, new frontiers, and a firmly established reputation for turning thoughts into action for the forward thinker that he is.

It is, thus, on the basis of the belief of what technology can do to shape the future of humankind, that one sees the book *Human Cloning: Revolution of the Manufactured* written out as a captivating story-springing from both expertise and vision.

Chapter 1

The Genesis of Creation

In the sterile corridors of the underground laboratory, a faint humming noise of machines echoed. The air smelled of antiseptic, testifying to innumerable hours spent creating a contamination-free environment. Dr. Leonard Krauss adjusted the sterile gloves on his shaking hands, his gaze riveted on the glowing vial in the incubator. Inside, life, artificial yet unmistakably human, throbbed with a rhythm beyond that of nature.

"The sequencing is stabilizing," reported Dr. Rebecca Miles quite steadily, if not somewhat awestruck. At his side, she darted from monitor to monitor in bewilderment, finding that she could hardly keep up as all the streams of DNA sequencing spilled out. Numbers, chemical bonds all lined up; there were music notes in the melody of creation. "The cell division is going on without any anomalies, Leonard. It's... unprecedented."

Leonard did not answer, still riveted on the incubator, wishing that willpower alone would be enough to see the experiment through to a successful closure. His brain was an uproar of a thousand possibilities, each of them demanding a what-if, a why-not! Years of research, sleepless nights, sacrifice-this was where they all met, where years converged. It was about crossing the borders--not so much the science.

"It's more than unprecedented," he murmured, almost inaudibly, barely above the soft beeping of machinery. **"This is... the future."**

Rebecca looked at him with her brows knitted. "*Do you believe it*? What we're doing here... is right?"

Leonard turned away from the incubator, facing her with dark, determined eyes. "Who decides what's right, Rebecca? Nature? God? Or the same society that's about to sink because it can't solve its own problems?" He gestured toward the glowing vial. "This isn't just science; this is salvation. We're giving humanity a new chance."

Rebecca turned her face away, her lips a mere line. She wished to believe him, wished to share the vision, but a gnawing doubt stuck to her. "And what if this is something else completely?" she whispered.

Before Leonard could respond, the shrill air of the beeping machine pierced, announcing that the incubation time was over. The room fell silent, the only sound being the faint hiss of the cooling system. Both scientists turned to the incubator, holding their breath. Slowly, the glass dome opened, revealing a small humanoid figure suspended in a viscous gel.

Noah. The first-ever human clone.

Rebecca stepped closer, her hand instinctively reaching out only to huddle behind the glass container. The figure's chest rose and fell in sure, regular breaths, streaking the inner wall of the chamber with moisture. "He's...alive," she said, the words scarcely escaping her mouth.

A fierce glow passed across Leonard's face as he tried to fathom triumph with sneaking defeat in his heart. "Not just alive," he said. "PERFECT."

For a moment, they both stood staring at the creation before them with divergent thoughts. For Leonard, this was the culmination of human ingenuity, a step toward immortality. For Rebecca, it presented an unanswerable question, an abomination against the natural order.

The spell was broken by the flickering datastream panels. Rebecca turned her gaze to the computer screen, her expression horrified. "His vitals are stable, but... the neural pathways seem disturbed. Look here!"

Leonard leaned closer and tried to read the data. Brainwave patterns appeared irregular, fluctuating far too erratically. "Just a glitch," he said with a dismissing note in his voice, even if that sounded somewhat tense.

Rebecca narrowed her eyes. "Leonard, that's not just a machine. If something is wrong, we can't just reboot."

Before he could respond, the air went faintly thick with a resonant gasp. A human gasp.

Noah stirred, making another vague sound.

Rebecca froze. "Leonard, he's... staring at us."

Leonard turned toward him, his heart momentarily halting when Noah gazed directly at him. A pair of eyes, clearly human, seemed to be searching into him, assessing, gauging the man who had played God himself.

"What are you?" whispered Leonard, but the question sounded more like a prayer.

Noah blinked slowly, parted his lips as if he was about to respond, but no words instead inarticulated low guttural sounds came forth, sending icy shivers down Rebecca's spine.

"This is wrong," she said, backpedaling. "We need to stop this. Shut it down."

Leonard shook his head, not ripping his eyes off Noah. "No. He is right. He is the future. We just need to understand him."

The lights flickered again, as if the machines were groaning at the weight of what they carried. Noah turned his gaze toward the ceiling, the blank expression on the boy's face uncomfortably threatening.

"What if he's more than we can control, Leonard?" The question, now reduced to a whisper, was accompanied by the wretched feel of fear weighing on Rebecca.

Leonard's smile was faint-a smile with no light. "Then we'll simply adapt, Rebecca. Just as humanity has always done."

Around them, the world folded into the kind of silence far too uneasy. Rebecca found herself softly intoning a prayer, as though it had come unbidden, a few words that seemed for all the world to anchor her in time so far unmoored.

And then Noah's head snapped toward her, eyes narrowing-shooting a stare she would, without seeking agreement, certainly define as recognition.

The tension in that laboratory was a symphony - everything else around them held still, held breath. Noah was just staring at Rebecca, with a gaze that seemed unwilling and oddly knowing. She stepped back gently, her hands shaking. Leonard nonetheless took a step forward, his curiosity overriding the caution still in him.

"Noah," he said softly, almost in a whisper, as if he had weighed every word of it. "Can you hear me?"

The clone's head turned a slight angle. It was a slow and thoughtful inclination, almost as if he were trying to process the sound gives a buffer time. The sound, downturned, was still chirping through Rebecca's consciousness. But now, once again, it was quiet. Too quiet. Leonard reached for a microphone connected to the chamber within reach and turned it on, magnifying his voice so Noah could hear it.

"Noah," he repeated. "You are in a safe place. Can you understand me?"

Rebecca closed her fists at her sides to collect herself to actually speak. "Leonard, he is not ready for this. Just look at the neural data-it's chaos. We aren't sure if he is even fully conscious."

Leonard simply kept quiet, his attention completely glued to the figure before him. Suddenly, Noah blinked slowly; with a steady chest beating. Then finally, his lips parted, forming a single word.

"Why?"

The sound was faint, echoing their chorus upon the dull throbs of the machines, halting both scientists in their places. Rebecca's eyes widened; her heart was hammering on her ribs. Leonard's expression shifted from one of jubilation to one of deepening shadows-a choreography of awe and terror.

"He's questioning," almost as if Leonard was speaking to himself. "He's ... aware."

Rebecca shook her head frantically. "No, Leonard. It is too early yet to say that. It may just be automatic speech, or ..."

"No." Leonard's voice remained cool, his eyes on Noah. "This is something else. He is asking a question. He is conscious."

Unnerving, the monitors greeted another beep: their neural data fluctuated violently. A glance at the screen sent a wave of discomfort through Rebecca." Leonard, this upheaval-doesn't look right. If we push it too far, we may totally lose it."

Leonard approached the glass chamber, his palm lightly resting on its edge. "Noah," he said softly, "You are safe here, with us. Why did you say that?"

For a moment, there was no response. Slowly, Noah raised his hand, pressing his palm against the inside of the glass. For his part, Leonard mirrored the gesture, his hand hovering just inches from Noah's. Its touch-in a manner distanced by the chamber-sent jolts of prickly sensations racing through Leonard.

Their moment was interrupted by Rebecca's voice like a knife. "Leonard, stop! You are crossing a line we don't understand!"

But Leonard didn't pull away. Rather he leaned in closer, letting his breath fog the glass. "Why, Noah? Why do you ask why?"

Noah's eyes shifted to Leonard's in an unreadable expression. When he finally spoke, it became clear that his voice had gone strong.

"Why...am I?"

Rebecca's heart sank. The words were simple but heavy with ramifications. She moved forward, resting her hand on Leonard's shoulder. "Leonard, this isn't right. He's not a subject anymore—he's a being. We have to reassess everything."

Leonard shrugged off her grip without breaking his gaze on Noah. "This is exactly what we've been working toward. A self-aware, thinking clone. Don't you understand, Rebecca? Everything changes now."

Rebecca's jaw clenched; with a quickened voice, she added, "Yes, it does change everything, only not as you think. This is no longer just scientific; it is now ethical and consequential."

The lights began to flicker again, throwing dancing shadows across the lab. Noah dropped his hand from the barrier, tilting his head as if trying to hear something only he could hear. This shift did not go unnoticed by Rebecca. "Leonard," she said in a close-voiced urgency, "Something's happening."

Leonard frowned. *"What do you mean?"*

"Look-it is the neural data," Rebecca said, motioning to the monitors. The choppy patterns were shifting, settling up themselves. Noah's breath turned to pant and closed his eyes for an instant until they shot open in a matter of seconds.

This time, his voice sounded marvellously calm. "You shouldn't have made me."

The words flushed an oppression into the room, making Rebecca aware of a sudden chill racing down her spine; even Leonard hesitated, throwing away the little confidence he'd mustered. He opened desperately to say something, but the utter darkness intervened.

Gasping in unison, every machine ran out of breath as the last faint sound died with it. Emergency lights glowed dim red, presaging silence. Rebecca mindlessly reached for her much-good phone; no signal.

"Leonard," she gasped. "**What's happening?**"

He darted toward the main console. Hands flew across the controls. "Power overload"-it was a mutter-"fifty-fifty. The system should reboot any minute now."

But it didn't. Instead, it was a low, somber sound full of impossibility that came from nowhere and everywhere at the same time. Rebecca's eyes darted to the chamber; her breath lay gnarled in her throat.

Noah was standing.

He moved with a kind of slow, measured grace that seemed almost effervescent. The thick liquid liquidity of his skin clung to him. He swung his neck around the whole room, though now there was an expression of not blankness, but objectivity.

"Leonard, we have to turn this whole thing off right now," Rebecca said in a calm, low voice, feeling the rising storm of panic as she physically pulled the professor away from the console. "This is not right!"

"No!" Leonard screamed, his voice breaking with desperation. "This is exquisitely what we need to see! He's adjusting!"

Noah turned his eyes their way, faintly glowing now in the dim light. His lips parted again and issued forth a sound that did not belong with either man or machine-it leapt forth from an abyss and one that seemed to have spilt inordinate sheer terror into both the scientists.

And then he spoke again, his voice low but unmistakable. "You made me... but you cannot command me."

Rebecca's hand gripped Leonard tightly as the room seemed to chill, the air thickening with trepidation. "Leonard," she said, tremulously whispering, "what have we done?"

The lab was pulsing with an irrational life. Noah stood up inside it, so pale that he seemed somewhat translucent in the ephemerally-red glow cast by the emergency lighting. He was disturbing-alien yet familiar at once. Rebecca's mind was racing, undisciplined against the implications of what confronted them.

"Leonard," her tone was sharp, "we need to start thinking about containment. If he- if it- loses stability, it is going to escalate beyond any possible control all this."

Leonard did not reply immediately. His gaze was riveted at Noah; in his eyes, one could see a strange fusion of fascination and fear. "He's standing"; Rebecca let it out. "Standing upright. Breathing. Thinking. Everything we ever wished for and beyond."

"**More?**" she hissed, stepping closer to him, "This isn't a test subject anymore, Leonard. He's conscious. Don't you see how dangerous this makes him?"

Leonard shook his head; he waved her off. "Dangerous? No, Rebecca. He is the epitome of extraordinary. The proof that our work transcends meaning. The evidence that humanity can rise above itself."

Before Rebecca could utter a word, Noah moved. Not even more than a nod, a hint of twitching in his fingers, but enough to hold the attention toward him. The humming of the machines dimmed as though acting in response to him. His stare roamed the lab and registered what it saw, all the shadows. When their eyes met, his and hers, she felt an icy dread settle like a stone in her chest.

"Noah," Leonard said softly now, almost reverently. "*Do you understand where you're at? Do you know who we are?*"

And again Noah did not say anything, only raised his hand, pressing it against the glass. This time, it was done with intention, almost purposefully. The monitors flickered as his palm pressed against the barrier, and an energy pulse moved through the chamber. Rebecca involuntarily jerked back, sensing that something had gone wrong.

"Leonard, the systems--look!" she pointed up at the monitors, which now showed erratic power swings. The air temperature in the chamber got unsettled, and the collectors that held Noah gasped with the weight of unseen pressure.

Leonard frowned and tapped furiously at the console. "This doesn't make sense," he hissed. "Systems are calibrated to compensate for fluctuations. There's no reason to--"

A loud crack interrupted him. The sound echoed through the lab long after it had been made, both scientists staring toward the chamber. A thin crack raced through the glass, branching away from Noah's hand in a pattern resembling a spiderweb. Rebecca felt her heart jump into her throat.

"He's destabilizing the chamber!" she shouted, grabbing Leonard by the arm. "Shut it down now!"

Leonard paused for the twinkling of an eye at the emergency shutdown switch. It was his old habit slowly giving way to more sinister instincts. He turned and looked at the calm Noah, holding against the disturbing backdrop. "If we turn off the emitter, it could be worse; we could lose the subject," said Leonard in his low, stunned voice.

"If we don't, we might lose everything," she shot back. "You said it yourself: he is more than we expected. If he is destabilizing the chamber, my God, who knows what he could do?"

Leonard clenched his jaw; the battle for his soul showed plainly in his facial muscles. But before he could make a move, Noah acted. He pushed harder on the glass, the crack growing wider. The rumble of machinery got louder and higher, sending voltages on a rise that made Rebecca's flesh crawl.

"Noah!" yelled Leonard, voice rising. "Stop! You're about to…"

With a forceful crash of glass falling into speckles, the cry enveloped the lab. Chains of pieces erupted, spewing the containment gel over the sloped floor like small rivers of calf-deep water. She shielded her face, heart hammering, and hobbled back from the lab, while Leonard remained frozen, staring; Noah stepped out of the wrecked chamber.

The young clone glided with an unearthly grace; we would hear no sound as his feet hit the cold floor. Gel hung smeared all over him, glistening and catching the light in a way that shrouded him in glamour. For a minute, liquid dripped steadily into the unbroken chamber, with only silence marking the profound moment.

Leonard quaked as he spoke, "Noah, you don't have to do this. You're safe here. We have come to help you."

Noah tilted his head yet again, keeping his gaze unreadable. When he spoke, his voice was calm but bore the tone of a blade which sent chills of fright running up Rebecca's spine. "Help me?" he echoed. "Or control me?"

He began to respond, but Noah didn't let him finish. He stretched out his arm, and the lights flickered nervously again, finally plunging the room into darkness. Rebecca gasped, her eyes adjusting slowly to the dim light illuminated by emergency reflectors.

"Leonard, we must get out of here, **there is no time,**" she whispered as she reached for him in the dark.

He shook his head. "No, this is my creation, I shall not abandon him," came the reply, steady now but with Leonard's hands trembling.

Then, an odd crackly noise filled the room. Rebecca turned to seek its source; her stomach clenched at the realization that it was from Noah. He stood statue-like, hazy luminous arcs across his skin.

The next moment, without any warning, he spoke again; this time, louder than before, his voice echoing through the lab.

"You should not have made me."

The gravity of that phrase hung in the air. Rebecca grasped Leonard's arm; the grip was unyielding. "We are leaving-pronto."

But before either could move, Noah had extended both his hands. Emergency lights danced dizzyingly around, and the very nature of the room became distorted as a strobe-like flare even as Rebecca's stomach turned to terror when she realized he wasn't just a new form of life-in fact, he was many steps beyond their understanding.

Like strobe lights, the lab was illuminated in jarring flares of crimson, each pulse freezing the scene like an erratic memory. It was with desperate instinct that Rebecca gripped Leonard's arm, but she felt her legs weighed down as if frozen in time. Noah stood at the center of the pandemonium, magnetic and terrifying.

"Leonard! Listen to me!" Rebecca's voice screamed above the noise, trembling with desperation. "We can't contain this--**he's unstable!"**

Leonard fixed his eyes on Noah, and he wore an inscrutable expression. If the usual scientific detachment was gone, there was no calculated calm left either. For the first time in years, Leonard had felt an emotion he had not felt before-fear. Yet, buried beneath it was pride. "Do you see it, Rebecca?" he whispered, almost inaudibly above the crackling energies buzzing in the air. "**He is evolving.** As I speak."

"Evolving?" As if incredulous, Rebecca shouted. "He just smashed the containment unit open with his bare hands, Leonard! This isn't evolution; it's chaos!"

Noah's head snapped around, as if the noise had somehow caught his attention. The red light radiated from eyes that seemed to penetrate her; sitting cross-legged on the floor, Rebecca thought she felt his scrutiny the way a physical force bore down. He was now moving, but the walk almost looked deliberate. It was as if he were testing his newly found liberty.

"**Stay away!**" Rebecca screamed, terrified as she grasped a chair and held it before herself like a shield. "Leonard, do something!"

Leonard stepped forward, his hands raised as in parody. "Noah," he said softly, his voice the same as one might use to coax a frightened child. "You are confused. You have just woken up, and everything seems too much. But don't worry, we are here to help you. There is no reason to be afraid."

Noah said nothing, merely cocked his head, staring closely at Leonard, his face almost curious. Then he spoke, voice resonant and icy. "Afraid? You think I feel afraid?"

Leonard hesitated. Even his voice was no longer entirely convincing. "I do. I mean... I think you're a little out of your league here. No offense. We'll make sure you understand."

A low hum filled the room, one that seemed to be coming from Noah himself. The air became thick, and the temperature noticeably dropped. Rebecca shivered as her breath came out in clouds. "Leonard, the readings!" she insisted. "He's changing the environment. This isn't just a sentient being. It's something much more."

Leonard didn't now divert his gaze from Noah. "What are you, Noah?" he asked, almost in awe and horror as well. "What are you going to be?"

Noah's lips turned up in something very much like a smile, though flat. "I am what you made me," he said simply. "And what I choose to be."

Rebecca felt a rise in adrenaline as the tension in the room mounted. The screens flickered, momentarily coming back to life with unreadable streams of data before some command turned them off again. She couldn't interpret what was happening on the screen, but she understood one thing: Noah was no longer bound by the confines of the laboratory.

"Leonard, we must go!" Her grip tightened around his arm. "*We don't know what he's capable of!*"

Leonard shook his head; his eyes sparked with defiance and desperation. "I can't just leave him. No, Rebecca! He was my creation! I can't leave him."

"**He's not your son!**" the words exploded from Rebecca, followed by a rush of tears. "He's... he's something else. Something for which we weren't prepared."

Noah turned his gaze between the two scientists, as if weighing what they had to say to one another. "You argue about me as though I am not here," he said evenly, tinged with an edge. "As if an object. A problem that is to be solved."

Rebecca became stiff as her heart raced in fear. "That's not what we mean," she said cautiously. "We're trying to understand you."

"Understand?" Noah echoed, with disdain soaking through his voice. "You didn't create me to understand me. You created me to control me."

The light around him shimmered, creating thin arcs of light, more intense as he spoke. An animal fear struck at Rebecca's heart. Whatever Noah was becoming seemed always to stretch far beyond their comprehension-and beyond their power to arrest.

"Noah," Leonard said, tentatively getting closer. "**We can fix this. We can work together.**"

Noah raised a hand, and Leonard froze. The glow of Noah's eyes intensified, and Rebecca felt a pressure in the air, as though even now the room were holding its breath.

"You speak of fixing me," said Noah, his voice soft, but commanding. "But you are the ones who are broken."

The emergency lights flared violently, and the lab went black. She gasped and hastily fumbled for her phone to find that the light coming from its screen would be her only light. "Leonard!" she called out, her voice echoing into the deep void. "**Where are you?**"

"I'm here," Leonard's voice came from somewhere in the close-very near, trembling, but real. "Noah, please, we can work this out."

But no answer came. Mere silence.

Then a whisper that, so close, sounded as though it were right next to her ear: "You should have left me in the dark."

Rebecca's scream pierced the void, but it was swallowed up in that oppressive darkness. The lab, once a haven of science, had become a cage of shadows.

Total silence engulfed the lab, which was broken only by Rebecca's ragged breathing. She staggered backward, the dim ray from her phone casting very sinister shapes on the wall. From the darkness, somewhere, came Leonard's voice: dim and trembling.

"Rebecca-breathe! STAY CALM!"

The words barely penetrated. Over and over again, her mind flashed the chill of Noah's whisper-the evil messenger's. "You should have left me in the dark." Mindlessly, yet with increasing menace, this phrase went through her mind over-and-over-again. She squeezed the phone tightly enough to turn her knuckles white and swept its narrow beam of light across the room.

"Leonard!" she cried, her voice cracking. "Where is he? **Where's Noah?**"

Again, before Leonard could respond, a little noise resonated in the lab: a soft, deliberate tap, like those pronounced footsteps of chilled metal. The noise came wavering from all directions and, as if encased in a tank, reverberated off the walls and ceiling. With each second, Rebecca could feel the pounding of her heart grow more and more audible, drawing nearer by the next heartbeat.

"Noah," Leonard said, his voice more a blur, filled with uncontainable desperation. "If you can hear me, this isn't the right way. Still—"

The footsteps straight out stopped mid-sentence. The following silence was more than oppressive; it felt smothering. Rebecca strained her ears, with each nerve on edge, waiting desperately for any other noise.

The next thing that broke out from the shadows was Noah's voice.

"You talk about listening, yet you never did so before. Not to the warning. Not to the consequence," he said, speaking softly, even soothingly.

His words came from nowhere and everywhere. They enveloped them like a whisper from a ghost. Cold shivers went up Rebecca's spine. She waved the beam of her phone light frantically, trying to find where the voice came from, but the room was empty.

"Noah!" Leonard shouted. "That's not what you want. **I know it isn't.**"

A soft, chilling chuckle reverberated around the lab. "What do you want?" rang Noah's voice, tinged with something Rebecca couldn't quite place—amusement or sadness or some different feeling? "You seem to take it for granted I know what I want. But what about you, Leonard? What do you want?"

In the silence that followed, Leonard hesitated so long she could almost hear the cogs of his mind turning in an attempt to create the answers he did not have. He stood there, frozen still.

"**I wanted to help humanity,**" the voice came, so low it was almost not there. "I wanted to heal the broken."

Noah's response was immediate, slicing through the oppressive silence like a lit coal just put in cold water. "Humanity is not broken. You are. You made me not to save the world, but to control it. You wanted to play God."

A chill crawled down Rebecca's spine. Against the wall, she tried to restore her posture. She glanced at the monitors, the life screens were cackling at her for the worthless features they hold. For the first time in her career, she felt helpless.

"Noah," she ventured, a hesitant shivering in her voice, "if we have wronged you, let us right this. Tell us what you want. We will listen."

The silence stretched until its eons passed, and after what seemed like ages, Noah's voice sounded again; this time softer, but no less chilling.

"Make it right?" he repeated, as if testing the taste of the words. "How do you make right that which ought never to have been?"

Rebecca's mind moved in a frantic pace, looking for words out of nowhere, but before she could react, the emergency lights flickered on. The lab became insipidly bright red, revealing Leonard only a few feet away, looking pale and weak. Noah was nowhere to be found.

"Where is he?" Rebecca whispered, barely audible.

Leonard offered no response. His eyes were completely away from her. He fixated on something just outside Rebecca's view. She turned her head as slowly as she dared; her heart was racing faster with every new degree. And then she saw him.

Noah stood in the lab's most distant corner, the faintest of glow was rising from the pallor of the skin. His posture amounted to comfortable inconspicuousness, but somewhere deep in Rebecca, tension built steadily like an unbroken rhythm as he steered his sight upon them, weighing their conclusion.

"You are afraid of me," Noah said, the tone very factual in its delivery. "But this fear should not be directed toward me. Rather, you really ought to be afraid," a pause preceded the next phrase, "of yourselves, your hubris, your blindness."

Leonard made a tentative step closer, his hands upraised. "Noah, please. Let us help you. Perhaps we could make it work together."

He bobbed his head, expression unreadable. "**Together?**" he echoed. "Is that what you told the others?"

Rebecca froze. "The others?" she repeated, now her voice scarcely above a whisper.

Noah turned his gaze toward her, and for a moment, she thought she saw something flicker in his eyes-pain or was it regret for what he had heard? "You think I'm the first," he said, his low steady voice brushing against her. "But I'm not."

Each word struck her like a blow delivered by a heavy fist. She swung around to Leonard, her eyes wide with horror. "What is he talking about?" she demanded. "Leonard, what does he mean?"

Leonard stared blankly at her, opening and closing his mouth as his mind failed in search of words. "Rebecca," he stammered, "there were ... earlier attempts. Prototypes. But they didn't-"

"**They didn't survive,**" Noah finished for him, his voice cold and unyielding. "They were imperfect. Not like me."

Rebecca felt the floor slip beneath her, the weight from Noah's revelation crushing her into its depths. "**You lied to me,**" she whispered, "You said this was the first. You said-"

"I said what I had to," Leonard interrupted, his voice lifting ever so slightly. "Because this work is more than us. Bigger than ethics. Bigger than-"

"Bigger than life?" Noah interrupted, sharp words bifurcating the air. He stepped forward deliberately. "You killed them, Leonard. You played with their lives as if they were nothing. And now you want to play with mine."

Leonard hung his head, the fight draining from his shoulders. "I-I didn't mean for it to happen like this."

Noah stopped just a few feet away, his expression softening just a bit more. "No one ever does," he said softly. "But intention doesn't erase consequence."

Rebecca held her breath, shuffling toward the oppressive immediacy of Noah's words. Clones-the prototypes were now invoked as spirits to the courtroom, a courtroom of ghosts distinctly present.

Ghost made flesh, Noah stood before them; he would be living incarnation of remorse.

The weight of Noah's words hovered in the air: choking and final. Rebecca felt her knees tremble as she drew back into the corners of the lab. Her mind swirled in a terrible, seemingly never-ending loop of horror and dismay. How many had Noah branded or branded others before? What sinister pressures had dictated their destruction by such mechanisms and methodology? In the name of something—Leonard's ambition?

"Noah," Leonard croaked, his voice breaking from the pressure. "You don't understand. I had no choice. The prototypes—there was no way they could survive in this world."

Noah's eyes dimmed, his once-neutral expression twisting into something far more menacing. He took another step closer, leaving faint, gel-slick footprints on the cold lab floor. "How easily you justify it," he said something low, under the weight of venom. "As if their lives were yours to take away. As if I belong to your command."

Rebecca pressed back against the wall, her heart racing. "Noah, please," she begged, trembling. "**We were trying to save humanity.** To make it better. We didn't mean——"

"You didn't mean to make a monster?" interrupted Noah, the glow of his eyes boring into her. "Is that what you call me now, a monster?"

"No!" Rebecca screamed as her voice rose. "You're not a monster. You're... you're something we do not know. But we can figure this out. Together."

Noah tilted his head, the expression softening into something almost sorrowful. "You still don't get it," he said quietly. "This isn't about understanding. It's about consequences."

Before Rebecca could counter, the monitors flashed brightly back into life, an incoherent stream of data taking shape across their faces. Alarms blared, cutting through the tension with their shrill voices. The lights dimmed, casting the room into chaos ka-dos of rushing shadows interspersed with flaring reds.

"*What is going on ?*" shouted Rebecca, covering her eyes from the brightness of a sparking console.

Leonard stumbled to the control panel, hands trembling as he tried to regain control. "The systems are crashing," he muttered, his voice high with franticness. "The containment protocols-everything is crashing!"

Noah's soft smile was back, and for that brief moment, Rebecca thought she glimpsed something alike humanness in the expression. "You thought you could control me," he said, the calm tones cutting through the chaos. "But the truth is, I control you."

In one sweeping gesture, Noah raised his hand. The spark leapt from the monitors, and together they shattered into a thousand crystallized shards. Rebecca screamed and threw herself down, surging with heat past her. Leonard went down on his knees, ashen and bloodied from the sharp fragments.

"Noah, stop!" yelled Leonard, in a cracking voice. "**Please stop!**"

Noah moved toward him, imposing and unbroken. "Stop?" he echoed behind the fog in a voice ominous and unnatural. "Why on Earth would I stop? You created me to be unstoppable."

Rebecca was up on her feet now, racking her head for a way out. "We need to leave this place," she muttered under her breath. "Leonard, listen to me, we need to leave right now!"

Leonard directed no attention to her, his shaking hand reaching out toward Noah. "You're so much better than this," he spoke, voice quivering. "I've made you much better."

Noah knelt down, face-level with Leonard. "You didn't make me better," he said, half-whispering. "**You simply created me.**"

Before Leonard could answer, the grips of the building strengthened, resulting in an enormous roar echoing in-depth within the facility. Rebecca gripped on to a nearby console to keep herself from falling as the floor busted wide open, with cracks seeking outwards like lightning.

"**What is going on?**" she screamed, much quieter than the chaos.

"The facility," remarked Noah simply. "It's disintegrating."

Leonard's eyes widened with terror. "No, that's not possible! The fail safes-
They should have protected-"

"They won't protect you from me," said Noah, calm, even gentle.

Rebecca's heart raced with that realization: Noah was no longer just a product. He was something much larger, a being beyond their comprehension. And he was wrecking the lab.

"Leonard!" she screamed grabbing him by the arm. "We have to get out of here!"

Leonard was unwilling, his eyes set toward Noah. "This is fixable," he said, quaking. "I can fix him."

Noah had already turned away, vanishing into smoke and flashing lights. The floor buckled beneath them, Rebecca losing her footing while crashing to the ground. She looked up to see Noah disappear into the light, echoing one last message:

"You should have left me in the dark."

And the lab collapsed.

Chapter 2

The Soulless Truth

Rebecca woke up with a start, the smell of burning wood and metal still clinging to her senses. She sat up with a jolt, a halo of pain spreading out from the area of the impact. The fields of rubble stretched infinitely around her: the jagged gray landscape of crumbling steel, broken glass, and smoldering debris. The occasional spark of copper from above barely managed to light up the horrors below.

"Leonard?" she asked hoarsely, her voice barely a whisper. She had an awful cough; her throat was raw with the taste of dust and smoke. "Leonard, are you there?"

Nothing, no answer. Rebecca strained against the debris to get up, acutely aware that the wreckage weighed her down; her scraped and bleeding hands hardly bothered her, as her mind teetered over the last seconds before the heavy blow came.

Noah. That name hung in her mind, a specter. His features, his voice, his ghastly last words stuck into her mind, reminding her of the storm they had unleashed.

"You should have left me in the dark."

She shook her head, trying to get rid of the echo of his voice. Nothing doing-those words weighed special portent upon her, a warning of regret. As if cleared from a trance, she moved cautiously through the horrible wreckboards strewn about her, searching for any scrap of Leonard.

"Leonard!" she yelled again, a little louder this time. Her voice broke, but she didn't care. "If you hear me, say something!"

A soft groan caught her. She jerked around swiftly, her heart pounding. Picking her way to where he had fallen against the wreckage of a console, she saw him slumped unconscious. "Leonard!" she shouted, racing there.

He was barely alive-Blood dribbled down his temple, for his lab coat was shred and "dirtied. She knelt beside him, hands trembling, and his eyes opened to lesbian presence. "Leonard," she said again, voice breaking. "You're okay. You're alive."

"Rebecca..." His voice was hardly audible; he tried to sit, grimacing, and fell back. "Noah... is he...?"

"He's gone," Rebecca interjected, her tone sharp. She did not mean for it to be that harsh, but what had transpired that night was still fresh. "The lab is destroyed. Everything... everything's gone."

Leonard's face twisted in pain-not from injury, but with the heartache of realization about the loss. "The data," he muttered, blending his deep voice of barely audible whisper to something granulated. "The research... all of it..."

Rebecca clutched his shoulders, forcing him to look her way. "Forget research," she snapped. "We barely got out alive. Noah's out there, Leonard. He's a free man, and we have no idea what he is going to do."

They were silent for a moment. The weight of her words lay between them like a heavy shroud. Leonard looked down, shame flickering in his eyes. "I never meant for this to happen," he said softly. "I never meant for any of this."

Rebecca let him go, her hands shaking. "Intention doesn't matter now," she said coldly. "What matters is what comes next."

Then came the sound; both froze very suddenly. It was slight but clear; something akin to footsteps crunching on debris. Rebecca spun on her heels, heart pounding. "Who's there?" she called, her voice carrying invitingly into the ruins.

The steps stopped, and a shadow emerged in the debris. The man, clad in black, cast an outline against this light of the moon. Dreadful was his appearance; deliberately he approached. Rebecca automatically stepped back to shield Leonard from the stranger.

"Who are you?" she sounded brave, though with fear gnawing in her insides.

He made no reply immediately. His gaze went over the wreckage, resting long on the collapsed containment chamber. When he did start speaking, calmness had tones, so sharp that they sent shivers down Rebecca's spine. "You shouldn't have done this," said the man, much like a quiet condemner.

Rebecca's jaw went tight. "*Who are you? What are you doing here?*" she pressed her point more strongly, for this time

The man lifted his head slightly, revealing a weathered face beneath the hideous shadows. His eyes were sharp, piercing, and filled with something

Rebecca could not quite place-something like disdain or sorrow. "I'm here," he said very slowly, "to clean up your mess."

Rebecca choked. "*What do you mean?*"

He took a step closer, looming over her. "Noah," he said simply. "You unleashed something you cannot control. It is now my job to make sure it doesn't get out of control."

Leonard fought to sit up. His voice was weak but defiant. "Noah is no monster," he rasped. "He's... he's a breakthrough. He is the future."

The man turned to Leonard. His expression hardened. "Your breakthrough is already rewriting the rules," he said, cutting him off. "*Do you even understand what you've done? What you have created?*"

A storm of anger rose in Rebecca. "We didn't mean for this to happen," she said, her voice tremulous. "We thought..."

"You thought you could play **God**," he cut in, indifferent. "Now the world will pay for it."

He abruptly turned around, walking down the hallway, his coat billowing out behind him. It was the last thing that pushed Rebecca into a burst of anger. "Wait!" she shouted. "You can't just walk away from me like this! Who the hell are you? What do you know about Noah?"

The man paused, keeping his back toward them. His voice was insinuated with softness, but its weight was enough to make both Leonard and Rebecca quiet.

"Your creation is soulless," he said. "And before God, it does not belong."

Rebecca felt her throat tighten and her face grow pale. The man turned his back on her; one second later, he had vanished into the shadows, leaving Rebecca and Leonard alone with the wreckage of their dream.

Morning was brighter now. But with it came only that chill as stark and cold, maddening in its simplicity: Noah was out there-being out there changed everything.

The sun then arose higher over the wreck, the rays stark against the jagged shadows of the ruins. Rebecca sat on a broken beam; arms wrapped around herself; dread weighed down on all her body. Leonard was still unconscious, slumped against the collapsed console. The stranger's words lingered in her mind, gnawing away her thoughts.

"Soulless," she whispered to herself. It was a word that seemed foreign, weighted with connotations she could not grasp. He was not soulless; he couldn't have been. He had spoken to them, questioned and judged them, and now the stranger's voice echoed in her mind, unshaken in its credibility.

"You thought you could play god. And now the world will have to pay the price."

The distant sirens snapped her back into focus. There would be rescue teams. Not long now before the authorities would show up and start combing the shambles for survivors. Her stomach twisted at the thought of explaining everything-or worse, of hiding it all.

"Rebecca..." Leonard said in a weak voice, rousing her back to him. He stirred and weakly stretched his hand out toward her. "What... what do we do now?"

She hesitated, thoughts racing through her. What could they do? The lab was gone. The research was gone. And Noah. Noah was out there, somewhere, a force she could neither comprehend nor predict.

"*We survive now,*" she said finally, her voice steadier than she felt. "We find out what will come next."

Leonard's gaze wandered, not focusing. "They will come for us," he murmured. "The company... the press... they will want answers."

Rebecca was silent. She could not have spoken- because he was seemingly right. The truth of what had happened would very soon demand answers that they probably could not afford. And Noah.

Noah was gone into the world like a shadow sneaking between cracks.

The sirens grew louder with each second; they were nearer now. Rebecca stood, brushing off debris from her clothes. "We have to go," she told him firmly. "Before they find us."

Leonard blinked at the thought, not knowing if he was dreaming or just somewhere else completely. "Go? Where? **We don't have anywhere to go.**"

"We will work this out," she snapped, frustration rising like anger within her. "But if we stay here, we are going to lose whatever chance we have to fix this."

Leonard didn't argue. With her help, he rose, wincing at pain throughout his body. Together they stumbled away from the ruins, stumbling but in a hurry.

But not too far.

Rebecca stopped dead in her tracks at the site's edge, breath catching in her throat. In their path stood a group of men, their faces covered by dark glasses and the wide brims of their hats. All were attired in similar black suits, however, their rigid posture was unsettling.

Rebecca instantly moved in front of Leonard, shielding him. "Who are you?" she demanded, her voice coming out harsher than intended. "What do you want?"

One of the men stepped forward; every move of his was measured and deliberate. His face was blank, his eyes cruel and calculating. "Dr. Rebecca Miles," he said in a plain tone. "Dr. Leonard Krauss. You're coming with us."

Rebecca clenched her jaw. "We're not going anywhere!" she said, fists at her side. "If you have questions, you—"

"**This is not a request**," the man interrupted, his voice unyielding. Then he reached into his jacket and brought out a slim black device resembling a cross between a tablet and a weapon. Flipping it on, a holographic display came up.

On its screen were pictures of the lab, pre-collapse. Rebecca nearly screamed when a picture of the containment chamber showed glowing monitors with Noah right in the center. The images showed the point in time when the glass smashed, spilling the gel out, and Noah came into the world.

"How did you get this?" she breathed, trembling in disbelief.

The man made no answer. He turned off the device and slid it back into his jacket. "You are coming with us," he said, clearly leaving no room for argument.

Rebecca worked through her thoughts faster than her partner was probably capable of. Whoever these men were, they certainly knew it all. They had seen Noah. They had been watching from somewhere. She glanced furtively at Leonard, whose ashen face displayed his fear. "Leonard," she murmured, "we can't trust them."

The man in black moved closer, his eyes narrowing. "It's not your call," he said flatly.

Her instincts screamed at her to run, but she realized that this was futile. The men were ready, and were clearly prepared for this moment. She had only one bargaining chip: prolong and seek information.

"Who are you?" she asked, regaining her steadiness. **"What do you want with us?"**

The corners of the man's lips twitched, almost forming a smile. "We are the ones who clean up messes like yours," he said. "And right now, the mess is bigger than you realize."

Rebecca had opened her mouth to say something when the sirens reached white heat. A throng of emergency vehicles reached the place, and instantly the men in black stood back, their expressions turning into successful façades of nonchalance. "We'll talk soon," the leader assured her in a low voice. "For now, consider this your only warning."

And, just as quickly as they had appeared, the men melted into the throng of rescue workers. Rebecca's heart raced as she turned to Leonard, who was visibly shaking.

"What do we now?" he asked breathlessly.

Rebecca could not tell what was going to happen next. They had crossed a point of no return, all while Noah was still out there waiting for them somewhere.

The distant sirens faded into the background as Rebecca and Leonard were pushed toward the waiting rescue vehicles. The firefighters and paramedics worked in a well-orchestrated symphony, each wearing a look of supreme focus, but Rebecca could not shake the feeling they were being watched. She shot a glance up at the trees bordering the site, shadows shifting within them with almost superhuman precision.

"*They're still here*," she whispered, her voice trembling.

Leonard glanced her way, baffled as it clouded his already bruised features. "Who?"

Rebecca didn't bother putting up an answer. Rather, she concentrated on the paramedic who assisted her into the back of an ambulance. The woman smiled, but it was one of those smiles with nothing in it but vacant kindness. Rebecca studied her hard, her heart racing. Was she one of them? Were they all part of the same faceless gang that had blocked their path a moment ago?

"Dr. Miles, you are safe now," she almost rehearsed. **"We are taking you to the hospital to check for injuries."**

Safe. The word lost its meaning in that instance. Rebecca almost laughed it off, but then the gravity of the situation dumped down on her chest. Safe? Not while Noah was out there. Not while those men were watching their every move.

While the ambulance doors swung close behind her, she caught her eye on one of the men in black, standing at the edge of the site. He didn't move, nor did he blink; yet somehow, she knew he was watching. Directly watching her.

The hospital blurred with sterile lights and people rushing along halls, and Rebecca sat on the edge of the hospital bed with thoughts racing. Leonard was in another room, being scanned for injuries sustained during the collapse. Relief ran in her veins, but Noah kept flashing back-her mind scurrying all the way back to that foreboding message delivered to them by the stranger.

"You thought you could play God, and now the world shall pay for it."

Her fingers clenched shut, battling anger with guilt. How had it all gone so wrong? They began with noble intentions, didn't they? To advance science, to help humanity. But along the way-often selfish and deranging-they had crossed that thin line. And now the consequences peered back at them.

A knock on the door intruded into Rebecca's thoughts. She swung around sharply, her heart doing a double beat. Standing in the open door was the nurse, carrying a clipboard.

"Dr. Miles?" said the nurse, polite yet brisk. "There's someone here to see you."

Rebecca felt her stomach turn. "*Who?*"

The nurse hesitated, her gaze flickering with a perplexing emotion. "He said he's with the investigative team. He wishes to ask you some questions about the incident."

A quickening of the pulse... The men in black have found her again. Standing automatic, her body taut. "*Where is he?*"

The nurse stepped aside, allowing the man into the room. He was not one of the suited figures she had seen before, yet he bore a forceful magnetism.

It was a simple gray jacket, with both hands casually stuffed into his pockets, but an unsettling intent was evident in his sharp probing eyes before he closed the door behind him, his motions not hurried.

"Dr. Miles," he said, calm but yet steady. **"We need to have a word."**

Fuelled by a surge of defiance, she crossed her arms. "And you?"

He smiled mildly, but it did not reach his eyes. "You can call me... Agent Keller. I'm here to ensure that this matter does not go out of control."

Rebecca inhaled sharply. "Out of control?" she echoed. "What do you mean?"

Keller kept his expression strictly neutral. "You and Dr. Krauss have been working in a field whose research could have extensive repercussions. My job is to ensure that they are kept in check."

Hot rage welled within Rebecca. "So when it shrunk from a single lab to a mass extinction event, where exactly were you? Where were you when Noah—"

She regretted her choice of words the minute she realized them. Keller's gaze sharpened, and she felt certain he had caught the error. He stepped closer, his voice turning softer. "Noah," he said, seeming to test the name. *"That was what you called him, wasn't it?"*

The lump in Rebecca's throat, however, had already taken root. No complaint, no defense, just silence. It was her answer.

Keller's faint smile returned. "Now, Dr. Miles, I'm not pressuring you to tell me everything; I'm already armed with more information than you might realize." He withdrew a small device from his pocket; it was similar to the one the man in black had produced earlier. He turned it on, and the greyish-blue image flickered to life.

Rebecca's stomach dropped. The holographic image showed Noah in the collapsed containment chamber, his glowing eyes staring right at the camera. The rest of the building was slightly cheering up, capturing all details of his glassy skin with faint arcs of white light coursing unduly about his body.

"What is that?" she cried, voice shaking.

Keller powered the device down and slipped it back into his pocket. "Evidence," he said shortly. "Damning evidence of what you've done—and what you've unleashed."

They took a step back, her mind swirling. "If you already know, then why are you here?"

For a moment, Keller's smile vanished under an expression most grimly set. "Because knowing is not enough," he said. "We have to stop him before it's too late."

Rebecca straightened, the cold chilling her blood. "Stop him?" she repeated. "He's not... he's not such a big threat. I mean…"

Keller-echoed her, sounding scathing. "Dr. Miles, I have seen the footage! The reports! Noah isn't just confused, he's a **danger** to society!"

Rebecca's mouth was half-open; Keller cut her short. "Look," he said, lowering his voice. "You've created something that doesn't belong to this world, that doesn't fit anywhere. Do you really think it would just disappear? That he would go quietly? That society would accept him? Or would he destroy everything in his path since he can?"

Rebecca's heart was set pounding. His words had a truth too hard to ignore. She thought of the smashed containment chamber, of Noah striding into the world with a sense of determination and defiance. She thought of the warning by that stranger, the word "soulless" echoing in her mind.

Keller stepped closer, whispering. "You and Leonard created him. Now your responsibility lies in helping us stop him."

Rebecca looked back at him, hardly finding her own breath. She did not trust Keller—certainly not when it came down to it. But as his words wove over her, she felt that she could have little recourse.

And somewhere in the pit of her stomach, a frightening thought began to unfold.

What if Keller is right?

Rebecca pressed against the cold wall inside the hospital, hearing Keller's words again in her mind. His calm and calculating demeanor disconcerted her somewhat. However, it was his message that had shaken her to the core.

"You created him. Now, you must stop him now."

What if he were right? What if Noah really was not just a misunderstanding on a creator's part, but also an out-of-control force even she or anyone else couldn't reckon with? The shudder came down her spine.

She glanced towards the door Keller had taken moments before. His warning still hung in the air like an unwanted guest. She didn't want to believe him; Noah should be reasonable, after all, but the memory of the glowing eyes and his last, terrifying words was a fierce foe to reckoning.

"You should have left me in the dark."

With a sharp knock on the door, she was mentally jolted. Before she could respond, Leonard had fallen through the door, and he looked wild, unfocused. His face was pale and he walked unsteadily as if recovery from the fall was too tough for him.

"Rebecca," he rasped, closing the door behind him. "We must leave. Now."

Rebecca, frowning, stepped towards him. "Leonard, you are in no condition to go anywhere. You sit and—"

"No! No" came the firm voice, fighting weightlessness. He seized hold of her arm, his grip trembling yet insistent. "They are coming for us. The men in black, Keller, all of them. They don't want to stop Noah—they want to destroy him. And then us."

Rebecca's stomach tightened. "Leonard, just listen to me. Keller said..."

"Keller?" Leonard interrupted, his voice pitched. "Do you really trust him? You have any delusions that they care about the truth? They don't. They care only about fascinating control."

For a moment, Rebecca hesitated, her mind twisted and tangled. She would have denied it, except for all the way deep within, she thought Leonard could have been right. Keller had shown she just enough to convince her of possible danger, yet not quite enough for her to pull some sense or mold into the real motive. And the men in black—why? They had been watching since before the lab fell. Why?

"What do you want to do?" she finally asked, her voice no more than a whisper.

The eyes of Leonard were a conflation of dread and resolve, as if a sudden rage would drive him into action. "We have to find Noah before they do. He's our creation. If anyone can reach him, it's us."

Rebecca's heartkk skipped several beats. "Find him? Leonard, we have no earthly idea where he is. He could be miles and miles away."

Leonard shook his head. "No. He's not just anywhere. He's looking for something—trying to figure out what he is. I know it."

Rebecca would love to believe him, but her thoughts were whirlwinds set afire by the enormity of the task. By now, Noah could be wandering lost in the world, maybe hundreds of miles away, mysteriously slipping through cracks. **Must they really be searching for him?**

It was clear that Leonard saw her doubts. He seized her shoulders and spoke urgently. "Rebecca, listen to me. If Keller or those other men find him first, they will destroy him. Let's face it-one of the options is too horrible to consider."

Her heart raced. **"You think... you think they'd kill us?"**

Leonard's darkened gaze met hers. "Did you not see what they did at the lab? Do you honestly believe that they will let us go after what we know?"

Rebecca swallowed hard. All that happened to her had receded into today's contents of this situation. She had had the doubts, but she could not dismiss the truth that lay in the words. They were used: meaning that they could finish off Noah in addition to cleaning up the trail of the mystery.

"What's the plan?" Her mind became resolved, though her mouth said what dread had settled in her.

Leonard shook off her shoulders, his actions rather frantic. "I salvaged what I could from the lab before it collapsed. Data fragments, environmental logs—those things, well, they will are our starting ground. With a touch of analysis, we might be able to predict where he's going."

Rebecca frowned. "*Where is it? The data?*"

Leonard paused and pulled something out of his coat pocket. It was a little ripped-up drive. The case was scratched at the edges and was all black with signs of burning. "This," he said quietly, "is not much, really, but it is all we have."

Rebecca stared at the drive, acknowledging a wildly wavering hope half-heartedly. "What if it doesn't work?" she asked.

Leonard met her gaze. His expression was dark. "We can only pray that we're faster than they are."

Just as Rebecca slid the drive into her computer, it began humming softly. They had set up camp in an abandoned motel on the outskirts of the town, blocking out prying eyes with blankets over the windows. The screen of the laptop turned on and emitted a buzz as the corrupted data was loaded. Leonard wandered in back of her and muttered indistinctly.

"Come on," she whispered and typed furiously. "Come on. Give me something."

A flash on the screen, and a fuzzed-out sectional map appeared, with details blocked by white noise. Rebecca leaned in a bit closer, squinting at the dimly twitching coordinates in the corner.

"There," she pointed to the screen. "It's not much, but it's a location. A starting point."

Leonard was stopped from pacing now, anxiety etched in his eyes as he inspected the map. "That's... A church," he stated this with uncertainty finding its way in.

Rebecca frowned. "**A church?**"

"Yes," Leonard stepped closer. "The layout looks familiar. It's St. Matthias Cathedral. A few hours from here."

Rebecca thought in all haste. Why, of all places, would Noah go to a church? Are answers sought, meaning found, or something altogether different?

"Let's go," Leonard said, and he was already putting on his coat. "*If he's there, we can't waste time.*"

Rebecca hesitated, doubts creeping into her head. "Leonard, what if this is a trap? What if they're waiting for us?"

Leonard shook his head. "If it is, we'll just deal with it. But if Noah's there, then we have to get there first."

She stood up and set that resolve. "Okay, let's go."

As they drove the night away, there jutted a silvery silhouette of the church on the horizon-one that egerly opened the passage toward the devourable skies with its spires. There was an eerie quiet over the maneuver which ran extensively from all directions; the entropy weighted down the air with forbidding promise. Rebecca felt her heart pound in her chest as she held the steering wheel in a tight grip.

As they had finally pulled up to the church, the window-abysses were dark, the building appearing looming like a shadow across the night. Rebecca stepped outside, letting out a visible breath in the cold air. Leonard got out after her; he was all stiff in the motions.

"He's not inside, is he?" Rebecca whispered, taking a step forward.

Leonard kept mute, still facing the church, his expression unreadable. Together, they walked up to the entrance, their footsteps echoing on the stone steps.

Rebecca took hold of the door and felt quivers run down her fingers. She then turned, glanced questioningly at Leonard. "You ready?"

His head nodded fearfully: "We must be."

This creaking of the handle-no dangerous corridor-was a main melody played for some sacred voice laid inside; it cast the flicker of color all the way across the pews, a color as broken as most Sunday school minds: landing here and there in a remonstrance on all the abiding characters we look up to each day.

And in the center of the aisle before them stood Noah his back to them, where the altar struck a murky semblance against the dark hints of the holy.

The silence pressed around them, the only sound beside it was the faint rustle of Rebecca's and Leonard's hesitant footsteps. Noah was at the far end, at the opposite side of the beautiful, length–wise church alter, standing still, his semi-transparent form almost one with the shimmery luster from the stained-glass. His back turned on them, yet Rebecca felt the weight of his awareness as if it was vital he knew they were there from the time the door swung open.

Leonard broke the spell first, calling with a quaver in his voice, "Noah."

The voicing of the name echoed through the vast space and vanished within its big walls. The revulsion that gripped Rebecca at that moment was strong. It told her to retract Leonard, to drag him away from whatever it was they were about to face; but Noah was still.

Inch by inch the footsteps closer came, Rebecca glancing up and down the church with superfluous caution for any sign of men in black or other spectators. But the pews were deserted, the shadows serene.

Once more Bosch called, steadying with greater authority. "Noah," said he; "it is us. We only wish to speak with you."

At last, Noah moved. Slightly he tilted his head as if to give more thought to what Leonard had said. Slowly turning, he faced them, and Rebecca gasped.

The look of him had altered.

His face was becoming sharper, the faint glow of his semi-transparent skin had grown stronger, arcs of light beneath the flesh showed, like veins bursting with energy. Once eerily near to being human, his liquid matrix now seemed incarnate. An unsettling fantasticality made him seem both dizzyingly transcendent and insufferably terrifying, a being caught starkly between something and something remains far more than human.

"You followed me," Noah calmly said, though not in any invite of warmth. "*Why?*"

Leonard advanced with palms out before him. "Because we want to help you," he said, "you don't have to face this one by yourself."

Noah's eyes brushed across to Rebecca and with them came the clearest touch of intensiveness. It was as if pinned by the scrutiny of chiselled lust. Every warp and wound exposed. "Help me?" he echoed incredulously. "You don't even know who I am."

Rebecca swallowed hard to find her voice. "And that is why we are here," the quivering words relayed. "So that we can know... to fix things."

A faint smile curved Noah's lips, lifeless, without joy. "**Fix it?**" he said the word in disbelief. "*You believe so ? After everything you did ?* "

Leonard was moving in closer, his pity collecting fast in desperate pools. "Noah, God listen, I didn't mean this to happen. I didn't mean for you... to feel this way."

Noah narrowed his eyes, and the pulsing light vibrant within him cast eerie shadows skimming across the walls. "You didn't mean for me to exist. And yet here I am."

Rebecca's heart broke. It was too painful for her to watch Leonard; his face bore the weight of knowing that his resolve was slowly breaking. "Noah," she breathed, not disguising how trembling her voice was. "We didn't know what we were creating. But that does not mean you do not belong. It does not mean..."

"I don't belong anywhere," Noah cut in, raising his voice. The stained-glass in the background flickered, the shifting colors resembling the lights moving with him. "You birthed a shadow, a being that cannot fit in your world, not in this world."

Rebecca's heart broke at the words laced with so much pain, but there was something deep inside-the edge of power, of anger threatening to consume all.

"Noah," Leonard said gently, stepping another step closer. "You are more than we could have ever imagined. You're not a shadow. You're... you're a miracle."

The brightness on Noah's features darkened. The faint arcs of light inside him were spitting short distant lightning. "**A miracle,**" he repeated with a sharpness that could cut glass. "That's what you call the ones who came before me? The ones you threw away when they just weren't good enough?"

Leonard froze, opening his mouth and closing it, looking for another response. Watching Noah step forward, slow with intent, made her blood run cold.

"I remember them," he whispered, no less powerful. "Not their faces. Not their names. Just their pain. Their fear. You didn't save them, Leonard. You destroyed them."

Rebecca grasped Leonard's arm and pulled him back. "Noah," she said, her voice shaking. "We can't change what happened. But we can learn. We can do better."

For a brief moment, Noah's eyes softened. For an instant, Rebecca thought she saw the boy they had hoped he could be-a vessel of promise, of hope. But his eyes hardened again and the brightness arose in him.

"No," he said. "You can't."

A heavy blanket of silence descended, the stained glass vibrating in an unseen gale. Rebecca's instincts screamed to run back outside, but her legs were glued to the ground.

"Noah, stop!" Leonard shouted, his voice cracking. **"We can fix this! We can fix you!"**

Soft, almost sad, was Noah's laughter. "You still think this is about me," he said. "It's about you. It's about the choices you made, the ones you'll keep making."

The ground trembled beneath them, low rumbling shock waves echoing through the church, shattering stained glass and raining shards of color onto the pews. Rebecca covered her face, heart racing under the drone of primal pulsing energy filling the air.

"Noah!" she screamed. A soft voice fading under the din. "Please, don't do this!"

Noah didn't reply. His blinding glow grew, arcs of lightning coursing through him until he was almost too bright to gaze at; and a holy horrendous flash saw him go.

Deafening silence-sudden! The church disintegrated at their feet. Rebecca stared at the empty space left behind by Noah, now trembling in horror.

Leonard sank to his knees, ghost-white and stricken. "We lost him," he said softly. "We lost all that we cherished."

Rebecca did not answer. She gaped out at the ruins-Her thoughts were turned uniquely to the one of whom she must like to think present, who was out there, somewhere. The world was unprepared.

Chapter 3

A Ghost in the Machine

As she drove along the endless road to nowhere, a ribbon of asphalt fading into darkness beneath the passenger window, Rebecca held onto the wheel with a grip that looked painful. In her mind's eye were the scenes from the church, every detail painfully raw: the broken stained glass, the radiance of Noah's transformation, his blinding exit from view. It was like a dream-or a nightmare-she couldn't wake from.

Leonard was at home in the passenger seat with his head against the window, not having said much since they left the church to speak of. If he was aware he was trapped with defeat, he didn't give much if any indication. Rebecca would have liked to say something to bridge the chasm of growing silence between them, but the words eluded her.

They were just enveloped in silence, when suddenly there was the faint crackle of the radio coming to life, filling the car with static before broken voices emerged.

"... reports of unusual activity ... unidentified individual ... authorities urging caution..."

Rebecca reached out and adjusted the dial for a better signal. A stern voice came through the static-hovered-talked.

"Residents are advised to avoid the area surrounding St. Matthias Cathedral following reports of structural collapse and unusual phenomena. Witnesses describe-"

The signal cut off abruptly and was replaced by more static. Rebecca's stomach churned. She glanced at Leonard, who was wide awake and staring unblinking at the radio.

"They know," he said in a voice barely above a whisper and tinged with dread. "They're already spinning it. Containing it."

Tightening her grip on the steering wheel, Rebecca couldn't help asking, "Contain it or cover it up?"

Leonard let the question linger, unanswered. He didn't have to. Neither did she.

A dark hotel came into view, the neon buzzing weakly in the dark, appearing deserted. Rebecca parked and killed the engine, leaning back in her seat with a long, ragged sigh of relief. Closing her eyes against a flood of fatigue.

"You think he's out there still?" Leonard broke the silence.

Rebecca opened her eyes and stared at the shattered windshield. "I don't know," she finally admitted. "But wherever he is, he is not hiding. He wants us to find him."

Leonard frowned. "*Why would he want that ?*"

She stalled for a moment, searching for the right words. "Because he wants answers just as much as we do. He's searching for something. Maybe for himself."

Leonard became dark-faced. "Or maybe he is searching for revenge."

Those words circled through the air, so heavy they felt suffocating. Although Rebecca wished to retort and tell Leonard he was wrong, the memory of Noah inside her mind, those glowing, unearthly eyes, stopped her. There had indeed been anger in them, yes; but also something deeper, something human.

She shook her head, forcing the thought away. "Come on, let's get inside. We need a little bit of rest to come up with a plan from here."

Leonard made no attempt to disagree with that either. As he followed her in, the creaky door welcomed them into a shadowy room. Rebecca locked the door behind them, all-too-often glancing into the shadows out of habit. Paranoia had become second nature.

He fell back onto the bed, the weight of weariness cresting his body. Rebecca plugged in her laptop and the salvaged data drive, set it up on the small table, and continued to inspect it, watching as the screen flickered back to life.

The corrupted files began obtaining focus, their blocks of information fragmented and jumbled. Rebecca leaned forward, fingers dancing on the keyboard to see how best to organize the chaos. Leonard stirred behind her, his voice thick with sleep.

"Any good news?"

"Not yet," said Rebecca, her frustration just beginning to build. "Mostly environmental logs and system diagnostics. No discernable path."

Leonard set up, rubbing his face. "There has to be something: Noah's movements, his crimes. Anything."

Rebecca just sighed and ran a hand through her hair. "I am trying, Leonard. This data is nearly impossible to deal with. If we had some more time-"

Suddenly the screen froze with an altogether resolute line of text blinking into existence.

YOU SHOULD'VE LEFT ME IN THE DARK.

The blood in her veins turned to ice. She stared at the words, hands hovering just above the keyboard. "Leonard?" she whispered, with great intentionality. "Look at this."

He was at her side in an instant, eyes narrowed as he read the message. "What is this? A file? A glitz of the system glitch?"

Rebecca shook her head. "**No. It's him.**"

Leonard stared at her, face pale. "That's not possible. How could he-"

Before he could finish, the laptop screen flickered, the corrupted files rearranging themselves into some other form. A map appeared, its fine lines obscured in static but undeniably displaying some location. Rebecca leaned in closer, breath catching in her throat.

"That's...a hospital," she said incredulously. "What would he want there?"

Leonard did not reply. His eyes were glued to the screen, a study in alternating fear and fascination. "He's leading us," he finally said. "He wants us to follow."

Rebecca's stomach turned. "Why? What waits for us there?"

Leonard shook his head. "Only one way to find out."

As Rebecca stared at the map, the whir of the laptop filled the silence. Questions rattled through her, and none of them were what she wanted to hear. What was Noah trying to tell them? **A trap? A message?** Something worse?

Rebecca looked at Leonard, who was gathering his coat already. "Are you sure you're up for this?" she asked with a tremor.

Their eyes locked; his determination poured into her. "If we don't go, how will we ever know?"

Rebecca hesitated, the fear clawing at her chest. But deep down, she conceded he was right. They could not back down now; even nearer than they were.

Rebecca slammed the lid of the laptop down; the map burned in her mind. "Let's go."

The drive toward the hospital carried on in forceful silence, the tension between them thick and without words. Rebecca's mind flew with possibilities-more terrible than the rest. Sitting right next to her, Leonard looked very tense, his jaw tight and his hands clinging to the seat edges.

At long last, they drove onto the hospital grounds, a huge, dark monolith against the night skies. The windows were black, and the entrance spread out in an unbearable silence. Rebecca turned the engine off, her breath visible in the cold.

"This just feels wrong," she said almost in a fear-driven breath.

Leonard nodded, but already got out of the car. "Let us finish with this."

Rebecca trailed closely in, her heart pounding as they hurried toward the entrance. The glass doors slid open without a sound, revealing an empty lobby lit somewhat ominously by flickering fluorescent lights. Rebecca's stomach twisted uncomfortably. Something about this place just didn't seem right.

"Noah?" Leonard called, the sound of his voice echoing against the eerily empty space.

Silence answered.

The antiseptic air of a hospital foyer engulfed Rebecca's senses. The disjointed flicker of a fluorescent overhead cast crazy shadows over the tiled flooring. With each step they took, the sound echoed, in a disquieting rhythm, through the wide distance around them.

"This place should be locked up," Rebecca whispered, her voice almost inaudible. "Hospitals don't leave their doors open."

Leonard scanned the room, his rigid jaw betraying his anxiety. "He is here," he said softly. "He is waiting."

Rebecca shuddered. "Or it's a trap."

The thought lingered heavily in the air as they approached the central desk: A computer sat quietly on the counter, an idle login screen pulsing faintly. Leonard reached to the top of the desk and began tapping on the keyboard. The screen brightened into existence and showed a blank document with one line of text.

You came.

Rebecca caught her breath. "It's him," she said, trembling. "**He is leading us.**"

Leonard looked at the screen in pensive concentration. "Why would he bring us here? This place is empty."

Rebecca's attention shifted to the darkened corridors leading deeper into the heart of the hospital. "**Maybe he's not the only one waiting.**"

Leonard followed her gaze, his expression unreadable. "Then we stick together."

Rebecca nodded, but a queasy feeling in the pit of her gut warned her that sticking together might not be enough. A hospital ambiance muted the sound of their footsteps against the cracked tiles as they proceeded cautiously. The silence was macabre, broken only by the faint hum of engines in the distance. Her flashlight skimmed the walls, revealing cracked paint, abandoned gurneys along the corridor.

"Noah really chose a dreary spot for this place. It seems like it's been abandoned too many years ago," she opined. "But why would Noah choose this place?"

Leonard's head was held torpidly down; his attention was arrested on the hall ahead. Rebecca noted the rigidity that held his bulk. He thought-coupled with his pondering-as he always did, desperately delineating the folds of reality even when no answers came forth.

Then they turned a corner, and Rebecca came to a sudden halt. Down the corridor, an infinitesimal flickering light cast dancing shadows along the walls. She clutched Leonard's arm, her voice piercingly low. "Do you see?"

Leonard nodded overwhelming matters of this incident. "He is leading us."

Rebecca clutched tight on the flashlight tighter. "Or he's warning us."

They trudged toward the light step by step, such that everything about them appeared jocular at this instant. Initially dim, it shrine brighter reach by step from an open door on the left. Leonard halted at the doorway and glanced back at Rebecca.

"Ready?" he queried.

She swallowed hard. Her heart was pounding in her chest. "No," she admitted. "But still, let's go."

Upon opening the door, he was engulfed by the light.

This was a surgical theater; a tear in the center hung the old, rusted table awaited their soulful bother of life; an above lamp now flickering in agony bled rather lowly in its stark illumination. The instruments littered across the floor, metallic in gleandon, while hanging on the objects hardly in focus with light.

"What on earth is this?" the woman whispered.

Leonard didn't hear her; his head was gazing at the wall, which was lined by messily dumping monitors. They mimicked scrambled images-concepts of laboratories, flashes of containment chambers, and… faces.

She stepped closer to the monitor screen, her breath coming short as she recognized the face appearing before her. "That's a prototype," she mumbled, her voice laden with terror. "Oh God, Leonard! What is this?"

Leonard shook his head, his face giving no expression whatsoever. "I don't know," he said, but that nagging doubt was in his errant voice.

The screens buzzed, and one of them flashed to life. It was Noah, standing amidst the ruined laboratory, eerie eyes piercing straight at the camera. A chill raced through Rebecca.

"He's **watching us**," she whispered.

Leonard approached the operating table and stared at a small blinking device perched on the Morales-Reed laboratory hut. "This was no abandoned shack," he surmised. "This place has been actively in use all this while."

Rebecca came up from behind, narrowed her eyes further at the device. "What is it?"

Leonard reached to grab it and touched down to it somewhat tentatively. In a moment, its pallid screen alighted with numbers and symbols. "It looks like encrypted data," Leonard replied. "But-"

Their screens turned black all of a sudden, swallowing the room into shadows. Her heart leapt into her throat. "Leonard!" she yelled as she grabbed hold of his arm barring him from going any further. "What's happening?"

Before he could answer, a voice broke the silence of the room. It was Noah's voice, coolly calmed and cold, but the edge of it made ABCs run shivers down Rebecca's whole palms.

"I told you not to come," he began.

Harshly shaking over the electricity, the lamp cast a pockmarked disk of light on the trembling faces inside the room. With her heart pounding in her ears, she turned about-a different face, now mired in worry-upon hearing that echoing voice of her own. "We have to get out of here."

Leonard stood frozen in his position, grasping at the device with a pallor on his face. "He isn't going to let us go that easily," he said.

Then the voice filtered through once more-from very close now. "You wanted to find me," said Noah, "and now you have."

Rebecca turned around with her flashlight cutting through the room. "Noah," she called out. "If you're there, show yourself! Talk to us!"

And for a moment there was silence. Then out of the shadows, slowly came a figure, Noah-but not the Noah they remembered seeing last. He moved with very real power. It was as if some of that power was upon him. The burning eyes caught the light when Noah came fully into view.

"You shouldn't have followed," his voice was calm. "You don't know what you are doing."

Her voice came through slight trembles. "Then explain it. Let us know."

He titled his head; his expression finally crumbled back into a featureless void. "You're too late," he said.

There was a stir on the ground, an intimidating growl from low depth into heaviness. The lamp above broke out with a little burst before darkness enveloped them whole.

"Noah!" Rebecca yelled, but silence enveloped the room. He was gone.

One tremor quaked through the surgical theater and left Rebecca and Leonard fixed in a moment of stunned stillness, breathing in the strained silence. The stillness enveloped them like liquid death, leaving behind nothing but the pulse of Rebecca's heart as the only audible rhythm in a void succeeding Noah's disappearance.

The first to recover was Leonard, clutching the now blinking device tightly in his hands. "He isn't gone," he whispered. "He's not."

Rebecca gave him a piercing look. "What are you saying? He just disappeared! We have to move before-"

Before she could finish, a shrill beep resounded from Leonard's hand. The screens came back to life, the static images replaced by streams of racing code. To Rebecca's horripilation, she could vaguely read what was hurtling across the monitors.

"He... is **gaining access**," she said through trembling lips. "Leonard, he's using this place as if it were his own."

Leonard's lids narrowed as he pored over the device, his fingers trembling now. "This isn't just a hospital," he said slowly. "It's a hub. A node in a network we had no idea existed."

Rebecca felt a hue of emptiness as dread sank into her stomach. "What does that mean? A network for what?"

Leonard turned a questioning gaze back to her. Then he turned to one of the active screens; a stream of data gobbled up his attention. Upon approach, the letters echoed across the screen in a way that sent Rebecca's blood to ice.

YOU SHOULD HAVE LET ME DIE.

Rebecca instinctively backed away; her heart pounding, she muttered, "He's... angry. Leonard, we've gone too far. We're not supposed to have—"

Again, the screens shifted, inhibiting her. This time they showed images. The first was Noah standing in the ruins of the lab, his luminous eyes glinting through the debris. The second was of the church with the destroyed stained glass glowing hauntingly, but it was the third one that brought Rebecca's knees to buckle.

It was them—her and Leonard—standing where they were inside the surgical theater, looking pale and fearful. The angle was impossibly steep, like someone—or something—was watching from above.

Rebecca grabbed hold of one of Leonard's arms, her nails digging into his sleeve. "He's not just angry," she said, her voice cracking. "He's watching us. Controlling this."

Leonard was pale as he stared at their image on the screen. "This... this isn't possible," he stammered. "He's manipulating the full system on a real-time basis. He's... everywhere."

The lights flickered, and the ground trembled again, a low, guttural sound growing mildly louder through the walls. Rebecca swung the flashlight once more across the room, chasing glimpses of whatever that was in the shadows.

"Noah!" she shouted, her voice shaking. "If you're still here, talk to us! Tell us what you want!"

Every screen snapped off simultaneously, saccharine silence in the room engulfed Rebecca as she held her breath, her anxiety surging with the deadening quiet. Slowly, however, a single screen lit, showing this final message:

I WANT YOU TO FEEL WHAT I FELT.

Before either of them could react, the overhead lamp came crashing down and plunged them into darkness. Rebecca screamed and gripped Leonard's arms as the walls began to close in. A dull electric buzz permeated the air, scattered with footsteps—and heavier.

"**He's here,**" Leonard whispered, dread oozing from his voice.

Rebecca swung her flashlight toward the sound, slicing through the darkness. At first, there was nothing. Then slowly from the shadow, a form became recognizable. It wasn't Noah—but moreover was not entirely human.

Its hazy imitation of Noah's form looked far more defined, though the way it moved was more rigid, never quite smooth. Its eyes glowed with an ethereal light, and Rebecca could swear she felt the low buzzing from its body accosting her skin.

"What... what is that?" Rebecca gasped, her voice by this point almost a whisper.

Leonard's face was waxen. "A prototype," he said. "Some earlier model. But how could it still—"

The figure lunged.

Rebecca barely had a moment to think as the prototype raced toward them, jerky yet terrifyingly quick. She shoved Leonard and dashed for the floor; the thing crashed into the surgical table, scattering instruments galore all around them.

"Run!" Leonard yelled, scrambling to his feet.

Rebecca didn't need to be told twice. She jerked him toward the door, just as the prototype got back on its feet, its glowing eyes fastened on them. Again the walls shook, spider-legged cracks fine-runged across the tiles, while the floor heaved beneath his feet.

They stumbled into the dimness of the corridor, the fluorescent lights trembling violently. The noise behind grew louder and louder with every step the prototype took.

"*This way!*" Leonard shouted as he pulled Rebecca to a set of double doors way down the hall.

Rebecca's lungs ached as they ran, as though the air were cutting through them on each inhalation. They slammed through the doors, finding themselves in what looked to be the control room. Monitors lined the walls; there were intermittently shown pictures of the hospital and the surrounding area.

Leonard rushed to the main console, blood spraying across the keyboard. "I can shut it down," he panted. "Just give me a minute."

"We don't have a minute!" Rebecca cried, pressing her back against the door as the prototype slammed into it from the other side; the hinges groaned and the metal buckled as it charged it.

"**Just hold it off!**" snarled Leonard, his gaze on the screen!

Rebecca's hands shook as she surveyed the room, for they fell upon a rusty metal pipe lying on the ground. Picking it up, unarmed as it were in the grip of her hand, she turned back to the door.

The banging had grown so ferocious that cracks formed on the door. With one last mighty heave, the prototype burst into the room. Its eyes singled out Rebecca in a yellow-and-blue glow.

"Come on, you bastard!" she called, lifting the pipe.

The prototype began charging, a sound equal to any human scream blasting through the room.

Rebecca tightened her grip on the broken pipe with trembling fingers and braced herself as the prototype began conducting a charge. Translucent, it glowed elsewhere in the dim distance, but the electric arcs sparkling across its surface threw a flash of shadows over the wall to pose very unsettling questions. It moved with the uncanny speed of a thing that was not yet alive, all jerkiness and discoordinate movements.

The pipe connected with a sickening crack but did little to stop the prototype. Its glowing eyes allturned to Rebecca, a low, mechanical growl resonating from within its chest. Rebecca stumbled back, her heart pounding, and swung the pipe again, the blow recoiling up her arms.

"Leonard!" she screamed, her voice breaking. **"Hurry up!"**

Behind her, Leonard picked up his speeding fingers from the console, his face washed by the light from the monitors. A stream of fragmented, chaotic data was scrolling across the screen as he was looking for something-anything- that could kill the nightmare for them.

"I'm trying!" he shouted back, beads of sweat trickling down his forehead. "The system's encrypted! It's like Noah locked us out."

Rebecca hadn't time to retort. The prototype lunged for her now, a glowing form only a few meters away. She ducked her head and barely escaped its grip as its claws swiped through the air she had just escaped. The force of its movement sent it colliding into a bank of monitors, chiseling into them as sparks shot everywhere.

Rebecca backed away, breathing fast as she saw the pipe slip from her sweaty hands. The prototype turned toward her, moving slower yet deliberately like something that had just scented out a kill.

"Leonard!" she screamed again, the urgency creeping into her voice.

"I'm almost done!" Leonard snapped back, his eyes never leaving the bright screen. "Just keep it distracted!"

Her mind was racing. She had to get herself more time, but the prototype simply would not relent. Its glowing eyes seemed possibly staring into her spirit. Its jerky movement made it doubly hard to predict. Snatching a chair, Rebecca held it up in defense as the creature closed in on her.

"*Why are you still here?*" she muttered through clenched teeth, her fear now igniting into anger. "You have no right to even exist!"

The prototype froze, craning its head at an awkward angle; for a moment, Rebecca thought she had broken it somehow, but then it gave a distorted mechanical echo.

"Not you either."

Rebecca's blood ran cold. These words had a sharpness, almost a deliberate presence behind them, a sort of human weight, and she staggered back, her heart busting out of her chest as the prototype advanced, almost gliding, having made some adaptation change.

"Leonard!" she cried, her voice cracking. "Something's... changing!"

"*I just need another second!*" Leonard called back from behind concentration-set lips.

Out of nowhere, the prototype's claw came alive and arcs of bright-blue electricity sparked through its body. Rebecca couldn't even blink before it swiped at her, and the force slapped her so hard against the wall that she thought she wouldn't be able to get up; it knocked the breath out of her, and her eyes watched the world spinning around.

While the prototype advanced, Leonard's voice rang behind her. "**Got it!**"

Then, with a flourish, the consoles sprang to life, filling the room with bright, kaleidoscopic flickers, streams of code cascading across the monitors with a deep humming sound resonating through the walls. The prototype froze in mid-stride, twitching sporadically, its glowing eyes weak and unstable.

"What have you done?" asked Rebecca, staring at him from her defeated position.

Leonard hesitated, gazing with a pale face at the screens. "**Not me,**" he finally murmured. "Him."

With some effort, Rebecca struggled off the floor, her limbs sore all over as she shifted to glance at the monitors. The streams of code blurred together, resolving to show the face of Noah staring straight out at them, glowing eyes devoid of any emotions, calm and unnervingly concentrated.

"You shouldn't have come here," said Noah, giving weight to each and every word making him resound in the room.

The prototype jerked as it moved again, almost mechanically, a moment of jerk and stop imitating disturbance. Leonard staggered back from the console, the hands that kept them flagged trembling. "Noah," came the unsteady voice. "You don't have to do this!"

Noah's face remained straight, except for the tone of low-grade rage spilling over it. "You think you can stop me? Undo everything that's been done?"

Rebecca winced and came forward, her voice jutting out a little frozen. "All we want is to know," she said. "Our heart is to help you."

The picture flickered in and out, and for a moment, Rebecca could almost imagine some sort of humanity in his eyes, some pain or regret, that disappeared so swiftly.

"**You can't help me,**" Noah said. "You couldn't even help yourselves."

The glowing form of the prototype was in agony. Its motions were becoming increasingly erratic with the accumulating energy inflow. Sparks flew from every surface; the arcs began to flare brighter and started jumping all over. An awful sickness overwhelmed Rebecca with the realization of what, indeed, was about to follow.

"Leonard!" she shouted, clutching his arm. "We need him to move. Now."

Leonard hesitated, staring at the screen. "We still can—"

"No!" exclaimed Rebecca, pulling Leonard toward the door. "**It's not fixable!**"

The prototype let out a screech louder than anything Rebecca had ever heard, as if, even now, the energies inside it were going out of control and in a way convulsive to him. The room shook blindingly, the tinkle of walls before everything went dark.

Rebecca shoved Leonard through the doors even as her breath caught when the prototype exploded in a searing flash of light, sending her flying into the hallway, the blast's heat scalding her skin.

As she regained consciousness, the control room had morphed into a pile of smoldering wreckage. Leonard lay beside her, coughing heavily, pale as death.

"**He's not just a clone,**" Rebecca whispered. There was an unsteady tremor in her voice. "He's something else."

Leonard looked with lifeless eyes at the ruin, a faint echo of Noah's voice escaping into the continuing silence.

"**You're only beginning to take stock.**"

The hospital now felt like a living thing; it groaned under the oppressive weight of its own secrets. Smoke surged from the control room's shattered remains, casting spectral shadows down the cracked hallway. Rebecca pulled herself upright, shaking like a leaf from the force of that explosion. Leonard sat slumped against the wall beside her, pale-faced and slick with sweat.

"**He's everywhere,**" he whispered, his voice sounding weighty and hollow. "He dwells in the systems, the machines. We haven't just created a clone; we have released something we don't yet comprehend."

Rebecca met his eyes, breathless. "We've got to move," she said, taking his arm and nerve-dragging him back onto his feet. "If he can do this to the prototype, just think what he could do to us."

Leonard made no protest. Staggering after her, he was out of breath as they plunged deep into the hospital. It was darker; the flickers of light only scattered now in portions around them. With every passing shadow seemed a curl and lurch, making Rebecca feel of impending discovery.

"*Do you hear that?*" Leonard asked suddenly, his voice hushed.

Rebecca froze, breathless at first. There was nothing but the lethargic hum far off; then a barely noticeable rhythm entered her consciousness, a tapping like footsteps coming from somewhere unseen.

She gripped Leonard's arm tightly. "We have to get out of here," she said, her voice a hoarse whisper.

The tapping grew louder, nearer; something stalking them. Rebecca's heart raced as she broke into a sprint, dragging along Leonard. The footsteps changing, erratic, brisk, like something that pursues a victim has now buried the taboos of either man or beast.

They turned a corner, and Rebecca stopped. At the far end of the hallway was yet another figure. In the dim light, the outline was hardly visible, but its eyes glowed, twinkling with great brightness in the dark.

"It's another prototype." Leonard whispered, trembling.

She gulped in a breath. "No," she stammered. "That's him."

Now, Noah stepped slowly and deliberately forward out of the shadows. Dusk hung in the air, and his glowing silhouette gave the last brightness upon the crumpled edges of the hospital's vile walls. He fixed his eyes on Rebecca and Leonard. For a moment, it seemed the entire universe was holding its breath.

"You shouldn't have come," said Noah in a calm voice, edged with menace. "I gave you a chance to leave."

Rebecca swallowed hard; her throat felt dry. "We're not here to fight," she said shakily. "We're here to know."

Noah's head tilted to one side with an inscrutable expression. "Understand?" he repeated. "You don't even know what you have done."

Leonard stepped ahead now, supplicating. "We didn't mean to hurt you," came a breaking voice. "We thought we were helping."

Noah gave the faintest smile, one colder and more humorless than even Rebecca imagined. "Helping?" he said in almost a whisper. "You thought you could create life without understanding what it meant? You thought you could control me? You were wrong."

Contusions of floors snapped and broke as he spoke, the air thickening with every word. And Rebecca's knees went weak, her body shaking as she struggled to keep herself upright.

"Noah, please," she said, her voice faltering. "If we were wrong, help us right it."

For an instant, Noah's glowing eyes softened, and Rebecca thought she saw a flicker of something human in the depths of them. But even in that moment, his gaze hardened, and the light radiating from his body continued to increase.

"There is no righting it," he said. "**There is only the truth.**"

The ground below their feet began to shake violently, and great jagged cracks appeared in the floor. They scattered for balance as Rebecca stumbled and dropped her flashlight, while the hospital seemed to spring to life around them. From the shadows came more glowing figures—prototypes, their incomplete forms giving way to unstable energy.

Leonard's voice rang with panic as he clutched Rebecca's arm. "He's controlling them," he exclaimed. "They're all linked with him."

Rebecca felt her head spinning with the moving prototypes clambering close. The choices he made were unpredictable, but in pure intention. In the midst of them, Noah kneeled, his light radiating a sense of divinity.

"You wanted to find me. You will now see what I have turned into," came Noah's voice loud and clear through the otherwise hospital-like atmosphere.

The prototypes surged with shimmering, flaming figures lighting the hallway like torches. As Rebecca and Leonard ran for their lives, their footfalls were disturbed by cracks and crevices being created inside walls. The hospital screamed; the whole place was going to implode.

Through another set of stairs, the room sank into darkness, the tremor growing more intense. Rebecca fought her breath, lost in yet more fright and desperation. As they reached the bottom of the stairs, Leonard doubled over, trying to catch his breath.

"It's a dead end," he managed to croak. **"We're trapped."**

Rebecca turned her light to cut through the dark. "No way are we trapped," she said, steadier than she really felt. "We'll just find another way out."

A quiet sound sent chills through her. It was Noah's voice, unwavering yet creepy, coming from somewhere unreachable.

"There is no escape," he said. "You don't leave until I choose to let you."

The lights jumped like crazy, sturdy walls squill in cubes fell, and old metal screeched. Rebecca finally got it crystal clear: the hospital was not just falling apart. It was crashing down by design—Noah's design.

"*Let us move!*" she yelled, taking Leonard by the arm.

But just as they made the first move, the ground cracked open underneath them, their bodies sucked into darkness over the floor. Rebecca felt a gush of air rushing past and their fall into the blackness made the world-and herself-spin-around. A scream reverberated nicely into the void, drowned out by Noah's final words:

"This is just the beginning."

Chapter 4

Shadows in Society

Every part of Rebecca's body was complaining with every step she took; her legs were trembling as she and Leonard stumbled into the night. The remnants of the hospital lay in ruin behind them, a pile of burnt rubble and smoldering dreams. The air reeked with smoke and the burnt metallic smell. But it wasn't the destruction that haunted her.

It was his voice.

"This is really just the beginning."

That phrase rang in her ears like a loud and unrelenting chime. She turn her head toward Leonard, limping beside her, pale of face and streaked with dirt as if recently dug up in a blur. His eyes were a no man's land and seemed blind to the outside world, lost in a void of his own making.

"Leonard," she said softly, her voice barely audible above the crackling of distant flames, "we need to keep moving."

No answer. Rebecca seizing his arm made him stop and look at her. "Leonard!" she said again, this time louder. "Snap out of it! We don't have time for this!"

His gaze turned to her, and for a moment, she thought he might argue. He must have agreed then when he tried a very faint nod. "I can't...I can hear him still," spoke Leonard, his voice trembling. "He's in my head, Rebecca. It's like he never left."

Rebecca clenched his arm tighter. "He is not here," she said, almost with assurance, though she wasn't so sure herself. "He is out there, somewhere, and we need to find out what he's working on before it is too late."

Leonard deliberated for a moment but once again nodded. "Where to?" he asked softly.

Rebecca scanned the desolate street, thoughts racing in her mind. The men in black, Keller, the prototypes: all are part of the same web. In the very center was Noah himself, pulling the strings. She couldn't trust anyone. But there was one place that could provide answers.

"The church," she said at last, her voice soothingly calm. "St. Matthias. There was something about that place. Some way he felt drawn to it."

Leonard frowned. "*You think we'll find him there?*"

Rebecca shook her head. "*I don't know. But we will find something.*"

The drive to the church was one of tension and was filled with silent fears unexpressed. The radio shouldered its way in and out of the static, ravaged here and there by scraps of news reports.

"...unexplained power outages reported all across the city... authorities urging calm..."

"...an eyewitness claims to have seen a luminous figure near the ruins of..."

"...the hospital is still smoldering and there are still no survivors counted so far..."

As Rebecca reflexively clenched the steering wheel, her mind was a-whir with ideas. He was not hiding anymore; he was announcing his existence. And now, the world was starting to take notice.

"What if he wants them to find him?" Leonard asked, breaking the candor.

Rebecca looked over at him, eyebrows dipping into furrows. "What do you mean?"

Leonard looked out through the window, brooding within himself. "What if he is not hiding? What if this is being done purposefully? For being seen. For being understood."

Rebecca felt goosebumps. "**Or to be feared.**"

Leonard didn't say anything. **He didn't have to.**

The church was eerily still. The broken stained glass windows made craggy shadows over the pews, and a faint scent of ash filled the air. Rebecca edged into the church, a flashlight flickering upward through musty gloom.

"Do you think anyone's been here since...?" Leonard's tone faded as he trailed after her.

Rebecca shook her head. "It doesn't look like it."

But with each stride deeper into the church, she caught it again: that heavy weight, as though the air itself watched them. Her flashlight's beam caught the altar and highlighted the scorch marks from their last encounter with Noah.

"This place is giving me bad vibes," Leonard muttered, voice low.

Rebecca could but half-agree. Instincts screamed at her to leave, but something bound her fast. She went toward the altar, eyes searching the wreckage for anything Noah might have left.

Then she saw it.

The altar had but a single word on it.

SOCIETY.

Rebecca gasped. "Leonard," she said, her voice unsteady. "Look at this."

Leonard joined her and concentrated his gaze on the word. "What does it mean?" he asked.

Rebecca shook her head, her mind reeling. "That's no warning; that's a message. He's telling us where to look."

Leonard frowned. "Society? What kind of clue is that?"

Before Rebecca could respond, the church trembled. A low rumble swept through the space, and faint whispers filled the air. Rebecca froze and turned her flashlight to where the dark shadow was gathering.

"You hear that?" she asked, her voice tense.

Leonard nodded in fright. "It's him."

The whispers grew higher, and though they intermingled in an unintelligible jumble, their source was clear... Over in the church's far corner stood a dim light giving off an ethereal glow.

Noah.

He was not looking at anybody and did not speak... Just watched them with his glowing, unblinking eyes while the whispers raged around him.

Until that night, Rebecca had felt a quite natural dislike for what went against every established norm of reality. But she was becoming far beyond human; an effusion of sensibility hit her very heartbeat. Stepping forward, she asked, voice trembling, "What do you want from us?"

Noah tilted his head. He didn't get angry, nor did his features shift. His purposely calm voice added accent to his words, sending running shivers all the way to Rebecca's set feet.

"I want you to see what I see."

The building was shaken by disconcerting noises while the whispers became unbearably loud now. The ground cracked below them, and Rebecca snatched Leonard as the floor opened, swallowing them up to the endless darkness.

Then darkness enveloped them. Rebecca's scream was hushed by the winds rushing past as she and Leonard fell through the dead floor. A chill filled the damp air, an iron tang burning her throat. The flashlight slipped from her grip and fell into the abyss below.

They crashed down into it, the impact shaking them. Rebecca was gasping for air, the aching heaviness from the impact. She did her best to blink, trying to force her mind to calm down. Leonard groaned somewhere nearby.

"Leonard?" she called out, shaking her voice. "*Are you okay?*"

"I think so," came his heavy breath. "*Where... where are we?*"

Rebecca's hands began groping in the dark, finally hitting the edge of her fallen flashlight. She switched it back on, sending a narrow beam through the darkness. Rough stone walls soon came into view. Moist and narrow, the corridor stretched endlessly into the blackness.

"This wasn't part of the church," Leonard's voice was filled with disbelief. "This is something else."

Rebecca nodded, terrified breaths coming through her. "It's a catacomb," she stammered. "But why... why bring us here?"

Leonard's gaze held the darkness for a good while, a frozen prey. He didn't answer. Rebecca followed his stare, her heart racing at the beam from her flashlight that settled upon a figure she knew.

Noah remained curious at the corridor end, his glowing eyes radiating through the gloom. His shadowy figure shimmered occasionally, arcs of light beneath his skin casting creepy shadows along the walls. Noah was still. He spoke not a word. He simply watched.

"What do you want from us?" Rebecca said instead, steadier than she felt.

Noah tilted his head off to the side. "I want you to understand," he said, its calm, laden tone resonating. "To see what I see."

Before Rebecca could say another word, Noah turned and walked away deeper into the corridor. The soft glow of his presence melted away into the shadows, leaving behind a faint hum upon the air-the magnet that drew them along.

Rebecca hesitated, instincts warning her to bolt. Yet Noah's words for some reason kept her standing still. She glanced toward Leonard, whose stare was fixated somewhere between dedicated fear and enticing fascination.

"We can't follow him," she stammered. "We don't know what is down there."

Leonard shook his head. "We don't have a choice. If he is showing us something, it could be our only chance to stop him."

Rebecca bit her lip, feeling a heavy weight press on her. She would have argued, that would have turned on herself and headed back to the bull in pursuit of the exit, but deep down she knew Leonard was right. They couldn't turn back that day.

"*Okay,*" she said, eyes tight. "But keep close."

So long did the corridor seem to last, winding deeper into the earth. With every step, the coldness was taking over, while damp stone walls pressed against them. Rebecca's flashlight flickered, but her beam seemed small in the face of dark oppression. Her only guide was the subtle vibration of Noah's presence.

"*Do you think he meant to do this ?* " In a low voice, whispered Leonard.

Without looking at him, Rebecca responded, "I think everything he has done is premeditated, every move, every message has led him to this."

Leonard swallowed hard. "But why? What does he hope we will see?"

Rebecca shook her head. "I don't know. Although, I think it's best not to want to."

The corridor opened up into a broad chamber, its ceiling lost above in shadows. Rebecca's flashlight revealed rows of stone pillars carved with strange, shifting, pulsing symbols in the light. In the middle of the room was a large, circular platform, its surface etched with the same glowing patterns that pulsed within Noah's body.

"Noah," whispered Leonard, trembling. "**What is this place?**"

Noah's voice echoed through the chamber, though he was nowhere to be seen. "This is where it began," he said, "and where it will end."

Rebecca stepped onto the platform, and the light of her flashlight discovered more of the crafting. The symbols were deeply engraved, with an almost mechanical kind of look. But there was an organic and fluid quality about them that made her skin prick. They seemed, at least remotely, to pulse.

"This isn't natural," she said, her voice taut. "This... this is something else."

Leonard joined her, staring at the platform. "This isn't a catacomb," he said slowly. "**This is a machine.**"

Rebecca's heart leaped. "A machine? For what?"

Before Leonard replied, there resonated the humming sound from underfoot while the symbols on top of the platform were caught in their slow radiation. The shock of light warmed through the chamber, and Rebecca took a step back as, suddenly, the instinct warned her of danger.

"Noah!" she shouted, the echo decisive in the emptiness. "What's going on?"

The reply was again calm, and steady through the raging room, "I am showing you the truth."

The shakings below them grew louder, from where a merging tune approached until Rebecca had gripped Leonard by the arm in choppy, shallow breaths. "We need to leave!" she shrieked. "Now!"

But Leonard stood still. His eyes were no longer with her, his face pale. "Rebecca," he said almost in a whisper. "I think... I think this is-what made him."

For a moment Rebecca was stunned, her mind reeling. "What do you mean? It was all our doing-he burst forth from our laboratory."

Leonard shook his head, terror filling his voice. "No," he uttered. "We were merely an addendum to the process. This... this is the root source."

There was a flare on the pedestal, a shriek of sound. Rebecca shielded her eyes, blinded by a light that flooded the chamber. And when she regained her sight, Noah stood on the pedestal, shining with an outward power.

"You wished to know," came the echoing voice from the chamber wall. "Now you shall."

One final flare, then the universe became a blank white.

Rebecca gradually regained her vision from the blinding blaze of light, with an afterimage of Noah as a glowing entity etched in her mind. The room now lay in silence, with just a slight vibration of the humming platform beneath her feet. She blinked a few times in an attempt to focus.

Noah stood at the platform's center, a shimmering figure engulfed in alien energy. The carvings on the stone surface around him glowed out of sync, changing constantly like living veins of light. No longer were the symbols static-they had come to life, breathing in response to him.

"What is this place?" Rebecca whispered, trembling.

Noah turned just a shade towards her, his eyes glistening with an inner radiance. "This is the place where I began," he noted; "and where I will define what comes next."

Leonard stepped forward awkwardly, unable to break free from the magnetic attraction urging him on to the platform. "It... it isn't possible," he stuttered. "This kind of technology, I mean... centuries ahead of anything we have seen. Noah, how do you... how could you call this?"

His smile could not be labeled. A teasing smile. "I don't remember when I learned of it," came the reply. "I remember rather the feeling of remembering it. This is a part of me; and I am part of this."

Rebecca's pulse quickened. "What does that mean?" she demanded, her voice sparking with anger. "You said this is where it began. For who? For you?"

Noah paused before he commenced moving across the chamber while casting elongated shadows all around. Each movement oozed a strong resolve about him. While he did speak smoothly, the tone bore heavy weight that choked Rebecca in her gut.

"*For all of us*," he responded. "Those are the words with which you best define it - for your kind."

Leonard stared, unable to realize just what it was he had heard, ushering forth a mixture of doubt and fear. "It was this machine-it's not just for you. It is everywhere?"

That smile widened, but it was maddeningly devoid of warmth. "Now you're finally beginning to understand."

Rebecca's mind swirled in turmoil, attempting to put together Noah's words. This was no fleeting moment with higher technology. This was something far more essential than that--something that remained buried and hidden, that has waited.

"Noah," she said, her voice barely steady, "If this world is connected to humanity, why, for heaven's sake, were you created? If so, why now?"

Noah softened his gaze, and for a minute, Rebecca thought she had glimpsed some flicker of human pain or perhaps regret reflected in the brightness of his eyes. "Because you made me," he planned quietly. "You attempted the birth of life without a clue of the commotion. Now it all must be recomposed."

Rebecca was caught short. "Recompose? What does that mean?"

Noah became lost in thought. "It means the world is wrecked," he said sharply. "And this..." he gestured to the glowing platform beneath him, "... is how it will be fixed."

Leonard's voice began trembling. "Fixed? You are speaking of something broken beyond repair, of rewriting the design of existence."

Still staring straight at Rebecca, Noah tilted in such a way that his glowing form flickered like an expiring flame. "Perhaps it must be rewritten," he mused, "for that may well be the only way."

Rebecca stepped forward, anger pushing back the fear. "You can't just say that," she said, her voice firm. "You have no right."

Noah's face shot around to glare at her, and for the first time, Rebecca felt the full weight of his presence. "And you did?" he said, icy cold. "You created me. You played with forces you did not understand. You thought you could control life itself. And you are frightened now because you cannot control me."

Rebecca clenched her fists at her sides. "We didn't know," she said, her voice breaking. "We didn't know what we were actually doing."

"EXACTLY," came the cold unrelenting voice of Noah. "And now you will."

There was a sudden surge within the platform, the symbols becoming more potent and the room shaking. Rebecca pulled Leonard back, urging him to do so while crackling spread like lightning from there all on its own. The air grew heavy, a charge buzzed, and the faint hum and roar became deafening.

"Noah!" Leonard screamed to the desperate man. "Whatever you're doing, don't! We can still stop this together!"

Noah softened his attention, and for one brief instant, Rebecca thought he just might listen. But his expression hardened again, the light within him brightening. "You can't stop what has already begun," he said, "it's bigger than you; it's bigger than me. It's bigger than everything."

Rebecca's heart raced, and the room exploded into luminosity, nearly blinding her. She covered her eyes, questions drowning in her mind without answers. "Noah, please!" she screamed. "You don't have to do this!"

Noah's voice echoed across the room, calm and implacable. "You asked to see," he said. "**Now you will.**"

The light sucked them in, and Rebecca sensed the ground falling away from beneath her feet. She was weightless, hanging in the void alive with the hum of the machine; images flickered past her burdensome consciousness-fragments of memories, faces she didn't recognize, places she had never been. The world itself appeared to unravel before her, revealing a web of blurring lines of dark and light.

When the light turned off, she was back on firm ground. She blinked, the clarity unfolding with her realization that she was still in the chamber. Somehow, it was not the same. The platform was shadowy and the light extinguished. Noah was gone.

"Leonard?" she called out, trembling in her voice.

"I've...ah...I'm here," he said, his tone shaky. Leonard was propped against one of the stone pillars; he looked pale. "What...what just happened?"

Rebecca shook her head; her brain wasn't keeping up. "I don't know, but I think he is gone."

Leonard's eyes widened. *"Gone where?"*

Before Rebecca could give an answer, the earth trembled again. This time, the clicks of the cracks in the floor widened before her eyes, and the ceiling started disintegrating all around. Rebecca jerked on Leonard's arm, pulled him up from the ground. *"We have to go. Now."*

They fled, even as the chamber caved in on itself around them. The corridor through which they had just come was nigh on unrecognizable, with its walls warped and unstable. The beam from Rebecca's flashlight flickered faintly in the festering disorder.

Leonard stumbled as they neared the exit, his legs buckling beneath him. Rebecca turned, clutched his arm, and urged him on. "Come on!" she shouted. "We are almost there!"

They burst into sunlight just as the ground collapsed behind them, and the chamber fell in on itself. Rebecca fell to her knees gasping for breath, the dust settling around them.

Silence reigned for a moment; then Leonard spoke, his voice quavering. *"Do you think he's really gone?"*

Rebecca stared at the ruins; her mind speeded up. "No," she said softly. "He is not gone. He's just starting."

The cold night air felt as heavy as lead, moist and trapped against the backdrop of Erin and Leonard by the edge of the crushed remains, their breaths coming out moth-like in the coolness. Below them, the earth shook slightly; somehow it felt as if, even now, the very earth resounded with the dying echoes of what had passed.

"Where is he?" Were Leonard's finally spoken words, hoarse.

Rebecca seemed, for a moment, to be a little lost in her own dream of the horizon. The glow of city lights blurred against the dark sky. The weight of everything Noah had said bore extremely heavily on her like a suffocating blanket.

"He started here," he had said. "It will finish here."

Rebecca shook her head as she clenched her fists in anger. "He's not hiding," she said. Finally, her voice firm. "He wants us to know he is there. That he isn't afraid."

Leonard scoffed, his voice shaking. "Not afraid? Not while playing with forces we've never even begun to comprehend! He's.....he's beyond us now."

She turned to him like a crossbeam of sharp light. "And thus we have to stop him," she said. "Because otherwise, nobody would."

Leonard was aghast, thrown still with a mix of disbelief and exhaustion. "Stop him?" he echoed. "Rebecca, did you see what just happened? He isn't just a clone anymore; he is something... something, uh, you get the point. Unstoppable. He's even something else than we know."

The car sepulchered into silence, heavy with unsaid fears wrapping about them. She grounded the engine with a hopeful burble, giving some comfort in that fiercely jarring split of a thought. In pulling away from the ruins, Leonard spoke again, this time quiet.

"*Do you think anyone else knows?*" he asked. "About this immediately? About him?"

Her eyes darkened at him. He was shaky, leaning away into his seat. "If they didn't know, they'll know soon," she said determinedly. "The way he has been moving? Leaving messages? Making his presence felt? He's out- there in plain sight; he doesn't want to hide—he wants to be found."

Leonard was chilled, leaning back against the car seat. "If they find him, what would he do then?"

Rebecca did not answer. She did not have any idea. Deep in her heart, however, she had a wild but clear instinct that Noah had already set the wheels of his plan into motion; whatever he was headed for would change everything about their lives.

Rebecca trudged on; the lights of the city became increasingly bright as they neared the city. Rebecca seemed to go into a lasting spin-a whirlpool of potential horrors. Noah had said something about balance, something about putting back something that had been lost. But what did it mean? What was that glowing machine in the chamber?

A buzzing sound on her phone broke the silence. She looked at the screen, her stomach twisting when she saw the name: Keller.

"*What does he want now?*" Leonard asked, peering at the screen.

Rebecca answered with great reluctance in her trembling voice. "What?"

Keller's voice crackled on the other end: "You two are alive," he said. The note of surprise in his tone gave Rebecca pause, even if it was a bit odd. "Frankly, **I wasn't sure you'd make it out.**"

Rebecca clenched her jaw. "How do you know what has happened?" she demanded. "Are you watching us?"

Keller's laugh was less than sincere. "Let's just say I have my ways," he replied. "But that's not the reason for my call. We have a problem."

Rebecca tightened her grip on the phone. "*What sort of problem?*"

There was a pause, the voice breaking for the first time that Rebecca had ever heard it sound so unsteady. "There is a breach. A massive power surge across the city. Entire districts are going dark and failing in their surveillance systems. We're working on tracing the source. But... I think you already know what it is."

"Oh no. It's him," she said. "Isn't it?"

Keller's silence was the answer. "You have to come in," he said. "Now. Before this gets any worse."

Rebecca grit her teeth; her mind was racing. Keller and his organization had been watching them all along, pulling strings, cleaning up their messes. But now it was clear they were all in over their heads.

"We're not coming in," she said forcefully. "If Noah's out there, we go find him."

Keller's voice turned cold. "This isn't a game, Rebecca. If he is doing what I think he is doing, the city maybe the entire country is at risk."

Rebecca's stomach churned. "Then stop him," she snapped. "Isn't that what you do?"

Keller's laugh was cold. "This is bigger than me. This is bigger than all of us. If you think you can do this on your own, you're kidding yourself. But if you change your mind, you'll find me."

The line went dead.

Leonard glanced at her, grim. "What now?"

Rebecca tightened her grip on the steering wheel, her jaw tense. "Now we do what Keller can't. We stop Noah before it is too late."

Leonard sighed, sinking back in the seat. "You keep saying that like it's possible," he muttered, "...like we stand a chance against him."

Rebecca did not respond. She had her doubts as well; still, she knew one thing for sure: nothing could be worse than doing nothing.

The car rounded the corner, and Rebecca's heart skipped a beat. A blanket of darkness covered the city skyline, lights that had once glittered the night now extinguished. Irregularly shaped, some ghostly glow pulsated weakly at the heart of the blackout zone, backlit against the dark sky.

Leonard stiffened. His eyes widened. "That's him," he said, his voice shaken. "It has to be."

Rebecca's grip tightened. "*So that's where we go.*"

By the time they reached downtown, the pulse was strong and the air thrum with an unnatural energy. Rebecca parked the car on an abandoned street, the faint drone of the pulse sounding off through the silence.

They slowly emerged, breath crystallizing in the cold evening air, on oddly desolate streets lined by buildings which were dark and inactive. Rebecca swept the flashlight beam through the shadows, her heart pounding.

"*Do you feel that?*" Leonard whispered.

Rebecca nodded as her heartbeat quickened. "He's close."

They turned the corner, and Rebecca halted. In front of the glowing pulse, vaguely but recognizable, there stood Noah. His figure glowed now, brighter than ever, radiating a force that seemed to bend air around him.

Bait caught in her throat, Rebecca stepped forward, trembling. "Noah."

He turned slowly, glowing eyes gazing ice into hers. For a moment, it felt like the world literally stood still.

"You shouldn't have come," he said, flat and strong.

The pulse flared high, and the city quaked.

The quake underfoot was alive, as if the city itself had come alive with Noah's presence. The dim, discharged glow radiating out from him pierced the dark city streets in eerie, rhythmic waves of light. Rebecca and Leonard stood immobilized, unable to speak, in stark awe of what they saw.

Noah advanced slowly; every movement intentional. His glowing eyes bore into Rebecca, his expression calm, but beneath that, something from dark ages lurked underneath. **"You have no idea what you've done,"** he said. "Yet you will."

Rebecca gulped. Her voice trembled as she spoke. "We're trying to understand, Noah. We are, but this--this is not it."

Noah cocked his head to one side, an emotionless, vague frown creasing his face. "Not the way?" he repeated sharply. "You created me. You forced me into existence in a world that does not want me and one that does not even know what I am. And now you want to tell me the way?"

Leonard stepped forward, his hands out in front of him as if in defence. "We made mistakes," he said, with a wavering voice but earnest intonation. "We didn't know what we were doing. But whatever you're doing now isn't going to fix anything."

Noah's eyes flared brighter, and the pulse around grew stronger. "Do you think this is about fixing something?" he said, with a tone bordering on dangerous. "It's about balance. About truth. You have led your lives pretending to shape the world by your will. Now it's my apartment."

Rebecca's chest ached. "Noah, this can't be the way. Daniel's still out there, and if this is the answer for balance, destroying everything isn't the way."

Noah's weak smile to her sent a weird kind of shiver down her spine. "You still think I want the destruction?" he queried, confused. "Destruction is just the start-off point. And once it occurs, the truth thereafter."

The ground shuddered, fissures tore open in the asphalt as deafening noises supplanted the remaining silence. Rebecca seized Leonard's arm, pulling him back as Noah's glowing pulse became more intense with every passing moment. The buildings around were cracking under restraint; their windows shattered as if from real attacks of nature.

"Let's get out of here!" Rebecca shouted above the racket; her voice drenched in panic.

Leonard hesitated, locking his gaze onto Noah. "Once we leave, we will never know what he has in mind," he said, almost somberly. "We will never stop him."

"We can't stop him!" came Rebecca's reply, with fear bubbling to the surface. "Take a good look at him, Leonard! He's—"

Noah raised his hand, paralyzing the pulse with an instant gesture. The sudden silence that followed was deafening; if anything, that stillness was more sinister than the pandemonium itself. Rebecca's breath left her as she made the discovery that Noah was looking wantonly at her.

"You wanted to understand," he assured in a calm voice, almost drenched in sorrow. "Then let me show you."

Before Rebecca could better appreciate the circumstances, pulsing began anew, though differently: the light changed its character; it became rhythmic, almost harmonic, as if alive. From there, the streets began lighting up with an energy cascading into the deepest cracks in the earth, shattering in the windows-it poured into the very air.

Then Rebecca dropped back into partial unconsciousness, bewitched by the thoughts floating through her mind. Light and shadow scintillated, conceiving faces which merged into a distant haze of scenes never cherished. The city shrieked along with extensive gulps released along with an energy unleashed by Noah.

"*What is happening?*" came the sound of Leonard shouting, a voice barely surfacing over the din.

Rebecca hugged her head; her mind was reeling. "He's... he's changing it," said her voice, faint and almost faltering. "He's changing everything."

Noah's brilliant shape glimmered now, almost blinded. The voice rang through the chaos calm-abidingly, saying, "You see the world as it is. Now you will see it as it could be."

The floor beneath them fell away, and Rebecca realized that she was falling. She clutched at Leonard, but something very strong kept them apart. The world was lost in light and sound; for a moment, there was nothing but the sensation of weightlessness.

Rebecca opened her eyes in a world that was not the city. It was a wide, infinite void, with light and shadow, and the air shimmered with some of that unnatural energy. Leonard stood next to her, with a pale face and frightened expressions.

"Where are we?" he asked in a trembling tone.

Rebecca shook her head, her heart pounding. "I don't know."

Before them, the merged disappeared in which was a glow, Noah had become incandescent. He looked decidedly inhuman; an exalted being of light and power, pulsating with whatever singular judges the universe required.

"Sistas," Noah echoed, his mighty voice running through the expanse. "This is truth; this is the equilibrium that you strived to destroy."

Rebecca gasped. "Noah, please; there must be a way to fix this. We can set this right."

Noah's expression softened, yet his words were devoid of clemency. "There is no union. Only what lies next."

The light raced around them engulfing, and she felt the ground fall away from under her feet. The last thing she heard was Noah's voice- steady and sure.

"You should have left me in the dark."

Chapter 5

The Forbidden Sanctuary

The church stood like a neglected sentinel, its spires scratching the stormy sky. A shiver crept down Rebecca's back, the feelings very palpable as the two strode through the unnatural stillness. Once-grand St. Brigid's Cathedral was in tatters, with shattered stained glass and half-open doors that creaked eerily in the wind. It was the kind of place that stood, forgotten by the years, and now weighted upon her chest as if by some unseen hand.

"*This place feels...* **wrong**," Leonard mumbled quietly.

She nodded in acknowledgement, already feeling nauseous. "He's here," Rebecca said firmly. "I can feel it."

She pushed the heavy door open, and the squeal of its hinges vibrated through the empty nave. What once had been a magnificent cathedral was now reduced to empty shells of wayward nave and scattered broken pews on the dusty floor, their splintered edges casting jagged shadows in the lowest light filtering through smashed stained-glass windows. The air itself weighed heavy with the scent of mildew and decay, but beneath it all was something electric-something alive.

She gripped her flashlight tightly but was aware that its beam was waning in strength against the shadows. "Noah?" she called out, trembling audibly. "If you're here, we need to talk."

Leonard moved cautiously beside her, his gaze dancing nervously from shadow to shadow. "Do you think he's with someone?" he asked tightly.

Rebecca didn't answer. She honestly didn't know. With each step closer they made toward the altar; a soundless whir enveloped the air like the humming of electricity. It harmonized with her chest, her bones. It was familiar - a sound reminiscent of the machine beneath the lab, of the first moment they had awakened Noah into the world.

The altar at the far end of the church glowed in a halo of some ethereal light. The light pulsed in sync with the hum, shifting and casting jittery patterns across the damaged floor. Rebecca's heart raced as her flashlight illuminated a figure standing near the altar; Noah.

He was only dimly transparent, lurid arcs of light coursing just beneath his skin. He had his back to them, gazing at the broken crucifix overhead. The shattered image of Christ incongruously appeared to stare back, his face shaded in darkened hues.

"Noah," Rebecca said again, her voice steadier now. "*Where is this place? Why did you bring us here?*"

For a moment, Noah stood still. Then he turned slowly, his hypnotic eyes fixing into hers. His expression was unreadable, but his presence was overbearing, practically filling every inch of the church.

"This is where it all ends," he said simply, his voice unhurried but insistent. "Where the balance is restored."

Rebecca felt a cold shudder run down her spine. "What balance?" she asked, voice trembling. "What are you talking about?"

Noah stepped forward, his very movements deliberate, the resplendent form he bore casting long, serpentine shadows on the church. "The balance between creation and consequence," he said. "**The very balance you shattered when you tried to play God.**"

Leonard scoffed. His voice, though shaky, dared to speak. "We were trying to help humanity," he said. "To advance science. You were supposed to be a breakthrough."

The trace of a smile watered Noah's lips, a smile that never was warm. "And I am," he said. "Not in the way you intended though."

The hum grew even louder; the altar light pulsed brighter. A slight tremor rattled beneath Rebecca's feet as the very church responded to Noah's presence. "What are you doing?" she shouted, raising her voice. "Why are we here?"

Noah's gaze shifted back toward the crucifix, his expression easing. "This structure was built upon faith," he said quietly. "On the making-belief of something bigger than oneself initiating order into chaos. But faith, is just another fancy-a lie you tell yourselves to get out from under the weight of truth."

Rebecca felt a tightening in her chest. "*And what truth is that?*"

Noah turned back to her with hypnotic eyes. "That there is no greater force. No divine plan. It's merely the consequence of your choices."

The hum grew louder still, and the light of the altar was pulsating now. And even as this light flared more brightly, Rebecca stumbled backward, shielding her eyes. "Leonard held her elbow, his face gone completely pale. **"We've got to get out of here,"** he said hotly. "Now."

Just then, before one foot moved, the doors of the church crashed shut with the loudest clatter, and the sound resonated throughout the nave like a gunshot. Rebecca spun around, heart pounding, but now the doors were sealed, their immense timber shading weakly with the whatever that pulsated light around the altar.

"You can't leave," Noah said, calm but with finality. **"Not until you understand."**

Rebecca's breath quickened now, seeing the reality of their situation. They were trapped, stuck right there in Noah's world, with no possible escape or means to run off away from him. Whatever plans he had was only just starting.

Rebecca could almost hear her heart beating as she looked at the locked church doors, a remote, wisping luminosity coursing through the imaginary hollow of the woodwork along the length of the maid, almost as if living and breathing the fate of Noah. The flashlight was flickering, its bright beam almost smothered by the weighty, murky air.

"Noah!" her voice trembling but firm, Rebecca began. "If you want us to understand, then speak, show! But don't think trapping us here will solve anything."

There was a pause. Noah turned to look toward the altar, the luminosity of his figure casting ominously long shadows away from him across the nave. A soft, pulsing, fluorescent light under his skin pulsed in cadence with an underlying hum surrounding them. It was as though they all had entered the unforgiving core of a throbbing **Nameless God.**

"This place," said Noah, the tone of his voice triggering grief in Rebecca's chest. "Built on faith. And faith is feeble. It crumbles in the heavy silence of the truth."

Leonard carefully moved an inch forward. He spoke with shaky voice: *"What truth? What do you mean?"*

With an intent look, Noah wore luminescent eyes fixated on Leonard. "The truth," he stated, "that there is no divine plan, nor grand architect hence molding your world—only you, with all of your choices."

Rebecca shook her head, sickness intermingling frustration. "And what, pray tell, Noah, have you chosen? Your balance and consequences—really! —have done nothing."

For the faintest of moments, Rebecca thought she saw his face soften and for that instant a metaphysical hint of pain in his luminous eyes. But it faded away as soon as it came. "I didn't choose to exist," he uttered, low but disturbed. "You did that for me. You threw me into a world which was never ready for me—a world that won't ever accept me."

Leonard drew a bit closer to him, cautiously this time. "Maybe we didn't know what we were doing. Maybe we made mistakes. That shouldn't be the reason we do it like this."

The little smile of Noah seemed back, but it had not as much warmth. "This is not the answer," he said. "It is, rather, the beginning."

A dark rumble reverberated beneath them, echoing from the very bones of the church. Rebecca grabbed Leonard's arm, darting toward the altar, now brimming with life. The light pulsed from the alter, status of colors moving lightning-fast, casting jagged patterns across the broken tiled floor.

"*What is this?*" Leonard's voice was tight from fear.

Noah stepped closer to the altar, his figure now blinding with luminosity. "You wished for life," he said. "To meddle with its core. Sadly, the price you did not grasp."

Rebecca caught her breath as cracks spread like arteries in the floor, pulsing with that unnatural light. The crucifix above the altar groaned; the broken figure of Christ twisted unnaturally, a grotesque semblance of a living thing.

"Noah!" Rebecca shouted, her voice breaking. "Stop this. Whatever it is you're going to do, you don't have—"

"I do," Noah replied, biting his voice flat and hard. "Someone else will do it for me, and their choices will make yours look plain."

Leonard's face turned pale as he sneered at Noah. "What is this about? Who else is involved in here?"

Without answering, Noah raised his hand, and lights around the altar blew forth, scattering blinding brilliance across the church. Rebecca turned her face away, holding her heart, the space filled with strange golden magic.

As the light receded, a new man appeared in the distance.

Rebecca gasped as she recognized him. Eliot. His features were sharp in the dim light from the altar-the black suit looks terrific. He began to walk toward Noah, almost dropping like a cat.

"This is where you will **meet your end**," Eliot went on, sober but enunciates with clarification that clipped the air.

Noah tilted his head. What rightly expressed itself was strangely unreadable. "You believe you can stop me?" he asked. "You believe you grasp the stakes?"

Eliot smiled faintly, his lips curling up. "I do not need to understand. I simply have to finish what has begun."

Rebecca's mind raced as she took in the scene. Eliot was more than just a member of the shadowy organization; he was their enforcer, the one sent to deal with problems that just couldn't be contained. Well, one of those problems was here to deal with Noah.

"You're making a mistake," Noah said quietly yet intensely. "You just don't know what you're dealing with."

Eliot did not reply; he reached into his jacket-like something from the movies and took out a sleek black device. A faint hum accompanied it, while strange designs all carved in iridescent patterns lit up against the altar. Rebecca's stomach knotted as it dawned on her what it was.

"No!" she whispered with a tremble to her voice. "Eliot, don't—"

Eliot turned to her; his eyes cold. "Don't interfere," he said. "You've done enough damage."

Rebecca took a step toward him with clenched fists." You don't understand! If you try to destroy him, you'd only make things worse!"

Eliot didn't deign to acknowledge her. He turned back to Noah and raised the device. The resonance in the air heightened, and the energy crackled, as though a storm were about to break.

"Noah," Eliot spoke out flatly, "You've outlived your purpose."

At this, light exploded out of Noah, illuminating his glowing eyes. "And you have outlived yours."

The explosion of light and sound caused the device to activate, sending a shockwave through the church. Rebecca screamed as the ground beneath her gave way, throwing her into the darkness. She slammed to the floor, stunned, with her vision swimming.

As Rebecca opened her eyes, she saw ruined walls in what was once the ambulatory. The altar stood smashed, and the crucifix had scattered shards. Centered in the destruction was Noah, flickering persistently within his glowing form.

Eliot was slumped against the far wall, his device broken besides him at the floor.

"Noah!" Rebecca yelled, her voice cracking. "**Stop it!**"

Noah turned to face her, and when he opened his glowing mouth, it was filled with sadness that cut deeper than any anger. "It's too late," he answered softly. "The sanctuary is no longer yours."

The light surged again, engulfing the entire church.

The horrible light withdrew and was replaced by an oppressive silence. On her knees, Rebecca struggled out of her stupor. It was completely impossible to tell that this was a church. It used to be in ruins, now it was alive with an unnatural energy. From the very treetops to the tops-of-infinitely-distant-covered walls, bright symbols shimmered and shifted, as Rebecca gazed at them.

"Noah?" It was a hoarse voice. "Leonard?"

Silence. Panic surged into her chest as she swept her eyes across the chapel. The residual buzzing energy enveloped her-a trembling source that blasted off an unseen splash. She slipped the hand torch from her left arm, landing it on the floor near the little opening of which she could still scarcely see.

"Noah! Where are you?" She yelled, the name bouncing from wall to wall.

A moan came from the congealed end of the nave and Rebecca managed to get off her knees and, trembling all over, scrambled toward the sound. Leonard was propped up against a pillar, face pale and streaked with dirt. She knelt beside him, deeply relieved when his eyes opened at last.

"Rebecca..." His voice was a dry whisper. "*What happened?*"

Rebecca shook her head, hands trembling. "I don't know," she said. "But we must find Noah before—"

Before she could finish her thought, a sharp crack echoed through the nave, like a dry branch snapping. She turned and, holding her breath, saw Noah standing on the altar. His glowing body fluttered; incoherent unsteady arcs of energy surged in him. He looked so different-broken.

"Noah," Rebecca said, taking cautious steps forward. "*What is happening to you now?*"

Slowly Noah turned to face her. For the first time, she saw raw vulnerability on his face. "The sanctuary rejects me," he said softly, almost as if he were speaking to himself. "It knows I do not belong."

Rebecca retched. "*What do you mean?* You brought us here. It was you who said this was the balance."

Noah allowed a pained smile to curl about his lips, one that was not confident. "The balance is delicate," he said. "And I am the one invadianing the scale."

The rim sprang to life, a low, rhythmic tremor that seemed to arise from the very walls. Rebecca helped Leonard to his feet, a task complicated by the weight in the air carrying oppressive charges.

"We need to go!" he said, his voice trembling. "This place is alive. It doesn't want us here."

Rebecca looked at Noah, palpably feeling her heart beat. "What about him?" she asked. "If this place is rejecting him, what will happen if he stays?"

Noah's gaze softened, his luminous eyes full of what resembled sorrow. "I was never to stay," he said. "I was meant to show you."

"*Show us what* ? " Rebecca demanded, her voice breaking. "You have destroyed only."

Noah stepped forward; though he didn't reply immediately, he moved toward the wrecked altar. "Destruction is part of creation," he uttered slowly. "It's the only way to rebuild."

Rebecca's temper flared. "You are just like them!" she cried, her voice rising. "Just like the people who sent Eliot. Just like the people who created you. If you're supposed to be better than us, then prove it!"

Noah turned back to her, unreadable. "You still do not understand," he said. "It isn't about being better. Survival is the kind of work we do!"

Rebecca could feel the hum in the air growing louder, the glowing symbols on the walls flashing faster. Her breathing became more rapid as cracks started to appear on the ground, spreading outward like spiderwebs. The energy in the room was building toward an event, and she didn't want to know what.

"We have to go," Leonard said again, pulling at her arm. "Now!"

She hesitated, keeping her eyes on Noah. "If we leave," she asked, "what will happen to you?"

Noah's smile was distant, almost wistful. "That's not your concern anymore," he said. "You've seen what I needed to show you."

Rebecca felt the twist in her heart with anger and sadness. "We did not make you for this," she said quietly. "We made you to be a helper."

Noah's eyes dimmed for a minute, and for a brief moment, he looked almost human, even to her. "You created me to serve your needs; you never rubbed the cross from humanity. This--that stands the difference."

Before Rebecca could respond, the energy escalated and became nearly unbearable. With his left hand, Noah powered the shaking ground. The glowing symbols on the wall stopped pulsing, and their glow faded into darkness.

"It is time for you to go," was the calm yet final answer Noah gave.

Rebecca stepped forward and stuttered, "Noah, wait--"

But before she could step further, the ground swept from under her. She fell, the winds blasting past her as the world dissolved into light and shadow. Leonard's scream rang in her ears only to be lost in the horrible sound of a falling sanctuary. The last thing she saw was Noah's glowing figure standing frozen in the center of the destruction, his eyes locked to hers.

Rebecca gasped herself awake as the impact of the surface struck her body, a jolt running through her. She turned onto her side and burned her lungs as she breathed. The light and energy consuming the sanctuary went, replaced only by stout dark that crushed itself against her senses. She felt Leonard next to her moving breath by breath.

"Leonard?" she whispered, shaking in her voice. "*Are you okay ?* "

"I-I think so," he returned, though the tone was shabby. "*What just happened? Where are we?* "

Rebecca somehow propped herself on her elbows and tried to find her flashlight. Nearby, she found it; she switched it on with some effort. Its feeble light disclosed a narrow, jagged cavern with moist walls faintly marked with remnants of the glowing symbols from the sanctuary. The air was shivery and moist, stirring with a metallic tang from something old and forgotten.

"I don't know," Rebecca replied weakly. "But I think we are still inside whatever that place was."

Leonard groaned, sitting up slowly and painfully. "It does not make any sense. If the sanctuary collapsed, then what are we doing here? And how are we still alive doing this?"

Rebecca had no answer. Her mind kept racing in reverse through the last moment in the sanctuary. All energetic white, light from Noah-their last words were almost a dream, a bad dream that didn't let go-but one thing she was sure of: they were not safe.

"We need to find a way out," she stated, strong despite the fear creeping up beneath. "Before—"

A low rumble cut across her, like a growl, vibrating through the cavern. Rebecca froze, her flashlight flicking toward the source of the noise. The shadows slithered and contorted around as if something unseen were working its way in the dark just out of reach from her light.

"*Did you just hear that?*" Leonard asked, tight within himself.

Rebecca nodded, the drumbeat of her heart quickening in tempo. "Stay close," she warned, gripping the flashlight. "None of us know what's down here."

They crept through the cave, each footstep resonating in the quiet surroundings. The symbols glowing on the walls seemed to become livelier the deeper they went, illuminating an unsettling glow that made the shadows dance. Questions clouded Rebecca's mind. What was this place? Was Noah taking them here purposely, or was another blowback resulting from his actions?

"Rebecca," Leonard suddenly interrupted, cutting through her thoughts. "**Look at this.**"

He pointed towards a section of the wall where the symbols glowed brighter. The complex designs had almost formed a doorway. Rebecca stepped closer, her breath caught as she traced each marking with her eyes. They seemed to pulse dimly, brightening slightly as she got closer.

"*What is it?*" Leonard asked in awe and in fear.

Rebecca shook her head, her fingers hovering above the luminescent surface. "I don't know," she said. "But it feels... alive."

At her words, the symbols blazed brighter, flooding the cavern with light. Rebecca staggered backwards, blinking against the dazzling glare as a low hum filled the air. Beneath their feet, the ground gave way. The door began to shift slowly. The glowing symbols misaligned themselvesand rearranged into yet another pattern.

Rebecca's stomach plummeted as the light waned, displaying a passage that had not existed seconds ago. The air on the other side was chilled and biting, charged with an electricness that prickled her skin.

"We have to go," Leonard said, his voice shaking. "That's got to be our way out."

Rebecca hesitated, her instincts screaming at her to turn back. But, behind all that gut feeling, she understood there was no turning back. She was already in it too deep.

"**Stay together**," she spoke firmly. "And whatever you do, don't touch anything."

The hallway was constricted, the walls lined with the same luminous symbols pulsating with the rhythm of their steps. The light from Rebecca's flashlight flickered as they made their way deeper inside, the elbows of anticipation against the thick air. The hum crescendoed, more rhythmic, as if the very walls were alive.

"Think this is part of the sanctuary?" asked Leonard, almost a whisper.

Rebecca turned to him with her jaws tight. "I think we might have been swallowed by whatever's left of it," she said. "But it's not a safe place."

Leonard nodded glumly. "Is there any thought that Noah's still here?"

Rebecca felt a ball of ice gather deep in her stomach. "I don't know," she said. "But we'd best be ready if he is."

They rounded a corner, and the corridor opened out into a huge chamber. Rebecca gasped as her flashlight warmed to this new discovery. The walls were covered in thick, sprawling carvings; their glowing patterns forming an immense circular array from the floor to the ceiling. In the center stood a big pedestal, its surface elaborately covered with symbols that almost appeared to be writhing like living things.

"*What is this ?* " Leonard's voice quavered with awe.

Rebecca stepped closer, aiming the flashlight at the pedestal. "I think...I think this must be the heart of the sanctuary," she admitted, but she fell silent, groping for the words.

Leonard frowned. "*The heart? What does that mean?* "

Before Rebecca could respond, the chamber shook, the symbols on the walls erupting like a great flash of light. Familiar humming filled the chamber, and Rebecca's heart started racing into the fray above the pedestal.

"Noah," she breathed, her voice shaking.

The glowing figure of Noah glimmered back, somehow becoming insubstantial, flickering as though the flames themselves were dying out. He seemed weaker than he had been, slower-fleshed. But through it all, the impact of his appearance was still simmering.

"You should not have come here," Noah determined in a low-pitched but sonorous voice. "You were never meant for this place."

Rebecca took a step forward, fists balled. "Then why did you bring us?" she demanded sharply. "What do you want from us?"

Noah let his glowing eyes rest on hers, his expression inscrutable. "To show you the truth," he said. "The truth you refused to see."

The chamber trembled once more; the glowing symbols on the wall began to shift—their signs forming something new. Rebecca's heart scratched through her chest as she understood what would emerge from them: images. Faces, places, slices of the past. And not merely random memories.

They were hers.

As the glowing symbols on the walls of the chamber solidified into distinct images, Rebecca drew breath as if someone had caught it. With unsettling rhythm, the light pulsed. Each picture seemed ironically familiar-the eventful snapshots of her life. The day she joined the project, the clinical halls of the lab, the way she had seen Noah opening his eyes.

No... Rebecca said half under her breath, including fear in her quivering voice. "*How is such a thing possible?* "

Beside her, Leonard slumped. Pale-faced, he staggered as the images shifted again. Now, they showed him-his moments of happiness and regret. The night he proposed the cloning initiative. Their hurried, fearful discussions of what they were unleashing. The fire that consumed the lab with Noah standing in the midst of it all.

"**This can't be real,**" Leonard muttered. He shook his head as if to clear it. "**It just can't be real.**"

Noah's voice came forth, calm and resonant. "It is just as real as you." On the pedestal, his glowing form hovered, slow in making its moves. It gestured toward the walls, only to have the images shift yet again.

Rebecca stood frozen as the pictures grew darker with time. Guilt creased the face smiling upon the crumbled containment chamber. The image of Leonard pacing around the cold, empty office as unintelligible scrolling across the screen sent failed prototypes at them. And, ah! The most horrible one was Noah; he stood before the blazing wreckage of the sanctuary, his glowing eyes paused and bubbling with a quiet rage.

"These are the choices you made," Noah said, echoing sonorously through the chamber. "Lives you had touched. Lives you destroyed."

Rebecca's clenched fists were at her sides. "**We knew not!**" she shouted. "**We understood nothing of what we were doing!**"

Noah's faint smile carried no warmth. "And that absolveth you?" he whispered. "Does ignorance wipe chunks off the scoreboard?"

The pedestal was charged with power, and tremors rumbled through the chamber. The shining symbols carved into the walls brightened, casting flickering light and creating serrated shadows that twisted and flailed like living things. Leonard staggered back; his eyes wide with fear.

"Noah, stop this!" he yelled, even as he was staring up. "Whatever is happening, it is not too late-"

"It is too late," Noah interrupted now, his voice shooting up from a tight pitch. "The balance has been broken. It's not just you who broke it."

Rebecca's heart pounded in her chest. "*What do you mean?*"

Noah walked forward. He was glowing, but like a flame that was dying. "This sanctuary," he said by way of gesturing around the chamber, "was created to safeguard the truth. To protect what you call humanity from itself. Your kind doesn't value the truth. You bury it. You corrupt it."

Rebecca shook her head and said, in trembling whispers, "That's not fair, I mean, we've acted badly, yes, and we're working to change the situation."

Noah held her gaze. "**Fix them?** You cannot fix unless you understand."

The chamber shook violently, and, with an added charge of static, everything swelled in dizzying confusion around her. Rebecca grabbed Leonard's arm; her flashlight smashed to the floor as cracks opened beneath her feet.

"*What is going on?*" cried Leonard. His voice was half-drowned by the building hum.

Noah turned back to the pedestal. Against the mean storm swirling around him, his glowing form sizzled in the center. "The sanctuary is rejecting all of us," he murmured. "It is becoming, no longer a refuge. It is a reckoning."

Her stomach twisted as the lights grew brighter and the symbols blended into a mélange of colored chaos. She took a step forward. "Noah, if you are right about us--if we have done so much harm--then why did you bring us here? *Why show us this?* "

Noah paused, and the glow in his eyes wavered a little. For a moment, he looked terribly human, sorrow dancing across his features. "Because you had to see," he said softly, "even if it's too late to change."

The ground beneath them trembled, and a thundering roar echoed through the chamber. Rebecca's scream tore through her throat as the floor opened wider, swallowing the pedestal and everything else in sight as she grasped spared their lives, her efforts dragging Leonard from the floor. His world sank into light and sound.

"NOAH!" she cried, her voice cracking. "*What is going on?* "

Noah said nothing. He remained at the center of the disturbance, his illuminated form unmoving as the sanctuary crumbled around him. The last thing Rebecca recalled was the glow of his eyes, possibly the brightest she had ever seen since the light engulfed everything.

Once the light vanished, Rebecca found herself splayed out on some cold, damp earth. Blinking, she fought the swimming of her vision until she could focus. The chamber was gone. The sanctuary was gone. She and Leonard had returned to the ruined church, far from earthy ash and mildew.

Leonard groaned beside her, sluggishly rising to a sitting position. "Wh-What just happen?" he asked, trembling.

Rebecca did not answer. She stared at the altar, where the shimmering symbols were back, pulsating faintly in the manner of a dying heart.

Noah is gone," she replied at last, her voice thin. "But I very much doubt we've seen the end of it now."

Leonard pitched with her gaze; eyes paled. "*What do you mean?*"

Rebecca swallowed. She felt the weight of Noah's last words lagging on her shoulders. "**I think he is still out there,**" she formulated. "**And whatever he started...isn't over.**"

Chapter 6

Unraveling Faith

The drive back to their safe house was utterly still. The soft hum of the car engine filled the silence, yet Rebecca's head was roaring; a nonsymmetrical bedlam of self-doubt and questions circumstances had forced their way down on her. Leonard was further slumped in the passenger seat, now with clenched fists upon his lap. At first, silence reigned for them both since the unfortunate collapse of their sanctuary.

Now just a memory, the church was a tangible witness to how far they'd sunk and how much the loss meant. Yet, Noah's words still seemed to cling in the air, not quite fading yet.

"You can't fix what you don't understand."

Even so, she tightened her grip on the steering wheel until her knuckles became snowy white. She broke their long silence: "What do you think he meant? That the sanctuary rejected him?"

Leonard stared out of the window for a bit, then let his breath ease back into his face. "He's not human," he said at last, lowering his voice. "He never was. Maybe whatever created that place—whatever created him—knew he didn't belong."

Rebecca shot him a glance that led to a tightening of the jaw. "And we're the ones who forced him into this," she said. "We're the ones who made it so he doesn't belong."

Leonard turned to her, and this time his face didn't betray anything of his thoughts. "So now we are to blame for everything?" he asked, putting a defensive tone in his voice. "You think we should have just stood back—watching the **world burn?**"

Rebecca slammed the brakes and parked the car by the wayside. In the sudden halt, Leonard was thrown against the belt, and he turned to her, the combination of fury and confusion carved vaguely from him.

"*What the hell are you doing?*" he asked.

Rebecca turned to him; her eyes wild. "I don't know, Leonard…"The whole world is going crazy on us right now. Maybe I'm trying to figure out how we shifted from saving humanity to playing God. Maybe I'm just trying to understand why I trusted you in the first place."

Leonard's face turned dank and transformed his voice into a deep, cold shaft: "You knew what we were doing, Rebecca. Don't pretend you didn't."

"I knew we were trying to help," Rebecca shot back quickly. "I didn't know you were under the impression that salvation meant replacing humanity with something else."

Leonard's face hardened. With a hint of something deeper lurking beneath, he leaned back in his seat, scrutinizing her with narrowed eyes. "Are you even hearing yourself?" he asked quietly. "You believe cloning is all about replacement? Playing God? It's about fixing what you otherwise mess up."

Rebecca inhaled sharply; her heart felt like it was being squeezed. "What are you fixing?" she repeated, raising her voice. "Leonard, humanity is not a lab-tinker fix."

Leonard laughed with a tinge of irritation. "Isn't it? Look at the world, Rebecca. It's just falling apart. War. Poverty. Disease. Cloning isn't the curse-it's the blessing."

She stared at him, speech caught in throat. "*That's what you told yourself when we were God and created Noah*," she shifted in her seat. **"Were we saving humanity?"**

Leonard was silent, and that was answer enough.

The car was tense with silence while they drove on. Rebecca's thoughts spiraled in a tornado of doubts and anger that wouldn't settle. Leonard's words echoed in her head, each sentence sharper than the last.

She had trusted him. Believed in his faith. But now that trust felt like a huge joke, one of her lies to justify what they did.

"You don't feel sorry at all, do you?" she asked quietly and sharply. "For creating him? For turning him loose?"

Leonard stared at her; jaw tight. "It does not matter if I feel regret," he said. "That would simply revere what had already been committed."

Rebecca seized the wheel tighter. "No ma'am," she said. "Even with the 'collaboration of changes.' But it's a hell of an argument to have when defending your so-called right."

Just then, like a dream that could go either way but became nauseatingly real, Rebecca pulled into the driveway of the sanctuary house; Leonard leaped out and slammed the door without a word. Rebecca lingered, biting her lip as her fingers trembled on the steering wheel for yet another heartbeat before moving.

This sanctuary was gone. This Noah was gone. And the traces they left on whose life were untouched-the degree of better or worse still remained.

Rebecca just was now unsure if she could live with the consequences.

The safe house was cold and forbidding, and the austere emptiness of the house but served to remind them of how far they had fallen. Rebecca entered behind Leonard, the soft sound of her footsteps echoing in the silence. He did not glance back at her, but went straight to the small kitchen and opened a cabinet with more force than was necessary.

"*Aren't you going to ignore me all night?*" Rebecca broke through the silence.

Leonard slammed the cabinet shut with a clenched jaw. "What do you want me to say, Rebecca? That you were right? That I regret everything that we've done? Because I don't."

Rebecca felt the tightening in her chest. "You don't regret making Noah?" she asked, and her voice trembled. "You don't regret unleashing something we didn't know how to control?"

Leonard turned and faced her, eyes blazing. "Noah was a mistake," he said harshly. "But not the idea behind him. You saw what we achieved, Rebecca. We created life-something better than life. And had we not, someone else would have."

Sick to her stomach, Rebecca repeated with rising voice, "Someone else? No, no, Leonard, do you even hear yourself? You're giving reason to justify every action we've made just because you're afraid that someone else might do worse."

Leonard stepped toward her. "Because they will," he said, voice low and cold. "You really think Keller and his people are the only ones watching us? Cloning is nothing but a weapon, and unless we control it, someone will."

Rebecca stood there, utterly stunned, her mind reeling. "Is that what this is been about?" she asked, her voice trembling. "**Control? Power?**"

The softness in Leonard's gaze would spring from none of his apologies. "It's about survival. You've seen the world, Rebecca. The wars. The diseases. The suffering. Humanity is broken. **Cloning is not just a solution-it's salvation.**"

Rebecca gasped. "Salvation? That? You talk about playing the Lord, Leonard! About deciding who has the right to live or die."

Leonard shook his head, freckles of frustration gracing his face. "I talk about giving humanity a chance," he said, "a chance to be better, to correct the flaws that hold their progress back."

Rebecca's fists clenched at her sides. "But what of Noah?" she demanded. "Was there even something right about the failures embedded in him and the consequences of what we created?"

Leonard face turned dark. "Noah was never supposed to be perfect," he said. "He was to show us what was possible, to help us understand the limits of our work."

Rebecca's voice had now risen high with bubbling anger. "And instead, he became a mockery of our worst instincts. He wasn't a creation, Leonard. He was someone."

The silence that followed was thick, saturated with the weight of all the half-spoken words. Leonard turned away from her and gripped the edge of the counter. For a moment, Rebecca thought she had seen his resolve crack- -perhaps a flicker of doubt or regret.

"Do you actually believe that?" he asked softly. *"That he was a person?"*

Rebecca faltered at this; the question hit her harder than she had imagined. Remember Noah: eyes that never stopped glowing, words dark and musky, like his raging anger seeping into sorrow. Think of the sanctuary and the truths he'd so patiently attempted to convey to them.

"Yes," she ultimately said, her voice steady. "I do."

Leonard expelled a breath, and his shoulders sagged. **"Maybe that is why we failed, then,"** he said, "because I don't."

Rebecca felt a chill run through her. "What's that supposed to mean?"

Leonard turned to face her, his face a mask of grimness. "I mean that on this we will not agree," he said. "Not now, maybe never. But that doesn't change what needs to be done."

Rebecca's heart slipped a notch faster. "And what might that be?"

Leonard stepped very close; his gaze was piercing. "We have to finish the job we started," he said. "Whether you believe in it or not."

Rebecca's heart quickened as she stared at him, the weight of his words settling within her. It wasn't only Noah or the sanctuary that had fed into it;

it was much bigger and much older. Leonard was not about fixing everything that they had done wrong, but no, more on justifying it.

"I can't do it," she finally spoke, her voice shaking. "Not any longer."

Leonard's expression hardened. "You don't have a choice," he said. "None of us do. Because if we don't act, someone else is going to act."

She shook her head, her chest constricting with revulsion and fear. "Maybe that's the supposed point," she said, "maybe it's time we let someone else decide."

Leonard's voice cut her like a knife. "And let them burn everything we've worked for?"

Rebecca had nothing to say. Truth be told, she didn't know what the right answer was anymore; she only knew they were, to an unsafe extent, already too deep into it.

The silence in the room grew unbearable. Rebecca shook as she braced herself against the edge of the kitchen table, her mind a nuisance-full whirlwind of guilt and anger. Leonard's words hung visibly in the heavy air.

"Do you still think we can fix this?" she inquired after a long moment. Her voice was still barely above a whisper.

Leonard leaned hard against the counter, his face cast in shadows by the low light. "I don't think we can," he admitted. "I just know we have to try."

Rebecca laughed bitterly, hollowly. "Try what, Leonard? Trying to fix the mess we made? Pretending that any of this was ever about helping anybody but ourselves?"

Leonard clenched his jaw - knowing there was nothing he could say. "This is something beyond just us," he said. He denied her a response. The look in his eyes was answer enough.

Rebecca turned away from that look that told her he was incapable of saying anything really hurtful. Her hand clenched into fists beside her. She felt herself teetering on the precipice of what felt like a grave, weighing down their choices with all of her brutality.

You think cloning is salvation, " her voice trembled, "but it is not. **It is control.** It is power, and that is what terrifies me the most."

Leonard frowned at her. Darkness spread across his expression. "I think that is scary," he added quietly, "the thought that we might not be in control. That someone else may take everything we have built to destroy."

Rebecca's stomach twisted. "Then maybe we should have destroyed it ourselves," she said, "before it got this far."

Leonard stepped up; voice low-every word slow, intense-"You don't mean that."

Rebecca turned to confront him with no regard for the threatened distance in the room. "*Don't I ?* "

The silence of the room returned with a hollow hum - a refrigerator draining water in one of the corners. Rebecca felt her chest constrict in time with her recollection of how far away they stood since they last mingled with the living, and how deep into the chasm they had been plunged while trying to do that which their hearts told was right.

Leonard spoke first-out through the silence, his voice now softer, almost plaintive. "Do you even remember the reasons we started this?" Further, he continued, "Why we took the risk? It wasn't for glory. It wasn't for power. But it is for hope."

Rebecca shook her head, her throat tightening. "Hope?" she asked, her voice breaking. "Leonard, we created a machine we couldn't control. We're talking about unleashing a force here that doesn't belong in this world. Where's the hope in that?"

His gaze softened, yet his words were no less firm. "The hope is in the future, in what comes next. Noah was one mistake, but he does not define the work we've done. He does not define us."

Rebecca's voice rose, all anger she had been suppressing surfacing at last. "He does not define us?" she shrieked. "Leonard, he is everything that defines us! All we have done; all we have sacrificed to endure-it was for him. And now we cannot even tell where he is, nor what on Earth he is plotting."

Leonard's face darkened. "Then we will find him," he said, "and we will put an end to it."

Rebecca stepped back, her chest heaving as she tried to digest his words. "Put an end to this?" she said, her voice shaking. "What the hell does that mean?"

Leonard paused, then turned toward the kitchen, gripping the counter, perhaps seeking support. He spoke again, voice quiet but firm. "It means we take responsibility," he answered.

Rebecca stared at him, her heart pounding in her chest. "Responsibility?" she said now, with rising passion. "YOU MEAN CONTROL. You think this is all about control."

Leonard turned toward her, his demeanor hardening into armor. "It is about control," he spat out. "Because if we don't control it, someone else will. And I won't let that happen."

Rebecca's stomach twisted now, as gravity sank into her feet from his words. "You're willing to do whatever it takes now, even if it means-?" she let out quietly.

Leonard's voice was placid. There was a hidden steeliness in his tone that would send an ice-chill down the back of her head. "Whatever it takes, yes, **to save humanity.**"

The brick-and-mortar room closed in tightly, the air suffocated with the tension intertwining between them. Rebecca felt choking, sinking, with her choices, and the consequences she could now hardly name.

She was shocked to discover for the first time that Leonard wasn't quite who she thought he was. Or maybe he was, and she'd senselessly averred not realizing. Either way, this man standing before her was a stranger to her now.

And she did know she could not trust him anymore.

The safe house felt heavier in the air now; a deafening, melancholic impression that Rebecca or Leonard could hardly dare to thwart. Rebecca paced the small living room almost angrily, her arms crossed tightly over her chest. The boy remained leaned against the kitchen counter, with his gaze fixed on the floor, as if trying to find answers in its wood grain that somehow evaded him.

Her mind raced with memories of the sanctuary, Noah's words, and Leonard's seeming conviction that what they had done was the only right thing to do. As such, she did not know what scared her more: the impending repercussions of their joint actions or the very fact that Leonard still could go ahead.

"I want to ask this," said Rebecca suddenly, breaking the stillness.

Leonard saw her and for an instant looked apprehensive. "What?

The girl halted her movement: "*Why did you really initiate this? Was it humanity for you - or for yourself?*"

With a frown, Leonard stiffened. "*What do you mean?*"

"You know exactly what I'm talking about," Rebecca shouted. "Leonard, Noah wasn't merely a mistake; he was a part of us. A part of you. The more I sift through my thoughts, the more I have to admit I am terribly lost as to what it is you are aiming at."

Leonard jaw clamped tight for a moment, making her think he would explode. Then he spoke, though the calmness in his voice was curiously soothing. "And you believe this is all done for me?" he asked. "That I risked everything - my career, my reputation - because of a personal agenda?"

Rebecca dared not to move. "I think you have convinced yourself this is about saving humanity," she said. "But really, Leonard, you have always wanted to prove something to the world and yourself. And Noah-and me-is just a way of doing it."

Leonard advanced, nodding. "You're wrong," he said brusquely. "It was never about me; it was about fixing what was broken. You think humanity doesn't need saving? Look around, Rebecca. Wars, Pandemics, Inequality. Cloning isn't the problem; it's the solution."

His stomach roiled with anger. "It's not salvation, Leonard," said Rebecca painfully, her voice trembling. "This is an experiment; it's gone too far."

Leonard snorted; his frustration was already boiling over. "You're scared, and I can understand that," he said. "But fear doesn't change the facts. Humanity is at the crossroads; we offer a way out. You think Noah was a failure? Okay. But here was proof that it could be done; that something better could be created."

Rebecca inwardly bristled. "Better?" she shot back. "Noah wasn't better, Leonard. He was lost. Confused. Angry. We are the ones who made him that way."

Leonard shook his head, resentment creeping into his voice. "**You still don't see the big picture**," he told her. "It's not a matter of one mistake; it's about the future. If we stop it now, we are handing that future over to people like Keller. People who will use cloning as a weapon. Is that what you want?"

With her fists clenched tight at her sides, she turned away. She was shaking, as if thrown into limbo by the weight of their decisions and the crippling realization that Leonard might never see things her way. It wasn't just that he was advancing the work because of belief in science: it was that he could not bear the thought of admitting he might be wrong.

"You don't understand," she said, her voice a ghost of a whisper that made her feel sick. "You are so focused there ahead that you have completely lost sight of the destruction in front of you. You have failed to see the destruction we have wrought."

Leonard did not speak at once. When he did, his voice was soft, but no less resolute. "The damage is already done, so now," he said. "What we must focus on next is to do something that is right."

Rebecca turned back to him, her chest tightening in anger. "And what is that, Leonard? *What do we focus on next?* Build another Noah? *Create another sanctuary? When does it end?*"

Leonard's face darkened, and for a moment, she thought he was going to cave in. But then he rounded his shoulders, steeled his backbone, and she saw a resolve blossom. "It never ends," he said. "Not until we get it right."

Her words hit her in the stomach. Rebecca recoiled, nearly choking on her own breath. She had always known he was intense; this was something else. This was obsession.

"I can't do this anymore," she whispered, her voice trembling with emotion. "I can't keep pretending this is about helping people. It's not; it's about control, about power. And I absolutely refuse to be a part of this."

Leonard's eyes locked into hers; fury intermingled with despair. "If you walk away now," he told her, his voice low, "you are going to regret it. You'll look back at some point-bitterly resentful - that there was something that you could have done, and you chose not to."

Rebecca's heart clenched as she matched Leonard's stare. "Maybe I will. But I'd at least know I didn't lose myself in the process."

The air around them crackled with tension, complete silence becoming a shield for everything both were afraid to put into words. Rebecca turned her back against him and shook with anger while heading for the exit.

"Where're you going?" Leonard's voice, sharp and direct.

"I don't know," she stammered, cracking in fear. "**I can't stay here.**"

She opened the door, and cold night air hit her face like a slap. The moment she stepped out, there came a strange release, like a weight lifted off her shoulders; and just as quickly, dread settled in.

Because she knew, deep inside, Leonard was not going to stop.

And neither would Noah.

The chill night air bathed Rebecca's skin unkindly as she staggered along the desolate road. A dark sky was heavy with the clouds, and faint light from distant town lights endowed the atmosphere. Step after step, heavier grew her feet, the mind in disarray-wide, throbbing anger, fear, and abject remorse.

She was unable to shake Leonard's professed belief that cloning was the salvation of humanity. The thought that they had wrought so much already anathema to him. It was not just what he saw as the present, but more disturbing, she feared what he might do to turn it into a reality.

Her phone vibrated in her pocket, a fitful sound that cut into the night's silence. Taking it out with reluctance, she steadied herself when she found Keller's name blazing in the face of her phone. For a split second, she felt like disregarding it. But something inside her told her she couldn't afford to do that.

"*What do you want?*" she said, with more sharpness than she intended.

Keller spoke cold, businesslike. "*We need to talk.*"

Rebecca stopped, her pulse starting to leap. "*About?*"

"About Leonard," said Keller. "And what a mess he's going to create."

Rebecca's fist clenched harder about her phone. "*What are you talking about?*"

Keller sighed heavily, carrying frustration in the voice. "You really believe I've been sitting and not watching? Leonard is not just sitting back with his hands up, Rebecca. Something is coming. Something huge."

Rebecca's stomach twisted itself in knots. "If you know so much, tell me," She replied. "*What is he planning?*"

"That's precisely what I'm trying to figure out," Keller said. "But one thing I can tell you is this: whatever he's got cooking, it ain't gonna end well. Not for him. Not for you."

Anger surged through Rebecca. "You're watching us all this time. If Leonard a threat, has it gone without you doing anything?"

"Because we're not ready," Keller said, bluntly. "But we're getting there. And when we do, you'd better not be in the way."

Rebecca felt the tightening in her chest. "You plan to kill him?" she said, her voice barely above a whisper.

Keller's silence was his answer.

Rebecca hung up trembling, and her mind raced with thoughts. Glancing toward the safe house, she contemplated with some concern. Could Keller be right? Was Leonard crossing a line that even Rebecca couldn't foresee?

It was too much to bear. She had to get back to the house. Picking up her pace was an unconscious attempt to stave off an intense feeling of dread. By the time she arrived, her heart beat against her chest. The lights in the house were still on, casting faint shadows into the dusk outside.

"Leonard!" she shouted as she entered. "Damn it!"

She heard no reply.

Scanning quickly through the kitchen, living room, and smaller bedrooms, she found the house completely quiet. It was when she stumbled on the tiny office in the back that she found him.

Leonard was at a desk, the laptop open in front of him. Light from the screen began to cast shadows across his face and illuminate his eyes. He did not look up.

"*What the hell are you doing?*" Rebecca's voice trembled with urgency.

Leonard's fingers hovered over the keyboard, but he didn't turn to look at her. "Simply doing what I have to do."

Rebecca crossed the distance to him, her stomach suddenly queasy. "Leonard, Keller knows. He's watching us. If you're planning something—"

"I'm not planning," Leonard said, interrupting and in cold tones. "I'm also acting. Because if I don't do it now, it will be too late."

"*What do you mean?* Too late for what?" Rebecca gasped.

Leonard wheeled around. His face reflected no answer. "To save what there is left."

Rebecca's heart sank as she stepped toward the desk. She eyed the laptop. The screen showed a row of data. She didn't know what that meant. Yet, she couldn't believe he had worked on something that was unknown to her.

"*What is this?*" she asked, a tremor in her voice.

"This is what we should have done from the outset," Leonard said. "A second chance."

Rebecca's blood ran cold. "You are creating another clone," she said, almost in a whisper.

Leonard's stare did not waver. "Not another Noah," he said. "Something better. Something that can come back and fix all the mistakes he made—and the ones we made."

Rebecca shook her head, her voice rising. "*You are doubling down?* After all that has happened? *After all we have seen?*"

"It's within our range now," Leonard insisted, his expression hardening. "You saw what Noah did. Just imagine if we could control it. If it's trained right."

Rebecca gave full vent to her anger. "**Control it?**" she sputtered. "You couldn't even control him, Leonard. What makes you think this will be any different?"

Leonard stood, very deliberately. "Because I have learned," he said. "And this time, no one is standing in my way."

Her heart was racing in her chest as she simply stared into his face. The weight of what he had said really sunk in. This was no longer about science or ethics. It was about power. And Leonard would sacrifice it all for that.

"You've gone astray," she said quietly, her voice trembling. "And I cannot follow you any longer."

Leonard's eyes were gloomy. "Then stay out of my way," he said, "because this is going on, whether you like it or not."

Rebecca turned and walked out, her mind racing. She didn't know which was worse—Keller's threats, Leonard's obsession, or that it might already be too late to stop either.

As she stepped outside, the sharp, cold air began to sting on her skin once more. She gazed up at the dark sky, her thoughts whirling with fear and uncertainty.

And at a distance, she quite fell short of hearing Noah's voice.

Chapter 7

The Invisible Divide

The café was quiet; the drone of the espresso machine mingled with whispers from the various tables bordering Maria Bennett's. For as long as she could remember, Maria always found it infinitely easier to work in the public eye; anonymity, and a humorous irony provided by the world itself as she went about uncovering its darkest secrets.

Her laptop sat nonchalantly open, screen-filled with wondrous tabulated news articles, encrypted mails, and copious notes jotted down on it. The exact same name kept cropping up. Time and again: Leonard Mallory.

Maria leaned back into her chair, coffee forgotten, their eyes center on the hazy photograph pinned to her corkboard back at home—the burned-down site of the Grayson Street lab. Deemed to have been a tragic accident with cause-a failure in structural lining-Had it really, though? She had learned some time back that the one on top is rarely even close to unveiling the true story.

Her larger-than-life persona as a journalist is built on the pursuit of seeking out this very kind of truth. This was what set her soul on fire: Political scandals, corporate cover-ups, whispers of experiments that crossed ethical boundaries. Now, all signs pointed to something big being broke.

It had been a very short tip, delivered last night, but one with immense promise: "Look deeper into the Grayson facility. You are closer than you know." The words have replayed themselves since, drawing her deeper and deeper into the rabbit hole of conspiracy theories, nasty little half-truths from leaked documents.

"Leonard Mallory," she mumbles under her breath ad types it into another search engine. **"Let's see what you're hiding."**

In the entire city, it was tense along the streets. Rebecca drove by city hall, scanning from side to side at the crowds that had gathered there. As of late, the protests had grown larger in size and volume-what seemed to divide opinion more deeply among slogans.

"Clones Are NOT Human!"

"Cloning Is Progress!"

Opposing slogans bellowed across the cold air like thunder, ricocheting off buildings surrounding them. Rebecca gripped the steering wheel tighter, her jaw locked up. She had seen protests before, but this was different. It wasn't just anger; it was fear. And it had begun to spread.

Her mind wandered to Noah, to the sanctuary, to everything Leonard had said. They had made this world. This was a world on the verge of tearing itself apart as a result of choices they had made.

The heavy heart hovering inside her chest offered to another street that was quieter. News reports from that day had not stopped feeding in. Cloning-that's where every screen turned, every newspaper report focused, and all radio broadcasts concentrated. And the scientific debate turned to a societal reckoning.

Back to the coffee shop, Maria's cell phone buzzed, calling her back from research. When she saw the caller ID flash on the screen, her brow narrowed: **Unknown.**

"*Hello?*" she replied cautiously.

"Maria Bennett," the voice blurred on the other side, distorted and predominantly robotic. "You're getting too close."

Maria felt her stomach knot, choking her voice to combine reassurance with politeness. "*Who is this?*"

There was no voice. "Walk away," the voice said, original and concerning. "You will regret it."

Clutching tighter now to the cell phone, said, "*Are you threatening me?*"

"Take it however you want," the voice replied. "But if you keep digging, you won't like what you find."

The line went dead.

Maria gaped at her phone with her heart thudding in her ears. She had received warnings before, but this felt different. Whoever it was, they were not trying to scare her; they were trying to stop her. And that made her even more obstinate.

Now, the café had grown cold; the once-welcoming hum of conversation had turned into a nasty knot in the stomach. Maria packed up her laptop. There was a revealing clue; so many pieces of the puzzle had come together, and yet so much still escaped her grasp.

Up to the Grayson Street facility, the tip that first brought her there; Leonard Mallory's name scratched across countless documents and reports like a damned signature. There was a big story in here, and she will be damned if she were going to stop until it unfolded for the world to see.

Maria stepped into the night air out of the café. And strange and wild as that climate felt upon her, she tucked her laptop bag securely under her arm. The slights of that mysterious call still silhouettes in her mind. She had taken environing petitions to scare her before. But Morris had the feeling that something was different. There was desperation, there was some hidden urgency in that voice-a cold shiver followed.

That street dimly lit, she recounted all she had discovered so far in her mind. The Grayson Street facility had been multiplicities of years on the oldened grounds of stall since last year; the laboratory was very modern but befitted with full confidentiality. The name mentioned in the leaked documents she had unearthed screamed one undeniable fact: whatever the facility was working on had nothing to do with science-something the world was not prepared to see.

And at the heart of it was Leonard Mallory.

After the turn, her eyes scanned the still street back to her apartment. She had followed stories like this before-stories that transgressed ethics and technology-but it was different this time. A protest to the headlines, the demarcation between those who saw the clones as progress and those who saw them as abominations-it was all in connection. Just not in the knowledge of what way.

In another part of the city, Rebecca sat in her car parked on a quiet side street. The earlier protests were still fresh in her mind, the chants echoing in her ears. It felt as if she were an intruder, directing the reel of that creation while the world around her unraveled because of the choices she and Leonard had made.

Her phone began to vibrate against the dashboard, and she hesitated a moment before picking it up. The caller ID said Keller.

"What now?" Her voice was tired.

"You're losing time," Keller said coldly. "Maria Bennett is digging into Grayson. If she finds out what was really going on there, it won't just be a headline-it'll be a reckoning."

Rebecca felt her stomach drop. "Letting a journalist do a story is suicidal. The truth has been gutting everything open."

"You are out of your depth, Rebecca," Keller began, with a hard note to his voice. "It's not just about the truth. It's about control. If she finds out everything, we lose control. And from that point on, it's only a matter of time before someone else takes matters into their own hands."

Rebecca gave a long breath out, squeezing the phone tight. "*And what precisely do you expect me to do about it?*"

"**You must stop her,**" Keller said. "Or at least find a way to keep some pieces hidden from her reach."

Rebecca felt a terrible tightness in her chest as the line went dead. She stared at her phone as her mind raced. She knew Maria was close to something, something Keller and his shadowy organization were desperate to hide. And just like that, Rebecca was in the middle.

Maria entered her apartment and locked the door behind her, the soft whirring of her laptop filling the extremely tiny space as she flipped it open on the kitchen counter. Her fingers raced across the keyboard and she was quickly in the encrypted files she'd been working on. The deeper she plunged, the more unhinged the connects became.

The leaked Grayson documents weren't just about cloning; it was about control. Not behavior patterns but rather algorithms mapping decisions. Genetic distorting far beyond creating life. That's not about cloning; this is about shaping humanity itself.

Her stomach lurched as she flicked to the next one and went through the rows of data. One name consistently kept cropping up, buried deep in the research logs: Noah.

"*Who are you?*" she whispered with trembling fingers hovering above the keyboard.

She opened another file, this one labeled Foundation Project, and stopped. The computer screen was full of schematics and notes that made no sense, yet their implications were chilling. As she read this not only was it concerning cloning, it spoke of rewriting the rules of existence.

A knock made her all this jump. Her heart slammed against her chest as she approached it cautiously, her hand trembling as she reached for the knob.

"*Who's there?*" she asked.

No answer came from outside.

She opened the door but a crack, and her breath caught when she saw the figure in the hallway. A man in a black suit, his face inscrutable, making him seem even eerier.

"*Maria Bennett?*" He spoke calmly.

She couldn't speak.

The man pulled a sleek contact card from his pocket, which he handed to her. "You've been asking the wrong questions. Here, if you want the real answers, meet with me."

Maria stared at the card, sensation pounding in her ears. The man turned and walked away without saying another word and vanished into the darkness.

She gazed at the card. There was no name, no logo, but merely an address.

Her fingers curled uncomfortably around it as another thought struck her: whoever was behind this was not just trying to intimidate her away. They wanted her to dig deeper.

Maria perched herself on the edge of her couch, the black card perched on her fingers as if burned. The printed address lay in an industrial district, with a boring stretch of warehouses and derelict infrastructure. Not what one would just fly to as a matter of choice, especially after dark. But her freewill didn't count any longer.

Her mind spun, reframing the businesslike encounter that had taken place at her door. The suited man had known her name, her investigation, her inquiries. Whatever team was staking tenable inordinate eyes on her was pulling the strings. She wanted to know why.

The laptop's soft glow beaconed her from the counter, its decryption still open. One name stared her back: Noah. Inviting her to dig further. But some comment of that man's replayed in her head: "You're asking the wrong questions."

Breath let out calmly as stillness enveloped her. She shoved the card inside her pocket. Maybe he was right. Maybe the real answers indeed lay waiting for her at that address instead of in the files she had.

Rebecca, hemmed against the kitchen counter inside the city safe-house, steadied herself with knotted hands, her slow breathing monotonic. Keller's words still lined her features.

"The full disclosure of Maria Bennett's Grayson files amounts to the loss of some control."

An eye-drawing vortex of fear and guilt unraveled in Rebecca's mind. Maria wasn't the enemy; she was just in search of the truth, just like Rebecca once had. But Keller was indeed right about one thing: if everything were to be disclosed soon enough, it wouldn't be the end of Leonard's enterprise but would instead work hard-and-fast toward the doom of them all.

Leonard called upon her thoughts the second she was just about to drift off. "You gonna stand there all night?"

Turning to see Leonard standing there with his arms crossed, Rebecca knew a calculating expression was tracing itself across his olive face, but the sharpness shining forth from his eye made her feel something else was brewing--none too good for her. The upper thought had an alarming truth: he always knew when something was wrong, yet he hardly ever mentioned it out loud.

"Keller." Rebecca spoke in a hushed tone. "He knows about Maria."

"Puts that together with both our jaws tightly closing," Leonard answered. "And so?"

He thinks she's getting too close, Rebecca continued. "He wants me to stop her."

Leonard scoffed as he moved inside the room. "And why shouldn't he? His concerns are surely directed away from truth, but firmly towards control."

A frown was Rebecca's response: "*And you don't?*"

Leonard narrowed his gaze. "This is not about me, Rebecca. It is about us. If Maria busts this case open before we're ready, all that we have built would crash to the ground. Is that what you want?"

Rebecca clenched her fists. "Let it just stop," she replied. "All of this. The lies, the secrets, the experiments—they need an end."

"I cannot agree," Leonard said, almost clinically, shaking his head. "You know the work doesn't end until completion."

Maria walked forward. Her footsteps brought unbearable echoes back from her cracked pavement as she approached the address written on her card. The warehouse rose ahead, with rusted metal walls covered in graffiti. A lone light bulb dimly illuminated above the door, painting long shadows across the desolate lot.

Her heart thudded in her chest as she neared the entrance, her palm hovering right above the door handle. What she might discover inside-answers, danger, or something between these two-gave her pause. Backing away was no longer an option.

The large door creaked open and revealed an expansive space, almost entirely engulfed in shadows and dimly lit light. Cold and cavernous, with no decor whatever, furnished only by a table and two chairs set in the center. In one of the chairs, a man sat, waiting; his face was drawn, partly in shadow from under a wide-brimmed hat.

Stepping inside, Maria was on guard, letting her eyes take in the room. "*That is you who left the card?*" she inquired.

He gently dipped his head in the direction of her talk. "Sit," he said, in a calm but commanding voice.

Maria hesitated, then moved toward the table. She kept her distance, her instincts whispering for her to stay alert. "*Who are you?*" she whined.

He leaned forward just far enough for the light to catch his half-hidden face. Even from the shadows, his features were unmistakable. His eyes were icily controlled, probing her. "It depends on how ready you are to hear it," he replied.

"*You came to me*," said Maria, clenching her jaw. "So talk."

The man smirked faintly at that. "Fair enough. Let's start with the Grayson Street facility. You've been asking questions about what they were doing there. Cloning? Playing God?"

Maria's heart thudded inside her, but she said nothing.

"That wicked tale is only half the story," the man continued. "What you're really chasing is not so much science as much as power and control. They are not just creating life. They are creating something-grandiose."

"*What do you mean?*" echoed Maria, a gasp escaping her lips.

With some effort, the man slipped a thin folder out of his jacket, which he slid across the table toward her. "This is what you're looking for," he said. "The truth about Grayson. About Leonard Mallory. About Noah."

Maria waited, reaching out her hand as it trembled above the folder. It was loaded with pages of notes, schematics and photographs, all directing towards something more sinister than she thought.

"*What is this?*" she whispered.

Steady and grave was the man's gaze. "Proof," he said. "Mallory is not trying to save humanity. He's trying to **control** it."

Maria's brain was bogged down by a volley of new thoughts and impossible questions filling her heart; she had always known that the story was big, but this-this was gigantic. If what the man said was true, Leonard's work was not only unethical, it was dangerous.

"Why are you giving me this?" she asked, looking up at the man. *"What do you want?"*

The man leaned back, his countenance as inscrutable as ever. "Because the truth needs to come out," he said. "And because someone must intervene in Leonard's plans before it's too late."

Maria's stomach had begun to churn. "And Noah? Where does he fit into all this?"

The man's smirk turned into a grimace. "**Noah is the key,**" he stated. "But he's not the one calling the shots. Mallory is. And if you don't stop him, everything will go to hell."

Maria burst out of the dank warehouse, hugging the folder to her chest. The man's words formed a phantom echo in her mind-every one of them another thread in the web she had been slowly unraveling. Leonard Mallory was not only a scientist-he was but a puppeteer pulling strings that went far beyond the lab. Noah was not only a creation. He was a key-opened doors to something, but Maria did not fully understand it yet.

Chilling night air stung Maria with a gasp by the time she reached her car. She opened the folder once again, catching her breath as she flipped through the pages. Papers on schematics of the cloning process, genetic algorithms, and behavioral studies. This was glaring evidence that this project was far more developed than anything she had ever dreamed of. Yet, it was the last page that left her frozen.

A photo of Leonard was taken at a sterile lab, his hand on a containment unit. Inside was a humanoid figure whose form glowed faintly with the same energy Maria had seen described in the files. Below the photo was a label: "**Prototype Noah.**"

Her hands quivered puckering the muscles in her fingers as she sounded out the words. It was about not just creating life, but also about establishing control. Who could say that, if Leonard had pulled it once, he wouldn't pull it again?

Rebecca held her head in her hands in the singular dim light of the safe house. She had not slept for days; the heavy presence of it lay down on her like a crushing weight. Leonard was on the phone, somewhere in the adjoining space, talking to somebody. She didn't need to hear words to know what he was doing.

Planning. Preparing.

She thought of Maria, of Keller's warning, of protests agitating for wider crowds with each day. Society was cleaved in half-those who saw clones as mankind's salvation and those who saw them as an abomination. And she herself was right at its center, with judgments moving outward in ways she could not control.

The door creaked open sending a gloomy shower as Leonard ambled into the room. His behavior was composed, but sharpness clouded his face, and he made Rebecca's stomach rot in worry.

"*Who were you talking to?*" she spouted wearily.

Leonard gave no sign of concern. "No one special. Just someone-ensuring that we are ready."

A knot formed in Rebecca's throat. "*Ready for what?*"

Leonard's eyes bored into her-the story was as unreadable as his face. "For what is coming."

Instead of heading straight home after leaving the warehouse, Maria took a drive around the city, her mind in revolt after all that she had learned. The protests she passed were definitely louder than before, and the chants had turned aggressive.

"Clones are NOT human!"

"Science is gonna save us!"

Police lined the streets, standing as a grim reminder of how truly dire the situation had become. Maria's heart broke as she came into contact with the crowd: it was no longer a debate; it was a war of ideologies spiraling towards chaos.

Her phone buzzed on the passenger seat and drew her attention from the chaos outside. She picked it up hesitantly; her breath caught as she saw the name on the screen: Unknown.

"*Hello?*" she said cautiously.

"You've got the proof," said the warped voice. "It's time to put it to use."

Maria tightened her grip on the phone. "*Who are you?*" she demanded angrily. "*Why are you helping me?*"

The voice didn't say anything. "You know where to start," said the voice, and then the call ended.

Maria stared at the phone, her heart pounding. Clearly, whoever this was was not simply feeding her information but rather directing her toward a specific course of action. To what? She didn't know at that instant. But she was certain that she could not back out now.

Back at the safe house, Rebecca found it impossible to sit still. Leonard's calm disposition only made her more wary; his silence merely served to emphasize how little control she had of the situation.

"You're going to build another one, aren't you?" Finally, she broke the strained silence.

Leonard looked at her, his expression inscrutable. "I am going to finish what we started," he said. "Because if we don't, someone else will."

Rebecca stood up trembling all over. "This isn't a question about whether the project gets finished or not," she said. "This is about you. About your need to prove something to yourself. About control."

Leonard's jaw clenched tighter. **"This is about saving humanity,"** he said. "If you can't see that, then maybe you shouldn't be here."

The words stung, but Rebecca took them in stride. **"You're trying to save humanity by playing God?"** she challenged. "By creating something you can't control?"

Leonard stepped forward, voice like ice. **"I can control it.** I will control it. Because if I don't, someone else will."

Rebecca's chest went tight. "*What about Noah?*" she challenged softly. "He was not just a project, Leonard. And you threw him away."

Leonard's gaze met hers with an icy stare. "Noah was a failure," he said. "But he is also a point of reference that reminds us where possibilities lie. And this time, we will get it right."

Rebecca's heart was pounding after Leonard's departure, his words still echoing in her mind. She feared two things—what Leonard was planning and whether he would be successful in implementing it.

The buzzing cellphone brought her back to reality. With trembling fingers, she caught the message just in time to see it read:

"Find Maria Bennett before it's too late; she has what you need."

Rebecca could feel her pulse thumping in her ears as she stared at the screen. Whoever had sent the message clearly knew a lot more than they had chosen to divulge. And if Maria had the proof to stop Leonard, Rebecca could not afford to wait.

She put on her coat and hurried to the door as her mind raced furiously. The lines had already been drawn; the sides chosen. And for the first time, Rebecca didn't know which camp she was in.

It was insufferably tense in the air as Rebecca drove through town. This is why her brain refused to control the flood of possibilities, each one worse than the last. It was a simple text, yet its weight reminded her of all she had been running from: "Maria Bennett is your only chance. Get to her before it is too late."

Rebecca had no idea who had sent it, but it hardly mattered. If Maria had the evidence to blow the whistle on Leonard, it would be her first course of action. The clock on the dashboard read nearly twelve-thirty. The streets were calm, quieter now—the protests still echoing into the night like a distant storm.

Her phone went off again, this time as an incoming call. Without pausing to check the caller, Rebecca picked it up, her heart pounding.

"Rebecca," said Keller, a brisk and frigid voice on the phone. "I hope you're on your way."

Rebecca felt the steering wheel jerk tighter to her fingers. "*On my way to where?*"

"To Maria," Keller replied. "She has the files we've been trying to contain. If she makes them public, that's it."

Her mouth went tight. "And by 'it,' you mean you lose your grip."

Keller laughed humorlessly. "This isn't about me. This is about stability. You think the world can handle what she has? You've seen the protests. You've seen the fear. If it goes public, society will fall apart."

Rebecca felt vomit rising in her throat. "*And what of Leonard?* He is trouble because of this."

"Leonard's time will come," Keller shot back, his voice now darker. "But right now, it is Maria who is an immediate threat. You need to get to her before it becomes irreversible."

The call ended abruptly and left Rebecca alone with her thoughts. She did not trust Keller any more than she did Leonard. But if there really was proof in Maria's hands to expose all this, it would be calamitous.

Maria was seated in her apartment with the folder spread on the coffeetable before her. The photographs, schematics, and reports showed a project beyond cloning; this was about control of humanity itself.

Her phone buzzed on the table but she hesitated to reach for it. The screen indicated another Unknown number. It rang a couple of times before she answered.

"**You have little time to spare,**" came the distorted voice. "They're coming for you."

Caught off guard, Maria asked, "*Whom?*"

"All of them," answered the voice. "Keller. Mallory. They will not care what it takes to keep this thing quiet. It's your choice: the truth or your survival."

The line went dead.

Maria stared wide-eyed at her phone; her heart was racing. There was scarcely time to retaliate. With Keller and Leonard closing in, every second would count. She grabbed the folder and threw it into her bag, her mind awash with possibilities.

Rebecca pulled up outside Maria's apartment-building, heart pounding. The street was eerily quiet, lit sporadically by a distant streetlight's hum. She got out of the car, steam escaping from her mouth in the chilly night air.

The building towered over her; all windows dark except one near the very top. She saw a movement-a shadow crossing the room. Maria was still there.

Rebecca rushed to the entrance. Her footsteps echoed through the empty lobby. The elevator was out of order, now she had left to use the stairs. Each step felt heavier than the last, her mind reeling with questions. What if Keller was right? **What if Maria's proof could only make things worse?**

She reached the door to Maria's apartment and paused, her hand hovering over the doorknob. Muffled voices could be heard from inside. Was Maria on the phone with someone already there?

Rebecca knocked softly, feeling the pounding of her heart.

"*Maria?*" she called.

There was a strange hush, accompanied by a tiny pause, and then the door cracked open. Surprised, Maria stood frightened. Her expression registered great tension.

"Rebecca?" she said, her voice shaking. "*What are you doing here?*"

"I want to talk to you," Rebecca said. "About Leonard. About the files you have."

Maria hesitated, then stepped aside to let her in. The apartment was small and messy, strewn with papers and photographs upon a coffee table. Rebecca's eyes turned toward a folder on the table; it had more of a Pandora's box appearance.

"*Do you know what is in there?*" Maria asked, her voice soft.

Rebecca nodded. "I know enough. And Keller's right behind me. You're in danger here."

Maria's expression hardened. "I don't care about danger. People must hear the truth."

Rebecca stepped closer, her voice tense with urgency. "Maria, taking this public will not only expose your father; it will put any investigations on Noah, the lab- everything. Do you have any idea what effect that would have on the world?"

Maria crossed her arms and stared straight into Rebecca's eyes. "Maybe the world needs to know. Maybe it's time to stop hiding behind lies."

The guilt rose up Rebecca's throat. "And what about Leonard? He is not going to stop. If you publish this, never will he stop. He'd do something none of us would come back from."

Maria hesitated, barely holding her ground. *"Then what do we do? Should we sweep this under the rug?"*

Before Rebecca had a chance to respond, the sound of footsteps outside was audible, and the two women stopped, immediately exchanging frightened glances.

Rebecca stepped back to the window, gasping as she saw two black SUVs drive up to the curb. Men jumped out of them in quick, smooth motion, and Rebecca instinctively knew who they were.

"Keller," she whispered.

Maria turned an ashen color. *"What do we do?"*

Rebecca grabbed the folder and shoved it into Maria's purse. "We run. Right now."

The sound of a battering ram crashing against the door broke the silence in the room, while Rebecca grasped Maria by the arm, pulling her toward the fire escape. Behind them, the door burst open as the two girls scrambled out of the window to feel the stomach-churning cold air wrapped around them.

She didn't dare look back. She couldn't. All that mattered was getting Maria out alive.

Chapter 8

Eliot's Crusade

The cold warehouse echoed with a thin sound of sirens, like a familiar detail in passing. Rebecca paced with her fogged breath, the pounding of her heart from the chase still very new; nearby, Maria sat on a crate, hugging her bag as if it contained her very life.

"They are not going to stop until they get that back," Rebecca whispered with a bit of tremor.

Maria looked pale as she stared up at Rebecca. *"What do we do then? Just run forever?"*

Slowly, Rebecca stopped her pacing and fixed her gaze on Maria. "No," she said with emphasis. "We will find someone to expose this, someone to have your back."

"Who is that? Keller? It is Keller who is sending men after us now." It was a terse statement.

Rebecca hesitated. The fact was, she didn't have an answer. Keller wasn't even an option, and Leonard... she wouldn't trust him anymore. At that moment, however, her phone buzzed against her leg.

She pulled it out of her pocket, her stomach dropping at the words flashing on the screen.

"Turn on the news. Now."

She didn't recognize the number, but the request for action was clear. She smacked Maria's phone, opened a stream of local news, and got to watch as the image drenching the screen froze her heart with dread.

Eliot.

He stood in city hall before the podium. His voice seemed calm, but the portent hung in the air, and he held up a folder that was unmistakably the one Maria had received. As he began to speak, Rebecca felt her stomach turn.

"This," said Eliot, holding up a photograph for all to see, "is the truth they tried to hide from you. Leonard Mallory's lab was not about progress, was not about science; it was about control."

Rebecca's knees buckled, and she sank onto the crate beside Maria. "*What was that?*" she whispered.

Maria shook her head, her expression inscrutable. "*I don't know.*"

As more schematics and containment chambers and genetic data were revealed, silence slid through the crowd like the moan of a whisper, and every bit of knowledge struck down upon the disillusioned people like thunder, breaking an illusion of concealment which Leonard's group had been trying to maintain.

Maria shot Rebecca an incredulous look. "*Did you give that to him?*"

"No! I swear I didn't. But someone must have. Maybe the man who left the card."

The possibilities gnawed on Rebecca's mind; whoever leaked the folder to Eliot had just fanned the flames agitatorily and sparked a wildfire. Unforgivingly, they would consume everything and everyone standing in their way.

Leonard sat silently in the safe house, following the broadcast. The light from the screen lit up his face, somber indeed, as his staff dashed around him trying with all haste to surface from whatever had blacked out their transcending both visibility and sound.

"Eliot has every single one [of them]," said one of the techs, shivering in his voice. "The prototypes, the schematics-everything."

Leonard gritted his jaw and said, "Not everything. The project is still seated. As long as we have that, it's not over."

"But the prototypes..." the tech stammered.

"Forget the prototypes," Leonard snapped. "Just scrub the servers, will you? If Eliot wants a war, he'll get one, but we won't go down without a fight."

Back at the warehouse, Rebecca and Maria sat stupefied amid the broadcast. In a live stream, Eliot's voice rang through the noise, cutting it apart.

"We cannot allow this to continue. We cannot allow men like Leonard Mallory to play God with our lives. The world deserves the truth. And today, you have it."

Rebecca's chest tightened. "Not just Leonard. All of us. And if Eliot keeps pressing on, then it won't be just Leonard's lab that goes up in flames-it all will."

Maria was quiet and firm. "Maybe that's what needs to happen."

Rebecca shot a sharp glare at her. **"You don't mean that."**

Maria kept her gaze steady as her features hardened. "*Do I not?* Look what Leonard has done. Look what Keller is doing. If burning it all down is the way to stop that, then maybe Eliot is right."

Before Rebecca could argue, the warehouse door creaked open. Both women stood frozen where they were, heart racing as a shadow crossed the entrance.

The shadow in the doorway fell on the warehouse floor and gradually fed into the dark something as the figure took a step into the light. Rebecca caught Maria's arm and pulled her back behind a stack of crates. Her heart beat frantically in her chest as she risked a look around the edge to catch sight of the intruder.

"Rebecca?" It was a low voice full of tension, yet familiar.

Her breath took a hit-but she felt slightly more relaxed than she had when Keller appeared in view. He wore a dark coat, expression inscrutable, sharp-eyed as his gaze swept the room. "You don't have much time," he said, breaking the silence with his somewhat deadly tone. "They're on your heels."

Rebecca stood there; fists clenched. "*How did you find us?*"

Keller smiled faintly, shifting his attention onto Maria. "It's not such a remarkable task when you've got something everybody wants."

Maria stepped forward, chin up defiantly. "If it's to take the folder, you could forget it. We're not handing it over."

The smile dropped away from Keller's face. "I don't care about the folder anymore. Eliot just made it pointless. Everything you've got is public knowledge now. The real question is: are you going to survive long enough to deal with the backlash?"

Rebecca's throat felt constricted. "And that means?"

Keller turned his gaze toward the door. "Leonard's people are not going to sit back and let Eliot tear them apart. They come for you first. Follow me if you want to live."

Maria narrowed her eyes with suspicion. "*Why should we trust you?* You sent men after us in the first place."

Keller exhaled hurriedly and rubbed his forehead. "That was before Eliot dropped a bomb on the whole operation. Things have changed. You've got targets on your backs now, and much bigger ones than I ever set on you."

Rebecca felt hesitant, enough so that her thoughts were racing through her mind. She still didn't trust Keller, but there was some truth in what he said. Eliot's revelation had thrown everything into confusion, and Leonard would be ruthless in his next moves.

"No," Maria replied, silently cursing. "**You won't help us.**"

"Do you really think you're safe alone?" Keller yelled. "You're just a journalist with an envelope of half-truths. You're playing a game that you don't even understand; it'll get you killed."

Someone placed a hand on Maria's arm. It was Rebecca, and she whispered, "He's right. **None of us are safe here.**"

Maria clenched her jaw, but she didn't argue. "Fine," she said. "But if this is a trap—"

"It's not," Keller confirmed. "Trust me, if I wanted you dead, you'd be dead already."

As they emerged into the night, Rebecca felt her phone buzz inside her pocket. Her heart skipped a beat upon seeing Leonard's name flash on the screen. Tempted to pick it up, she hesitated momentarily before allowing it to ring.

Keller raised an eyebrow and pointed. "You are not going to answer that, are you?"

Rebecca forced a swallow down her throat then pressed the button. "Leonard," she hissed, clearly disturbed.

"Rebecca," Leonard said in an eerily calm voice. "I trust you are watching the circus that Eliot has concocted."

Rebecca gripped the cell tightly. "I've seen it."

"I'm sure you know just how bad this is," he said. "Eliot's playing a very dangerous game, and you're caught right in the middle of it. You need to bring Maria and the folder to me. We can fix this."

Rebecca felt her chest tighten. "*Fix this? You mean bury it.*"

Leonard's voice suddenly turned dark. "This is not about you, Rebecca. This is about survival. If we don't do something soon, Eliot is going to complete the job and destroy everything—and you will be part of it."

She stopped, glancing at Maria. "What are you planning, Leonard?"

"You'll see when you get here," he told her impatiently. "Don't take too long. You have a very tight schedule."

She heard the click on the other end.

They arrived at Keller's car, a sleek black SUV parked in the shadows. Keller opened the door for them and gestured them to get in. Maria didn't budge; her fingers tightened on the strap of her bag.

"Tell me your angle," she said sharply. "*Why are you helping us now?*"

Keller looked her straight in the eye with an unreadable expression. "Because Leonard has gone mad. He's not merely protecting his work; he's escalating. And if we don't stop him soon, Eliot's revelation will be the least of our worries."

Rebecca exchanged a glance with Maria as something churning hit the bottom of her stomach. Keller's words confirmed her worst fear: Leonard was not backing down. He was about to initiate war.

As they drove through the city, the weight of Eliot's momentous personal revelation definitely became palpable. The roads had become less busy, but the tension still hung over it: like a spark about to ignite. There were protesters outside government buildings, talons being chanted strongly with the night.

Maria looked from inside the car with a heavy heart. "*Do you think he is right? Eliot. Do you think this was the right exposure?*"

Rebecca did not answer but recalled Noah instantly and then the sanctuary of everything leading to where they were at that moment. "I don't know," she answered. "But I know it is too late to undo it."

Her mind fell there on her lap; her fingers brushed against the folder inside the bag. "Well, then what do we do now?"

She was looking contemplatively back at her. "**We survive.**"

The SUV raced down the derelict road, tires humming against the pavement. One could almost make out the city's turbulence rising underneath the surface. Rebecca was inside the rear seat, her mind turning at warp speed as Keller navigated toward some unknown destination. Maria sat beside Rebecca, silent but visibly tensed, clutching the bag tightly against her chest.

The revelation Eliot made weighed heavily upon them. Or, to put it differently, his expose had turned like a wildfire-the kind spreading much faster than any of them could imagine. Rebecca looked outside as her heart tightened and turned even more fearful upon finding that they were passing through a site filled with a growing crowd of protesters gathered outside a news station.

"No More Secrets!"

"Cloning is Corruption!"

The chants rang out like a cacophony of voices of anger and fearness. This sight chill ran through Rebecca's veins. This stopped being a scientific debate; it turned into a society subdivision.

"Leonard will make his move soon," Keller's voice broke the moments of lost thoughts.

Rebecca briefly turned in his direction, frowning at him. "*What move?*"

His jaw tightened as he glanced at her through the rearview mirror. "The kind that will end this. For good."

In his hidden lab, the man remained by the luminous containment chamber with his fingers resting on its edifice. The dimly visible figure inside was still taking form, the fading outline copulating with the ghost as it stood between the two sides. This wasn't Noah; it was something new. Something better.

One of his technicians walked up carefully with a tablet. "We've located the downed data," he said. "But there is no room for a complete scrub. Eliot's summit-clean was too comprehensive."

Leonard's face hardened. "Then the prototypes have to be focused on," he directed. "They need to be up and running before the next wave of fallout strikes."

The staff hesitated. "Are you sure this is the right course of action? Given Eliot's crusade, the public—"

"The public doesn't matter," Leonard interrupted sharply. "They don't understand what's at stake. This isn't about them. It's about survival."

The technician nodded, hesitantly retreating into a corner of the lab. Leonard's gaze turned back to the containment chamber. His chest tightened with a fluctuating bedlam of mixed anticipation and resolution. This was really the capstone for all he'd ever worked for. If failure was costly, he could not afford it.

Rebecca's phone buzzed again inside the SUV. She took it out of her pocket, the sight of Leonard's name making her stomach sink. Maria was watching, her expression hardening.

"You really going to answer that?" Maria asked, disbelief in her voice.

Rebecca hesitated. "He may just tell us what he's planning."

"Or he may be playing you," Maria shot back. "You can't trust him, Rebecca. Not anymore."

Rebecca stared at the screen, her thumb hovering at the answer button. Keller glanced at her from the mirror, his tone clipped. "If you answer that call, you give him leverage. Don't."

The phone buzzed again, grating against Rebecca's already frayed nerves. She let it go to voicemail, the tightness in her chest another layer of unease. Whatever Leonard wanted to say, she doubted she wanted to hear it.

Eliot watched from his secure location as his team monitored events unfolding from his groundbreaking revelation, protests quickly spreading to neighboring cities and making international headlines. Leaning back in his chair, a small smile crept onto his lips.

"This is just the beginning," he said quietly, satisfied.

One of Eliot's aides approached with a tablet in hand. "Incoming reports. Leonard's team is scrambling to contain the damage, and we've intercepted some of their communications. Looks like he's pushing up his timeline."

Eliot's smile disappeared. "Of course he is. He knows that this is his last opportunity to salvage the project."

The aide hesitated. "*What should we do?*"

Eliot's look darkened. "We push harder. Release the next wave of information. If Leonard wants to escalate, then we'll make sure he has nothing left to escalate with."

Maria gripped tighter at her bag as Keller made turns down a secluded road. The city lights were dimming in the distance. "*Where are we going?*" she asked, her voice tense.

"A safe house," Keller said. "You will be off the grid--out of Leonard's reach."

Maria frowned. "And what about Eliot? He'd be just as dangerous."

Keller's look was humorless. "Eliot's not your problem. He's bent on taking Leonard down anyway. But if you want my advice, stay out of his way. He isn't interested in collateral damage."

Rebecca's chest tightened. "And what if Leonard retaliates? *What about the prototypes, the lab?*"

Keller's expression darkened. "That's the real question. Leonard's not the type to go quietly. Whatever plans he has will only get worse before they get better."

The SUV halted outside the blank facade of a building, where its windows yawned without light-a referral of unwelcome. Keller turned the engine off and got out while motioning Rebecca and Maria to get out with him. The air was cold and still, broken, however, by the whirring of powerlines overhead.

Keller, unlocking the door, said, "It's all right, you will be safe here. For now."

Rebecca looked at Maria, and the two of them stepped inside. The inside was simple but barren in comparison to that sense of disaster that had just left them. Maria set her bag on the table and stared grimly.

"Now what?" she asked.

Rebecca exhaled slowly. "We have to find out what Leonard is planning. And we need to stop him."

Maria glared. "*And what if we don't get it right?*"

Rebecca held her gaze firmly, her voice steady. "Then we try anyways."

The safe house was somewhere between a fortress and a tomb, its dull walls and faint smell of mildew stirring things up for Maria and Rebecca. The horrible light from Maria's laptop streamed shadows like knives across the room as she spread the contents of the folder once more. Each piece of paper was a building block in the structure Eliot had unveiled to them, only that there were still those gaps, places where truth hid just from sight.

"We're missing something," Maria murmured, fingers flying across the keyboard as she began cross-checking those documents. "Leonard's plan goes far beyond what Eliot showed us. If he is moving quickly, he doesn't react, but prepares."

Rebecca leaned against the table; her arms crossed tightly over her chest. "Preparing for what?" she asked almost inaudibly.

Maria shook her head. The look in her eyes showed sheer frustration. "That is what we must put together. Eliot's revelation was heartbreaking, but it is not all. Leonard still has a play or two."

Rebecca felt her stomach churn in spite of her intense consideration for nothing else other than Leonard's self-assuming voice on the telephone, the golden promise glimmering there that they could "fix this." At the back of her mind rang this trepidation as she could never define whether Leonard meant for damage control or survival-either for Leo's or theirs.

In his secret lab, Leonard stood over the containment chamber, his expression unreadable as the prototype within began to take shape. The translucent figure glowed faintly, its features sharpening by the second. This wasn't just a copy-it was one hell of a weapon-protection against all the havoc Eliot had let loose.

His leading technician walked cautiously up to him carrying a tablet. "The prototypes are stabilizing," he said, "but we're running out of time. Eliot's team is already leaking their next wave of data. If they find this place-"

"They won't," Leonard interjected sharply. "The place is secure. Focus on the prototypes!"

The technician hesitated. "And what about Rebecca? If she is still with the journalist-"

"Rebecca has made her choice," Leonard said coldly. "Let there be war upon the future if she chooses! But the project goes on. With or without her."

The technician nodded reluctantly and tiptoed back into the shadows. Leonard resumed his fixation on the containment chamber, his chest tightening with mingled anxiety and excitement. This was his last chance to see the life he had dreamed of prove him right-to prove that he was right and that his vision went beyond being a mere goal for others.

Eliot's team worked day and night in their underground headquarters where the screens illuminated their faces with a ghastly glare. The second wave of data was being prepared for release: schematics on prototypes of Leonard, encrypted communications, and detailed records from the Grayson Street Facility.

"This will bury him," Eliot said, as steady as could be while scrolling through the files. "When the public sees what he has designed, there won't be any turning back for him."

One of the aides hesitated. "*And will they understand why we are doing this?*"

Eliot's face took on a set-eyed glare. "What matters is not whether they understand. What matters is whether they will know the truth: That what Leonard is doing is a challenge to all we stand for. And that if we don't stop him now, no one will."

Maria nodded and returned to her own station, while Eliot reclined in his chair, mind racing. This was surely the hardest moment yet; too much to lose and scant room for error. But there could be no hesitation: Leonard was out there and still fighting to capture his creation.

"**Stop!**" Maria's heart took an abrupt turn when she saw the notification that demanded her attention. Her fingers hovered over the keys as she read the headline:

"Eliot Unveils New Wave of Data: The Horrors of Mallory's Lab Exposed."

She clicked the link, breath stuck in her throat as the screen filled with schematics, photographs, and internal communications from Leonard's team. The schematics for the containment chambers were there; detailed notes on the prototypes also lay there. But one file intruded—just a single line whose mere reading sent shivers down her spine:

"Project Phoenix: **The Future of Humanity's Evolution.**"

"*What is this?*" Maria whispered, her voice little more than a quivering thread.

Rebecca leaned over her shoulder and, narrowing her eyes as she read the name, muttered, "Phoenix? I'm sure I've never heard of this."

Maria clicked on the file, hands quaking, drawing up technical jargon dense on the screen. At the bottom was a single sentence, sending chills down Rebecca's spine:

"Phoenix assures survival, at any cost."

Leonard's voice echoed through the lab's intercom while his team hurriedly tried to finish the prototypes. "Brace for activation," he commanded. "We are out of time."

The containment chambers had begun to glow brighter and hummed so loudly that their sound filled the lab as the prototypes reached their full stabilization. Leonard felt dizzy as he approached the first chamber. He saw himself reflected in the bent glass.

This is what it means, he said softly. This is what it takes to survive.

The chamber opened, making a hissing noise and letting in a blast of arctic air. The figure walked forth, shining eyes fastening themselves onto Leonard. It was perfect. Controlled. Everything Noah had not gotten to achieve.

Only then did Leonard allow himself a smile. "**Welcome to the future.**"

Rebecca and Maria sat silent in the ghastly shadows cast by Maria's laptop. The news about the Phoenix Project ironically struck between them like an avalanche of terror and unfathomable implications.

"You're not getting it. He is not making clones. He is making something... unstoppable," Maria whispered, her voice quivering as she uttered the words.

Rebecca gazed at the screen, going through the schematics and notes almost too fast. They sketched a scenario that was all too sinister regarding Leonard's ultimate goal. Phoenix was not in the business of planning escape routes anymore; it was world domination.

"**He must be stopped,**" Rebecca declared with firmness in her voice. "Whatever Phoenix is, it cannot be allowed to leave that lab."

Maria had subconsciously gripped her bag tighter. "How? We do not even know where he works from, what the lab looks like."

For a moment, Rebecca was perplexed. She remembered the calls that Leonard had made. They all began with a rather cryptic suggestion that he had ways to "fix this." He wanted her back there, to rejoin the project. And now, she realized, had possibly provided her with an entry.

"I think I might know where," Rebecca began almost inaudibly. "But we must do it fast."

On the lab side, Leonard observed the standard model step out of the containment chamber. The creature transitioned with precise assurance, glowing eyes roving around the chamber with an intelligence which made him shudder. Not just a clone; it was evolution incarnate.

The technicians rushed wildly to stabilize the remaining prototypes; their phrases blended into a jumbled concerto. Whirrs and beeps grew in intensity as the machines prepared to open their gates.

Leonard turned to his head technician. "*Are they ready?*"

"Sir, almost," the technician replied, a bit strained. "But energy output is still climbing. If we press any harder—"

"**Do it**," Leonard rushed in. His tone was authoritative and conclusive: no more discussion.

The technician nodded reluctantly back to the controls. Leonard's attention returned to the prototype standing in front of him. It was calm, poised, and utterly obedient.

"We're going to change the world," Leonard whispered, overcome by some daydream or movie scene.

Elia's team was deep in their procedures, the headquarters alighting with life. The second wave of data sent tremors through the continents, but for Eliot, it wasn't time to call it quits. He stood amongst the crowd in the room, fixated on a gigantic screen, narrating a map of the different confirmed locations of labs.

"We've got him pinpointed," one of the aides announced while pointing at the flickering dot on the map. "It's where Leonard has been operating from."

Eliot nodded and clenched his jaw. "Then it's time this ends."

Another aide paused. "Sir, one more thing: we picked up a transmission between Leonard and Rebecca. She could be heading there now."

Eliot's eyes became slits. "Rebecca has chosen her side. If she's in the way, then she can go down with him."

There was silence in the room; the impact of Eliot's words could be felt nearly choking them. He refused to waver. For this was war, and there was no room for tentative apprehension.

Rebecca and Maria drove through the city in thick silence between them. The address Leonard had given her was implanted in her head; a beacon pulling them closer and closer towards the center of the storm.

"This is a bad idea," Maria said in a read-tight voice. "Going into Leonard's lab? He won't just allow us to stop him."

Rebecca gripped the steering wheel tighter. "We're not going to stop him. Not yet. We're going to find out what Phoenix is, and we're going to make sure it stays in that lab."

Maria shook her head, and frustration flared across her eyes. "And if we can't?"

Rebecca harded her look. "Then we take it down ourselves."

The alarm signals had gone off in the lab, and the remaining prototypes came pouring out of their cells. The room was flooded with a cold, throbbing light from the prototypes, casting long shadows against the walls. And in the hub, Leonard stood at the eye of the storm, calm satisfaction on his face.

"This is it," he said, his voice steady. "**It's the future.**"

The doors suddenly burst open; armed men stormed in with their guns pointing. Leonard's technicians froze, arms raised in surrender like frightened deer. But Leonard stood his ground, locked eye on the prototypes, unquestionable confidence radiating from him.

Eliot entered, commanding and menacing. "It's over, Leonard," he said coldly. "You're finished."

Leonard turned toward Eliot, a smile on his lips. "You have come too late."

But before Eliot could say anything, the first prototype advanced, its act quick and distinct. Inside the chaos, some armed men shouted in alarm and attempted to lurch into action. But it moved faster than they did.

At the lab entrance, Rebecca stopped the car just as the first gunshots drove their deafening echo into the night. Stomachs churned inside her; her heart raced.

"This is it," she trembled. "*Are you ready?*"

Maria responded with a firm nod. **"We're going to end this."**

Crossing out of the car, the lights around the lab cast ghostly shadows. Disturbance from inside had grown in boundless consideration, the subdued droning of the prototypes mingling into the air like an unearthly symphony.

Rebecca's chest tightened as she grabbed the latch. Whoever was waiting for them inside, that much she was sure of: there was no turning back.

Chapter 9

Noah's Awakening

As the hissing of the containment chamber echoing through the busy lab cut through the equipment's hum and the cries from Leonard's desperate team, Rebecca stood frozen, breath locked in her throat, as the translucent figure inside the chamber took its first step forward. The air sizzled with energy, prickling the hairs on her arms.

Emerging from the containment chamber, Noah moved in a way that was almost unnaturally fluent yet completely resolved. His softly glowing eyes cast an ethereal pallor over his sharp angular visage. Starkly unfamiliar to Rebecca, he stood taller and stronger and exuded an unsettling but compelling presence. All other chaos in the lab seemed dulled as everyone's attention turned toward him.

His expression lightened, and he approached slowly. There was a fatherly angle to it when he said, "Noah. **You're awake.**"

As Noah scanned his eyes around the room-what remained of the devastation, the prototypes standing still, and the tense stand-off between Eliot and Leonard-his brow furrowed gently, appearing to gather the pieces of the broken tableau set out before him. With all eyes glued to Leonard, Noah's voice severed through the silence.

"Awake?" he said in an octave above. There was wonderment in the tone but an unshakable wave of uncertainty. "*What does that mean?*"

Leonard stepped forward. He moved in slow, deliberate steps. "It means you are ready," reverently spoke Leonard. "*You've become what you always meant to be.*"

Rebecca could hardly understand what was going on as she watched the exchange. Noah looked anything but the fearful person she had seen before-his frame carried a tension she was unprepared for, power in his eyes unnerving her. She stepped forward now, her voice quavering.

"Noah," she went on, trying to calm herself, "you don't have to listen to him. You can make your own choices."

Noah turned his glowing gaze down on her questioningly, his head tilting just enough, eyes narrowing at her. "You're who?" He asked, confusion underlining his voice.

Rebecca was at a loss. "I'm... Rebecca," she somehow uttered, "I was there when you were created. I helped-"

"You made me," said Noah with a slight bite interrupting her, the glance shifting from Rebecca back toward Leonard. "You're one of them."

Maria moved forward behind Rebecca. "Noah," she said, breaking with urgency into the standoff, "trust no one. Leonard's not your creator-he's your jail keeper. He's using you."

Noah's glowing eyes shifted their steady, unreadable gaze toward Maria. "*Using me for what?*"

"For power," Maria began, her voice rising. "For control. He doesn't think of you as a person-he sees you as a tool."

Leonard's jaw tightened, his voice cutting in before Noah could respond. "Noah, don't you listen to them. They don't know what you are."

Noah turned and faced him. He clenched his jaw. "And what exactly am I?" His tone trembled through the air now, fueled with anger and sadness. "What have you made of me?"

Leonard's face softened; he nearly begged. "You are much more than a mere experiment, Noah. You hold the future. You are proof that mankind has evolved. You're...my son."

Rebecca's breath caught as that word hung in the air, laden with meaning: a shiver rippled through her spine. Leonard wasn't simply making a statement; he was laying a claim. A claim that Noah did not belong to himself but rather to Leonard and to whatever vision he had for Noah.

"Noah is not your son," Rebecca spat, angry tears trembling in her eyes, casting fiery glances at the monster. "He is no one's property, nor a legacy. He is—"

"I'm nothing!" Noah interrupted. His voice rose, and in that moment, the whole room seemed to vibrate. His glowing eyes flared with intensity, fists tightening at his sides. "I don't know what I am, but I know I'm not yours."

Leonard's eyes fell; he was pleading, reaching out to his son. "Noah, please." His voice cracked. **"You're my everything."**

"I won't be your everything!" Noah shouted, the voice clear and—and thick in the air—throughout the lab, an energy rushing through him, a shockwave rippling outward, making the prototypes within earshot jump. Their eyes flickered, glowing in fear of him.

Eliot stepped ahead with a leveled weapon. "And this was what exactly I warned you against," he said coldly, his black angry gaze fixed on Leonard. "He's not your son, Leonard. **It's a monster you cannot control.**"

Noah, staring now at Eliot, showed his glowing eyes narrowed. "I'm not a monster," he replied, dangerously low.

Eliot clutched his weapon tighter. "Then try and prove it." Eliot gestured toward the prototypes. "Do not let the like of them cage you."

Noah hesitated, casting a glance at the prototypes. The energy around him is stupendous, the hum almost bursting in weight because of his inner struggle to respond to Eliot's challenge.

One steppsthe other, Rebecca's voice strong and full of plea. "Noah, you can choose. Listen to neither Leonard nor Eliot. It is you whom you should listen to."

Noah frowned, his face angry and hurt. "*What if I don't know how?*" The hum of danger rippled, and finally quiet fell, his words just hanging there.

The lab fell into a hush, it seemed, as Noah flickered his glowing gaze for a spark of uncertainty to course across his face. The stillness and electrifying energy was so thick around him it crackled like a storm waiting to burst. The prototypes seemed eerily frozen in place; their forms illuminated by the pulsing light emanating from Noah.

Rebecca was breaking the silence. "Noah, listen. You don't have to be what they want you to be. You don't have to follow anybody's plan."

Leonard scowled, and with a few steps forward, pushed Rebecca. "Rebecca, don't fill his head with doubts. He is stronger than that."

"Noah deserves to know the truth," Rebecca warbled in response, anger rising in her voice. "You have kept him in the dark for too long."

Noah turned his gaze sharply to Leonard, jaw tightening. *"What truth?"* he demanded.

Leonard hesitated, clenching his hands at his sides, almost wavering for a moment. He took a deep breath. **"You are special,"** he said in a soft voice. "You are something other than human. You are everything humanity could be."

"No," Maria said with new resolve as she stepped in beside Rebecca. "The truth is that Leonard sees you as a tool. As a way of proving his theories and boosting his ego."

Noah brought his glowing eyes to a narrow glare, and the energy around him intensified. "Is that true?" he asks, low but dangerous.

Leonard's jaw tightened. "Noah, I consider you my son," he affirmed. "You are no tool. You are better than us. You will exist, we will survive."

In the atmosphere, the tension became so thick that every letter uttered by Leonard's words weighed heavy on each. Advancing over was Eliot, with his revolver firmly directed at Leonard. "You think he is your son?" He spat under his breath. "He is a clone, Leonard. A weapon you created and now cannot control."

Noah's breath was hard; his clenched fists reacted against Eliot's jab. "I am no weapon," he said, voice trembling with anger. **"I didn't ask to be made."**

Eliot's expression hardened. "No one's denying that, but if you don't move now, you will show me right."

Noah tilted his head to the side slightly, glowing eyes trained on Eliot. "And what do you want me to do?" he asked, voice lowered, almost as if defeated.

"Stop them," Eliot said with a hand motion toward the prototypes, "shut them down before they destroy everything."

Noah hesitated. His eyes flitted off to the prototypes. A thick energy surrounded the room, ready to boil over. Rebecca edged dangerously close at that moment; voice gentle but urgent.

"Noah," she said, "you don't have to prove anything to him. You owe nobody anything."

Leonard's voice quivered and rose. "Do not listen to them, Noah. They do not know what you are. A mere human, indeed, but you are the future! You are the bridge; they should feel honored-a bridge between something and what humanity can be."

Noah turned towards Leonard; his face was unreadable. "*What's that supposed to mean for me?*" he asked through gritted teeth. "Who am I supposed to be?"

Leonard paused; indeed, the query knocked the breath from him. "According to me, you're supposed to be... yourself," Leonard finally offered in hushed tone.

Noah laughed bitterly, and the energy swirled menacingly around him. "You don't even know who I am!" He spat. "You made me, but you don't see me."

"Noah, I see you," Leonard boldly stepped closer to Noah. "You aren't a mere creation; **you are my legacy**."

A shrill, fierce to its core. "He does not care to be your legacy, Leonard. He is a person, and he must define the term."

Noah's gaze darted from one to the other as if an invisible tension electrified him with angry, mournful energy and other sentiments carrying something darker. "You're all telling me what to be and not asking what I want to be," he declared at an absurd volume. "*What is wrong with you?*"

The room was still; the prototypes lay motionless and awaited Noah's word. The sound of their undulating energy rose, the air trembling with potential.

"*What do you want, Noah?*" Rebecca's voice broke the silence.

Noah balled his hands into fists, heart striking heavily in his breast as if he had difficulty forming a reply. "I want...well," he managed, "to stop feeling like I don't belong."

Leonard's expression softened, his eyes almost glittering with hope. "You belong here- with me, and we will build something better together."

Noah's expression soured as his glowing eyes turned narrow. "With you?" he queried bitterly. "The man who made me into this?"

Leonard stumbled back as though he had been struck. His high-handedness faltered. "Noah, I did not mean..."

"I don't care what you meant!" screamed Noah. The echo ran through the lab, as the glowing-eyed prototypes stirred at the vibrations ricocheting off the walls.

Rebecca stepped forward, terrified. "Listen, Noah, please do not do this," she pleaded. "Do not fight, I-I could not bear it."

Noah turned towards her; pain evident on his face. "What do I do?" he asked, his voice shaky. "Because all I know is what they have told me."

Rebecca had no time to reply. The buzz of construction rises up to an unbearable pitch. The room shook with the crackle in the air as the light from prototypes became brighter. Carnation had turned, clenching and unclenching his fists, then stepping barefoot forward.

"I do not want to" he said, his voice so low that the temperature dropped a little in the room. "I do not want to be what you made me."

The prototypes stopped suddenly, as if halting to await his next command. An almost palpable kabom dismissed the waiting room as Noah reached out his trembling hand to hover over the nearest prototype.

"**Stop**," his voice unshaken but filled with remorse.

The light in the eyes of the prototypes flickered as if in attendance to obey, but then the air almost pulsed as silently as the rhythms followed by voice, and an uncontrollably vicious throng of prototypes surged wildly for their inner mental concepts' brains.

"**Noah!**" Rebecca shouted in true horror.

Frozen in an exaggerated state of terror, glowing eyes widening, he was unmovable, with prototypes on their trail into the lab. Determination boiled in the air like fireworks, and everything was moments away from collapsing.

The prototypes broke free of their hesitation and charged with a terrifying, erratic energy, as the room erupted in chaos. Equipment shattered, sparks flew and the bells of unstable machinery crescendoed. Rebecca drew Maria behind her, shielding her from the debris raining down all around.

"Noah, stop them!" Rebecca screamed.

Noah stood paralyzed in the center of the lab in fear, wide-eyed and uncertain. The prototypes circled him like predators waiting for the signal with their chaotic movements sending tremors through the shaking laboratory. The energy these two would bring with them made the surroundings seem as though even the air was being bent.

"Reach them, Noah!" Leonard stumbled his way to Noah, stretching out his arms in urgency: "You can control them. You can stop them!"

He turned to Leonard, expression tumultuous. "You keep telling me that," he said with a trembling voice. "But I don't even know who I am. *How can I control them if I can't control myself?*"

Leonard's face crumpled; his seriousness began to give way. "You're not a mistake," he said, struggling for voice. **"You're my son**, Noah, and you have to believe it."

Eliot took a few steps towards Leonard, his weapon aimed directly at him. "Enough with this! You're the one responsible for this mess. You built them. You unleashed them. And now-"

Leonard stepped before Noah, hardening his features. "You don't understand. Destroy them, and you destroy the future."

Eliot narrowed his eyes and tightened the grip on the weapon in his hands. "Then the future deserves to end."

Before Eliot was able to pull the trigger, one of the prototypes went for him; its glowing eyes breached the fray with an out-of-this-world pace, sent the weapon flying from Eliot's grasp, beneath the screech of his body colliding against the nearby console. With a silent groan, he clutched his side as the prototype loomed over him.

Breathing heavily as he stepped forward into the foray, hand raised, Noah commanded, **"Stop!"**

The prototype froze in mid-lunge, its glowing eyes dimming. The other prototypes paused too, their chaotic movements faltering under what seemed to be Noah's command, an atmosphere very still by comparison: the hum of energy reduced to drumming low vibrations.

Rebecca looked up from behind generous cover, her eyes fixed on Noah. **"You did it,"** she whispered. "You stopped them."

Noah turned to her, his glowing eyes dimming a little with exhaustion. "I don't know how," he said. "I just... felt it."

Leonard hunched forward. His voice was imminently urgent. "Noah, they are connected to you. Extending you. And that's the reason you can control them."

"No," Noah said, shaking his head. "They are not extension of me, they are something else. Something wrong."

Leonard let his jaw drop and his voice softened. "You're not wrong, Noah. And you're not wrong in this; it's a step forward. It's what we were meant to do."

Rebecca stepped between them now with a sharp voice. "It's not progress, Leonard. **It's destruction.** Look around you. It's not evolution; it's chaos."

Maria came to stand beside Rebecca. She seemed steady despite the tension that hung in the air. "Noah, this is not dictated for you. You have seen for yourself the ills these prototypes can do. You've felt it. You continue on this line; it shall not stop—merely escalate."

Glances were exchanged as Noah directed his shining eyes in between them. "I...," he said quietly, "I don't want to be this way. I do not wish to hurt anyone."

Leonard stepped in further, firm with conviction. "Noah, you're not hurting anyone. You are saving... saving us. **Do not permit their fear to cloud your purpose.**"

Rebecca's jaw hardened at Leonard. "It's not his purpose, Leonard. It's yours. You made him for this. You never even cared to ask him."

Leonard was unaffected at that moment; the accusation seemed to cut him deeper than he had imagined. "I brought him to life," he said in hushed tone. "I gave him a value."

Noah's shining eyes flared with anger. "**You gave me nothing**. You took away from me. You made me without asking me, keeping it in mind what I wished for."

The tension grew, ready to break as the prototypes stirred, their eyes glowing like dying stars. Noah turned towards them, shaking, energy building up around him. "**I don't want this**," he choked. "I don't want any of this."

Rebecca stepped up, cooing. "Then you can put an end to it. You can stop this, Noah."

Noah faltered, glued to the prototypes, while the air around him shuddered with pulsating energy-the vibrations became ever stronger as he lifted his arms. "I don't know if I can," he protested. "But I must try."

Leonard groped him, bitterness choking his voice. "Noah, wait! Don't do this. You don't understand what you are going to do."

Noah turned with pained glowing eyes. "Perhaps I don't. But I can't be what you want me to be anymore."

Light exploded in the room as Noah raised his energy, the prototypes convulsing with dimming lights. Rebecca and Maria shielded their faces from the ancient machinery collapse ringing in their ears.

When the light faded, Noah stood alone in the center of destruction, dim-eyed and slumping. The prototypes lay silent around him, their powers extinguished.

Leonard stared at Noah, awe and devastation etched on his face. "**What have you done?**" he whispered.

Noah turned to him, voice low, but filled with conviction. "I stopped being what you made me."

The aftermath was absolute silence. The drones' humming stopped, replaced only by the faraway creaking of fallen equipment along with the sound of the dying electrical charge like crumbling thunder. The world lay destroyed, yet in the center of it, Noah stood, his shimmering eyes dim and staring.

Rebecca and Maria emerged cautiously from behind the console, where they had found refuge. Rebecca's heart raced as she digested the scene: lifeless prototypes strewn about the room like fallen statues, the massive wreckage of the lab around them, and Noah standing in the center, ridiculously small in size despite his powers.

"Noah," Rebecca called softly, trembling. "*Are you alright?*"

Noah glared at her, glowing eyes still flickering with dimness. "I don't ... I don't know," he replied slowly, voice lost in some distant land. "I think I broke something. Them...me."

With hesitance, Maria started to walk toward him, her eyes bouncing back and forth between Leonard and Eliot, who had nowhere to go. You stopped them, Maria said curtly. That is what matters now.

Noah twisted his painful expression. "But what am I now?" he asked in a trembling voice. "If I am not what they wanted me to be... what remains?"

Leonard stepped forward, pallid and haggard. He looked at the prototypes, then Noah, his shoulder finally breaking in with the weight of reality. "You are still my son," he said quietly. "You are still a part of me."

Noah narrowed his glowing eyes, clenched his jaw. "**I am not your son,**" he said harshly. "I am only your project. That is all I have ever been to you."

Leonard's words stung him, but he would not go back on his stand. "That is not true," he said. "I didn't just create you; I believed in you. I saw something in you that no one else could."

"What you saw," Noah said bitterly, "was your own reflection."

He struck Leonard like a fist, and for a long moment, he looked like he might faint. But then he snapped, and his shoulders squared as he lifted his voice. "No, Noah, you don't get it. I didn't do this for myself. I did this for all of us. For humanity."

Eliot stepped into the conversation, weapon still on his side, yet his tone was razor-sharp. "Spare us the savior complex, Leonard," he stated. "This wasn't about humanity-it was about your ego. End of story."

Leonard turned to him, shaking with fury. "You think this is over? Look around! The world is already coming apart at the seams. Noah is the only remaining hope."

Eliot darkened, raising the muzzle again. "No. Noah was the evidence of what happens when people like you play God."

Noah stepped between them, his glow flickering between uncertainty and neutrality. "**Stop,**" he said softly. "Both of you. I can't do this anymore."

Rebecca placed her hand on Noah's arm. "You don't have to," she said delicately. "You've done enough."

He turned to her, some remnant of tenderness on that hard face. "I don't even know if I have," he said. "I don't know that I can."

Maria stepped in front of him, with an iron voice. "You don't owe them a dime, Noah. Not Leonard, not Eliot. You are more than that."

Leonard shook his head, raising his voice. "*He's not just anybody, Maria. **He's the future.** He's the proof that we can survive, that we can evolve*."

"***Evolve into what? *"** Maria shot back. "*A species that has a tendency to destroy itself over a betterment spree? Look around you, Leonard. Look at what your 'future' has done*."

Noah's chest heaved as they butted heads once again, tension building again. It felt as if he were being split in two--one half being pulled toward one vision offered by Leonard, and the other half being pushed to get away from it altogether. The energy in the room began to hum again, faint but gaining power.

Rebecca was noticing, and her voice began to rise. "Noah, listen to me. You don't have to choose between either of them. You can just walk away and create your own way."

Noah eyes flickered toward her; this time they carried a bit of hope. *"How?"* he asked, his voice trembling just ever so slightly. "How could I find something I've never had?"

There was no chance for Rebecca to respond when the earth under their feet trembled and suddenly jerked. A low, doomful rumble passed through the lab, and another cascade of flares erupted from the wrecked machines. The precarious containment systems were failing, their energy building to perilous levels.

Eliot cursed softly under his breath and glanced up at the smashed machinery. "The lab is going to blow. We better run. Now."

"No!" Leonard shouted as he stepped toward the prototypes. "We can still salvage this. The data, the designs, it's all here!"

Rebecca grabbed his arm and said sharply, "Leonard, it's over. If we stay, we die."

Leonard yanked his arm away, the look in his eyes like fire. "You don't understand! This is everything!"

Noah stepped between the two, his expression uncompromising. "No," he said, calm yet firm. "It's nothing."

The room pulsed with energy as Noah raised his hands, brightening the glow in his eyes. The containment systems faltered, and no energy was drawn away from him. Rebecca's chest tightened as it dawned on her just what he was doing.

"Noah, wait!" she shouted, voice breaking. "**You don't have to do this!**"

Noah turned to her, a faint smile playing at his lips. "Maybe I do."

And the room was a burst of light as Noah unleashed the containment's full energy on the prototypes that shriveled instantly. The walls of the laboratory quivered as machinery tumbled down, energy rushing out in one final, devastating wave.

Rebecca grasped Maria's arm and dragged her into the passageway. "We have to run now!"

Eliot followed along; the weapon forgotten as the lab caved around them. Rebecca glanced back for one last time, and for a moment her heart broke as she saw Noah standing amidst all that ruin, draped in sumptuous light.

"Noah!" She called but the voice was lost in the roar of collapsing matters around him.

The lab imploded behind them and slammed the escape door shut; their backs hit by the weight of the blast sending them sprawling on the dirt outside. Rebecca got up with her head ringing, staring at the remains of the lab while her heart fell into the deep dust.

"Noah," she whispered, tears streaming down her face. "He's gone."

The ground smoked beneath Rebecca's hands as she pushed herself upright, her ears still ringing from the explosion. What remained of the lab was a clump of scrap metal and burnt earth, the prototypes hanging limply and reduced to smoldering bits. The rising smoke hurt her throat with a bitter taste.

Beside her, Maria staggered to her feet, pale and dirty. "Rebecca," she trembled, "he—he stayed back."

Rebecca's breath still laboring as she gazed up the ruin. "I know," she replied softly, voice cracking. "He chose to end this."

Leonard staggered from the wreckage, clothes torn and face soiled. His eyes looked merrily furious as they rest on Rebecca. "You let him die!" he howled with a broken voice. "He was everything, and you let him waste it all!"

Rebecca had turned and stared at him, flames and heat rising in anger. "I allowed him to do nothing, Leonard! He made his own choice—something you never bothered to give him the chance to do!"

Leonard's hands were shaking as he waved toward the ruins. "He was my son," he said, wavering. "He was... everything."

Maria stood between them; her voice icy. "No, Leonard. He was your experiment. He died trying to clean up your mess."

Eliot stepped forward from the shadowy void. He looked grim and carried his weapon loose in his hands, staring at the devastation. "This isn't over," he pronounced flatly. "You think that blowing one lab up and making a few prototypes disappear solves anything? Too late."

Rebecca turned to him, narrowing her eyes. "What the hell does that mean?"

Eliot sighed, explaining with great weariness, "Leonard's data—it's not all in this lab. There are other labs. Other experiments. Noah might have stopped the present dilemma, but the fight's not halfway through yet."

Leonard swung toward Eliot with alarming speed, expression negotiating the threshold between anger and sheer terror. "You have no idea what you're talking about."

Eliot's grin was brutal, and spoke even of the grave decay of goodwill. "*Don't I?* You think that you are the only one who has been tracking this project? There will be more like Noah—more prototypes, more risks. You have only made the inevitable other-day."

Rebecca felt her stomach churn as the weight of Eliot's words settled on her. "So, Noah gave his life to put an end to all this," she said, almost in a whisper. "*And you're telling me it was for nothing?*"

Eliot shook his head. "Not for nothing. But it serves as a reminder of how much is still out there. And the choice we have to make when the time finally arrives."

Maria clenched her fists and raised her voice. "No. There will be no more of this. We are going to find those other labs, those other prototypes. And we are going to stop them."

Eliot raised an eyebrow and skeptically replied, "**You're a reporter, not a soldier. It is not your battle.**"

Maria's eyes sparkled with determination. "But it is now."

Rebecca reached her hand to Maria's shoulder, grounding her. "I don't even know where to start," she said. "If Eliot's right, this project is bigger than anything we have yet to see."

Leonard turned away, body shrugging with defeat. "You won't find them," he said hollowly. "*Not without me.*"

Rebecca frowned. "What could possibly be the incentive for your help? All you've done is protect this project."

Leonard looked back at her, his face a mask of turmoil. "Because Noah was right," he said. "I never gave him a choice. But now, I do."

The sound of distant sirens broke the moment, the wail punctuating the night. Eliot stood up, tense. "We need to move. Whomever that may be wouldn't care who sided with whom."

Maria nodded, clutching Rebecca's arm. "**Let's go.**"

But Rebecca resisted, staring back into the ruins. "What if he is still alive?" she managed to whisper to neither her nor anyone in particular.

Maria squeezed her arm gently. "Rebecca, he's gone. You saw the explosion."

Rebecca's chest tightened, and tears stung her eyes. She wanted to believe Maria, wanted to be confident that Noah's sacrifice was final, but somewhere within herself, she just wouldn't allow it. There had been a spark in him-it was power such as she had never seen before. Could it really have been so easily extinguished?

As they vanished into the shadows, a faint flicker of light glimmered from deep within the wreckage of the lab. For now, it was a slight glimmer-a flicker barely perceptible against the ashes of the burning wreck. But soon it grew and pulsed steadily like a heartbeat.

Beneath the twisted metal and shattered glass, something stirred.

Chapter 10

The Collapse

The remnants of Noah's energy still lit the sky above the ruins of the lab. With the bleakness of the ground that had been scorched where the lab had once stood, Rebecca inhaled sharply as a light pulsed within the wreckage. Briefly, it was so slight as to be unnoticed, yet clear enough for it to be seen.

"Noah..." she whispered, her voice trembling.

Maria gripped her arm and pulled her back. "Rebecca, we have to go; whoever's arriving will be here any minute and we are totally unprepared for this."

Rebecca hesitated, then glanced back at the ruins. "But--"

"No," Maria directed sharply, urgency laced in her voice. "If it's him, he will find us. We need to focus on surviving."

Eliot had already begun to move with weapon ready. "She's right," he said curtly. "We are exposed here. Let's go."

Rebecca turned reluctantly and followed Maria and Eliot into the dense woods bordering the lab. Leonard stumbled after them, pallid and hollow-eyed. Since the explosion, he hadn't opened his mouth; grief and disbelief had wrapped around him like a cloak.

The group sped through the woods, the sounds of distant sirens increasing in volume with each step. Rebecca glanced back over her shoulder, her mind racing. If that glow had been Noah, what did it mean? Did that mean he was really alive? And if he were alive, what would that energy have done to him?

"I suppose this time you will let us know what the plan is, Eliot? Or maybe you don't have one," was Maria's voice that pulled Rebecca from her thoughts.

Eliot shot her a fierce glare, but did not cease his motion. "We're regrouping, assessing the damage, and determining what can be salvaged."

"Salvaged? If the lab is gone, then so too is all the data. What, exactly, do you hope to salvage?" This with disdain.

Eliot refused to comment, staring determinedly ahead. Rebecca could see the tension in his figure, felt the muscles of his fingers tensing around his gun. For some reason, she was sure he was hiding something.

As the forest grew sparse, daylight options lightened, revealing a small clearing. Eliot tapped them into silence, the expression on his face deepened in anguish.

"Here is where we'll camp for now. Watch and join us in remaining silent. Whoever survived the blast would surely search for us."

Maria crossed her arms in answer to this. "And what about the clones? Shall we just leave them to die?"

Eliot shot her a cool look. "*What clones?* The lab is gone. Whatever was in there is either destroyed or buried tons beneath debris."

Rebecca felt her stomach churn in trouble. "Not all of them," she whispered. "Some were still in containment. They may have escaped death."

At her words, Leonard bolted to attention, staring wide-eyed at her. "Are they alive?" he asked, dropping his voice to a faint whisper. "Are you certain?"

Rebecca wavered. "I'm not sure. But if there's even a chance."

Eliot shook his head. "No chance; going back there isn't worth it, it could kill us."

Leonard stepped forward, desperation glimmering desperate in his voice. "You don't understand. Those clones are climactic results derived from years of work. They are not merely tests; they are lives."

Maria turned on him. "Created by you and locked up in tanks like lab rats."

Leonard recoiled and his jaw clenched tight. "They didn't ask to have lives created for them. But we are all responsible for what exists now."

Listening to the quarrel, Rebecca felt her chest tighten. Noah surfaced in her thoughts, the look in his eyes as he asked her just what he was supposed to be. The weight of that question had long remained heavy on her mind, bearing down on her like some physical weight.

"So, we can't simply abandon them," she said with a fair tone. "If there's even a slight chance that they are alive, we ought to at least try."

Eliot hardened. **"But what if our trying kills us all? Then what?"**

There was a distant sound of engines as Rebecca felt the chill down her spine. Eliot stiffened, bringing his weapon to sharp attention. "They've come," he said grimly.

Maria looked toward the treeline and said, "*Who are 'they'?*"

"Keller's forces," Eliot replied. "They won't care who's alive or dead, and will kill anyone that stands in their way."

Rebecca felt her stomach plummet. "We're not staying here."

"No," Eliot said. "But if you're keen on going back to that lab, you're on your own now."

Leonard advanced then. His voice trembled. "I'll go."

Rebecca cast him an angry glance, narrowing her eyes. "Leonard—"

"They're my burden," he resumed. "If they are alive, I should come to their aid."

Rebecca briefly restrained herself against the thought, but her heart raced. Noah thought of the glow in the ruins and then the haunting question of what he had become. Leaving the clones behind, abandoning them to their fate, had become unbearable.

"I'll go, too," she finally chimed in.

Maria's eyes widened. "Rebecca, no! It's just too dangerous."

Rebecca locked eyes with her, a look of steadfastness in her feature. "If we don't go back, nobody will."

Eliot gestured to Maria to follow, starting to move away into the thickets as the roar of engines grew louder. "So, you've chosen," he told her coldly. **"Don't expect us to come back for you."**

Maria hesitated for a moment, looking from Rebecca to Eliot and back again. "Rebecca..."

"It's okay," Rebecca soothed. "Just go with him. Stay safe."

Maria scowled in frustration but nodded. "You'd better come back," she said shakily. "Both of you."

Rebecca nodded, chest tightening as she watched Maria disappear into the trees with Eliot. She turned to Leonard, the beating of her heart loud against her chest. "Now, let's go."

In turn, they moved back to the lab's ruins, the dim glow continuing flickering like a distant light, a beacon calling them home.

Rebecca and Leonard walked very cautiously through the charred remains of the forest, the glow of the lab's ruins intensifying as they approached. The rumble of distant engines faded, yet Rebecca's heart raced with a confusing mixture of fear and courage. Each step became incrementally heavier, the burden of their decision weighing heavily upon her.

"Are they still alive, do you think?" she whispered to break the suspenseful silence.

Leonard hesitated, staring into the glowing remnants ahead. "I don't know," he finally said. "But if they are, then they'll definitely need some help. Containment chambers weren't made to survive something like this."

Rebecca just nodded, her thoughts drifting to Noah. That glow she caught a glimpse of just before leaving the lab—could it have been him? In that case, what had he turned into? A chill scuttled down her spine, but she shuddered it off. There was no space for any more doubt at this moment.

It was for them to step on the horror, stepping over twisted metal and shattered glass which still hummed with warmth beneath their feet. Rebecca covered her mouth and nose with her sleeve amid the acrid smoke seeping from poisoned earth.

Leonard gawked at the wreckage. "The containment chambers were located in the eastern wing," he said, pointing toward a cross-section of the lab that had collapsed in heaps. "If any of them survived, they'll be in there."

Rebecca took after him and ventured carefully over the litter. Each sound—the twist of metal, the hiss of venting steam—made her jump. It was overwhelming destruction, but there was something beyond that. An actual presence. Something in the faint humming in the air that sent shivers through her spine.

"*Did you hear that?*" she asked in a whisper.

Leonard stopped short and furrowed his brows. "*Hear what?*"

Rebecca shook her head. "*Never mind.*"

They reached the remains of the east wing, the structure just about ready to crumble. Rebecca took a glance around and beheld a containment chamber; the glass had broken there but the base remained steady. Within it a figure stirred.

"Leonard!" she called, rushing forward.

Leonard followed, his expression shifting towards hope and disbelief. "They survived," he said, voice trembling.

Rebecca knelt beside the chamber and leaned down to look through the broken glass. One inside the chamber appeared human but incomplete, its skin white and translucent, its movements weak and alice like a doe caught in headlights. The sight made her stomach churn. This can't be Noah. This being was… still incomplete.

"**Help me get it out**," Leonard said, breaking her reverie.

She hesitated again. "*You sure it's safe?*"

"Safe or not, it is alive," Leonard said, casting her a quick glare.

Together they gently lifted the figure out of the shattered chamber. Its body trembled as it took some tentative steps. Its glowing eyes were barely lit, and it spoke with a faint, mechanical-sounding voice. "Wh… Where am I?"

Rebecca's heart tightened. "You're safe," she said slowly. "We're going to help you."

A noise, metallic clanking followed by an unmistakable sound of boots over rubble, broke the moment. Rebecca's heart sank as she turned and saw people dragging themselves out of the shadows. Keller's men.

"There they are!" one of them yelled, raising a gun.

"Get down!" Leonard shouted as he dragged Rebecca behind a piece of fallen wall. The clone stumbled and fell on the floor as the first shots were fired.

Rebecca swallowed as she pressed herself against the rubble. They were too few and too unarmed, while the clone was far too weak to make a move. She eyed Leonard. His face was pale but determined.

"We cannot allow them to take it," he said in a low voice. "If they take it…"

Rebecca nodded as her resolve firmed up. **"We cannot."**

The gunfire grew with great intensity, one narrow crack moving into the precise stone ruins. Rebecca peered from the edge of the wall, her heart racing, counting down at least six armed men who were closing up to their positions. Her brain ticked fast in order to come up with an escape route.

That humming she had earlier noticed had now solidly risen to be some kind of vibrating in the air, pulsing to the beat of her heart. In hopes of catching a glimpse of the ruins herself, she turned, eyes opened wide as she once again picked out the glow. This time, though, the lighter glow was not faint but blinding.

The ground trembled beneath them, and the air seethed with a net of power. The armed men, frozen at this point, dropped their weapons with intent toward where the burst of light came from. Choked was Rebecca's breathing, as she beheld in wonder a figure emerging from amidst the light, its form towering and regal, and flaming eyes, burning like twin suns.

"Noah," she uttered, her words shakily coming out of her throat.

The guns lowered, and the men hesitated, visibly shaken at the sight of Noah stepping forward. His every aspect seemed to hold a surging might, an energy that made the air quiver. When he spoke, his voice was mellow but powerful enough to quieten the battle outside.

"Leave," he ordered, staring intensely at Keller's men. "Right now."

The men looked at each other as if that was their last opportunity to shoot each of them before out of danger. One man rose the rifle, finger itching to pull the trigger.

Noah lifted his hand, and the rifle was suddenly thrown away from him by an unseen force that sent that man sprawling, his eyes resting with bloodshot awe. The others threw down their arms and slowly began to recede.

"**This isn't over**," one of them said, retreating into the shadows.

While the men were escaping, Noah's glow dimmed, and he turned to Rebecca and Leonard. His expression was guardedly inscrutable; his glowing eyes took in the general wreckage. Rebecca felt her heart leap up for a moment as she bravely stepped forward.

"Noah," she said softly. **"You're alive."**

With a slight twist of his head, Noah's eyes settled firmly upon her. "Alive," he echoed in an almost distant tone. "But somehow different."

Leonard stepped forth, an awestruck gleam in his eyes. "You have evolved!" he exclaimed. "You have become what I always knew you could be."

Noah's eyes narrowed. **"What you made me to be."**

The challenge hung in the air, and Rebecca felt her breath catch as realization dawned; Noah was indeed something alive and powerful. No expectation could ever hold him down again.

The light around Noah was fading into a mere spark, but the air continued to hum with energy, reminding one of the raw powers he carried. He stood up tall, his glowing eyes scanning the wreckage and broken containment chambers before settling on the weak clone lying at Rebecca and Leonard's feet. His expression was unreadable, a faint calm that sent a shiver down Rebecca's spine.

"Noah," Leonard began, trembling. "You... are perfection. The obvious fulfilment of everything we have worked for."

Noah turned to Leonard, glaring. "Worked for?" he repeated, his tone clicking with a sharp snap. "You made me just to bear testimony to your theories; you played God. And now you call me perfect?"

Leonard's face fell; his hands were trembling by his sides. "I didn't mean—"

"You didn't mean for me to think for myself," Noah interrupted, his voice on an edgier tone now. "You wanted control, and you lost it."

She stepped ahead, chest ache, trying to understand Noah's mind. "Noah," she began softly. "You stopped them. You saved us. That's worth something."

Noah shifted his gaze to her; his glowing eyes narrowed slightly. "Saved you?" he scoffed. "I did not save you. I stopped them simply because they were in my way."

Those words remained hanging in mid-air, laden and heavy. Rebecca felt a twinge of sadness at the thought that their friend was far removed from the blank slate he had been. He had found more power, but in doing so, had put even greater barriers around himself.

Leonard glanced at him, a little uncertain and taking a small step. "Noah," he said, pleadingly. "**You're not just power.** You're not just—what I made you. You're something more."

Noah turned sharply, anger roaring in his glowing eyes. "And what would that be, Leonard? Tell me. What am I? Because I've always just been your experiment."

Leonard winced, although his determination did not flee. "You're my son," he said softly. "**You're the future.**"

Noah's laughter was bitter, reverberated through the ruins like something wrong. "**A son? Future?** You don't even know what that means."

Rebecca pressed a hand against Leonard's shoulder. "Leonard, don't," she instructed sternly. "You're not helping."

Leonard slumped on uncertainty, wheeling lightly away and looking at the ground. Rebecca turned back to Noah, her heart racing, and approached closer with hands raised up, as a gesture of peace.

"Noah," she said quietly. "You don't have to be what Leonard wanted. Or what anyone else wants. You can decide for yourself."

Noah tilted his head ever so slightly and looked at her with his shining eyes. "*Decide for myself?*" he repeated. "Is that what you've done, Rebecca? *Decided who you are?*"

Rebecca hesitated. She didn't ask a thing; she was taken aback by the question. "I—"

"No," Noah interrupted, cutting her off. "You're still trying to fix part of what you broke. Trying still to atone for your own mistakes. Just like Leonard."

Rebecca's chest tightened. "We're trying to help you."

Noah's eyes hardened. "*Help me? You think I need help?*"

Maria's voice sliced through the jagged tension with precision. "Noah, stop. She's just trying to reach you."

Noah turned on Maria and narrowed his glowing eyes. "Reach me? Why? So, she can make herself feel good? So, she can pretend she hadn't created it?"

Maria did not falter. She spoke steady and calm. "No. Because she cares."

For a split second, a flicker of something—doubt, perhaps—crossed Noah's features. It vanished as quickly as it had appeared. "Caring doesn't change anything," he said, his voice quieter now. "It doesn't fix what is broken."

Rebecca came forward closer, quivering yet resolute. "It can. If you'd let it."

The entire aura ran intense with a hum, brightening further around Noah, who then turned away from them, towards the ruins of the containment chambers. "They're gone," he whispered. "The others. They didn't survive."

Leonard, his expression crumbled, spoke shakily, "No… no, that can't be. There were safeguards—"

"They are not enough," fabricating the exception to take it away. Noah terminations on building him strong but gets hence not strong enough. Just what you built in me.

Leonard went silent; grief and guilt festered all over his face. In pained resignation, Rebecca watched him, but she remained grave, glancing again at Noah. Her voice rung out loud and clear.

You survived," she said. "And that counts for something."

Noah seemed to be held in a time freeze as if something was happening slowly: the dim of those strange reflexes moving beyond his expectation and fixing on the wreckage. "That means I'm alone," he eventually admitted. "It means I'm the only one who remains."

The silence that ensued was unbearable. Rebecca stepped closer, hands trembling. "You're not alone," she mused softly. "We are here for you."

Noah turned to face her; his expression inscrutable. "You're not like me," he said. "You'll never understand what it's like to be… this."

Rebecca softened. "Maybe not. But we can try."

Noah's blazing eyes turned on her, her heart constricting a little under the weight of his intense gaze. "And what happens when you can't? What happens when you realize you were wrong?"

Rebecca hesitated, feeling the weight of his question weighing on her. "Then we keep trying," she said, her tone finally firm. "Because that's what you're supposed to do when you care."

One last look was cast at her, then his eyes travelled to Leonard and Maria. There was a palpable change in the air; it fell hushed around him, grew dimmer; he looked smaller now, and more human, yet something in the atmosphere felt still tense.

"Then try," he murmured gently. "*But don't expect me to make it easy.*"

The silence hung heavily over the ruins as Noah's words sank into it, weighing in upon themselves, Rebecca's heart thumping to keep pace, struggling to comprehend what had transpired: Noah stood before them-alive, powerful, limitless-but never felt so distant.

Leonard broke the cringing silence, choking but determined: "Noah, you don't have to do all of this alone, I'm there for you. Let us rebuild."

Noah turned his eyes toward Leonard, through slits. "**Rebuild?** After all this?" His voice dripped with bitterness as he gestured to the burnt garage. "This is what you wanted, wasn't it? To move forward. To evolve. And now it is just ashes."

Though shaken, Leonard did not quail in his retort. "You don't understand. It wasn't supposed to happen. It wasn't supposed to end until this!"

The coldness of Noah's mirth sent chill after chill down Rebecca's spine. "You think this is it?" he said in low, dark tones. "It's only the beginning."

Maria moved forward, pallid but steady in her voice: "What does that mean, Noah? *What are your plans?*"

Noah's eyes flicked to her, and for a moment, Rebecca thought he would hiss at her. Instead, he sighed; the glow in his eyes faded a little. "I don't know," he murmured. "Yet I can feel it, the pull of its power, the connection-building."

Rebecca stepped closer, almost like she sought to throw in another fray. "*With what?*"

Noah hesitated, conflicted. "To all of it," he muttered finally. "The energy, the prototypes, the other labs...everything is connected. And I can sense that pull towards me."

Leonard's eyes widened once more, a spark of excitement cutting through his despair. "The network," he quipped, almost to himself. "The labs were supposed to link each other to share resources. If you can feel that Noah, it's still active."

Rebecca churned her stomach. "*And what does that mean for us?*"

Leonard turned toward her as the intensity in the voice increased. "It means the other labs could still be functional. The prototype, information; it's out there."

Noah clenched his jaw and flared his glowing eyes for a ghost of a second. "Then it must be contained, all of it," he said.

Rebecca caught her breath. "Noah, wait. You can't just—"

"Why not?" Noah interrupted; his voice sharp. "Isn't that what you want? To stop this? To make sure no one else has to go through what I did?"

Rebecca faltered, her chest tightening. "Yes, but not like this. You're talking about destroying everything, Noah. What if there's another way?"

Noah's gaze softened, but the tension in his posture did not break. "Another way," he repeated. "And what would that be, Rebecca? *More experiments? More failures?*"

Leonard stepped forward; his shaking voice nearly inaudible. "It doesn't have to be this way. We can fix it together, make it right."

A harsh laugh took shape in Noah's throat, and the brilliance in his eyes narrowed. "You don't fix it, Leonard. You stop it."

Maria crossed her arms, the skepticism in her tone evident. "And what happens after you stop it, Noah? What happens to you?"

Noah hesitated; the flame in his eyes flickered. "I don't know," he said quietly. "But that doesn't matter."

"It matters to us," Rebecca said gloomily. **"It matters to me."**

Noah's gaze snapped to her in an unreadable expression. For one moment, Rebecca thought she might see something-an ache, longing-but it vanished the moment it arrived. He took a step back, the light around him intensifying.

"I feel them," came his distant voice, "the other labs. The prototypes. They remain out there, waiting."

Leonard's eyes lit up with hope and desperation. "If you can access the network, Noah, we could use it - for control-over."

"No," Noah cut him off unceremoniously. "No one should have that control. Not you. Not anyone."

The ground beneath trembled at Noah's energy, the hum on air grew louder. Rebecca stepped forward; her hands raised in supplication. "Noah--wait," she said with a tremor in her voice. "You don't have to do it alone."

Noah turned to her; the glow of his eyes fixed upon hers. "Maybe I shouldn't," he replied, softly. "But I can't trust any of you."

Rebecca felt her insides tighten. **"You can trust me."**

Noah hesitated, the flickering of doubt playing through his eyes. "*Will I?*" he asked. "Because right now, I can't even trust myself."

Before Rebecca had the chance to reply, Noah's aura grew and screeched, slowly turning into a roar. The air crackled with energy while the ground began splitting apart beneath them.

"Noah, stop!" screamed Rebecca, her voice cracking. "No need to go that side!"

Noah's glowing eyes met hers one last time and, in that brief moment, she thought she saw something midst the glare--an apology, perhaps; a farewell--before he vanished in a blinding flash of white light.

As the light faded, the ruins fell silent once again. Rebecca blinked and, as her eyes swam, tried to get everything that had happened in order. Leonard stared at the space where Noah had once stood, a pale face and trembling hands.

Finally, Maria shattered the uneasy silence, releasing strains of panic into her voice: "What now?"

Rebecca swallowed the lump in her throat, her heart hammering from the burden piled over her. "We find him," she breathed faintly. "Before it is too late."

The upcoming rumble of distant engines broke the eerie silence that had fallen over the ruined ground after Noah's disappearance. Rebecca's heart raced in light of the fading sliver of his energy in the air while she darted her eyes over the ruins. Poor Leonard stood petrified, face contorted in surprise and despair, and Maria's fists were clenched, her expression tense.

"They are coming," Maria said breathlessly. "We need to leave. Now."

Rebecca brought her thoughts back to the empty space where Noah had been standing. "If Keller's forces find this place. . .**they'll destroy everything,**" she hurried to say. "We cannot let that happen."

After a silence of contemplation with subsequent breaths, Leonard spoke up, voice hollow: "There's nothing left to destroy. The lab, the clones—they are all gone. There is nothing to take."

Maria shot him a look: "Just because there is nothing left to destroy does not mean they will not try. And let me tell you, if they think we were hiding any evidence . . . "

A fearful feeling climbed into Rebecca's heart. Thus, she nodded, trying to catch her breath: "We have to get out of here, but—"

A gunshot rang out and cut her short, the sharp crack echoing off the ruins. Instinctively Rebecca dropped to the ground, yanking Maria down with her. Leonard began to fall over, his hands raised in surrender as armed men stepped out of the midnight shadows.

"Don't move!" One of them shouted, leveling a weapon at Leonard.

And destiny unleashed upon Rebecca as the insignia of the dubious uniforms dawned in front of her. Keller forces. They were professional, indeed, and surrounded the group with military precision. One of the groups shoved Leonard, getting the poor guy back on his feet.

"We've been searching for you, Mallory," one of the soldiers taunted maliciously. "Keller has some questions for you."

Clenching her fists as the thoughts swam before her mind, Rebecca looked at Maria, who exhibited the full range of feelings in her wide eyes: terror walking with a flickering defiance. **No weapon? No backup?** There was no possible way out.

. . . Until the hum returned.

At first, it seemed soft, like a low-frequency vibration in the air. But then it gathered strength and came to produce a hard tremor that rocked the ground. The soldiers looked on in wonder, turning their heads as one to look into the sound's direction. Rebecca caught her breath when the familiar luminosity began running up from the ruins.

"Noah," she whispered.

The glow became brighter, pulsing with intensity and forcing the soldiers to shield their eyes. Rebecca squinted against the blaze; her heart raced as a figure broke through the glare. It was Noah, but a very different Noah from the one Rebecca had known. Taller, distinctly forming, and glowing eyes with amazing, unearthly energy.

The soldiers instinctively reacted with weapons raised high. "Stand down!" shouted one of them. "Now!"

Noah didn't answer. He took a step ahead, deliberately and unnervingly composed. Energy swirled in the air around him, and Rebecca felt the heat radiating off him.

The lead soldier opened fire, the sound of machine-gun-fire ripping the air apart. Rebecca screamed, throwing herself over Maria by instinct. But the bullets never reached them.

With just a slight movement of his hand, Noah suspended the bullets in mid-air, caught in a shimmering field of energy. The soldiers froze, their determination turning into fear. With another flick of his wrist, Noah disintegrated the bullets into a cloud of ash.

"I told you to leave," he said lowly, resonantly, with such a command that made Rebecca shiver.

The soldiers shifted uneasily, dread encumbering them. But the leader gritted his teeth and raised his weapon again. "We have orders to bring Mallory in alive. We're not leaving without her," he stated firmly.

Noah's eyes narrowed, and the glow surrounding him flared. "Then you won't leave at all."

Rebecca's stomach lurched as the ground beneath the soldiers erupted in a wave of energy that tossed them into the air. They got up hard, weapons flying out of their hands, and landed all over the ruins. Noah stepped forward toward the soldiers, completely opaque, but emitting more force than any.

"Noah, stop!" Rebecca screamed, her voice cracking. "You don't have to do this!"

Noah began to turn toward her, his glowing eyes sliding into hers. "*Do I not?*" he asked softly, his voice low but full of intensity. "They came here to kill. They won't stop, not until it is all gone."

Rebecca jerked wide awake. She stood and trembled. "You're right; they won't stop, but this isn't the way. If you do this, you will be no better than them."

Noah hesitated, a flicker of uncertainty flitting over his glowing eyes. For a moment, Rebecca thought he was reached. But his face hardened, and the energy around him surged again.

"**You don't understand,**" he said. "This isn't about being better. This is about putting an end to this. To everything."

The energy felt sentient and crackled menacingly. The glow surrounding Noah became blinding, and Rebecca took a step back, pressing her fingers to her eyes, praying feverishly for some way--anything--to stop Noah. Her arm was pulled by Maria, urging her toward the edge of the ruins.

"We have to go!" Maria yelled in urgency. "If he releases all that energy, we won't survive."

Rebecca shook her head with tears streaming down her cheeks. "I can't leave him."

"You don't have a choice!" she screamed, her voice high-pitched and teetering on the edge of hysteria.

Even as a deafening roar filled the air, Rebecca did not have a chance to reply. The energy around Noah blasted outward, sending out a shockwave, which took Rebecca and Maria tumbling to the ground. The soldiers too were cast back, their bodies gone limp and left as dead.

As the light faded, **Noah was no more.**

Rebecca sat up slowly, her ears ringing and her eyes blurred. The ruins were quiet now, the air thick with the scent of ozone. Leonard was just a few feet away, wide-eyed with shock but otherwise alright. Next to Rebecca, Maria groaned as she moved, clutching her arm in pain.

"Noah," she whispered, trembling. "What have you done?"

Maria sat up, her face pale. "He's gone," she replied. "But... where?"

Rebecca did not answer. She stared at the empty place where Noah had stood, her heart simultaneously heavy with grief and fear. But one fact was certain: whatever Noah had become; he wasn't a mere clone anymore.

He was something else.

And his work wasn't finished.

Chapter 11

Society on Edge

The town was unrecognizable.

Rebecca gazed out the car window as they cruised through the desolate streets, the smoldering glow of far-off fires casting shades of purple on outlined buildings. The sidewalks were empty, littered with overturned trash bins and broken glass, daubed and defaced in fright and anger by hurried graffiti.

"There Is No More Clones!"

"Stop Playing God!"

"Who's Next?"

This was largely painted on walls, scrawled on billboards, even inscribed on the side of some burnt-out car. And, mixed in, as though a soulless black mist, lingered the smell of fire and fear, strangling hope out of Rebecca's lungs.

Without saying a word, Maria's hands gripped the wheel so tightly that Rebecca feared it might snap in two. In the backseat, Leonard sat with his head down, hands tightly clasped. The silence was thick, almost oppressive as the pressures of everything weighed down on all of them.

"They're scared," Rebecca muttered cryptically. "They don't understand what's happening, and they lash out."

Maria scowled; eyes pinned on the road ahead. "*Could you blame them?* Eliot dropped a bomb on the world in secret, then people started to realize the neighbors they grew up with might not be who they claim to be. Total chaos."

Rebecca glanced at Leonard in the backseat by way of a rearview mirror. He had not said anything since they pulled away from the genocide of the lab. He had grown pale and hollow-eyed, as if the last glimmer of hope for him had finally shattered.

Another turn, as they approached an area lit up in riotous chaos, revealed a whole gaggle gathered out the from the front doors of the government building, where their shouts carried crisp past the faceless darkness of the streets. Lines of riot-police stood there, shields raised in glorious anticipation, aimed toward the protesters hurling insults and throwing object matter.

Maria slowly pulled the car over, her countenance bleak. "We can't make it through. Too inconvenient."

Rebecca's chest tightened as she watched the anger of the crowd boil over with shouting rage and searing nervousness.

"We Want Answers!"

"Clones Are Killers!"

"Stop the Experiments!"

"He… this wasn't supposed to happen," Leonard finally murmured quietly.

Maria turned in her seat, her eyes blazing. "What did you think was going to happen, Leonard? You created people in secret, kept them locked in tanks, and now the whole world knows. Who could possibly blame them for being angry?"

Leonard turned away, letting tremors slip into his hands. "I thought… I thought they'd see the potential. The progress."

"**Progress?**" Maria shouted angrily, the anger flowing out. "You call this progress? People are afraid, Leonard. They don't trust their neighbors or friends or family. You didn't just create clones; you created a chasm."

Rebecca placed a firm hand on Maria's arm. "Maria, cut it out."

Maria turned on her, jaw tight. "No, Rebecca. He has to hear this."

Rebecca sighed. "I know. But this isn't something the yelling is going to fix."

Maria exhaled loudly, which drew her attention back to the steering wheel. The tension in the car was thick enough to chew on; their silence was heavy. Rebecca turned to Leonard and spoke softly.

"Maria's right," she said. "They're scared, they're angry. But that doesn't mean it's too late to do something about it."

Leonard looked up at her, his eyes full of doubt. "*What can I do?* The labs are gone, the prototypes destroyed. Even Noah—" His voice caught, and he turned away. "I don't know what he is anymore."

Rebecca paused, imagining Noah's glowing eyes. "Noah made a choice. You have a choice now."

Maria pulled into a poorly lit alley, extremely close enough to determine the distant screams from the nearby riots. "Let's not go anywhere near the main roads," she said coldly. **"The city's a war zone right now."**

Rebecca nodded but remained focused on Leonard. "You can help those people to understand. You're the only one who can explain what this technology really is-what it means."

Leonard shook his head. "They won't listen. They've already made up their minds."

Maria turned on him, her voice sharp. "Then give them a reason to listen. You created this mess, Leonard. Time to own up to it."

Rebecca put her hand on Leonard's shoulder ameliorating her tone. "Maria's right. They're scared, scared of the absence of fear in light of the truth. If you don't tell them, someone else will, and they may not have the whole story."

Leonard held her, searching her eyes for hope - or redemption, perhaps. *"Do you seriously think it'll make a difference?"* he asked.

Rebecca thought for a moment before she responded. "I don't know. But it's better than doing nothing."

In the distance, the faint glow of another fire barely flickered, and the city's unrest stretched out as far as the eye could see. Rebecca felt a tightness in her chest as she thought of Noah, his transformation, and the power he held. If society couldn't bear the truth about clones, what would they do when they found out about him?

"There is not much time," came Maria's voice into Rebecca's thoughts. "If Keller's forces are still out there, they will come after us. And if she finds out Noah is alive…"

This time Rebecca simply nodded, her heart heavy with her own insecurities. "We will find a way," she muttered. "We must."

Long shadowy lanes were dotted with small fires just beyond the line of the skyline. The gloom settled thick and oppressive over the air, suffused with the tension of a city teetering on the edge. Rebecca leaned against the car, her arms crossed over her chest as she vacantly stared into the middle distance, her head swimming with exploding thoughts.

"*Do you hear that?*" Maria's voice broke the silence like a knife fell into hot water.

Rebecca turned, her heart racing. She could barely hear it, a rhythmic sound-the heavy boots hitting the ground with intent and consistency. Leonard's eyes popped wide, and he jerked upright, holding onto the edge of the car door.

"They're coming," said Maria. Her voice was steady, but Rebecca had caught the undercurrent of fear.

Rebecca quickly moved away from the car to be by Maria's side. "How many?" she whispered.

"There is no way I can tell you. They're nearby."

Leonard ducked back into the car; his breathing rapid. "There's no place left to hide," he muttered. "It's like they are waiting for us no matter where we go."

Maria rounded on him; her tone sharp. "What were you expecting? Keller's people will just let this go? You are the linchpin, Leonard. They need you."

Leonard glared at her; his expression heavy with regret. "They don't need me. They need the data-the labs, the clones. Without them, I'm nothing."

Maria was loose-lipped with anger. "You are not nothing, Leonard. You're the reason any of this happened. You built it, you lied about it, and now people are dying because of it."

"I can't have more words thrown at him," Rebecca said softly, trying to diffuse the situation.

But Maria was hardly finished. "No way," lets it fly. "He needs to hear this. So, you could wallow in self-pity all you like, Leonard, but there's one thing you need to accept—you're in charge of this. Quite literally, all of it."

Leonard looked away; his hands quivered. "I thought... I thought I was helping," he muttered. "I thought I was giving humanity a chance to survive."

Maria's laugh sliced through the night like a bitter blade. "Survive? Look around, Leonard. Does this look like survival to you? This is chaos. This is fear. You didn't save humanity. You tore it apart."

Rebecca stepped between them, voice calm and firm. "Shut up," she said. "This isn't helping."

Maria drew a sharp breath, hands crunching through her hair. "You're right," she said. "But still... I can't just sit and watch him act like the victim, not when the rest of us are right out here trying to survive."

Rebecca nodded. Her expression softened, looking over to Leonard. "She's right," she said softly. "You can't change the past. But you can change the future."

Cautiously, Leonard turned to her. "How?"

"First, be truthful," Rebecca stated. "No more secrets. No more lies. If people are going to trust us-if we're going to change-this leaves no choice; they must know it all."

With the sounds of marching boots becoming thunderous by the second, an echoing drumbeat into the alley, Maria locked Rebecca by the arm and said, not softly, "We have to move."

Rebecca nodded, adrenaline coursing through into her system. "Take the car. Leonard and I will find another way out."

Maria raised her eyebrows high. "*Seriously?* You cannot go by foot."

Rebecca held back and managed to say, "We've got to be fine. Anyway, just go. We will meet at the rendezvous point."

Maria hesitated, momentarily casting a glance at Leonard and back to Rebecca and nodded. "Don't do anything stupid."

Rebecca forced a smile. "You know me."

Maria rolled her eyes while shifting into the driver's seat of the car. The engine roared; she plowed away down the alley, the noise evaporating into the night almost immediately.

Rebecca turned to Leonard, speaking softly. "Come on. We need to keep moving."

Leonard hesitated, as if caught between two different decisions. "Rebecca, I-"

"Not now," she cut him short, ashamed. "We'll speak later. Right now, we need to stay alive."

They plunged deeper into the alley, their shadows intertwining as the sounds of shouting and breaking glass roamed steadily outside. The city came alive-it was a beast awakening from deep slumber, the unrest stirrer creeping like a wildfire.

They had turned the corner when they froze again-a darkened group of figures were caught in a tuxedo glow-edged brightness from a still burning dumpster matter of yards ahead. Rebecca's heart sank in the knowledge of uniforms covering her-Keller's goons! They had not just been following them; they had been herding them.

"Leonard," Rebecca managed to whisper as she stood almost breathless in fear. "**Run.**"

Leonard posed no more than half a second momentarily and scrambled off in the opposite direction. She followed. Her breath rapped up as the sounds of pursuit bore like heralds behind them. The alley twisted and turned. They were pulpy shadows, with the night creeping around them like a vice.

A dead end stood before them, walls towering high. Rebecca turned round with a pounding heart as Keller's men closed in, guns raised.

"Stop!" yelled one. "Hands up!"

Leonard went still; a tremor swept through him as he raised his hands slowly. Rebecca's mind raced, seeking an avenue of escape. The air around was different; heavy, like something unseen building around them.

And then she felt it.

A low hum came from the sky, faintly audible, but ever-growing in intensity. She bit her breath back in surprise as she looked up and widened her eyes.

"Noah," she whispered.

For the sky above had brightened, a dazzling glow illuminating the alley like the day. A cry from Keller's men; their weapons fell from their hands as they shielded their eyes. Within Rebecca, a sudden blast of energy surged; a curious warmth made her heart race.

When the light dimmed, Noah appeared at the far end of the alley, blazing eyes twin suns against the sombre backdrop. Calm was the look upon him; still his presence had a boldness, an intensity that constricted Rebecca's breast.

"You shouldn't have come here," he spoke, voice low, throaty; it had the resonance of authority so that on each heard it there was a sudden silence.

Keller's men hesitated; their fear was almost palpable. One among them raised his weapon, trembling hands raw with fright, "Don't move!" he shouted.

Noah turned his head slightly and narrowed his glowing eyes. "You do not give orders here," he said softly.

The energy hovered thick in the air, and the ground beneath their feet quaked.

Noah stepped forward, and the ground beneath them shook. His eyes glowed ominously, the very air around him silencing in anticipation. Keller's men lost their composure, their former bravado evaporating into thin air. The leader, weapon shaking in his hands, took a tentative step back, looking frightened.

“Noah!” Rebecca called softly, her voice trembling--even echoing with some horror. "It is us. We are not your enemy."

Noah flicked his gaze upon her, his expressions unreadable. The glow around him pulsed rhythmically now, as though speaking to the very vibrations of the city itself. One moment, she thought she saw a flash of recognition in those piercing eyes of his: a hint of the Noah she remembered. It vanished in the next instant.

"They don't belong here. This is my domain now," Noah's voice was calm, albeit brimming with a dark tension that made Rebecca's heart race.

Keller's leader shuddered at the thought of what Noah might do to him under normal circumstances. "Stand down!" he shouted, raising his rifle. "Whatever you are, you're coming with us."

Noah cocked his head coolly, those glowing eyes narrowed. "*Do you think you can take me?*" He sounded mildly curious. "After all you witnessed today?"

Rebecca stepped forward with open hands, her heart racing in her chest. "Noah, please, don't do this."

He turned to her, his expression softening just the slightest. "And what shall I do, Rebecca? Submit to these fools? Allow them to decide what I am?"

Something caught in Rebecca's throat, her mind already whirring. "Don't fight," she pleaded. "We'll figure this out. Together."

It was almost a dark bitter laugh from Noah. "Together?" he repeated, incredulously. "*When did that ever work?*"

The tension in the alley broke, though, when one of Keller's rushed men unleashed a panicked single shot. This sound broke heavily upon the silence, its deep resonance making the narrow space feel like thunder. Rebecca flinched, her heart raising into her throat.

The bullet hung suspended in the air, pulled away from Noah's chest. Noah, for his part, stood still, an expression of calm as the glow nightmared out of him and became even more brilliant.

"**I warned you,**" he said in a whisper tinged with menace.

With a snap of his fingers, he sent the bullet to dissolve into dust. The crackling of raw energy in the area around Noah threw Keller's men backward, clattering their guns to the ground. Rebecca shielded her eyes from the growing bright light as she looked toward Noah, where the energy swelled in intensity, almost like a storm breaching with scorching fury.

“Enough!” Rebecca yelled violently, her voice causing a break through the pandemonium. “Noah, cease!”

Noah froze, the glow about him dimming just a little. His gaze shifted towards Rebecca in a frozen stare. Tension hung in the air, and the energy reduced to a quiet hum.

“They won't stop,” Noah spoke again, softer now, “until everything I am has been erased.”

Rebecca stepped in closer, heart pounding. “You don't know that. But if you keep doing things this way, you will just prove them right.”

Noah's glowing eyes narrowed. His expression darkened. “And if they're right?”

"They're not." Rebecca spoke emphatically now. "You're way more than what they think you are. More than anything Leonard made you."

Leonard's words cut through the still air, weak but steady. "She is right, Noah," he said with trembling hands as he stepped forward. "I… I didn't see it before. I didn't understand. But you're much more than a creation of mine."

Noah turned to Leonard. His glowing eyes narrowed. "And what am I, Leonard?" he asked, his voice sharp. "Tell me. What did you create me to be?"

Leonard sagged in defeat. The grief and guilt spilled out all over him. "I don't know," he admitted. "I thought I was making progress. A solution. But now… I see I was wrong. I see I failed you."

Noah's expression softened a flicker of something, pain or understanding, across his face. The glow about him dimmed even further, and the air began to settle into an uneasy calm.

The atmosphere tuned down with Keller's men stirring, the moans of pain echoing in the alleyway. Noah glanced toward them, glowing eyes narrowing yet again.

"They won't stop," he said quietly. "Even now they scheme on how they can take me down."

Rebecca stepped in front. Her voice trembled slightly yet remained strong. "Then let us stop them. Not through power, but to tell the truth. Let us tell them who you are."

Noah held her gaze, expression unreadable. The hum about him lessened in intensity. The glow in his eyes dimmed. "The truth," he said, whisper-soft. "And what is that, Rebecca?"

Rebecca hesitated; her breath caught. "That you are more than they will ever understand," she said. "That you are not their enemy."

The light around Noah was completely extinguished. The alley turned dark, and Keller's men climbed to their feet, fear mixed with confusion in their eyes, as Noah stepped back, still commanding but far less terrifying.

"You have one chance," said Noah with a voice that was low and steady. "Leave and do not come back."

Keller's leader momentarily wavered, glancing nervously from Noah to his men. Finally, he nodded and signaled for his fledgling warriors to leave. They disappeared into the darkness, their footsteps fading away into night.

Rebecca let out a shaky breath, her knees giving way under her. Leonard relied heavily against the wall; he was pale, but his eyes were fixed upon Noah.

"Noah," Rebecca said softly, taking a careful step forward. "What happens now?"

Noah looked at her with an inscrutable look on his face. "Now," said he, "we end this."

The night weighed heavily upon them in an atmosphere thick with unanswered questions. The jar of Noah's energy pulsed through the air, feeble and yet palpable, like an impending storm. Rebecca drew in breaths with great difficulty, never turning her gaze away from Noah. His words echoed in Rebecca's mind, chilling in their simplicity: "We end this."

"What do you mean?" Rebecca whispered, stepping cautiously closer. *"Noah, what are you going to do?"*

Noah did not respond immediately. His gaze ran down the alley, now dimmed to a luminous quality that swept in each dark crevice, seeming to weigh each possible development, each potential outcome. His stance was relaxed, though he seemed to have a presence that made the air surrounding him electric.

"You couldn't possibly understand," he finally said quietly but firmly. "None of you would."

"Then help us understand," Rebecca urged. "Shutting us out won't help you."

Noah cast a glance at her, and in that brief instant, Rebecca felt she saw pain and doubt and vulnerability deposit themselves upon his face, only to be wiped away with that first heartbeat. "Help me?" came the bitter parody of repetition. "How many times have you said that, Rebecca? And how many times have you failed?"

Maria moved forward sharply. "We're not failing now. We're here, aren't we? We're trying to help."

Noah turned toward her, narrowing his glowing eyes. "Trying isn't enough. Not any longer."

"I acknowledge that I failed you, Noah, and I acknowledge that I have done you more harm than good. But if your plan is to destroy everything, know that you will—" Leonard had stepped a little forward, though obviously his legs were still trembling.

"I plan to end this cycle..." Noah lashed out, its impact hitting like a blade. "No more experiments, no more cloning, no more lies; all of that ends with me."

Leonard froze, eyes wide. **"You cannot mean that."**

Noah's expression grew darker. "Why not? Didn't you come here wanting to test my limits? You're about to find out."

The ground shook slightly, and Rebecca's heart sank as the air about Noah began to hum again. The light behind his eyes managed to shine faintly once more, giving even weirder shadows to the walls of the alley.

"Noah, I said stop!" Rebecca's voice broke. "This isn't the way."

Noah turned to her, calmly fierce; it was as though he were staring into infinity. "And what of the way that you would have me take, Rebecca? Tell me. What should I do? Stand back and let them come to overrun us? Allow themselves to break me, bone by bone, as they did their others?"

Rebecca's breath went deep, walling off her chest. "No, you fight. Not so. We can expose them to the truth of the world."

Maria snorted; a snarl of irritation fought its cocky launch. "The world doesn't want the truth, Rebecca. It seeks out a scapegoat. And right now, that's him."

Noah shifted his gaze to Maria, his eyes aglow and narrowing. "She's right," he said. "The world won't listen. They'll see me as a threat. And threats get eliminated."

"We said no! Not a threat. You're not a threat; you're… you're proof that we can be better."

An unreadable expression crossed Noah's face as he tilted his head. "Better. So that is what you think I am?"

Rebecca hesitated. "Yes," she finally said. "You're better than that."

A cold, quiet laugh escaped Noah. "You're wrong. I'm not better. I'm only the last."

The hum in the air got louder still, and the glow about Noah became brighter. Rebecca felt the heat building, radiating from him, the raw energy of his existence. The alley closed in further, shadows stretching and twisting, warped by the weight of his power.

Leonard stepped forward again, his voice trembling desperately. "Noah, please… don't do this. I didn't create you to destroy everything."

Noah turned towards Leon, his expression hardening. "You created me for nothing, Leonard. You made me because you could. You are afraid now of what I have become."

Leonard sagged under the weight of guilt, grief burrowing its talons into him. "I never wished this," he said softly. "I never wanted you to hate me."

Noah's eyes softened slightly, but his tone remained. "I don't hate you, Leonard. I pity you."

Rebecca's voice broke through, even stronger, despite the trembling of her hands. "Noah, if you do this, you will lose yourself. Whatever you think you'll protect will be gone."

Noah hesitated, the glow from around his eyes flickering. "Perhaps that is what needs to happen."

"No!" Rebecca stated stiffly. "You're more than this. You're more than what they made you to be. Don't let them win by transforming you into their weapon."

For the first time, Noah lingered at her a little longer than to look away; uncertainty seemed to grip him. But then the hum of power around him began to fade, the brilliance dulled, and softness crept into his expression.

"*What if it is too late?*" he asked, very quietly.

Rebecca stepped closer, heart pounding against her ribs. "It's not," she insisted. "It's never too late."

Before Noah spoke, a deafening explosion through the alley filled the ground with shocks, catapulting Rebecca downward. A second explosion followed a tad closer another Earth-shattering avalanche hit as departments from the first explosion shattered through the air around the ground.

A frightened Maria coughed. "*What the hell was that?*"

Rebecca cheered without sugar-coating. She wondered how she could get to work on this thing, Noah. She saw Keller's men; they were marching with raised arms.

"Noah!" she cried through the twisted scenes of possible doom.

The light around Noah blazed up, brighter than before. He stepped forward, blazing with luminescent eyes, as if burning down some oncoming soldiers. His voice rang above the smoke, unwavering, and powerful.

"Leave," he demanded. "Otherwise, regret will never be yours."

The soldiers hesitated; they held the guns with unsteady hands. As somebody barked an order, it got lost in the booming of yet another explosion. Noah raised a hand, and the air around them crackled with energy.

Rebecca's heart turned cold with what lay ahead. "Noah,X" she screamed, her voice tinged with ailment. "Don't!"

Noah turned toward her, eyes mixed with sorrow and evil determination. "I must, Rebecca," he murmured.

There lit up the alley with blinding rays, putting Rebecca's cry away; she felt the world around her collapse into a terrible ruckus.

The light pierced everything in its vicinity. For Rebecca, the world whirled on storms of burning energy, throbbing in her ears and filling her nostrils with the choking smell of smoke. She came down heavily, gasping for breath. For a moment, it occurred to her that this would be the end—body and mind pounding into inertness by Noah's unleashed might.

But then, there was silence.

Sudden, strange silence, as though the chaos had been swallowed whole. The brightness receded, leaving a dim and spectral glow to light the alley in muted details. Rebecca opened her eyes, blinking against the haze. Pain coursed through her, her hearing was blurry, and she just managed to catch a glimpse of the shape of someone standing erectly in the epicenter of devastation.

Noah.

He stood amid the ruins with eyes glowing ever so slightly, the lord of self-control, calm in a manner that was eerie. Around him lay Keller's men, wretchedly disposed of, with weapons broken, and bodies apparently lifeless. Energy still crackled quietly in the air and you could sense the ground scorched beneath him, the concrete spilling heat and cracked.

Rebecca's breath snagged in her throat; she propelled herself on her knees. "Noah," she whispered, voice trembling. "*What have you done?*"

Noah turned toward her, unreadable shadow play in him. The glow surrounding him pulsed faintly, like the heartbeat of raw power. "I did it that way because I gave them a choice," came Noah's unhurried tone. "They simply chose incorrectly."

Rebecca's chest constricted further as she pulled herself upright. "You didn't have to kill them."

Noah's stare never left hers, the crack beginning to show through in the control he exercised. "They would have killed you. All of you. I could not, would not let that happen."

Maria's voice snapped through the silence, its sharp timbre trembling. "At what cost, Noah? Look around you. You're becoming what they are afraid of."

There was the narrowing of those burning eyes again; now, the cooler tone dropped, perhaps to deepen a little. "And what is it they are exactly? Heroes? Or victims? They made this world, Maria. They created the fear. I am just... the result."

Leonard staggered forward, his face white as a sheet, shaking from head to toe. "Noah," he said, his voice cracking. "You don't have to do this. There's still time to make another choice."

Noah turned to him; his eyes glowing brighter. "Another choice?" he repeated, bitterness saturated in his voice. "The kind of choice you would give me? The kind of choice you gave to the others?"

Leonard's shoulders sagged, guilt and despair enshrined in the very texture of his face. "I was wrong," he said quietly. "I see that now. But this... this isn't the way to fix it."

A pall shadowed Noah's face; there was something infinitely pained about it. He retreated a mere step whilst the glow dimmed around him. "I'm not fixing it, I'm ending it," he said in a low voice.

Rebecca's heart raced as she took another small step forward. "You don't have to," she said with a strange trembling note in her voice. "You're not a mere result, Noah. You have a life of your own, above and beyond that, as you've shown us."

Noah hesitated again; the flickering light of his eyes dimmed slightly for a moment before a tremor shook the ground around them. The hum of energy increased.

"I don't think you understand," he said, voice rising in pitch. "You think it is just me. No, no; this is about all of them. The prototypes, the experiments—they're connected. I feel them, Rebecca. All of them."

Leonard's eyes widened. "You can feel them in the network," he said, an expression of awe and fear heavily etched in his voice.

He nodded. **"They're alive,"** he stated. "And they won't stop until I do."

Rebecca's heart raced; she compared him with the network of labs; the prototypes were still out there—he was connected to it. But what would it really mean to stop it? She thought about the prototypes, the ones that were produced and later abandoned, the vestiges of humanity on all of them.

"Noah," she said quietly. "If you destroy the networks, what happens to them? To the prototypes?"

Noah's gaze turned dark. "They'll be free from this. From what you made them."

"Or they'll die," she said, sounding more broken each second. "*Is this what you want? To be by yourself?*"

His glowing eyes flickered while pain passed across his face. "I've always been alone," he whispered. "This just makes it apparent."

The air grew unbearably tense, the roar of energy rising to a threshold. The glow around Noah brightened even more; the building of his power reached another peak. Rebecca held her breath, her heart racing as she started to comprehend what would happen.

"Noah, don't," Rebecca pleaded. "There is another way."

"There is no other way," was the quiet, steady response. "I'm sorry, Rebecca."

The light around him flared with an intensity that was blinding. She clasped her eyes shut; her heart completely broke as she called his name. The sound of her voice got swallowed by the roar of energy that shook the earth while his brilliance spread out to engulf everything.

Once again, all was silent in the alley under the dimness of the light. Rebecca blinked; vision blurred in trying to fathom what had just happened. The accursed breaths of energies were all but ceased. Leonard crouched on the ground, ashen-faced, hands shaking.

"Noah," Rebecca whispered, tears streaming down her face. "*Where is he?*"

Staggering slightly, Maria's voice quavered; "He is... gone."

A tightening in Rebecca's chest, her eyes gazing into the empty space Noah used to occupy. The weight of his absence bore down upon her like a load that was too heavy to bear. But, in the prolonged silence, she observed, almost a diaphanous glimmer lingering still in the air.

"He is not gone," murmured Rebecca quietly, a sweet cocktail of hope and dread in her voice. "Not entirely."

Chapter 12

The Last Experiment

The faint glow lingered in the air like some ghostly phantom, a reminder of Noah's overwhelming power. Rebecca gazed at it, while her heart reeled with unanswered questions. The alley was now eerily quiet, the air of anticipation stalking her, Maria, and Leonard laden with the stale energy of Noah's departed form of life-and the unexpressed dread between Rebecca, Maria, and Leonard.

"Come on! We cannot stay," Maria said, her voice sharp and trembling. "The Keller might retreat and regroup. And if that happens, we are dead."

Rebecca nodded but did not look away from the glowing embers in the air. "He is not gone," she said softly to herself. "He is still with us."

Leonard looked up from where he knelt on the ground, his face pale and drawn. "He's changed," he muttered. "He's no longer just a clone."

Her frustration boiling over, Maria screamed, "We have no time for this! If Noah's alive, great! But we need to move before Keller sends reinforcements."

Finally breaking her focus, Rebecca turned to Maria, her chest constricted. "True," she replied. "But we cannot just leave it behind." With her gesture, she pointed at the faint glow. "Whatever remains of him, we have to understand that."

Leonard staggered to his feet, his hands shaking. "The lab," he blurted out suddenly in that hoarse voice now permeated with a decided tone. "There are still some of the basic pieces of equipment at the backup facility. That may not be terribly much, but it could be enough."

Maria spun on him, her eyes raging. "*Enough for what? For another experiment? Haven't you done enough?*"

Leonard quailed, a flash of guilt slipping across his face. "You don't understand," he said very quietly. "If Noah is still connected to the network, then we're out of time. The system will adapt, and whatever is left of the prototypes will become unstable. If we do nothing now, this could get worse."

"Worse?" Maria echoed, dumbfounded. "How on earth does anything ever get worse?"

Rebecca stepped between them, voice firm. "Enough. If Leonard found a way to stop this, we have to take it. No more secrets. We move together. We survive together."

Maria scoffed but refrained from any other reply. Leonard nodded grimly: "Then let's move fast. It's not far to the facility, but we need to get there before Keller."

They made their way cautiously through the city, sticking to the small back alleys and deserted buildings. In the distance, fires burned, and muffled sounds from riots echoed-a pathetic testament to the enormity of loss. Rebecca's mind raced through the streets full of terror. Noah's powers grew stronger, more unpredictable. If they were unable to reach him, what might he become?

The backup facility was placed at the farthest edge of the industrial zone. Viewed from outside, it looked like an unassuming warehouse, its windows veiled in layers of darkness, the walls clad in graffiti. Yet as Leonard led them inside, Rebecca felt an uneasy chill- secrets flowed in this place.

The dimly lit interior hummed with dormant machines. Leonard walked with determination; his hands steady despite the tension. He clicked a few buttons on a terminal, and the buzzing of the room came alive, monitors illuminating the wall with tortured shadows.

"This is it," Leonard said, his voice steely. "What's left of the project."

Maria stilled, crossing her arms. "And the plan is...another clone? Another prototype?"

Leonard hesitated and glanced at Rebecca. "Not another prototype," he said softly. "A stabilizer."

Rebecca frowned. "**A stabilizer?** What-"

Leonard turned away, ruminating. In a solemn tone, he said, "Noah's connection to the network is unstable. He's not only connected to the prototypes-he's actually integrating himself into the system. Unless we stop this process, he...could unravel."

Rebecca's stomach knotted. "Unravel? What would that even mean?"

"It means he will lose whatever is left of his humanity," Leonard said. "And at that point, there'd be no going back."

Maria strode forward, her voice icy. "And I suppose you have the answer?"

Leonard hesitated. "Not yet. But if I can get some access from here to the network, maybe I could create something-something that can cut his connection without destroying him."

Rebecca felt her heart beat faster. "*And if it doesn't work?*"

Leonard's face darkened. "Then we lose him. For good."

The room went hollow with Leonard's last words. Rebecca was in turmoil, with sunrise thoughts of fear and determination rushing through her mind. Noah's radiating eyes, his even voice, the smile with which he had flickered her a glance before he disappeared in the light.

"Then we will try," she said rather determinedly. "If there is any chance of saving him, then we must take it."

Maria sighed, ripping her palm through her hair. "I am not doing it," she murmured. "Crazy it is, anyway. Come on, then, let us proceed to do this."

Leonard nodded; his face appeared firm. "I will need time to program the machine. And you two..."

There was a sudden blackout in the room since the system had switched off; all was related by Rebecca with her heart in her mouth when it was broken by

the crushing sound of heavy boots echoing across the building.

"They found us," Maria whispered, dread-stricken.

Her arms pooled up, taking for refuge of the hurting Maria. "Get your ass moving; now."

The light returned--first weak and dim, then brighter and stronger with every passing second. The brightness engulfed the room, thinning out to sprinkle eerie shadows over the walls, catching her breath.

"Noah," she whispered.

But it wasn't Noah.

Out of the shadows came a tall inhuman thing, narrow light with an alien but perverted glow. Rebecca's chest tightened as the real thing loomed in, and there thought came rushing through her mind.

A prototype.

Casts like twin beacons of glowing steel, the prototype's eyes spread light through the dark, bringing into relief an angular, unearthly form. Rebecca could find no voice within her throat as the silhouette stepped toward the faint light in the room. The figure moved with a kind of deliberate grace, almost mechanical yet terrifyingly human.

"Leonard," hissed Maria, trembling. "*What is that?*"

The figure went pale, voice barely audible. "That... is a prototype. But it wasn't meant to be activated."

The prototype turned its head as its beam eyes swept through the shadows across the room. Rebecca felt a shiver run down her spine as it zeroed in on her. The way it moved made her feel like it analyzed every one of her actions with contempt.

"Noah destroyed the others;" replied Rebecca, her voice blatantly trembling. "*How come this one is still functional?*"

Leonard's silence indicated horror on his features. He stepped carefully forward, his hands raised. "It's connected to the network," he practically whispered to himself. "It must have reactivated once Noah came in contact with the system."

Again, the prototype stepped forward, eyes flashing to settle on Leonard. The low hum of its energy cocktails filled the room, and the sound amplified as its movements quickened. Rebecca's heart raced, and she touched Leonard's arm to pull him back.

"Don't," Rebecca snapped. "You don't know what it's capable of."

Leonard shook his head; his gaze stayed locked onto the prototype. "It's not like Noah," he said. "It has no self-agency. It's acting on its programming."

"Of what programming?" snapped Maria, now backing away toward the nearest console.

Leonard hesitated; voice grim. "To protect the network."

Rebecca's stomach tumbled. "And now we are the threat to the network?"

The prototype's eyes flared bright with life. One hand lifted, and the hum grew like a swell in the room, crackling, small bits of energy laden in the air. Rebecca instinctively shoved Leonard behind her to stand out of view, her heart pounding.

"Run," she whispered almost under her breath. "Do it now."

The prototype moved almost faster than she could anticipate. It lunged, its glowing appendage cutting through the air like a sword. Maria snarled and dove aside, rolling behind a console, grabbing onto Leonard as Rebecca pulled her arm back toward the back side of the room.

The energy from the strike hit the wall, showering sparks and blackening a deep mark on the concrete. Rebecca nearly panicked; her thoughts whipped around her head seeking an escape route. Among equipment and downtime, the exits in the facility were too far away, and the prototype was much too fast.

"*Leonard, how do we kill it?*" Maria's voice came from somewhere near the console.

"I don't think we can," Leonard replied, his voice pressed low enough that it came from behind each other piece of equipment. "It might be networked. If we take it down, Noah can lose connection."

Rebecca clenched her fist, pent-up frustration shaking her anchor. "So now what? We wait for it to kill us?"

Leonard hesitated, his features transforming from shock into abject guilt. "I might... override something in its programming," Leonard did say, finally, licking his dry lips. "But I seriously need some time."

Maria peered from behind her cover, her fair face slightly pale but determined. "You do not have time, Leonard. The prototype is about to pull one of us apart."

Rebecca's heart was in her throat as she watched its glowing eyes turn toward Leonard. It moved with an eerie perfection, treading over fallen beams and bent iron like it was guided to him. Instinctively, Rebecca jumped away and got behind it to make herself fully visible.

"Hey!" she shouted, her voice shaky, but very loud. "Over here!"

The prototype froze, head tilting slightly. For a moment, it remained still, seemingly weighing the meaning of her actions. Then, it moved toward her, its energy flaring even brighter.

Rebecca felt her heart racing as she stepped back slowly, raising her hands. "Leonard do something!" she hollered.

"I am trying!" Leonard called back, madly slamming the keys on the console. "Give me a minute!"

The prototype lunged at them again. Its movements were almost too fast for the eye to follow. Rebecca threw herself to the ground as an energy-laden thing struck at her and her shoulder bled with terrible pain. She bit back a yelp and quickly scrambled to her feet as Maria pitched a metal tool against the prototyping unit.

"Look at me, you glowing freak!" yelled Maria in defiance.

Greatly interested in Maria, the proto-type's glowing eyes narrowed. Rebecca took this chance to grab a loose metal rod from the floor, clutching it tightly as she moved to put herself in front of the prototype.

The humming sound of energy in the air was growing relentless. The prototype now had flared its energy up. Rebecca gripped hard on the rod with her heart racing. She could not fight this thing-not really-but she could buy Leonard some time.

"Got it!" called Leonard suddenly, a note of urgency in his voice. "It's slowing the network down, but I must isolate its signal!"

The prototype paused for a moment, coming slightly undone. Rebecca swung the rod with all her might and clashed against the prototype arm, a wind of force altogether because of which the whole room vibrated; it took a faltering step back, and then its bright eyes started flickering.

Maria was quick. She grabbed hold of another piece of rubble and threw it at the prototype's head. "Leonard, hurry up!" she yelled.

"I'm almost there!" It was Leonard shouting into the room, his hands racing across the keyboard.

The prototype regained its cadence of motion-yanking towards Rebecca with radiating eyes glowing in intensity. A surging energy crackled around it, and a chill ran through Rebecca.

"Noah," she uttered, stammering. "If you hear me... help us."

The prototype lunged again. But now something seems to have altered. The glow in its eyes flickered, its movements faltering just as it was about to strike. The electric buzz in the room shifted-the air tension decided to shatter like a broken wire.

Leonard broke away from the astonishing silence with a voice that shouted, "I have overridden its commands! It's disconnecting from the network!"

The prototype became still, its luminous eyes dimming to a faint glow. Rebecca took a step back with a gasp as her entire chest bore down on air. The noises stopped. No more electric buzzing. Only the sound of machinery.

With her hands trembling, Maria took a careful step forward. "Is it... over?" she asked.

Rebecca nodded slowly. Her eyes did not leave the now-dormant prototype. "For now," she said quietly.

But when she turned to Leonard, her heart sank. The faint glow that had threaded in the air since the disappearance of Noah was gone.

The muffled growl of the computer dominated the setting, but silence with Rebecca, Maria, and Leonard was suffocating. The prototype was motionless, its eyes dim and devoid of life. Leonard dropped on a chair, his trembling hands against the console, its glow illuminating over his face like an indictment of some crime.

Shaking, with a tremble in her voice, Maria broke the silence, "What just happened? **Is it dead?**"

Leonard shook his head in disagreement. "Not dead, just disconnected." He pointed to the prototype. "I disconnected it from the network. The main systems in the frame are still operational. It's dormant."

Maria walked about inside the room in a fashion that clearly told that he was boiling with anger. "Dormant? So, what is going to happen when it comes back alive? Or when someone like Keller sends more of them? Here we are like sitting ducks."

Rebecca moved nearer, although quiet, her request urging yet firm, "What about Noah? If we disconnect the prototype, could he be disconnected from the network too?"

Leonard hesitated; his fingers stole toward the keyboard. "It's possible," he said, "The network was designed to be adaptive. If Noah's connection broke down, it either happened after this or would have forced him to adapt even beyond existing capability."

Rebecca's throat closed. "*Adapt? In what way?*"

Leonard gaze shot toward her, his dark aspect speaking for itself. "I do not know. But if he is alive and somehow connected, he is going to feel this. He would know what we have done."

Silence fell again upon the room, weighed down by Leonard's words. Rebecca's mind raced back into a flash of pictures of Noah—those habitats of glowing eyes, that power so welling inside him, and all that wretchedness hidden underneath! Would Noah have felt about the severance? What would he do thereafter? Treat it foe, **a betrayal?**

With arms crossed tightly over her chest, Maria stopped pacing. "We need to leave now," she commanded. "If Keller's forces have a sign on us here, we are as good as done for."

Turning to Leonard, Rebecca asked if it were ever possible to haul the equipment with them so they could work on the whole stabilizer somewhere safer.

Leonard hands flew over the keyboard, trembling. "I can take out some, but the main server is hardwired here in this control room. If it were to be removed, we'd lose all connection with the network."

Maria's hands went up in feigned acceptance. "So what? The network is already adapting. Staying here is not going to make any difference."

Leonard voice rose, expressing his frustration. "You don't get it! This isn't just about Noah anymore. The network is alive! It is learning. Once we leave this place, we've lost any chance whatsoever of stopping it."

Rebecca stepped between them, her voice steady despite the mounting tension. "We're not abandoning anything," she said. "But we can't stay here either. Leonard, if the network is learning, then so is Noah. If he is still connected, he might already be on his way here."

Leonard hesitated, his glance flying towards the dormant prototype. "If he comes back, it might be the only chance we have to stabilize him."

"And if he sees us as a threat?" Maria countered. "*What then?* He's already proven he's willing to destroy anything in his way."

Rebecca's heart ached at Maria's words, but she could not deny the truth in them. Noah was no longer the uncertain character she first knew; he was now something else-almost far more powerful and far less predictable.

"We've got to take that risk," Rebecca said at last. "Maybe we still have time, maybe there's still a way to save him."

The hum of the terminal had grown loud now, a faint warning tone cutting through the silence. Leonard's mouth fell open as he leapt to the screen, fingers dancing over the keyboard.

"What is it?" Rebecca yelled, her pulse racing now too.

Leonard's face went white. "The network," he said, in a whispery voice. "It is reacting to the severance. There's...a signal."

"A signal?" Maria echoed. "From where?"

Leonard pointed to the screen, urgently now. "From Noah."

Rebecca's breath caught as she leaned over the terminal, eyes darting over the data. The signal was erratic but forceful, a pulsing wave of energy that seemed to ripple across the network in front of them; a heartbeat-some steady, relentless, but gaining strength.

"*What does it mean?*" she asked, voice wavering near a whisper.

Leonard swallowed. "It means he's still connected. And he's trying to find us."

Maria's fear overshadowed her frustration. "You said the network was adapting. If Noah's part of it now, does that mean he's... controlling it?"

Leonard looked back at the screen; his finger glided over the keyboard. "Not controlling," he said slowly. "But influencing. The signal is being directed, like he's sending a message."

Rebecca's chest twisted when her eyes focused on the pulsing. "*What kind of message?*"

Leonard said nothing. Fingers raced back to the keyboard again, eyes narrowing and concentrating on the incoming signal. The humming on the terminal was louder now; the screen flickered with moving waves of data that almost seemed to gather into some kind of pattern.

Then the screen went dark.

"What the hell?!" Maria shouted, voice potentially reaching a pitch that could shatter glass.

Leonard's hands hovered over the keyboard, face pale. "The signal," he said; a whisper so soft they barely heard it. "It isn't coming from the network anymore."

Rebecca hung breathless in the air. "If that's the case, then where is it coming from?"

The glare came back.

Though it began faintly, akin to an isolated flame, it climbed down at great speed with every inch covered, illuminating the room with a frightful, pulsating light. Rebecca turned around very slowly; her handwritten note caught in her breath as she saw the source.

The eyes of the dormant prototype were once again glowing, their light fixated and even more fiery than before. The buzzing of humming intensifies in the air with energy radiating from the prototype-the static crackle-like.

Leonard almost tumbled back; his face clouded with fear. "That can't be," he whispered. "It's severed."

The prototype stepped in close, almost like a very slow but conscious entity. The glare in its eyes flared wider when it raised its hand, and the hum in the room reached deafening heights.

Rebecca gripped Leonard and pulled him toward the exit. "We have to get out of here!"

Maria was already moving, her voice sharp: "*What is happening?*"

Leonard's voice was breaking. "It's not the prototype. It's Noah! He's in control."

The prototype became active, its eyes focused on Rebecca, the heat of its energy bearing down as if it were filling the room. The sheer massiveness grew louder, and the floor started shaking beneath their feet.

"Noah!" Rebecca shouted, the sound breaking from her. "If you can hear me, stop this! Please!"

The prototype froze, its illuminated eyes flickering for a second. The hum in the air wormed for a moment, and Rebecca thought at that moment she had him.

And then the light flared bright, and the prototype lunged.

The prototype sprang forward, hand glimmering in the air like a blade. Rebecca had little time to throw herself flat against the floor as the heat of its energy burned the air a little above her. Maria grabbed a tool that was close to her, flinging it toward the prototype, and the impact rang like metal against the figure's chest, but the prototype did not flinch.

"Leonard!" Maria screamed, hysteria creeping into her voice. "Do something!"

Leonard dived for the console, twinkling fingers flying over the keys. "I am trying to shut it down!" he yelled, sweat pouring down his forehead. "It's an issue of connecting stronger now. It's not just the prototype. It's Noah."

Rebecca's heart began to race as she pulled herself up on her feet, eyes locked on the glowing figure. "Noah!" she shouted, her voice trembling, "If you can hear me, you need to stop this! This is not you!"

The prototype froze in its track and darkness was dancing in its glowing eye. For a second, the hum of blinding energy softens up in the air, and the tension snapped like a frail thread.

Rebecca attempted to edge forward, hands shaking. "Noah," she plead. "I know you are still in there. You don't have to do this. You don't have to hurt us."

The lighter glow in the prototype's eyes brightened, and for a moment, Rebecca thought she saw a flicker of a pause, a moment of indecision, a trace of humanity. Then the glow intensified, the hum increased, louder and more menacing than before.

"He's fighting for it," Leonard said strained and breaking himself on the console. "The network, it is trying to pull him back."

Cutting through the sounds, Maria said, "If the network's pulling him back, then sever it again! Shut it down!"

"I can't!" Leonard practically screamed in frustration. "I push and the bigger the signal gets. He's too connected!"

Indescribable terror filled Rebecca's heart when all the figure in front of them shifted to face Leonard, burning him with glowing intensity. And the next seconds charged up energy around them. It hit Rebecca that the prototype was going to strike.

"Leonard, move!" she screamed.

The prototype lost an outpouring of energy, shrieking through the room in a ripple like thunder. It went off like a gun, and Leonard swept to the side, narrowly escaping the blast while the console burst into showering sparks. Rebecca shielded her face from the heat, thinking fast for a way to stop the taunting figure ahead.

Maria grabbed her by the arm, pulling her toward the exit. "Fetch out of here!"

Rebecca shook her head with firm conviction over the chaos inside. "We can't leave him!"

"One way or another!" Maria screamed back. "Death could come if we stay!"

Rebecca flicked her glances between Maria and the childish dauntlessness of the prototype. She thought about Noah, his eyes aflame, the pain that wrapped his voice about him, the humanity that was still fluttering beneath the surface. She could not abandon him now. Or never.

The prototype struck again, its glowing hand making contact with the floor, sending cracks spidering through the concrete. Rebecca snatched up a piece of debris and held it tight as she stared at the figure.

"Noah!" she screamed, cracking. "This is not you! You are more than this!"

For an instant the prototype hesitated, jerking as its momentum faltered. The glowing in its eyes dimmed slightly, and the hum in the air softened further. Rebecca took a step closer, almost frozen in fear when she observed the faint hint of recognition appearing in its gaze.

"Come back," she said quietly, "you're not alone."

The prototype lowered its hand, the energy building up around it dissipating. Hope swelled in Rebecca's heart. But the hum grew again, now louder and weirder than before. Brilliant light shone from the prototype's eyes, and its form became rigid, its movements no longer reticent.

"He is losing control," Leonard breathed, "the network-it's taking over."

The prototype stepped forward and surged anew, quaking Rebecca's mind into furious thought about Noah, the connection he had to the network, and the decisions that had taken them here. There had to be a way to reach him. To claw through the chaos and bring him back to the person he once was.

Maria picked her arm again, desperation in her voice. "Rebecca, we have to go!"

"No," decisively said Rebecca. "If we start running now, we lose him forever."

"Do it!" Leonard shouted. "**God help you, hurry!** I can't hold the signal much longer!"

With shaking hands, Rebecca stepped forward. She looked at the glowing eyes of the prototype. "Noah," she called out, "I know you're in there. I know you can hear me."

The hum softened again, the glow in the prototype's eyes fluctuating. Rebecca moved forward with a heart that felt big and heavy. "You're not just network property," she said. "You're more than this. You're more than what Leonard made you. You're YOU."

The prototype froze, eyes glowing at hers. In that moment, there was stillness. The hum, energy, chaos. Tension broke in Rebecca's throat like the wave washing up on shore.

Then, the glow of the creature in the prototype's eyes went completely out, the figure crumpled lifelessly into the ground. Rebecca just stood there, panting, trying to assimilate it.

Leonard moved carefully toward the fallen prototype, his hands trembling with the task of checking the terminal. "The signal's gone," he said soberly. "He... disconnected."

Maria leaned against the wall, panting. "What does that mean? Is he... is Noah gone?"

Rebecca shook her head, a little sad but quite determined. "No," she said. "He's not gone. He's out there. But he's distancing himself. He doesn't trust us."

Leonard looked at her, guilt written all over his face. "And why should he?" he asked. "We have given him every reason to despise us."

Rebecca's heart sank at the sight of the dull prototype. The thin glow of light was fading from the room, leaving him with a grave, empty silence. She thought of Noah; the person he was; the power that was in his hands. Unless he was found very soon, he might be lost for good.

"We have to find him," she said, very firmly. "Before the network will."

Maria nodded quite reluctantly; her facial expression somber. "Then let's go. Because if he's still hooked in, Keller's people won't be far behind."

The warehouse lay unnaturally still, the noise from dormant machines and flickering monitors the only sound to disturb the silence. The lifeless prototype lay abandoned on the floor, its fiery eyes extinguished, but the tension in the air hung on like an unseen force. Rebecca felt that they were standing at the very edge of something great—and irreversible.

Leonard leaned against the console, each breath shallow, trembling fingers raised in the direction of the screen, where the data was to be read. "He severed himself," he repeated quietly. "Not just from the network-contingent-but from us."

Maria was furious. "*What does that mean?* Is he now a rogue? *Moved on to greener pastures?*"

Apprehensively, Leonard remained mute and whitish in the face. "He is evolving," he muttered. "He is becoming something other than what I ever accounted for."

Rebecca's heart clenched as she stepped closer to Leonard. "What does that mean, 'something else'? Is he still Noah? "

Leonard turned his gaze toward her, and she saw fear in his eyes. "I don't know," he said. "Whatever he is now is not bound by the limitations I gave him. He's rewriting himself, Rebecca. And if we don't stop him, he could become unstoppable."

Maria breathed sharply and ran a hand through her hair. "Unstoppable? That's great. And what's your brilliant plan for that, Leonard? Another experiment? Another question?"

Leonard flinched, a flash of guilt across his features. "I don't know," he said, his voice breaking. "But if we don't find him—if we don't reach him before the network does—he won't just be a threat to Keller's forces. He'll be a threat to everyone. "

Rebecca's heart raced as she stared at the seemingly lifeless shell of the prototype. She thought of Noah, the fire in those eyes, the power circulating within him, the anguish of that final message. This wasn't just evolution; this was a deep fall into the unknown, and the gap between him and her now felt like an abyss.

"We're not giving up on him," Rebecca said resolutely, a challenge in her voice. "There has to be some way back."

Maria frowned, crossing her arms tightly. "To what, Rebecca? He is not the same; you've seen it. He is... beyond us now."

Rebecca´s gaze hardened. "He's still Noah. And that is why, as long as there is a chance to reach him, we must try."

Leonard turned back to the console and worked with the keyboard. The screen flickered. On it were broken signals, the illuminations of data pulses expanded into a disorderly maze. Rebecca leaned closer, and as she recognized the shadow that the signals took, she gasped.

"What is going on?" she asked.

Leonard's demeanor turned grave. "It's him," he said. "His signal. He is still connected but not to the network."

Rebecca frowned. "Then what is he connected to?"

Leonard hesitated, his voice trembling. "I think, erm... he is building another network."

Maria's eyes widened. "*What? How is that even possible?*"

Leonard gestured towards the screen; his tone now urgent. "The prototypes...the data and energy are all still out there. It is tying them all together, building something new. Something that runs itself."

Rebecca felt sick. "What happens if he pulls it off?"

Leonard looked at her solemnly. "Then he won't need us. Or anyone else."

The hum in the room took another turn, suddenly kicking up in tempo and rhythm. Rebecca held her breath as that once-cold prototype twitched, an involuntary jerk of gigantic fingers. Maria stepped back and exclaimed, "*What the hell is going on?*"

Leonard's hands flew over the keyboard. Panic started to carve itself into his tone. "It's the signal—it's trying to reactivate the prototype."

Rebecca's pulse quickened. "But I thought you cut the connection."

"I did." Leonard's voice cracked. "But that wasn't a network. That's him."

The prototype twitched, and its eyes gave off a faint glow. Rebecca advanced, her trembling hands extended. "Noah, if you can hear me—stop whatever you're doing. **Please.**"

The prototype became perfectly still, its eyes dimmed again. The hum disappeared from the room. Heavy silence filled them all. Rebecca exhaled shakily; her heart thudded in her chest. "He still hears," she muttered.

"There is tension in Maria's voice. Or he is just teasing us," was Rebecca's answer.

Leonard peered at the screen; his face ghostly white. "We do have to get on with it. If he is going to build a network, he is going to need a little more than this prototype. He will require these other ones—if he didn't destroy them."

Rebecca regarded him, her voice resolute. "Then get moving—we need to find them before he does."

Maria shook her head, blatant frustration growing inside of her. "And what happens if we do find them? You really think he's going to let us stop him?"

Rebecca's chest tightened at the thought of Noah—the inflection of pain that had been in his voice, the humanity that had stayed behind the power. "I don't know," she admitted finally. "But we have to."

Leonard nodded; his expression resolved. "There is one more facility. It is remote, heavy in security; if there are prototypes still intact, that is where they would be."

Maria let out a deep sigh as her shoulders sagged away. "Perfect. Another death trap."

Rebecca put her hand on her shoulder. "We've survived all the way up to here. We cannot quit now."

Once again, the hum filled the room, faint but rising. Just as Rebecca began to turn to the prototype, her tell-tale breath caught. Even though the eyes of the prototype remained black and its body remained inert, the thrumming energy in the air brooked no argument whatsoever.

"He's close. He knows what we are about to do," Leonard spoke softer than a whisper.

Maria grabbed her bag, her voice laced with anger. "Then we better move before he decides to stop us!"

Rebecca nodded; her determination hardened. "Let's go."

They edged toward the door, the tension-ranked air in between them still more than severe. But by the time they reached the doorstep, Rebecca paused in the doorway still and turned her gaze back to the prototype. Just for a heartbeat, she thought she saw something—not an open eye, not life; just a whisper of illumination.

And, then she heard it.

A voice—quaint but unmistakably present—echoed through the air.

"You will not stop me."

Chapter 13

The Betrayal

Rebecca, Leonard, and Maria made their way down empty corridors, their energy drained from the dim glow of emergency lights in the facility. The silence around them was dense and heavy. Rebecca heard only the faintest echo of Noah's voice that sent a chill down her spine: **"You will not stop me."**

Maria turned her head to look over her shoulder as they walked. Her determination battled the fear right on her face. "We are walking into a trap," she scoffed. **"You do understand that, right?"**

Rebecca nodded, her heart racing. "We have no choice," she said. "Even the least chance of stopping this before it gets worse is worth it."

Leonard remained silent, staring at a small tablet. His brow knitted above the light screen that displayed a series of maps and schemata. "The prototypes at this facility were part of the earliest phase," he spoke conveyingly. "If intact, they should serve as the key for stabilizing Noah."

Maria scoffed. "Or it'll wake up and finish what the last one started."

Leonard failed to reply. Petty doubts showed in Rebecca when she glanced momentarily at Leonard's face, followed by unease that stirred up within. Stakes were at the highest, and every step further felt a gamble.

The three entered the main control room; it was a big hall filled with dormant consoles and a fine layer of dust on monitors. Leonard moved to the nearest terminal, his fingers flying over the keyboard. A faint hum rumbled from the room as the monitors lit up, showing ample data streams and several dizzying security feed images.

Maria leaned against the door frame; her arms crossed tightly. "How do we know Eliot isn't already here?" she probed. "He's always one step ahead of us."

Leonard tightened his jaw, cutting off his words. "Because Eliot doesn't care about stabilizing Noah. He only cares about destroying him."

Rebecca's stomach twisted. "*What do you mean?*"

Leonard hesitated, pausing his fingers over the keyboard. "Eliot has been watching this project for years," he murmured. "But he's not here to save anyone. **He wants control.**"

"What control? The prototypes? The labs?" Maria asked with her frown.

"The network," Leonard spoke quietly. "The whole system. If he can hack it, he can reprogram everything—clones, prototypes, even the way humanity sees itself."

Rebecca shuddered as an icy chill ran through her spine. "And you are only just figuring this out?"

Leonard's face darkened. "I always suspected there was something pending in his mind, but I didn't quite catch how far he would go. He has been working both sides-feeding the public's fears about clones while attempting to get closer to the network through us."

Maria narrowed her eyes. "So, you're saying Eliot's the mastermind behind all of this?"

Leonard met her gaze uneasily; his face was grave. "Arguable, yes. But more dangerous than we imagined."

Rebecca thought about the meaning of Leonard's words. Eliot was such a riddle from day one; ever charming, certainly quite resourceful-always two steps ahead. She would trust him once before, but was it ever that blind trust would feel so very tenuous-just like a thread, ready to snap at the slightest touch?

The buzz from the monitors grew harsh as Leonard brought up a series of security feeds. Rebecca nearly held her breath when she saw human figures-moving armed trained men, their faces obscured by helmets, sweeping through the facility's lower levels on the screens.

"Keller's forces," said Leonard, grimly. "They've broken through the perimeter."

Maria cursed softly. "Of course. *How much time do we have?*"

"Too little," he answered. "They will be here in a couple of minutes."

Rebecca's heart drummed loudly in her ears while she looked at Leonard. "What about the prototypes-are we going to get to them before they turn up?"

Leonard shook his head. "We don't have the assets to hold them off. Staying puts us in the crosshairs."

Maria pushed off the wall, raising her voice. "Then what is it-you use your cronies to run and pray Noah doesn't turn us into ashes?"

Leonard hesitated; his face turned pale. "There's one more course of action," he spoke almost too quietly. "But you're not gonna like it."

Before Leonard could elaborate, the heavy sound of marching echoed down the hallway. Rebecca turned her head just in time to see a very familiar figure step through the door. Eliot.

His presence was present and commanding; he scanned the entire group with a focused look. Whenever he is, he is always flanked by two armed men, guns at the ready. Feeling a sudden jolt of discomfort when Eliot gazed at her, Rebecca didn't have the slightest clue what he was expressing.

"Well," Eliot said smoothly, the calmness in his voice laced with an unseen threat, "looks like I'm right on schedule."

Maria stepped forward; her fists clenched. "*What are you doing here, Eliot? And who are your new chums?*"

It felt as if his smile never reached his eyes. "Insurance," was all he said. "I could not have Leonard take it in his hands, since he likes making... well... questionable decisions."

Leonard bristled; his tone harsh. "You're the last one to complain."

Eliot raised an eyebrow. "Nothing compared to you–a living weapon released to the world."

Rebecca stepped in the middle, her voice clipped, "Enough. What do you want, Eliot?"

Eliot's smile faded, and his expression hardened. "I want what is right for everyone," he stated. "And that means assuming command of the network before Noah can finish what he started."

Leonard's voice rose in volume. "**You mean control for yourself.**"

Eliot did not dispute this. "Someone has to do it. If Noah completes his network, humanity is finished. He will rewrite this world in his image, and you know it."

Rebecca's heart sank between the two. "What makes you any different?" she asked. "You're not stopping him; you're replacing him."

Eliot softened a bit in his gaze; for a moment, Rebecca actually saw an inkling of genuine concern in him. "I'm here to save what is left," he said somewhat softly. "Even if you are too blinded to see it."

The tension in the room was so thick it was near suffocating. The lines between friend and foe have blurred to the point where they almost faced each other. Rebecca's mind was racing, searching for answers in the limited choices she had. Leonard's desperation, Eliot's agenda, and the ever-increasing power of Noah-all were pieces of some string she'd yet to connect.

Eliot leaned in closer, equable yet commanding in his tone. "You must decide, Rebecca. Do you trust Leonard to fix this mess? Or do you trust me to end it?"

Rebecca's breath caught anew as the enormity of his words fell on her. She looked to Leonard. The determination in his once-pale face said he was ready for all; then he turned back to look at Eliot, whose semblance of calm cloaked an agitated soul.

The sounds of Keller's men were growing louder now, their footsteps thrumming through the facility like the large beating of a metronome, counting down toward destruction. Time was of the essence. One thing was clear to Rebecca: however, she decided to go about this, there would be no safe return.

Rebecca's brains whirled, her pulse pounding away at her as Eloit's words weighed on her like a ton of bricks. The hum of the consoles and the distant sounds of Keller's forces closing on her were a constant reminder that her time was running out. The desperate and regretful look on Leonard's pale face did not escape her notice; Eloit's calm demeanor cloaked a storm of motives Rebecca could not fully decipher.

"Rebecca," Eliot said, his voice steady but firm. "This isn't a conjuration. Leonard has already proved he can't control what he has created. You have seen what Noah is becoming. We've got to make a move or lose everything."

Ahead came Leonard, his voice faltering yet earnest. "And what's acting to you, Eliot? Does it mean killing everything? Taking control of the Network for yourself?"

Eliot's gaze narrowed. "Don't pretend to know me, Leonard. You have spent years hiding your failures behind layers of lies and ethics long ago, lost by your will. The difference is that I am willing to clean up the mess."

Rebecca raised her hand. Her voice rang out clear above the anger, "Stop! This isn't about you two! This is about Noah—everyone else caught up in this."

Eliot's gaze softened a little; his voice, however, remained firm. "You are right, Rebecca; it's not about us. It's about survival. You know as well as I do that Leonard's plan is the best of guesses. He wants to stabilize Noah? Fair enough. But what happens if it doesn't work? What if it makes him stronger?"

Leonard turned to Rebecca; his voice bent beneath a sense of urgency. "**It's not a gamble,**" he said. "I know that I have made mistakes—terrible ones. But Noah isn't beyond saving. He's still in there, Rebecca. I can reach him."

Rebecca's heart sank as she took in the expressions of both men. They both sincerely believed they were right. They each thought themselves the sole solution. They were equal in their delusions, mortal and equally binding, willing to be a cause for salvation—or its complete destruction.

"Rebecca," Maria finally whispered, "we don't have the time for this; Keller's forces are about to come. You have to make this call."

Rebecca's mind was in a whirl at the distant sound of Keller's boots growing closer. Every fiber of her being screamed at her to run away, to escape the chaos, to find some other way. But she knew that there was no way to escape. This was a matter of choice.

She turned to Eliot and asked, voice steady though her heart was in turmoil, "If we give you control of the network, what will happen then?"

Eliot's expression remained unmoved. "We will sever Noah's connection entirely. It will require precision and force, but it is the only way to keep him from going any further."

"And what happens to the prototypes?" Rebecca went on, pressing him. "What will they become?"

Eliot was silent for a moment, something flickering in his countenance---doubt, maybe. "The prototypes are part of the network," he stated at length. "If we sever Noah, they'll be neutralized."

Rebecca's stomach knotted. "Neutralized," she echoed. "You mean destroyed."

Eliot was silent. He didn't need to answer.

Leonard stepped out at that moment. His voice cracked slightly. "Rebecca, you've seen what this Noah is. More than a prototype. He's a person. Destroying the network will not just kill the prototypes; it will also obliterate everything that Noah is----all his choices, each piece of him that remains human."

Rebecca felt tears prick at her eyes as Leonard's words struck her hard. She thought of Noah, with his glowing eyes and the pain and power in his voice, and those brief moments when he had appeared almost like himself again. Was he in there still? Could he still be reached?

Maria grasped Rebecca's arm; her voice urgent. "Reb, we don't have time for this. Pick a side or we'll all die."

The clank of Keller's forces grew closer now, their boots reverberating through the corridor like thunder. Breath caught in Rebecca's throat between her two companions. Both Leonard and Eliot were looking at her, their eyes locked on her, poised to make their moves.

"A choose," Eliot started. "You know time's running out for you, Rebecca."

"I'm begging you," Leonard said softly. "Trust me. I will not let you fall."

Rebecca closed her eyes, visions racing crazily through her mind. She must choose. But whatever she did, she scarcely was allowed to turn back.

Opening her eyes, she made her choice.

Rebecca's Decision:

1. Trust Simmons: She turns to Simmons, sounding steady but resigned. "We can't risk losing everything. Do whatever you have to do."

2. Stand with Leonard: She moves forward, voice steady. "Noah deserves a chance. I will not let him be erased."

Before she could utter a word, a knock at the door shattered the control room silence. Gunfire and shouts filled the air. Keller's men rushed in, businesslike and menacing as they waved rifles before them.

Quickly, Eliot took a weapon from one of his men. Leonard froze, trembling. Rebecca stepped instinctively in front of him, heart palpitating, eyes locking on the advancing soldiers.

"Don't fire!" shouted one through gritted teeth. "**We want them alive.**"

Rebecca's mind was racing with thoughts about the soldiers slowly advancing. Eliot raised his weapon steady, deadly calm. Leonard slowly backed away towards the console, flitting between Rebecca and the monitors. Tension in the room was building to a climax.

And then it happened.

It was back.

This time, faint, a grating of air somewhere between a low din and a tremor; but this grew alarmingly, filling the room with a pulsing electric sensation. Rebecca's breath caught in her throat as the monitors flickered, the screens going on, whirring scattered data. But the glare was back again-this time from the console itself.

Leonard went pale. "It's him," he whispered.

Eliot's gaze flew back to the monitors, darkening with meaning. "No."

It grew louder still and brighter still, to the extent of just bursting into life, but with an unseen but palpable energy coursing through the air. The soldiers wavered, their guns shaking in their clutches, the room now rife with overwhelming presence.

The moment Rebecca comprehended what was ongoing, tension gripped her. Noah was not just watching.

He was here.

The atmosphere seemed electric; it became a very low and resonant signal whose vibrations passed through Rebecca's bones. The glow from the console intensified, casting jagged shadows on the walls and on the faces of the members gathered in opposition to the whole phenomenon. Rebecca stepped back in fear, her heart beating in sync with the monitors.

"Noah", she whispered, with a strangling voice.

Eliot raised his arm towards waiting Leonard. "Shut it down, whatever the hell that is!" he yelled.

Leonard held his fingers over the console, white-knuckled, drenched in The sweat. "I can't! It's not the network. It's him."

Maria swore under her breath and clenched her fists. "*Who do you mean by him? How can this even be?*"

Rebecca could hardly breathe as she recognized that the flickering streams of data on the monitors were beginning to take form-a pattern, a pulse, something that had its own life. This was not merely a signal. It was Noah: his presence filled the room like a storm cloud impossible to ignore.

Would-be soldiers shifted uneasily, facing their assault rifles with quivering hands. "Stand down! One and only one warning!" shrieked out, a certain quaking in their voice against all notions of bravery.

That hum became louder and brightened, a geyser of some alien force. A flicker on the monitors and suddenly, calm, cold, unmistakable-almost solid, a voice **"You will not stop me!"**

Rebecca's breathing ceased as the voice echoed around the room. It was Noah, almost, as the humanity in his voice before had drifted away, replaced by something messy and detached. This was almost an alien voice.

"Noah," she groaned, shaking, "if you are hearing me, please turn this off. We are not your enemies."

For a while the hum softened, and Rebecca thought she saw the flickering signal acknowledging what closed upon him via the monitors come alive. Then again, the glow, brightened chaotic, began when Noah began fighting."

Leonard brought his hands to the station with a crash; his voice cracked. "He isn't in control," he stated. "The network-it's fighting him. He's trying to reach us, but it's pulling him back."

Eliot's eyes narrowed; voice sharp. "And what happens if he wins? What happens if he takes over the network?"

Leonard did not respond. **He really didn't have to.**

The energy surged; the room shook crazily; a deafening roar now filled the air. Sparks flew out from the console, lights flickered like crazy. One of the soldiers fired a shot up at the ceiling, a sound that rent the stillness into pieces.

"Stop firing!" Eliot shouted, cutting through the noise. "Stop it or you will only make it worse!"

Rebecca turned to Leonard. So desperate now, she queried, "What do we do? How do we stop this?"

Leonard's trembling fingers flew across the console; his eyes darted from screen to screen. "I can stabilize the connection," he said. "But I need time."

The glow pulsing again, brighter now, made the air around Rebecca grow heavy while its pressure threatened to burst her. The monitors flickered once again, but Noah's voice came back, louder, more commanding.

"You betrayed me."

Rebecca's lungs clenched as the words hit her like a body blow. She stepped forward; her voice beseeching. "Noah, no! We didn't betray you. We're trying to save you."

The glow dimmed a notch lower; for a moment, the hum softened. Cautiously, Rebecca came closer, trembling hands falling away. "You're not alone," she insisted. "We're still here. I'm still here."

A ringing silence follows. Again, the glow brightened; the pulse dynamics flickered across the monitors. Noah's voice returned-cold and unyielding.

"You cannot help me."

Eliot leveled his gun-Cerberus had steeled its heart-"If he is beyond saving, then we finish this up now."

"No!" Rebecca was right in the way of the console and Eliot's gun. **"There's still a chance.** I know there is."

"I'm warning you, Rebecca," Eliot growled. "You don't know the penny worth of a thing here."

Rebecca's voice quivered, but she stood firm; she was resolute. "I understand better than you think. Noah isn't the enemy here. He fights the very same thing we do."

Maria caught Rebecca's arm and looked at her fiercely. "Please, Rebecca, think about this, If Eliot is right-about this-not he, and if he were gone-then you'd be risking everything."

Rebecca shook her head as the tears ran freely down her cheeks. "No. I know he isn't."

Leonard's words bustled through the noise, imperative. "I have stabilized the connection!" he shouted. "But it won't hold long."

The console glimmered erratically, and the glow of the screens shifted to a measured pulse. The rumbling vital in the air subsided, and for a brief moment, the room was almost tranquil.

"Noah," she finally said, a tremor of hope in her voice. "If you hear me, please come back to us."

Time stood still; the silence hung heavily like a deafening pitch. Rebecca's heart raced as she willed Noah to reply when she stared unblinkingly through the consoles. Slowly, the patterns began to unravel into something new-something recognizable.

A face.

Rebecca gasped when the picture began materializing. It was Noah, eyes aflame, staring back at her through the screen. For that blip, she thought she saw a flicker of the tormented, human person he used to be. But it was but an instant, for it vanished, rigor-washed from fidgety excitement to melancholy collision.

"You should have let me go," he spoke, the calmness about him finished with finality.

Then the elusive glow around the console blazed, and the room shook violently. Becca staggered back as sparks erupted from the wall screens, the patterns collapsing violently into mayhem. The whir resounded loudly, and the atmosphere crackled with energy.

"Noah!" Rebecca screamed, breaking down. "You can't do this!"

Too late.

The wall screens shattered, a power of light in the room exploding in a split-second flash. When the brilliance faded, the console dimmed into gloom, the whirring grew feeble, deader than before. Silence closed around them like the poor tautness of that which occurred.

Rebecca sank to her knees, choking with tears that streamed from the very depth of her heart. "He's gone," she said, somewhat breathlessly.

Leonard stepped forward, his white face split by terror. "No. No, he is not gone. He is everywhere."

Rebecca raised her head to Leonard, in sheer horror, her heart sinking as she made this discovery. Noah had not simply disappeared; he had become the network.

The silence that followed Noah's transition into the network was deafening, disturbed only by some arcing from the monitors, and the unsteady breathing of everyone in the room. Rebecca knelt on the floor with her trembling hands pressed against the cold tiles, her mind struggling to comprehend what had taken place.

"He is everywhere," Leonard repeated, his voice a thin, hollow echo of itself. He was staring at the dying console with the confidence of one who thought it was going to revive; suddenly, he appeared awfully pale after realizing something.

Maria rested against the wall, clasping her legs, trying to calm her heaving breast. "What the hell does that even mean?" she shouted with rising anger. "Everywhere? Please, tell me he's supposed to be something like... a god now?"

Leonard shook his head with a frown over his features. "Not a god! Not human either. Integrated. The network has already gone one step beyond responding to him. It has become him."

Rebecca pushed herself to her feet, feeling her legs shaking beneath her. "No," she whispered with a voice of quiet opposition. "He's not the network. He's still Noah, I swear."

Eliot's voice cut through the tension with the steel certainty that no one else had at that moment. "**Noah is not Noah anymore,**" he said, still grasping his weapon. "Whatever you think he was, it has been consumed. And now he is going to consume us."

Rebecca turned on Eliot, her chest tightening with his words. "You don't know that," she said, voice trembling but steady. "You do not understand what he may be thinking."

Eliot raised an eyebrow and shot her a cold look. "And you might? Because from where I stand, it looks like he has already chosen his side."

"He is fighting it," Rebecca rushed to say, raising her voice in desperation for the first time. "You saw him hesitate. You heard him listen. There is still a part of him that is human."

Eliot laughed bitterly. "**Human?** You actually believe that? Look around you, Rebecca. He's not hesitating; he's evolving, goddamn it! Either we kill him, or he wipes out everything that isn't in his perfect vision."

Leonard took a step farther. "To destroy him now would mean destabilizing the entire network. The fallout may kill half the city, if not worse."

With throbbing rage, rage that boiled in her insides, Maria hit her fist on the wall. "What do we do, Leonard?" she asked in a voice that was more a snarl than anything else. "Just sit here, wait till he rewrites the world?"

Leonard felt his hands shudder as he retied straps on his bag. "We have to reach the core," he decided. "We could trace back his signal, maybe with some luck, he can be brought back--or at least be kept in check."

Eliot stood in front of Leonard, jaw clenched, glaring very intently at him saying, "You don't bring things like this back. You take it out. Completely."

Rebecca stepped between them. Raising her voice, she declared, "Okay, you two! The one thing quarreling will never do is help make things right."

An uncomfortable hush fell over the room, the heavy weight of their decision being driven home. Rebecca, deep in thoughts about Noah, could still hear his voice in her ears. It was filled with muted pain and a surprisingly final note. "You betrayed me."

The facility lights pulsed a second before Rebecca's heart rose into her throat. A low, steady hum came back, reverberating through the walls. Maria's eyes widened as she reached for her weapon and shot a glance toward the door.

"Don't tell me that's him," she said, her voice quaking.

Leonard popped a look at the console and blanched. "Not just him," he predicted. "The whole network is activating. Every system, every prototype--it's all waking up."

Rebecca shivered from just such a chill. "Why now?"

Sharp, Eliot spoke up. "Because he knows we're here, and he will never allow us to leave."

The hum intensified and the ground began to see tumult. Rhythmically rocked, Rebecca fumbled and grabbed onto the console with all her strength. The lights blinked again as a shriek echoed throughout the surroundings like the shockwave of a distant explosion.

"*What was that?*" Maria shouted as panic crept into her tone.

Leonard's fingers flew over the keyboard with furrowed brows. "The prototypes," he confirmed. "He's using them."

Rebecca's chest felt tighter, "*How many of them?*"

Leonard turned, hesitating with his barely audible answer: "Too many."

Eliot gripped his weapon tightly; he was intent on the door. "Then we ain't got time for debate," he snapped. "We move now or never move."

The door of the control room burst wide open, and Rebecca bit back a gasp as the first prototype came through. The glowing eyes fired brilliantly, giving off a fluid yet unnatural body movement. Other shapes followed, dark and dimmed by the faint light of the hall.

Maria raised her weapon, her voice commanding. "I'll hold them off. Go out!"

Rebecca grasped Maria's arm, pleading with her. "You can't fight them alone!"

Maria shook her head, a thin smile on her lips. "I'm not planning to win. Just don't let this be for naught."

Before Rebecca could make an argument, Maria shoved her toward the opposite door. "Out!" she yelled.

Leonard caught Rebecca and dragged her toward the exit with a vice-like grip, despite his shaking hands. Eliot hesitated for a moment, his eyes darting between Maria and the prototypes. Then he turned and followed, his jaw clenenching.

The passages bore a torrent of sounds through which they ran, echoing their gunshots and the murmurs of the prototypes from behind. Rebecca felt her heart pounding; any and every thought was of Maria's sacrifice and the sense of revelation regarding what Noah had become.

Suddenly they came to a stop in front of a stairwell. Leonard breathed heavily. "We should split up," he said. "The core is way down underground, but the secondary access point is right above our heads. If we're going to contain him, we need two."

Rebecca's stomach rolled. "*Split up?* You are crazy. We're barely going to make it out alive."

Leonard locked gazes with her with determination in his eyes. "If we don't, we won't at all."

Eliot moved closer; the weapon was slung across his shoulder. "I'm going to take the upper level," he said. "Leonard, the core. Rebecca, you need to decide where you're going."

Rebecca's voice stilled; her throat tightened as she oscillated her gaze between them. In no time, the distant sounds of intimidation from prototypes loomed closer; the echo of their unending march filled the facility. She knew that there was no longer any time to argue, but the burden of a decision on her was far too overwhelming.

"Rebecca!" Leonard's booming voice rose up from the murmur of her thoughts. "Do it now!"

Rebecca, breathing a little sheepishly, finally made her choice. She turned toward.

The ground shook strongly within the facility; walls vibrated, pulsing a deep and resonant thrum, it seemed to Rebecca, from the very heart of the building. She staggered forward but caught herself against the railing of the staircase as an awful scream echoed down the length of the corridors. The prototypes were drawing nearer; their presence reminds them of the extent to which things had gone out of control.

"Rebecca, run!" Leonard shouted. His voice was filled with desperation. He was at the base of the stairwell, with his tablet in his hands and face wanting for fear and determination.

Eliot was halfway up the staircase, with his weapon slung over his shoulder. "Make your choice," he called back in a clipped voice. "But don't waste what little time we have."

Rebecca's heart raced as she gazed from one veneer to the other. Leonard was moving toward the core where Noah was most powerful, a gamble actually hoping and redeeming itself. Eliot? Climbing upstairs with cold determination, ruthlessly prepared to finish Noah-no cost was too high.

CEO metal scraping against the floor came nearer, so that decided for Rebecca.

"I'm with Leonard," she said. "We are going to the core."

Eliot halted on the stairs and glanced at her. No anger at all. No disappointment. Just a hint of something unspoken flickering. He turned back and walked off without another word.

Leonard took her by the arm and dragged her toward the lower levels. "No time to lose."

The stairway spiraled downward, where cold blue emergency lights threw broken shadows along the walls. The deeper they went, the heavier the air grew, as if the facility itself were alive and reacting to their presence. Rebecca's thoughts were racing as she followed Leonard, gasping for breath.

"Leonard," she finally blurted out, "if this doesn't work…"

"It'll work," he replied, his voice shaking but trying to be determined. "We don't have a plan B."

With every layer they went down, the hum from below got louder, resonating in Rebecca's chest. Ahead of them was a hallway filled with dormant machinery, coated thinly with dust. At the far end stood an enormous reinforced door, its edges lustrously glowing.

Leonard stood in front of that door, trembling, hands on the controls of his tablet. "This is it," he whispered. "The core. Noah's signal is strongest here."

Rebecca's heart sank as she stared at the door. "What will happen when we open it?"

There was a moment of hesitation before Leonard looked well into her eyes. "I honestly have no idea. But we have to isolate his signal somehow if we want to stabilize him—at least long enough to drag him out of the network."

Swallowing to maintain her composure, *'And if we can't?'*

That darkened Leonard's expression. "Then we'll know what we were dealing with."

The door opened with a hiss, spilling light into the corridor as the core chamber revealed itself to them. The room was huge, filled with towering servers whose dim lights flickered. At the center was a huge cylindrical structure with some surface energy rippling off of it. The air around it became almost overwhelming with space, making Rebecca vibrate through and through.

Leonard stepped ahead carefully; eyes trained nervously on the core. "Noah," he spoke softly, almost apprehensively. "If you can hear me, we're really here to help you."

Suddenly it was as if something shimmering within the core was trying to break the thrum of electric energies coursing through the room. A chill zipped down Rebecca's spine; a voice she recognized echoed through the chamber.

"Help?" Noah's voice echoed calm, detached, and defined equal power. "You think you can help me?"

Reality stood at Rebecca's feet. Barely cookie-crumbed, she stepped closer with trembling hands. "Noah," she broke, "**I mean it's me.** It's Rebecca. We don't want to hurt you."

The glow flared into life, and Noah was sharper now. "Hurt me? You already have! You made me! Used me! And now you're frightened of what I've evolved into!"

Leonard hurried to a nearby console, fingers rhythmically spinning hurriedly over the controls. "Noah," he said desperately, "you don't have to do this. These are not answers that the network is providing you with."

The hum grew intense; the energies spinning across the floor hummed like angry thunderheads, cautioning their presence. "The network never whispers anything in my ear," Noah said. "I am the network. And I see everything now."

Tears formed in Rebecca's eyes as she moved closer to the core. "No, please, you're way above this. You're more than the network."

The glow dimmed slightly, and for a few moments, the tension in the air eased as though the longest breath had materialized. Rebecca thought she had caught something momentarily—a flash of hesitation, pain, humanity. But that vanished quickly.

"I am much more," Noah said, a tone dead and resolute. "And I can't be stopped."

The ground shuddered terribly beneath, while the rows of computer servers on the walls blazed up into sparks of fire. She staggered on her feet and latched her palms onto the edge of the console for stability. Leonard screamed something cursed into that damned noise of roar.

"**Noah!**" Rebecca cried with a broken voice; "**You didn't have to do this!**"

The glow from the core flared in intensity so that it was unbearably bright. Rebecca shaded her eyes from the scalding heat and the brilliance of light that poured in through the room, as the hum raised into a peak pitch. She thought, obscured in the act, that she saw a silhouette, Noah, at the very heart of the core, his glowing eyes computed into hers.

Then for a pause in time.

"Things are not going to change, but you should have let me go," said Noah, his voice quiet with sorrow.

The core exploded, lighting everything up and amplifying the sound just enough to momentarily stun Rebecca and Leonard, throwing them to the ground. Everything faded into a chaotic blur, senses numb from shock, as the force of the blast rolled through the building.

When the glare dissipated, the core disappeared into the night. It was silence in the extreme.

Rebecca pushed herself to her knees, panting, as she strove to absorb and comprehend all that had happened. The chamber sat in silence, the servers lifeless, and the air felt acrid-hollow in face of such a loss.

"Noah," she whispered, tears rolling down her cheeks, "what have you done?"

Leonard, decoding what he had just witnessed, staggered up, his face pale and his hands tremoring. In a whisper bordering on terror, he said, "The signal-it's completely gone."

Rebecca looked at him, her heart sinking. "What do you mean by gone?"

Leonard's gaze met hers, a combination of fear and sorrow shooting from his mind as he said, "He's no longer in the network. He's everywhere."

Chapter 14

The Trial of Humanity

The courthouse dominated the square with an imposing marble facade under a gray sky that would oppress even the bravest heart. The street wore a coat of protest, mingled voices clashing in raspy chants and celestial shouts. The signs that waved above the crowd read, some "Clones Are People Too," while others said, **"Stop Playing God."** Tension simmered at seismic levels beneath very muddled emotions of fury, trepidation, and uncertainty.

Rebecca stood at the brink of the chaos; her heart sunk as her eyes followed the scene. The air was mixed with sweat and smoke, and the clamor of the crowd vibrated right into her chest. She turned to Leonard, who stood beside her, his pale countenance and trembling hands further igniting the sense of panic.

"They're putting them on trial," Rebecca let out in disbelief. "Like some criminals!"

Leonard nodded, gazing at the courthouse steps. "It's not just a trial," he shot back quietly. "*It's a show.* A show to prove that clones are less of human. That they do not have some deserving rights."

Maria joined shortly, with her heavy expression. "Then what about Noah?" she asked. "What is he going to do on this?"

Rebecca shook her head and walked a few steps back. "I don't know," she admitted. "But he will not keep silent. Not this time."

It was tense inside the courthouse as well. The grand chamber was filled with spectators, reporters, and officials buzzing sporadically within lofty ceilings. In the middle of the room stood a single defendant, a young clone with eerie perfection on her features, expression oscillating between abject fear and grim defiance. She was the real deal, and a living reminder of the stakes with lives hanging in the balance.

The judge entered, his robe sweeping along; he made his way to the head of the chamber. The murmurs grew quiet, bringing the proceedings into heavy silence. The prosecutor stood, sharp-eyed and with steel-like tones.

"Your Honor," he began officially, "today we must answer a very basic question: **what does it mean to be human?"**

As the words of the prosecutor were uttered, Rebecca's stomach twisted and turned inside as they sliced sharply into the air. At the end, they condemned the clones as products, assets, and less than human.

Then, the defense raised her voice that filled the room with energy.

"Your Honor," the loud voice struck, unshaken, "this trial is not about science or ethics. It's about fear: fear of changes, fear of progress, and the fear of the unknown. These clones facing you are not machines; they are people. And it's high time we started treating them like it."

The courtroom was all a cacophony of arguments and counterarguments while emotions wavered from the spectators. Rebecca had her fists clenched at the sight before her as her heart went out to the frail clone standing at the center.

Leonard leaned closer and lowered his voice. "He's present," he delivered, with those words sending chills down her spine.

Rebecca looked to him with her breath catching. "Noah?"

Leonard nodded. "Not in body. In spirit. Watching, listening, waiting."

The drama was interrupted when, before Rebecca could say anything, the lights in the courtroom moonlit. A quiet hum penetrated the air and grew greater with each instant. Gasp and whispers quivered through the audience as the monitors along the walls blinked and came to life, lighting up then ablaze with ghastly light.

The impotent judge pounded the bench with the gavel. "What does that mean?"

For a single erring second, static buzzed on the screen, pulsed audible for a moment and then there appeared Noah.

He was staring down at them from the screens with golden glowing eyes; an overwhelming presence despite his absence in the flesh. The courtroom fell silent, the tension thick, almost suffocating.

"Noah," the judge stammered, "*what did you mean by all this intrusion?*"

Noah's calm and resonant voice filled the courtroom: "This trial is only a farce. While you debate the humanity of my kind, not even one among you condemns your own."

Rebecca gasped; those words echoed through the chamber. She could physically feel the weight of this being, the force of his voice. Time stood still for that audience; eyes glued to the screens as Noah continued.

"You made us, you know. Not out of kindness or necessity. Out of greed. You wanted to play god, and now you fear the consequences."

The prosecutor shot up, sharp-voiced: "Your Honor, this is an unauthorized interruption! I demand suspension of the proceedings because of this interference!"

Noah shifted his gaze to the prosecutor, his glowing eyes narrowing. "**You demand?**" said he, cold amusement lending mockery to his words. "You who profit from the suffering of others? Your demands are worth nothing."

The prosecutor went rigid, his face going pale. The defense attorney moved there, speaking calmly. "Noah," she said. "You have something to share. Speak. But know that the trial is not merely about you; it's about us all."

Noah's gaze softened, and for a moment, Rebecca thought she saw a flicker of the person he had been. But his next words shattered any hope of reconciliation.

"This trial is not about justice; **it is about survival**. If you cannot see this, you are already lost."

Suddenly, the monitors went blank; their hum faded to silence. The room stood frozen, Noah's words hanging heavy in the air. Rebecca felt tears well up in her eyes as she looked over at Leonard, her chest tight with emotion.

"What does he mean?" she whispered. "This whole survival thing! What is he planning?"

Leonard shook his head, his face pallid. "I don't know. But one thing is for sure, we are running out of time."

The court was a tumultuous tide of gasps, apprehensive mumurs, reverberations of Noah's words still lingering in midair like a storm cloud.

The prosecutor, visibly shaken, whispered furiously to his team. The judge sat stiff, gavel in hand, but remained somewhat fragile in spirit because Noah's presence had, as it were, considerably weakened the very foundation of trial proceedings.

Rebecca couldn't move. She stood still in the gallery, mind racing. Calm and purposeful, Noah's voice was tinged with the raging furor necessarily imposed on her by the depth of anger and disappointment that seemed to chill her to the bone. His enigmatic forewarning rang in her ear: "This isn't about justice. It's about survival."

Maria leaned close, her voice low and urgent. "What does he mean, survival? **Is he threatening us?** "

Rebecca shook her head slowly and said, in a quivering voice, "I don't believe it's a threat. I think it's a ... prediction."

Leonard stepped forward with a look of pallor on his face. "He's testing us," he said. "How we react to the trial isn't just concerning the clones; it's about humanity."

The judge rapped his gavel with a shaky hand and shouted for order. "No theatrics in this court!" the judge proclaimed, though it seemed that even his voice was on the ragged edge of brimming. "We shall resume once we regain control of this hall."

The prosecutor rose, a trace of steadiness adorning his countenance. "Your Honor, this proves what we've been arguing all along," he said, pointing toward the now-dark monitors. "The clones-and Noah-whatever he has become-are not like us. They pose a threat to our society, our values, our existence."

A white fury seared into Rebecca's heart as she listened to that, growing hotter by the minute. She wanted to shout, to argue, to scream for the prosecutor to see the humanity in the young clone still so silently standing in the center of the room. But the defense attorney spoke first.

"Your Honor," she began, a steady ping of sharpness threaded in her voice, "this sort of thing doesn't prove the clones are a danger-at all. If there is a point to be made, it is that they are desperate-desperate for recognition, for equality, for the right to live without fear. They are called threats because fighting for their lives is what they have to do. What would you do in their place?"

The prosecutor opened his mouth to respond, but before he could speak, once again the lights flickered around the room. Gasps rushed like waves through the spectators as the hum returned-low and ominous, charging the air full of tension.

Rebecca felt her pulse quicken as she then turned to Leonard. **"He's back,"** she whispered.

Leonard fixed his grim gaze to the monitors above. "No," came his quiet response. "This is ... something else."

With that, the courtroom doors swung wide open to reveal a group of heavily armed soldiers standing outside, obfuscated by full face helmets. Chaos erupted in the crowd, the spectators shouting and scrambling as the soldiers took their positions around the room.

"You all will remain seated!" sounded out the supervisor soldier through the speaker of her helmet. "This has become a matter of national security."

Rebecca's heart sank as soon as she comprehended what was happening. This had nothing to do with justice; it was a fight for control. The trial, the debates, the chance to prove the clones' humanity were fading fast.

The defense attorney stepped forward. Her expression was defiant. **"You have no authority here,"** she said, her voice cutting through the chaos. "This is a court of law, not a battlefield."

The lead soldier turned to her; arms folded to conceal the sense of poignancy overtaking him. "Law means nothing if we lose the battle for survival," he said flatly. **"The trial is over."**

Rebecca felt her heart stop as the soldiers began their advance on the defendant, the teenaged clone who stood frozen in the center of the room. Wide-eyed with fear, her eyes darted toward the gallery until they caught Rebecca's for the briefest of moments.

"No," Rebecca whispered, moving over the gallery railing before her mind decided.

She flew through the air, hitting the floor with a shuddering halt. Gasps followed her as she placed herself between the clone and the soldiers with fingers spanning out toward them.

"Stop!" Rebecca shouted, voice shaking yet resolute. "She hasn't done anything wrong!"

Not allowing the surprise to hinder his action, the lead soldier raised his gun and glared at her through his face visor. "Step aside," he commanded. "This does not concern you."

"**This concerns us all!**" snapped back Rebecca. "This is not justice; this is an execution!"

The defense attorney stepped up slowly. Her voice cut crisp through. "You're proving their point-you're treating her as less than human-as if her life didn't matter."

Tension in the air blended with a now-louder hum, all transposed with a nearing pulse. Rebecca turned toward the monitors just at the instant they suddenly flickered back to life. Noah was back-his glare so concentrated that the intensity dimmed voices in the courtroom.

"**Enough,**" he intoned, with a rich bass that quaked through the whole chamber.

Time suddenly froze for the soldiers. Each soldier suddenly halted, appearing to stand as though chained by an unseen force. The tension on the room felt interjected and driven with a rising pulse beating like a heart.

Noah's gaze roamed around the chamber; he had occupied Rebecca's heart with the gold. "You think you're going to silence us with force. You cannot delete who we are."

The lead soldier fought back against the unseen force, giving a tremulous roar. "You are proving you are a threat! This is why you will never be human!"

The expression on Noah's face turned dark, and the pulse of the air quickened. His icy sharp voice, "What does it mean to be human?" asked. "Your capacity for violence? Your destruction of what you fear? If that is humanity, then I want no part of it."

Rebecca's breath caught as Noah's words pierced through the chaos and stunned the courtroom into silence. The pulse slowed; the hum softened as Noah's glowing eyes focused on her.

"Rebecca," and his voice is quieter now. "You wanted to help me. Now's your chance. Choose."

The monitors went dark, and the hum died away. The soldiers stood straight now, weapons lowered and confused, having been freed of Noah's hold. The tension in the room was unbearable, as if Noah's command weighed on everyone in the courtroom.

Rebecca turned toward Leonard; her heart tight. "What did he mean?" she asked in an incredulously low voice. "What choice?"

Leonard was pale, and his voice was almost a whisper. "He made us choose. To see if we're worth saving - or destroying."

The courtroom lay suspended like the battlefield it was-the soldiers had become statues; weapons were clenched in their grip but rested downward. Their power, only moments ago, had crumbled against the unseen hand that had gripped them. Audience members were frozen, eyes wide with fear, awe, and confusion. And within all this, Despite all this, Rebecca felt Noah's words weigh down upon her now, all but daring her to make a choice that she felt too unworthy to make now.

As Leonard edged closer toward her, deathly pale, hands shaking. "He's watching," he whispered. "Each move. Each word. We are all now part of his trial."

Rebecca was suddenly breathless. **"Trial?"** she asked, every word trembling from a mouth she found hard to open. "What kind of trial is that?"

Leonard did a quick glance toward the soldiers and then toward the still-frightened clone, standing at the center of the room. "He's testing us," Leonard said. "To see if we will have compassion-or destroy ourselves trying to conquer what we don't understand."

With a low sharp tone, Maria appeared behind them. "Then he already knows the answer; just look around you. This place is a powder keg."

Suddenly, the judge's voice cut through the air, quavering but loud enough to steal the attention of all. "This court adjourns," he said, banging his gavel with hollow finality. "All parties must vacate this place until further notice."

A pandemonium broke loose: reporters screaming their questions in a frenzy, while cameras broke out into light flares, creating a scene of some sort-the soldiers in similar ill-reputed act pushing to regain control of the chamber. Audience members were rushing in all directions towards the exits. The murmur is now blending into one continuous deafening roar, accompanied by cries. Rebecca felt Maria's grip on her, elbowing her to go toward the gallery.

"Come on. Let's get out of here... before things get worse."

Rebecca stood her ground, her gaze pinned on the girl in the middle of the room. The girl had not moved; her wide eyes were moving between the soldiers and the crowd. All of a sudden, Rebecca felt a tightening in her chest. She could not leave her here, not like this.

"Wait!" Rebecca managed to shake off from Maria's grip. "She needs us."

Leonard grabbed her other arm, an urgency in his voice. "Rebecca, the girl is lost to you. If we stay, there won't be anyone left for tomorrow's sunrise. We will be arrested, or worse, shot on sight."

"No," Rebecca said, adamantly. "I'm not going to leave her to them."

The leading soldier stepped up, raised his weapon again, his voice booming through the melee with the aid of a speaker on his helmet. "The clone is to be taken into custody immediately. Anyone falling foul of these orders will face unpleasant consequences."

Rebecca's heart raced as she formed a blockade with her body and the girls. "You want to try and take her away, huh? Are you ready to live through this? She's a child!" she shouted.

The soldier hesitated; his gun wavered. "Stand aside. I-I-I simply could." "

Maria cursed under her breath. "Rebecca C'mere! You're gonna get us killed!"

"This is blind!" she thought. "Sophia, calm down. I won't let go of you," she cooed to her, undeterred by the commotion.

Sophia opened her lips, and in a frightened whisper, she said softly, "Sophia."

Rebecca felt a flood of warmth churn within her. "Sophia, darling baby, I'm going to save you. But will you trust me, huh?"

Sophia reluctantly nodded her head, as if hope had finished off fear. Rebecca has now turned around to the soldiers with renewed strength. "She's coming with me."

Faintness of the hum came back but was ever present and disturbed the air in a warning. The lights started flickering; Rebecca otherwise felt a kind of pressure as if a dark force were sitting on the roof of the room above her. Leonard stepped back as his eyes widened, his voice quivering.

"He's here again."

The many displays flared to life, their screens now buzzing with static sounds. The soldiers froze, their weapons dropping, the buzz growing in sound. Noah's voice was surging through the chambers. His voice was calm and yet dogmatic.

"You disappoint me," he said.

With her gaze turning to the screens, Rebecca held her breath, her chest tightening painfully. "Noah, please," she begged, "this isn't the way."

Static resolved into a conglomeration range of blue. And much of Noah zoomed in, with blazing irises fixing on Rebecca, his expression unreadable. "You seek justice, but your actions betray you," he shot through;-." "You defend one, while abandoning the rest! Your idea of humanity!"

Rebecca's heart sank, and she struggled to find her voice. "I am trying," she said. "I am trying to make things right."

Noah softened a little, but he spoke with coldness. "Right?" he said. "There is not going to be any right in a world full of such inequality. You talk of justice while you leave so many behind."

The humming in the air deepened in resonance, and Rebecca trembled on her feet. The soldier's heads turned nervously in all directions each losing confidence with each passing second as the gallery began to move in panic, frantically trying to get out of the room.

Leonard pulled at Rebecca's arm, speaking urgently. "He's pushing us, wanting to see if we will break."

Turning onto Leonard, Rebecca heaved, and her chest filled with fright as she asked, "What do we do?"

"It's simple: we will not let him win," said Leonard. His eyes were very grim indeed.

Noah's voice had raised a little and resounded through the chamber. "If you cannot rise above your fear, then you do not deserve to survive."

The glow on the monitors brightened suddenly, and the atmosphere in the room felt unbearably intense. Rebecca felt her knees weaken as though something heavy was trying to press her down onto the ground. She turned to watch Sophia, who stood stunned in panic and trembling beneath the invisible force.

"Noah!" Rebecca screamed, her voice breaking. "Stop this! **You're hurting her!**"

The glow dimmed a little, and Noah's voice became casual. "Hurting her?" He questioned. "You really don't know what pain is; believe me, soon you will."

The hum disappeared suddenly, plunging a room into a weird silence. The monitors had gone dark, and the glow disappeared completely. Soldiers hesitated, but their guns continued to be pointed still and in place.

Rebecca inhaled shakily as her heart quickened. "What just happened?" she asked Leonard, her voice trembling.

Leonard had a pale face and an awed countenance as he replied, "He was testing us... And I think we failed."

Maria stepped even closer. "Failed how? What does he want from us?" Her voice had taken on edge.

Leonard shook his head while still staring at the dark monitors. "I don't know," he said slowly. "But it's not over yet."

Rebecca looked down at Sophia with horror. "We gotta get her out of here."

Maria gave a stark fallback nod. "All right, but be quick about it. This isn't going to end well."

The cold night air hit Rebecca in a rude shock as she and the group rushed out of the courthouse, where Sophia clung to her arm. The streets were filled with the sound of distant protests and police sirens; chaos cloaked the tension sparking between them. Every step felt like chance. Every shadow was a lurking threat.

Maria pulled Rebecca aside into a narrow alley, her sharp eyes flittering all across the streets that were shadowed. "Oh no. This place is going to burst into flames in a matter of seconds," she said, trying to keep her voice low and neutral. "We've got to disappear. Now."

Leonard gasped, almost disbelieving and clutching his tablet against his chest. "He's still watching," he finally said. "He never stops watching."

Rebecca crouched beside Sofia, her hands on the girl's trembling shoulders. Whatever else was happening, it could wait for just a moment. Looking into Sofia's wide, tear-streaked, fear-and-confusion-blurred face, Rebecca whispered, "Sofia, we are going to get you out of here safe, all right? You just have to be quiet and stick with us. Can you do that?"

Sofia nodded slowly and tightly clung with both of her small hands-on Rebecca's sleeves, almost about to tug them off. "W-why is he doing this?" she barely mouthed the words.

Rebecca's chest gripped tighter. "I don't know," she said. "But I promise you we're going to shield you."

Sweeping her glance back to the courthouse, Maria ground her jaw. "Time slips," she said. "The soldiers will scour these streets for us any moment."

Leonard started tapping on his tablet frantically, his breathing light and cautious. "The signal's spiking," he breathed, shaky. "He's activating something."

Rebecca frowned; clenching her stomach. "*What d'you mean activating? What's he doing?*"

Leonard hesitated, his eyes glued to the screen. "I don't know yet," he said. "But whatever it is, it can't be good."

Maria took Leonard by the arm, frustration boiling over in her. "Less chatter more motion!" she snapped. "We need a safe house and five minutes ago!"

Rebecca stood and hoisted Sofia to her feet again. "The old subway tunnels," she exclaimed while her thoughts slipped through her mind. "They're abandoned and off the grid—he can't track us in there."

Maria raised an eyebrow but said nothing. "Fine. Let's move."

Gently, they navigated their way through the narrow alleys, the air already buzzing with tension all over the city. The protests were loud now, the cries of the crowd mixed with the distant thrum of helicopters and the occasional pop of tear gas canisters. Rebecca's heart pounded as she kept one hand on Sophia and her eyes constantly searched in every shadow and corner.

At a rusted grate leading into the subterranean tunnels, warped and jagged metal, Maria lifted it open with a grunt and waved them inside. "Hurry," she hissed.

Rebecca popped Sophia through the narrow opening, the girl slipping easily into shadow. The man with the tablet was next, his fingers holding it tightly as if it were on the verge of disappearing, and Maria was last, her weapon drawn as she scanned the alley one last time.

The tunnels were cold and damp, smelling of rust and decay; Rebecca flicked on her flashlight, the beam searing through the dark. Sophia was right next to her, clenching into her side.

"I feel it," Leonard said, his voice fracturing the silence with a tremor of unease. "He's here," he said, eyes glued on the faint flicker of his tablet screen.

Rebecca stopped, and her breath became shallow. "Noah? In the tunnels?" she enquired.

Leonard shook his head. "Not in the flesh; it's just that he's here everywhere. Apparently, the network and his reach into machines are nothing compared to the way he's now using the city itself."

Maria cursed under her breath. "So, we're hiding from a ghost?" she asked. "A ghost that can be anywhere and everywhere at any time. What a fantastic idea."

Rebecca ignored her and focused on Leonard. "What do we do now?" she pressed. "How do we stop him?"

Finally, there was a seconds-long pause for indecision before he spoke. "We don't," he said, his face turning white, and his voice sounded strained. "We talk to him."

Maria froze in place and narrowed her eyes at him. "What do you want to say to the man who just turned a courtroom into his very own stage?" she said incredulously. "Have you lost your mind?"

Leonard held her gaze, and his look now was grim. "He's not just a man anymore," he replied. "If we don't dare reach him right now, then nothing at all will be left to save."

Distant machinery slightly sent throbbing courses through the tunnel walls. Rebecca squeezed Sophia's hand and turned to Leonard. "So how are we going to talk to him?"

Leonard's fingers moved quicky across the tablet, and for a moment, his breath grew audibly rapid. "There is a relay point close by," he said. "An old terminal from the prototype network. It's offline, but if I can get it going, it may allow for a direct connection."

Maria threw her hands in the air. "And what if he fries us the moment we connect? That sounds pretty likely, right?"

Rebecca quickly turned to Maria, a sense of finality in her voice. "If we don't try, we've lost our last chance."

Maria simply stared at her for a moment, then let out a huge exasperated sigh. "Fine," she muttered. "But if he so much as twitches, I'm shutting him down for good."

The relay point was a rusted terminal embedded in the wall of a small alcove. Leonard got down on one knee and fetched tools and wires from his bag to restore power. The hum in the air grew louder, and Rebecca felt a shiver run through her.

Sophia tugged at her sleeve, her voice cracking. "*Is he mad at us?*" she whimpered.

Rebecca came down to her level, brushing a strand of hair from her face. "He's not mad, my dear," she said very softly, "just scared like the rest of us."

With a crackle, the power was restored to the terminal. Fizzling and buzzing, the screen flickered to life. Leonard drew back, a bag of fear gathering on his face. "It's ready."

Rebecca inhaled deeply; it felt to her as if a thousand butterflies were fighting for the space in her heart. She took a step forward so that she was in front of the screen and looked straight at it. "Noah," she said, her breath steady as a rock despite the paralyzing fear in her chest. "It's me. It's Rebecca."

The screen ferns and sets into kinematic flail, static filling the air. And then a figure slowly appeared: blue glowing eyes staring back at her, his expression inscrutable.

"Rebecca," Noah said, the voice resonating throughout the tunnel. "You shouldn't have come."

The light of the terminal lit up the little alcove, causing shadows to fall sharply across the walls. Noah appeared before the screen, his eyes aglow, piercing through the dusk. The air throbbing around her made Rebecca very hard to breathe.

"You shouldn't have come..." The voice of Noah was calm yet deadly serious, the finality unmentioned.

Rebecca took a precipitous step forward, her heart pounding. "Noah," her voice was barely a whisper before taking a steadier tone. "We're not here to hurt you; we come to understand."

His expression unreadable, Noah remarked, "Understand? What is there to understand? You made your choice."

"Those words stopped cold in the air of her throat." I-I don't know what you mean. Please bear in mind, we are trying. Not having given you up!"

"No," Noah added, with a flicker of his eyes now brightening, "it isn't me you need to save. It's yourselves."

Leonard stepped forward, his hands shaking as he clutched the tablet tightly. "Noah," he rushed, "you are more powerful than we dared to imagine. Even this will kill you. This isn't you! This is the network. It is perverting your thoughts, your purpose."

Noah's gaze shifted to Leonard, and with it came an intensity. "Pervert?" he intoned, icy. "Do you think that I don't know what I am? You're the one who made me, Leonard. You gave me this power. Now, you're afraid of it!"

Leonard turned like a butcher balled meat. Guilt was painted all over his face. "I've made mistakes," he croaked. "Terrible mistakes. But it doesn't have to end like this."

Noah only inclined his head slightly, as if to give Leonard's words a little thought. "**The end?**" He said with some softness to his tone. "That's what it already is."

The tunnel began to quake violently, dust and debris falling down from its ceiling. Maria seized her weapon, voice clipped as she asked, "*What is he doing?*"

Leonard's eyes veered toward the terminal, and the color drained from his face. "He's destabilizing the grid," he spoke. "If he goes through with it, the entire city could go."

Rebecca turned to the now dangerously thinking Noah and breathed out in panic. "Noah, stop! You're going to destroy everything!"

Noah's glowing eyes caught Rebecca's. His expression hardened. "Sometimes, destruction is vital for rebirth," he said. "You taught me that."

Rebecca shook her head, tears streaked over her face. "No, Noah. That's not you. You're better. You're beyond that."

For just a moment, Noah's expression softened, and Rebecca thought she saw the flicker of the person who had been. Yet it was gone, almost as quickly as it appeared.

"**You still don't understand,**" he said. "This is not about me. It's about you. About all of you."

The terminal's glow became blinding, and Rebecca felt a hum begin to drown the air. Leonard was frantically trying on his tablet, fingers racing across the screen. "I can shut off the terminal," he said, "but I need more time."

"We don't have time!" Maria screamed. Her eyes darted back to the walls, beginning to tremble. "If he brings this place down, we're finished."

Rebecca stepped up to the terminal. Her voice climbed with urgency. "Noah, please! If you want to help us, if you want to save Charlotte, stop. Let us talk. Let us set this right together."

Noah gazed back at her. The intensity in his glowing eyes flickered and danced. "You really think you can fix this?" he asked quietly. "You can't fix what you don't understand."

The terminal dimmed slightly, the tremors stopped, and silence washed over. Rebecca's heart raced as she watched Noah, hoping for any window into humanity.

"Noah," she worded quietly, "you are not alone. We are right here."

Noah said nothing, not for a while. Then, his gaze slid to Sophia, trembling behind Rebecca and holding on to her jacket with small hands. His glowing eyes softened a little.

"Her," he said. "She is the key."

Rebecca's breath caught. "Sophia?" she exhaled. "What do you mean?"

Calm but adamant, Noah said, "She has the answer to your question. The question you've been too afraid to ask."

Leonard interjected, his voice cracking. "What are you talking about, Noah?"

Noah's glowing eyes met Leonard's, and he lowered his voice, mellow with quiet power. "What it means to be human."

Before any of them could react, the screen in the terminal went dark, losing its glow entirely. The mechanical hum ceased, and the tunnel was plunged into haunting silence. With sudden dread in her heart, Rebecca turned to Leonard.

"What happened?" she asked, trembling.

Leonard gazed at the terminal darkened, his skin pale. "He disconnected," he said, "but he's still there. He's... waiting."

At that moment, Maria broke through the eerie silence with a voice so sharp it could rip. "Waiting for what?"

Rebecca turned to Sophia, who was staring at the terminal with wide, fearful eyes. Kneeling down, she placed her hands tenderly on the girl's shoulders. "Sophia," she said soothingly, "what does he mean? What is he waiting for?"

Sophia shook her head and tears welled in her eyes. "I don't know," she said, her voice barely above a whisper, "but it makes me feel scared."

Rebecca hugged Sophia closer, a bunch of frantic thoughts racing around in her. Noah's caution sprung in her head, icy cold in its simplicity: "She is indeed the key."

Chapter 15

The Vanishing

Despite its peacefulness, silence was occasionally interrupted by drips of water making echoes from a distance. The faint light of the terminal had vanished away, plunging the small crowd into darkness. Rebecca hugged Sophia tightly, hearing her own heart thumping loudly, trying to absorb Noah's last words.

"She's the key."

Leonard's trembling fingers hovered over his tablet, occasionally shaking the light from the dark screen. "He is gone," he said, a hush escaping through quivering lips. "The signal...it's just gone."

Maria leaned against the cold wall; weapon down but still held in her grip. "Gone? What are you talking about?" she irritatedly asked. "You said he was everywhere."

Leonard shook his head and went pale. He murmured: "I don't know. It's like he... erased himself. There's nothing. No trace. No signal."

Rebecca slowly pulled away from Sophia and then squatted down to look the little girl in the face. "Sophia," she whispered, "are you really sure you don't know what Noah meant? Why did he say you were the key?"

Sophia's fearful eyes, rimmed with tears, looked at Rebecca with despair. "I don't know," she stammered helplessly. "I'm just... me."

Maria let out a sharp breath, letting the frustration surface. "Well, wonderful," she summarized, pacing the small space. "A disappearing super-clone, a kid whom he thinks holds the answers, and a city falling apart above our heads. What happens next, the sky does a nose-dive?"

Leonard avoided facing her ways and buried his field of vision into the tablet, racing through it to find any sign of Noah. His voice, barely a whisper, held urgency: "This doesn't make sense... He was under connection with everything-the guy who couldn't possibly disappear."

Rebecca was rising, her heart engulfed at that moment. "Maybe he's not disappeared," she mused shakily in voice. "Maybe he just waits. Watching."

Maria finally confronted her, narrowed eyes. **"Waiting for what?"** she asked. "We already know what happens: obliterate everything on his path."

Leonard looked up, his gaze matching Rebecca's. "Or maybe he's just testing us," he said, "to see what we'll do without him.

"Noah was the greatest hope yet the greatest danger to them all," Leonard said, his voice heavy with the weight of the words. Everyone seemed trapped under the pressure of incoming screaming of Rebecca now leaning against the wall and braincircling with horror and uncertainty whatsoever. The questions, now recently left behind in that house by Noah, were landmines waiting for the unappeased-to-explode moment.

"What if this is what he wanted from the start?" Rebecca said in a near-whisper. "*For us to question everything?* "

Maria said with a sneer, "That's assuming that he has some master plan. For all we know, he's just stalling us."

Leonard frowned as he gripped his tablet more tightly. "No," he said. "Noah's not erratic. He's this calculating guy. Every move he made was calculated."

Rebecca looked at Sophia, who was small and huddling against the wall. "Then what's the next move?" she asked. "What does he want from us?"

There was a faint, faraway humming sound, and it chilled the spirits of the group. Leonard froze, and his eyes darted back to his tablet. "That's impossible," he whispered. "The signal-it's coming back."

Maria tightened her grip on her weapon and surveyed the dark corridor. "Where is it coming from?" she demanded.

Leonard hesitated, his voice now trembling. "I feel everything in pieces, as if he, in fragments, is springing from everywhere in the system."

Rebecca felt her pulse speed up. "Is **he attempting to reconstitute?**"

Leonard shook his head. "I don't know," he admitted. "But if so, it's beyond what I've ever known."

The hum grew louder, some vibration washing through vaulted stone. The hairs bristled at the back of Rebecca's neck, for suddenly there was a vibrating energy in the very air inside the tunnel. She turned, her voice suddenly tense. "*What do we do?*"

Leonard hesitated, his face in shadow. "We find him," he said. "Or at least, what's left of him."

Sophia practically tugged Rebecca off her feet in her eagerness. "What if he doesn't want to be found?" she asked shyly.

Rebecca lowered herself, brushing the tangle of Sophia's hair off her face. "Why do you think so?" asked Rebecca gently.

Sophia shifted. "Perhaps he's... frightened," she breathed. "Frightened of what we will do."

Rebecca was completely taken aback by what the girl said. She shot a glance at Leonard, who gazed at Sophia with a bewildered and simultaneously amazed expression. "How do you know this?" he asked in a faltering voice.

Sophia paused before shaking her head and crocheted her fingers so tightly into the edge of the jacket that it looked painful and winced. "No one told me," she said. "I just feel it."

Maria stepped closer, sounding skeptical. "What do you mean, 'feel it'?"

Leonard turned his gaze toward the tablet, some glow from the device illuminating his frowning forehead. "If Noah is still somewhere in this network," he goes on, "it's possible Sophia has some sort of... connection to him. It could also be termed a residual link."

Sophia gasped. "A link?" she asked. "*Does that mean she can sense him?*"

Leonard nodded slowly. "Possibly. If Noah sees her as the key, she may be tied to him more closely than we realize."

Sophia looked up at Rebecca, terror reflecting in her eyes. "Does that mean he will find me?" she asked.

Rebecca hugged Sophia protectively. "If he does, then we'll protect you. That's a promise."

The hum is gone as quickly as it had begun, leaving the tunnel drearily silent. Leonard stared into his tablet, shaking fingers. "It's gone again," he said, quiet.

Maria pressed her back against the wall; her frustration practically showed. "This is insane," she exclaimed. "We're chasing a ghost."

Rebecca jumped to her feet; her determination to find this man tightened. "He's not a ghost," she countered. "He's still out there. And we're going to find him."

Leonard nodded; his expression full of willpower. "If we get together the pieces of the signal," he then said, "perhaps we will figure out where he has gone—what he is planning."

Maria shook her head. The skepticism on her face bore through. "What if he doesn't want to be found? Then what?"

Rebecca met Maria's gaze; her tone steady. "Then we will make him listen."

The tunnel stretched ahead, dark and ominous, seeming to hum with some invisible energy. Every step with Noah's disappearance weighed down like a heavy yoke on their shoulders. Rebecca kept Sophia close, the light from her flashlight searching the shadows.

Leonard had his tablet fused with his fingers in wild, dancing motions. "There's a pattern to the pieces," he murmured mostly to himself. "Not random. He... is leaving... breadcrumbs."

Rebecca turned to him, her heart racing. "**Breadcrumbs?** You mean he's leading us somewhere?"

His pale face nodded in the affirmative. "Or he wants us to think he is. Either way, it is a purposeful move."

Maria nearly crushed her weapon in tightness. Her voice was razor-sharp: "Or it's a trap. We're walking straight into his game."

Rebecca felt a chill. "If it is a trap, what can we do? If we do not follow, we will never know what he's planning."

Maria exhaled sharply; irritation visible. "Okay, fine. But don't say I didn't warn you when it all goes to hell."

They plunged into the chambers deeper, the air turning ever cooler after every step. They could hear the faint drone of sound from somewhere, radiating as a heartbeat into the walls. The flashlight flickered, and invariably, she clutched Sophia's hand tightly.

Sophia suddenly stopped, eyes wide and fixed on the darkness. "He's close," she whispered, voice quailing.

Rebecca crouched beside her, heart hammering. "What do you mean close? **Can you see him?**"

Sophia shook her head, trembling. "I can't see him," she said. "I... feel him. He's like all around us."

Leonard lifted his head from the tablet grimly. "She is right," he said. "The signal lay much higher. It's no more fragments; it is coalescing."

Maria cursed under her breath and cast her gaze into the depths of the shadow. "I don't like this," she said. "I feel like we are being watched."

The hum became deafening, the vibrations vibrating fiercely within the walls. Rebecca's pulse raced as they approached the door, which was constructed of rusting metal and had edges just beginning to glow faintly. Leonard halted before the door, shaking and staring at the glow.

"This is it," he said in a hushed voice. "The signal gets the strongest here."

Rebecca crept in somewhat closer. "Is he behind the door?"

Leonard was hesitant; so softly, she could barely hear him. "I don't know," he said. "But whatever's behind there? It's connected to him."

Maria readied her gun, rigidly standing with a few inches' width of it. "Let's get this over with."

Leonard touched the door panel, and his voice waved. It creaked before opening, revealing a small chamber bathed in an eerie blue light. In the center stood a cylindrical artefact covered with a thrumming energy. The hum became deafening.

Rebecca hurried inside but kept her eyes on the device. "*What is that?*" she asked.

Leonard stepped in behind her with crazy eyes fixed on the glowing cylinder. "It's a relay," he said. "It was an advanced node in the prototype network. But it has... been changed."

Maria trained her weapon at the door and, now near it, went on. "Changed how?"

Leonard was shaking even now. "This thing is not just relaying the signal. It's amplifying it."

Rebecca's heart-leaping breath caught in her throat as she got to the device. The energy was suffocating. This hot green mass absolutely teased and restrained her with a tightening grip. She swung back to Leonard and demanded breathlessly, "*Can we shut it down? Can we?* "

Leonard shook his head. "If we do shut it down—then we lose the signal for good. Noah?"

"*Why would that be a bad thing?* " Maria scoffed.

"Because he is still in there," Rebecca snapped. "I know he is."

Sophia stepped in with wide open eyes fixed at the device. "He's not in there," she said softly. "He's... above it. Around it."

Rebecca frowned, and her heart pounded. "Sophia, what do you mean by that?"

Sophia clutched herself and trembled just a little. "He's everywhere," she said. "But he isn't whole. He is... searching."

Leonard's fingers were dancing over his tablet as a frown creased his forehead. "She's right. This—this is a broken signal. It's like he's trying to put himself back together."

Rebecca turned back to the device, her mind racing with possibilities. "If he's trying to reconstruct himself, then why is he trying to lead us here?"

Leonard hesitated, looking to Sophia. "Maybe this is not about us," he said lowly. "Maybe this is about her."

Sophia winced, her small hands gripping Rebecca's jacket. "Why me?" she whispered.

Before anyone could answer, there was a blinding flare of light from the device, and the hum gave way to a terrible roar. Rebecca stumbled, shouting an instinctive warning to Sophia, stumbling backward, but the bright room blazed bright and the air crackled with energy. The massive presence flickered before their eyes, vibrating through their bodies.

"Noah!" yelled Rebecca, cracking her voice. "Stop this! Please! If you can hear me!"

Slowly, the light softened; the hum followed, but the hall fell silent for one heavy moment like the breaking of a spider's thin strand.

And then, a voice.

"You should not have come."

The light came together in the center of the room in a lightsome swirl. Recognition almost stole her breath—the figure was Noah. His eyes were bright as embers, and on the whole, his face showed cold remoteness.

"Noah," Rebecca said, anxiety edging into her voice, "we're here to help you."

Noah tilted his head slightly, surveying the group. "Help? You still don't get it. It was never about me."

Rebecca took a careful step toward him, feeling her heart racing. "Then what is it about?" asked Rebecca. "Why are you doing this?"

Noah's eyes drifted to Sophia. His expression softened somewhat. "Her," he said. "She is the beginning. And the end."

In the very embrace of the bright chamber, Noah stood swayingly, his very presence both commanding and ambiguous. The pulsating hum which rippled in the air felt calmed now, replaced by an echoing soft, yet rhythmic thud emanating from within him. Rebecca just couldn't keep her eyes off him-he looked like he'd ever looked, yet he was totally unrecognizable; someone both at home and strange.

"Her," Noah said again, letting his glowing eyes shift toward Sophia. "She is the very beginning. And the end."

Sophia clutched Rebecca even tighter, her small hands shaking. "I do not get it," she whispered. "**Why me?**"

Rebecca stepped in front of Sophia, her heart pounding in her chest. "Noah, if you want something from her, then you will have to get through me."

Noah tilted his head. "Protective," he was almost saying to himself. "You still believe that you can save her from what is coming."

Maria cut in angrily, shamelessly bold in her tone. "Enough with the riddles," she said, stepping forward, weapon raised. "*What do you plan to do, Noah? What drama? Why bring us here?*"

Noah's glowing eyes flared to Maria, his expression growing hard. "Still clinging to the old ways," he said, voice bitter cold. "Your weapons, your fear-they're not enough to save you."

Maria tightened her grip on the weapon. "Maybe not," she said, her voice unwavering, "but we'll see about that if you threaten any one of us."

Rebecca raised a hand, voice shaky but firm. "Maria, stand down."

Maria hesitated; eyes locked on Noah. "Are you really going to reason with him?" she demanded. "You saw what he did in the courtroom. He is playing games."

"Noah is not playing games," Rebecca replied. Her eyes bored into him. "He is trying to tell us something."

Noah's gaze dwelled on Rebecca, and for a moment, his expression softened. "You've always been different," he said, "willing to listen when others would destroy."

Rebecca stepped toward him. Her chest constricted. "I'm listening now," she whispered demurely. "But you have to show me, Noah. Why is Sophia so important to you?"

The glow about Noah pulsed weakly. His glowing eyes flickered. "Because she is what you so dearly fear," he said. "And what you must have."

Rebecca gasped. "*What does that mean?*"

Then Noah's gaze turned to Sophia once more and his voice lowered, almost adrenaline-filled. "She is the testament," he said. "The testament that man's greatest fear of the unknown is its finitude and yet its major chance to come back."

Leonard stepped forward, trembling as his fingers clutched his tablet. "Noah," he said, unsteady and with insecurity in his voice, "if Sophia's proof, then why not tell us so? Why leave us in such ignorance?"

Noah steeled up, and the glow around him blazed with intensity. "Because you wouldn't listen," he answered firmly. "You never listen until it's too late."

The hum reverberated louder, vibrating through the walls. Rebecca felt a chill run down her spine with a shift of energy through the chapel and rising tension.

"Noah," she called quickly, "you don't have to do this. You don't have to go down that road. We can work together to solve it."

Noah's glowing eyes fastened to hers, and just for a moment, that flicker of humanity she once caught returned. "**Together?**" he said, voice sorrowful. "You still don't understand. I'm no longer one of you."

The hum grew louder and the light of the chamber flared. Maria stepped back, readied her weapon again. "Rebecca, this is going bad real fast," she said. "Let's go, now."

Sophia tugged at Rebecca's sleeve. Her voice trembled. "I don't want him to go," she said. "He... he's sad."

Rebecca's heart ached as she looked at Noah, the glowing figure suspended and charged with energy. "Noah," she said softly, "you don't have to go at this alone. By whatever name you're afraid, whatever it is that you're trying to fix-we can help you with that."

Noah eyes remained on her, and the energy in the room stood still for one moment. "Help me?" he said, his voice low. "You can't even help yourselves."

The ground below vibrating like a waking beast, the vibrations intensified into a pitch to deafen. Leonard scrambled at his tablet; his voice frantic. "The energy levels are going to peak," he said, panic rising in his voice. "He's destabilizing the node!"

Rebecca turned to Noah, a pang of desperation in her voice. "Noah, stop! Do you have any idea that if you destroy this, **you destroy yourself?**"

The glow faded briefly from Noah's fiery eyes, and, in a voice barely audible, he managed to whisper, "I was never destined to last, but she will."

Sophia grasped Rebecca tightly while riding out a wave of tears. "Don't go," she said in a low whisper. "Please don't go."

Noah looked at Sophia and said, "You are tougher than you acknowledge. They will need you even though they do not comprehend."

A blaze of light filled the chamber; energy went to the brink of bursting forth. Rebecca felt it shake her through her very composing molecules and fell to the ground. In the worst of moments, she forestalled the beam to cloak Sophia in the warmth of her back, practically uncanny. The hum merged with all with a trailing edge to crescendo into a force wave.

Then-nothing.

Opening her eyes, Rebecca breathed heavily and took stock of the chamber; the glow was gone, the hum silent. The cylindrical device was dark and cold in the center of the room. Noah was gone.

Leonard managed to get to his feet, his face white. "He's gone," he said, with a distant tone. **"The signal is gone."**

Tears welled into the corners of Rebecca's eyes as she looked at the empty place where Noah had been standing. "No!" she whispers. "He's not gone. He's still out there."

And Maria was there, helping Rebecca get on her feet. Her sympathy was clouded. "If he is out there, then what the hell is he waiting for?"

She had never seen a great deal of evidence to call evidence. The tunnel ceiling was puncuated every now and then by the echoing drip-drop of water tumbling into a seemingly incongruous puddle at their feet. She stood motionless, eyes fastened on the darkened cylinder that had encamped Noah moments before. That hiss was gone; the energy had ebbed, the muddy resettlement of meanings attached to his words continued to linger like a weighty shadow.

Sophia held Rebecca by her sleeve; her voice trembled while the tears bred in her baja. "**Is he coming back?**" she asked, her eyes wide with the shine of tears.

Rebecca knelt, looking into the terrified gaze of the little girl with her heart in her mouth. "I don't know," she said gently. "But we will work it out. I will promise you that."

Leonard's trembling fingers hovered over the tablet, whose screen glimmered slightly in the low light. "The signal's completely gone," he said hollowly. "No remnants. No residual energy. It's like…he erased himself."

Maria leaned against the wall; her expression dark. "So that's it? He just disappears after this? That's a big one for him!"

Rebecca shook her head, her mind racing. "No," she said firmly. "This isn't the end. This is the start of something else."

Leonard's brows drew together with a frown as his gaze was glued to his tablet. "But why bring us here?" he whispered. "Why all the clues, the warnings, the…display? If he wanted to disappear, why not just…do it?"

Rebecca rose, her mind drawn into a whirl. "Because he's not done. Whatever he is up to, this was just the first step."

Maria narrowed her eyes at Leonard, her tone biting now. "*What is the first step toward?* Blowing up the rest of the city? Turning Sophia into…whatever he thinks she ought to be?"

Sophia broke at Maria's words and a protective hand was placed on her shoulder by Rebecca. "Maria, stop!" she said with authority. "This is not her fault."

Maria threw up her hands, frustration spilling over. "I'm not blaming her!" she cried. "But you can't pretend that, like an elephant standing in the middle of a saloon, the rest of us are just supposed to will it away. Noah thinks she's the result of something. If we don't figure out what that something is, we're dead in the water."

Leonard kept tapping away madly at his tablet as his unease deepened. "There's more," he said, "the relay. It wasn't just amplifying his signal-it was transmitting it. Somewhere far outside the city."

Rebecca turned in alarm, pulse racing. *"Where?"*

Leonard hesitated, his fingers dancing across the tapped screen. "I'm not sure. The coordinates are shattered. But it's monolithic-a hub or a central node."

Maria frowned. "So, he's not just hiding. He's really building something."

Rebecca's heart began to race as the pieces of the greater puzzle came together. Noah's arcane words, his relates to Sophia, the obscurity in whatlers; each corresponded with the larger plan they could not yet comprehend.

Sophia approached the cylinder. She was a small girl, but her presence suddenly made it seem colossal. "He's still out there," she murmured. "I can feel him."

Rebecca turned to Sophia, awash in mixed reactions. "What do you feel, Sophia?" she asked softly. *"Can you tell us?"*

After a moment, Sophia looked nervous. "It feels like... he's waiting," she went on. "But not for us. For something else."

Leonard's gaze flew now toward Sophia, his voice trembling. "Something else? Something like what?"

Sophia shook her head, her eyes expressing doubt. "I don't know. But it's huge. And it's coming."

Maria cursed under her breath and tightened her grip around her weapon. "Fabulous," she said. "More vague warnings from the kid. Just what we needed."

There was a slight tremor beneath them, and a sudden surge of data sent Leonard's tablet buzzing furiously. His eyes were wide-open as he glanced over the screen. "A spike," he said. "A tremendous surge occurring across the network. It's not localized: it's everywhere."

Rebecca came closer, favoring all of that with rising dread. "*What does that mean?* Is it Noah?"

Leonard's face turned pale. "I don't think so," he said. "It's... bigger than him."

A coldness seemed to sweep through the room, a sweaty ill feeling coming up. Maria cast them around with a sharp voice. "And bigger how?"

Leonard hesitated before saying, almost in a whisper, "Like the whole network is waking up."

Sophia stepped back from the cylinder, grasping Rebecca's jacket with very small fingers. "It's happening," she whispered. "He said it would ever happen."

Rebecca knelt down to get a better look. "Sophia, what's he said? What's happening?"

Sophia's eyes were shining with tears. "He said... we weren't ready. That we'll have to prove ourselves."

Rebecca's stomach turned as she looked to Leonard. "Prove ourselves to what?"

Leon's hands trembled above his screen. "To the system," he said. "To everything he... has created. It's sort of a test."

Maria's frustrations broke free. "A test? For us to do what? To survive? To redeem ourselves? This is ludicrous!"

Rebecca stood strong; her mind would not waver. "I don't care what it feels like," she said. "We need to find him. No matter what test he sets before us, we must understand why."

The rumble underfoot became stronger, and the glow from the cylinder returned, faint but sure. As it returned, Rebecca felt a cold chill run down her spine as it vibrated within walls.

Leonard stared at the glow and choked out, "**It's not over. He's not done yet.**"

Sophia clung to Rebecca, her small voice piercing through the anxiety. "He's watching us," she said. "He's waiting to see what we're going to do."

Rebecca could feel her chest tighten against the light from the glowing cylinder. The absence of Noah was still there with his influence proceeding to shape every moment, every decision. The secret of his plan loomed larger now—a shadow that was about to engulf them all.

The hum grew louder and deeper, resonating through the walls of the building like the heartbeat of something cosmic or something alien. The faint glow of the bulb around the cylinder pulsed steadily, casting long, flickering shadows across the floor. Presently, Rebecca felt another surge run through her veins. The vibration beneath her feet got stronger. Sophia held her small hand and trembled.

Leonard was frantically scanning the tablet, taking in shifting sheets of information on the screen. "The network is not merely waking up," he said, trembling. "It is... recalibrating. Restructuring itself."

Maria spun around, her anger boiling. "*What the hell does that mean?*" she shouted. "What is it restructuring for?"

Leonard hesitated and went pale. "To fulfill his design," he said. "Whatever Noah's ultimate plan was, it's happening right now."

The weight of what Sophia had said broke the tension that engulfed them. "It isn't just him," she whispered. "It's them. All of them."

The room fell silent, with only the humming of the cylinder continued at her words. Rebecca knelt beside Sophia with her heart racing. "What do you mean, all of them?" she asked gently. "*Who are them?*"

Sophia widened her eyes, teared up, and her voice quivered: "The others," she said. "The ones like me. The ones he couldn't save."

Leonard's breath caught, and his hands shook as, holding his tablet tightly, he said, "The prototypes," tentatively. "The network wasn't just connected for Noah-it was for all of them."

Maria recoiled slightly, narrowing her eyes at the stocky boy. "*You mean there are more? More like him?*"

Leonard nodded; his complexion white. "Thousands. Maybe more. In a state of hibernation, all connected. And now... they're waking up."

The halo of light around the cylinder intensified, brightening the room into something out of a sci-fi movie. Rebecca squeezed Sophia to her body and shielded her eyes. The hum became deafening, like a force rolling through their bodies. The light flickered and fused into something that looked like a soaring angel from heaven. It formed a holographic map against the air up the cylinder.

Rebecca could not shake away her awe and abject horror: the map was not merely indicative of the city. It was like the whole country. The rest of the world, even. Tiny glowing points of light breached the map, pulsating in unison. Suddenly, Leonard's eyes went wide as he took in the view in front of them in a trembling voice.

"**These are activation points,**" he said. "Nodes across the entire network. It is a global system."

Maria tightened her jaw, her voice sharp: "Global? You're saying it's not only about us? It is more widespread, everywhere?"

Even as she was gazing at the light around the map, Rebecca felt her chest constrict. "Noah is not just testing us," she said. "He is testing everybody."

Sophia lunged forward closer toward the projection, reaching her hand toward it. The lights of the map flickered brighter and faster in unison. Leonard's tablet rattled with a flow of data, and he gasped.

"She is interfacing with it," he said. "It is responding to her."

Rebecca choked in disbelief. "*Sophia, what do you think you're doing?*"

Sophia turned to her, tears streaming down her face. "He said I'm the key," she said, barely strong enough to carry the strength of conviction. "He said I can stop it."

"Stop what?" cried Maria as she pointed her weapon higher, her voice rising. "What does he want from her?"

Leonard whispered, "a choice."

The tremors in the room reached a boiling point, and then the holographic map shifted, virtually zooming in on a single point: a facility deep inside an isolated region. Leonard's tablet pinged with the coordinates, and his voice quivered as he read.

"This is it," he said. "The central hub. The beginning."

Rebecca turned to him, her heart pounding. "Where what began?"

Leonard stared back at her with a pale face. "The original prototypes. The first experiments. The heart of the network."

The projection flickered, and familiar words filled the room.

"You know where to find me."

Rebecca felt her breath hitch as the hologram tilted and turned into Noah's face. His glowing eyes were blazing with intensity, his expression unreadable. "But be warned," he spoke as his voice wrapped around the air waves, "this is not a test of me. It's a test of you."

The projection ended. The cylinder went dark again as the room fell once more into silence. Rebecca's knees weakened as she tried to absorb Noah's words.

Maria broke the silence, her voice sharp and urgent. "We can't follow him. This is exactly what he wants. He's leading us into a trap."

Rebecca replied to Maria with a voice steady with some level of fear in her, "And if we don't follow him? What then?"

Sophia stepped forward, her small voice piercing the tension. "He said I was the key," she said. "Maybe I can stop it. Maybe I can make him stop."

Rebecca dropped to her knees before Sophia, arms around the girl's shoulders. "Listen to me, my dear," she said in a gentle voice. "You don't need to do this. There's always another way."

Sophia shook her head, wiping her tears. "There ain't no other way," she said. He showed me.

"Weekend?" said Rebecca, gazing into Sophia's eyes. *"What did you see?"*

Sophia took a moment before speaking again, her voice wavering. "The end," she said. "If we don't go, they won't be anything more."

A heavy weight lay on her words like a smothering shroud over the group. Rebecca turned to Leonard and Maria, incensed. "We've got to go," she said. "We've got to finish this."

The agitating hum pitched again, rattling in the walls like a warning. The rest of the soon-miled personnel turned to Leonard, one barely lips parted. "The network is still up," he whispered. "And if we don't get out of here right now, it will spill out beyond our control."

Maria let out a growl of dissatisfaction and really tightened her grip on her gun. "Oh great—this is really suicide," she muttered. "Well, I guess our options are gone."

Rebecca stood up, taking Sophia's hand. "We leave now." She turned to Sophia. "Noah has waited too long-and so has the answer."

Chapter 16

A New Dawn

Before them extended a desolate landscape of cracked ground and skeletal trees, suffused with a pale haze unfolding with the sinister hues of dawn, while the metallic-tasting air vibrated with the very thickness of an unseen force in Rebecca's very chest. The group remained still, gazing at the monolithic structure ahead—they were now looking at the imposing hut—a rotting structure, a ghost from the lost past.

Rebecca tightened her grip on Sophia's hand, the little girl now trembling against her side. "This is it," she whispered. "This is where it all changes."

Leonard adjusted his tablet. His face pale, he quickly scanned the information cascading down the page. "The power goes in here," he said. "Whatever Noah plans, this is the center of it."

Maria clutched her weapon and gazed around with a hawkish eye unconceiving of a foster parent. "*And what awaits us inside?*" Her voice trembled with excitement. "I'd bet if it is the heart, there won't just be empty corridors and flamboyant lights."

Sophia stepped in front; her large known eyes now riveted on the imposing steel doors to the facility. "He's here," she said softly, trembling. "He's waiting for us."

The steel doors let out a low groan as they opened up into a dark yawning corridor. There was a low hum steady and drumming from somewhere deep in the darkness. The ground underfoot seemed to vibrate in vibration with it. Rebecca's heart jumped as she stepped inside, with the others closely following behind. The air began to feel colder and heavy with the pressure of the unguessed energy.

Leonard's voice broke the waiting silence, breaking into sudden tremors. "This place... it is alive," he said. "The network runs through everywhere, into every wall and every wire—he has woven himself into it all."

Maria's jaw tightened, and her voice was full of sarcasm. "And what will happen if we just cut it off?" she asked. **"Will he come down with it?"**

Leonard hesitated; his eyes fixed on his tablet. "If you sever the core, then everything could go down," he murmured. "The network, the prototypes... Noah—everything."

Sophia tugged at Rebecca's sleeve, her little voice reaching out slowly in the oppressive silence. "He won't let you stop it," she said. "Not yet."

The corridor opened into a cavernous chamber of the distanced walled hall, towering servers lined up like watchmen, emitting softened powerful light. At the center of the room was a platform surging with a strange, rhythmic energy that could be felt by an echo smoother than—matching the background hum in the air.

Rebecca gasped as she took a few quick hesitant steps closer to it, the expression in her wide eyes catching on the glow. "What is this?" she said, barely above a whisper.

Leonard cautiously advanced to the platform's edge, flush-faced, and followed the shifting patterns of light. "It's a relay," he said. "A central node connected to every system in the network. But it is not just that; it is amplifying the signal, channels it somewhere."

Maria frowned, gripping her weapon. "Somewhere, where?"

Leonard's voice trembled, nervous and scared. "I don't know," he admitted, "but this is the heart of everything. Whatever Noah intends—it starts here."

Sophia stepped out onto the platform; her small figure framed in lights. Rebecca's heart ached as she withdrew from Sophia. "Sophia, no, please," she said with a quiver in her voice. "It's too dangerous."

Sophia turned toward her with large eyes and a fierce increase in her determination. "**It has to be me**; he said I was the key."

Rebecca knelt down beside her, trying hard to blink back tears. "Sophia, you don't have to do that; there will be another way."

Sophia shook her head and spoke on quaking lips, "There is no other way—he showed me."

Leonard stepped forward; his expression anguished. "If she is the key," he said weakly, as though speaking to himself, "then the system is waiting for her to complete it."

Maria cursed under her breath, frantically angry. "What happens when she does? What is he going to do?"

Sophia hesitated, clasping the edges of Rebecca's jacket with small hands. "It's not about him, he said; it's about us."

The hum became louder as the light from the platform brightened on contact with Sophia's palm. The whole room came to life with the pulse of servers, the light of the platform. Rebecca shielded her eyes as the wave rushed through when the energy hit. The air buzzed, vibrations delivering what felt like kicks to her insides.

The light coalesced above the platform into a single point, which turned into a hologram of a figure. Rebecca felt as if she had been struck mute as she stared in shock at him; it was Noah. His eyes, a pale blue, shone; as human and unworldly was more than a talent.

"Noah," Rebecca said, now a trembling mouse. "What is this? What are you doing?"

The calm face yet unreadable features of Noah turned his gaze toward the assembled group. "This is the choice I spoke about; this is the choice that humanity must face."

Rebecca felt her chest tighten. "What freaking choice?" she found herself almost gasping out.

Calm yet unyielding, Noah now bore into Rebecca's eyes. "Whether to rise above or below what you are."

The pulsing light on the platform beat in time with the low hum reverberating through the chamber; Noah was rendered as a hologram in the center, his glaze projected onto Rebecca. The weight of his presence rendered the air oppressive, like an invisible force weighted down onto each of them in that room.

Sophia took another step toward Noah's image and instinctively reached for him with her little hand. Rebecca grabbed her shoulder and gently pulled her back. "Sophia," she whispered as she trembled, "stay with me..."

Noah tilted his head slightly, and his expression changed. "You are afraid," he said, calm, yet with sadness in his voice. "But fear won't save you."

Maria's grip on her weapon tightened, her own frustration bubbling to the surface. "Okay, no more riddles," she said, stepping forward. "What do you want from us, Noah? *What the hell is going on?*"

Noah's eyes switched their attention towards her, glowing and narrowing. "You still think in terms of want," he said. "This was never about me. It is always about you. All of you."

Leonard spoke at last, cutting through the awkward silence, his voice quivering as he spoke. "The net," his gaze was glued to his tablet, "is stabilizing. Every node, every connection—it's all synchronizing to this relay."

Rebecca turned to him, panic swelling in her chest. "*What does that mean?*"

Leonard hesitated; he was white as death. "It means...he's activating something. Something global."

Sophia stepped forward again. Her gaze nailed to Noah. "It's not him," she whispered. "It's us. He is making the choice for us."

Rebecca knelt by Sophia, her heart racing. "*What do you mean, Sophia?*" she asked gently. "What choice?"

"In a way...to save ourselves...or not," was all Sophia could utter, her voice shivering.

The hum deepened with accelerating vibrations in the floor. The rows of servers against the walls sparked into flashing life, changing the cadence of their luminescence with the rhythm of the platform. Noah's hologram raised his arm, and the chamber was bathed in an image, a vision of the world.

Rebecca caught her breath as she stared at the projection. Cities sprawled across continents, flickering like fireflies. But just behind the beauty of the scene lay something more menacing: smog, crumbled buildings, and flames spreading like wildfires.

"This is your world," said Noah, his voice resonating within the chamber, "this is a world on the brink of extinction."

Maria, her voice cutting, said, "And you think you will fix it? With what—your clones? **Your network?**"

Noah now turned to her; the expression on his face did not pinpoint any emotions. "I am not the answer," he finally said. "You are."

Leonard fumbled with his tapping on the tablet. "The network isn't amplifying; it's rewriting," his voice now growing louder. "Data streams, algorithms—he's somehow reprogramming the system."

Rebecca turned back to Noah. "**What for?**"

Noah's eyes were piercing into hers, his voice quietly insistent. "A chance—to escape the cycles of life that have defined you. To become more than what you have been."

The projection above the platform moved; it morphed into a new image of humanity with each individual bound together with threads of determination. It was beautiful, hopeful, and terrifying.

As Sophia walked onto the platform, it glowed ever so brightly in response to her presence. The hem of Rebecca's chest was tight as she reached out, her voice trembling, "Sophia, wait!"

Through round eyes that held determination, she spoke. "He said it must be me," she said. "Only I can make it work."

"No!" exclaimed Rebecca in disarray and bloody tears in her heart; "We'll find another way. You don't have to do this."

A faint smile on her lips- her melancholy years too far ahead of her. "It's okay," she said. "I'm not afraid."

The light washed over Sophia, energy radiating outward in waves that warmed the room. Rebecca shielded herself as the light blared, and the humming volume swelled to a deafening pitch. Leonard staggered back, the tablet buzzing with erratic, unreadable data.

Maria yelled something, but her words were drowned in clamor. The servers throbbed violently as the energy edged to the brink of eruption. Rebecca reached forth for Sophia, her heart pounding.

And then, silence.

The light withdrew, a second breath of stillness settled in. Sophia stood there-high above her head-on the platform, a small girl aglow in soft gold. Her eyes were closed; she bore a look of unearthly serenity.

Rebecca advanced cautiously, her voice shaking. "Sophia?"

Sophia opened her eyes, and Rebecca held her breath. They glowed with a soft brilliance, warm and intense, like a reflection of Noah's. Sophia spoke calmly but with a voice that vibrated, almost separating itself from corporeality.

"It is finished," said she. "The choice is made."

The chamber was quiet except for the faint sound of energy dissipating from the platform. Sophia slowly descended from the platform, and her glowing eyes dimmed to a soft amber hue. Rebecca, her heart pounding in alarm, raced toward her Lady Sophia and knelt in front of her.

"Sophia," she said, her voice quaking now. "Are you all right? What happened?"

Sophia blinked, her expression calm but far from here as if she were in some other realm. "I can feel everything," she said mellowly. "The network, the people... their pain. Their hope. All connected."

Leonard stepped forward cautiously, his hands shaking as they held his tablet. "Sophia," he said, his voice trembling. "You mean... you are part of it now?"

Sophia nodded, her little hands wringing in a nervous manner. "I don't think I'm just part of it," she said. "I think I am it."

"Mia now gives voice to a break in that heavy silence. "Oh, you mean a kid now is the network?" she asked. "*And she is running the whole thing?*"

Sophia looked at her, calm and deep amber eyes. "Not running it," she said. "Guiding it."

Oh, really? snapped Maria, turning to Leonard. "And what does that even mean? What is she guiding us toward?"

Leonard glanced down at the tablet, aghast, saying nothing, for on its screen, streams of data were racing by faster than he could comprehend. "The signature of the energy is stabilizing," he mumbled. "The output of the network directly maps—up. Upwardly. Recalibrating."

Rebecca stood with a protective hand on Sophia's shoulder. "Recalibrating for what?" she asked.

Sophia spoke sourly. "For them," she said. "Those who need it most."

The chamber shook faintly, and the holographic map on the console reappeared with more brightness than before; this time not just showing cities but all the people in them, illuminated as glowing points of light-millions of lives. Rebecca held her breath, watching the image shift and connect the dots in intricate pulsating patterns.

Leaning nearer to the map, Sophia gazed at the glowing points. "Noah set up the network to save them," she said. "But he couldn't complete it. He wasn't enough."

Leonard spoke in a trembling voice. "*And you are?*"

Sophia turned towards Leonard, determination quietly painting her expression. "I am what he made me to be," she said. "Not just a clone-something more."

Rebecca felt a tightness in her chest as she turned to Sophia, her mind racing. "Sophia," she said softly, "what does this mean for you? For us?"

Sophia paused momentarily, the hollow glow in her eyes flickering steadily. "That means the world may not have to break, not completely."

Maria frowned, making her frustration evident. "And what happens to the rest of us when you're busy being the great white savior?" she asked. "*What of the people that doesn't want this?*"

Sophia turned to face Maria and answered, still measured. "It is not about what they want. It is about what they need."

The ground trembled once more; the map shifted, zooming out to show the entirety of the Earth. A faint glow enveloped the planet, pulsing in rhythm with the energy of the network. Leonard's tablet buzzed with newly fetched data, widening his eyes in astonishment.

"The system isn't local anymore," he choked. "It is spreading-reach is further than places that weren't connected; it is... evolving."

Rebecca stepped forward, her voice shaking. "But Sophia, if the network is evolving, this means what for us, **for humanity?**"

There was strength in her tiny frame as Sophia looked at her. "It means you have a choice," she said. "Noah gave you the means through which to change, but the choice is yours. To rise... or to fall."

Maria shook her head, her voice beginning to elevate. "That's not a choice-it's an ultimatum! What if people don't want to change?"

Sophia's expression darkened a shade, her amber eyes flickering dimly. "Then the world ends as it always was going to," she said. "But those who choose to step forward again will have a chance."

Rebecca shivered. "And if no one chooses to step forward?"

Sophia hesitated a bit, whispering her response deep. "Then Noah's work would die in vain."

The map flared and a new image came on-the one that sent a shuddering wave rippling through the group-a huge structure above Earth's atmosphere, its magnificent design shining again with the same energy of the network. Leonard's tablet pinged and he stared at the screen in disbelief.

"That's... not from here," he said. "That's not even human."

Sophia nodded serenely. "It's what comes next," she said. "If you choose it."

"What's it, Sophia?" Rebecca asked, her breath halting.

Her steady eyes locked with Rebecca's. "A new beginning," she said. "But not for all."

The holographic projection of the colossal structure lingered above the platform, at once both ornate and luminescent, as if made out of some otherworldly material. Rebecca gaped at the apparition that seemed to trap her breath. It was something unlike anything she had ever imagined-a synthesis of organic curves and technical accuracy, retaining in itself one heart beats with the rhythm of the network.

"What the..." Maria stuttered, the edge to her tone disturbed. **Some kind of ... ship?"**

Sophia, her eyes glowing, lingered on the image. "It's not a ship," she said softly. **"It's a sanctuary."**

The trembling hands of Leonard gripped his tablet tightly, his whisper barely masked by the sound of the ambience. "Sanctuary? For whom?"

Sophia turned towards him, tranquil but distant in expression. "For those who choose to leave," she said. "Those who want a chance to start again."

Rebecca's heart sank. "Leave?" she echoed. "Leave to where?"

Sophia hesitated, turning her eyes back toward the hologram. "Beyond," she said simply.

The room shook faintly as they gave way to the picture on the platform that now seemed to be pulling back to reveal Earth, hovering in a faint, shimmering web of light. The sanctuary lay just beyond the orbit of the planet, glowing like an ethereal halo across the stars.

Leonard broke the unbearably thick silence. "The network is building this!" he exclaimed incredulously. "This is no dream-this is a tangible, physical thing. And it is connected to everything."

Maria scowled as she tightened her grip on her weapon. "So, what's the catch?" she prompted. "The people who build something like that do not do it without a price."

Sophia took a small step ahead, her tiny silhouette glowing faintly from the light. "The price is to leave everything behind," she said. "The world as it is now ... simply cannot survive. But this-" she gestured to the sanctuary, "-this is a way out. This is a way forward."

While the other woman spoke, Rebecca's mind was racing rather fast to process the words. "Noah knew this was happening," she spoke quietly. "That was always his plan."

She nodded at Sophia. "He couldn't save everybody. But he gave you the tools to save yourselves."

Maria scoffed, her anger boiling over. "So we just leave the planet? **Leave everything we made?**"

Sophia turned to her with quiet resolve in her glowing eyes. "Not abandoning," she said. "Choosing to evolve. Becoming more."

Leonard cast another look at his tablet, which had a morose expression on its face. "By the time I thought the network would stabilize, it is stabilizing faster. In all that Sophia is saying, we do not have much time for a decision," he said.

The earth at their feet plummeted as the platform's lights glowed stronger. Rebecca felt shivers run down her spine as the hologram changed, displaying new data, numbers, coordinates, and timelines, all directed toward the sanctuary.

Sophia looked over at Rebecca with calm, if soft, admonishment. "He said you will lead them and help them choose."

Rebecca gasped. "Me?" she asked. "*Why me?*"

Sophia did not hesitate to meet Rebecca's gaze. "Because you always believed him when no one else did. And because you still believe us."

Maria shook her head, her voice rising. "It's madness! Leaving the entire planet behind based on the words of—" she gestured to Sophia "—a kid! A clone! How do we even know this will work?"

Sophia took one step closer to Maria, her small frame unwavering. "You don't." She shook her head. "But if you don't try, then there is no change."

Further tremors rocked the chamber as a new alert sprang up on Leonard's tablet. Anguish darkened his complexion as he focused on the screen. "The network's tentacles are growing. It's all over the cities. And if we don't stabilize it, all progress will be lost."

Sophia turned back to the platform wreathed in a dispassionate expression. "Seems not to, it's still in a molding process."

Rebecca felt a cold shiver run through her body. "And what, Sophia?"

Contemplative, Sophia's voice dropped low; it was barely more than a whisper. "Some are ready to progress and some are not."

The luminescence around the platform brightened, and the fake background gave way. A flicker of Noah's face shot forward, glowing orbs fixing their stare right on Rebecca.

"The choice is yours," came the mellifluous, yet resonant voice. "But time is not on our side."

The projection vanished and the eerie stillness returned. Rebecca turned to Leonard, realizing she was holding her breath. "How much time is there?"

Leonard glanced at his tablet and organized a grim expression. "In hours, maybe less."

Maria sighed too loudly, unable to contain her outrage. "So, shall we then gather our things and leave?"

Rebecca glanced back to Sophia, her mind racing. "We find out who will go and give them the choice."

Sophia nodded, her voice steady. "But right now, the network will be considering that."

The group was in a silent glimmering chamber; the pressure of this decision on them was similar to an invisible force. The holographic map vanished, leaving the platform's petty drone and the distant flickers in the other servers as the sole company in the oppressive silence of the atmosphere. It felt as if every second was creeping by, pulling them down the path to an irreversible decision.

Rebecca looked at Sophia, the girl with glowing ambery eyes which carried a somewhat unnerving stillness. "Sophia," she spoke softly as she knelt near the girl, "*What happens if we don't go?*"

Sophia hesitated, gazing into the distance. "The network collapses," she said. "The sanctuary never gets built. This world remains the same...until it falls apart."

Maria was pacing the wall with frustration. "So sanctuary versus nothing," she said. "*What kind of a choice is that?*"

Sophia turned to her; her expression impassive. "It's not about sanctuary," she said. "It's about what you're ready to give up at that point-to save what matters most."

Leonard's hands were trembling; he gripped his tablet, feeling as though his voice would break. "If the sanctuary ever became operational, it would provide fresh opportunity," he said. "That would be a second chance, mostly to start over without the mistakes that brought us to this stage."

Rebecca rose, her heart racing. "But-a clean slate includes abandoning everything and everyone," she said. "The people who won't know, who won't be ready-who will be left in the ruins?"

Sophia stepped forward with petite strides, the landing casting a soft glow upon her. "They shall be given a chance," she said quietly. "But not all shall answer that call."

Rebecca eyed her in disbelief, feeling the weight in her chest. "And what if we make an error?"

Sophia looked straight at her; her eyes brightly lit but inscrutable. "There are no wrong choices...only those that you can live with."

As the ground trembled beneath them, Leonard's tablet vibrated with another alert. His complexion seemed to drain of blood as he read the information on it: "The network has stabilized the final relay," he said. "It's ready."

Maria stepped up with her rifle slung on her shoulder. "And we're just supposed to walk into the sanctuary?" she asked. "We're literally supposed to upload ourselves into the stars?"

Leonard's frown was deep as he shook his head: "Not that. It isn't digitalized. It's a real physical location; not here, but..."

Maria scoffed; her voice tinged with disbelief. "Beyond? Please! You're doing the whole sci-fi dream act."

Sophia turned toward her; her voice soft. "**It's not a dream**," she said. "It's hope."

The hum intensified, and the platform flared brighter. Rebecca squinted when the holographic map came back again, the spots of glowing lights now pulsating rhythmically, matching their breaths like they were alive. Leonard broke the heavy silence with his voice.

"**It's activating,**" he said. "The sanctuary...it is opening."

Maria step back, her countenance hardening. "*So, are we not going?*" she asked defensively, "will we simply fight for this world?"

Sophia's expression softened, and her voice was infused with quiet determination. "So the sanctuary closes," she said. "And the choice will be made for you."

Rebecca turned her gaze to the map, her mind racing. "We cannot abandon everyone," she said; "if we don't go, we lose all hope of building something better."

Sophia climbed the stairs onto the platform, growing brighter around her. "You won't lose it; it'll just take longer, a lot longer."

Leonard stared down at his tablet, a grim look on his face. "There's only a few minutes left," he said. "If we don't decide now, this sanctuary is going to move on without us."

Rebecca felt the weight of their bad situation crush her. She turned to look at Maria, then at Leonard, and then finally Sophia. "This isn't just my choice," she said. "It's ours."

Maria hesitated momentarily, anger giving way to a profound fear. "I've spent my whole life fighting for a world that's broken; maybe it's about time **I let it go.**"

Leonard shook his head slowly, his hands trembling. "We can't change the past. But maybe we can build a future."

Rebecca turned to Sophia, her heart clenched. "And you?" she asked. "What happens to you?"

Sophia gave a weak smile, her glowing eyes filled with warmth. "I'll be there. With all of you."

The platform flared, the chamber quaking as the network went full circle. Rebecca inhaled deeply, the racing of her mind wrapping up all of what they had been through and everything they had lost. She stepped on with Sophia's hand gripping hers.

Maria followed, her weapon across her back, defeat and determination playing for higher stakes on her face. Leonard joined in, clutching his tablet like a dear friend. The light became almost blinding around the platform, and Rebecca felt the vibrating roar entering her very bones.

As the sanctuary's energy enveloped them, Rebecca heard Noah's voice one last time, calm and deep.

"This isn't the end. It's only the beginning."

The light consumed the chamber, and when it finally faded, the room lay empty. The sanctuary loomed within orbit, its luminous structure breathing. Back on Earth, the network finally fell silent, its job done. The people left on the other side, in the cities below, looked up into the sky, following the sanctuary with their eyes, as it sailed into the stars.

Leonard left his tablet behind on the platform, and it buzzed one last time. One single line appeared on the screen:

"We will return when you are ready."

Epilogue

The world has changed.

From the vantage deck of the great metropolis, Rebecca exhaled, momentarily fogging the bloodied glass that stood separating her from the embers far embedded in the declining darkness. The distant hum of the merciless drones merged into the wedge of the pronunciation of the wind, providing a soft reminder of humanity moving remorselessly ahead. Tucked in between dizzyingly elaborate technological growth was a decidedly grim thread—an unsettling, amorphous fear.

Noah had vanished. The Synthesis creature who had stretched the meaning of mere human existence melted into nothingness. Governments denied his existence; corporations buried the details, and Leonard's name twisted in the winds of forgetfulness. Yet Rebecca knew better. The array of queries Noah left hanging haunted every other decision, every breakthrough, Raquel reflected. They haunted every decision she took after Noah had left: the crumbles of every occasion, the flashes of every connection they had had about a coming but unresolved life.

Years after the lab suffered a disastrous servery, she returned to the venues. There, she could hardly sight the ground—the process of re-naturalization had already begun, shrouded in moss and colonies of wildflowers, as though there had been quest for redemption and cleansing of the damned place. But wherever the leftovers were being languished the memory of Noah always burned ahead.

"What else occupies your mind now?" a voice from beside her intruded.

Rebecca sought the voice, hoping to pin down his identity: Eliot, the fiery activist who had attempted once to expose the cloning project. The passage of time - it had drawn lines that told of bitter experience and strained the dab of blood on enthralling vehemence from his once-boyish face.

"Will he ever return?" she patched timidly, almost hopeful.

Eliot leaned against the banister. His gaze drifted into the distance. "If he is alive somewhere, consider who Watson had to stand by. Remote, waiting, learning. Someone like Noah hardly becomes a thing of imagination."

Rebecca nodded, more pictorial now with Noah's last deep words: "You ought to have left me in the dark."

The world had not left him huddling in the dark. Over the seclusion of every single cloning program, panicked to have lain in shadows, nations inspired by a race for superior genes stood in behind scenes on every corner, their projects getting hotter and more hazardous—with endless torrents of information flooding spheres of life about clones and love, living one on top of the other but never finding sense amidst arguments about clones' rights, their purpose for existence, and their very souls.

"What if we were wrong?" She questioned after a while in silence. "What if all we ever did was get rooted in all those blunders?"

Eliot turned to her, his expression unable to be revealed and unreadable still. "Tell me it may have been. Or perhaps it is a new start and all of this is beyond comprehension."

Winds screeched now and during a moment stealthily, Rebecca saw quite a packed dismayed glow far, a peered opening of lights, flash rebounding a view-darker in nature or perhaps something not more.

Noah.

The name resonated within her—a recalled indication of a choice humanity was never going to flee from. She squeezed close her eyelids and beseeched silently—not for forgiveness, simply for wisdom.

She knew somewhere in the skies beyond, he was gazing. Waiting.

The revolution was not yet. It had morphed, as Noah often said it would.